monsoonbooks

THE ROSE OF SINGA

Peter Neville was born in Devon, England, in 1933. He came of age in the RAF, while serving in Singapore and Malaya during the Emergency Period in the early 1950s. When not tracking down Communist terrorists in the jungles of Malaya or avoiding capture by his own military police in the red-light districts of Singapore, Neville took the time to fully appreciate his new surroundings and fell in love with the East. And when his five-year tour of duty in the RAF ended, he returned to Singapore and went on to enjoy other lively adventures there and around the world.

Peter now enjoys a more relaxed lifestyle in Florida with June, his wife of forty years. This is his first novel.

Peter Neville

THE ROSE OF SINGAPORE

monsoon

monsoonbooks

Published in 2006
by Monsoon Books Pte Ltd
Blk 106 Jalan Hang Jebat #02–14
Singapore 139527
www.monsoonbooks.com.sg

First published in 1999
by Neville International, Ilfracombe
as "The Awakening of the Lion: Singapore"

ISBN-13: 978-981-05-1727-4
ISBN-10: 981-05-1727-0

Some of the names of people mentioned in this book have
been changed to protect their identity.

Cover image courtesy of Jazmin Asian Arts, Singapore.

Printed in Singapore

10 09 08 07 06   1 2 3 4 5 6 7 8 9

To Rose

GLOSSARY

All italicised words are in Bahasa Malaysia except where indicated. (Ch.) Chinese, (Hi.) Hindi.

Amah: Chinese nurse or maidservant

Atap: roof thatch made from palm leaves

Baju: traditional blouse worn by Malay women

Baju kebaya: traditional clothes (specifically the blouse) of the *Nyonya* or Straits Chinese (*Peranakan*) woman

Basha: a simple hut or temporary shelter

Cheongsam: (Ch.) traditional Chinese long, slender dress worn by women. The dress has a high, closed collar, is buttoned on the right side of the dress, has slits up the sides and hugs the body

Ikan bilis: small, dried fish eaten as a snack or used as a flavouring ingredient in Malay cuisine

Kampung: village

Kebaya: voile fitted blouse, often elaborately embroidered, open fronted and pinned together with gold or silver three-piece broaches (the word *kebaya* is derived from the Arabic word *kaba* meaning clothing and was introduced via the Portuguese language)

Kelong: large marine fish-trap

Kris: straight or, more commonly, wavy-bladed (usually ceremonial) dagger

Lalang: a kind of long, coarse, weedy grass

Parang: machete or cleaver-like knife used to cut through thick vegetation and as a weapon

Qiu qian: (Ch.) traditional Chinese ritual in which a believer, wishing to know the answer to a question or to know what the future might hold, offers incense to the god of the temple, tells the deity his worries (or asks a question) then throws two semi-circular objects called *yao bei* on the floor; should each *yao bei* land on a different side, which is an affirmative result and is known as *sheng bei* (*seng bui* in Cantonese), he proceeds to the next stage of shaking a bamboo canister, from which one stick falls to the floor; he must then throw three consecutive *sheng bei* to ascertain if this numbered stick holds the right advice for him (if three consecutive *sheng bei* are not achieved, he must shake the canister again for a new stick); with three *sheng bei* he shows the numbered stick to the temple custodian, who consults an almanac to derive its meaning

Samfoo: (Ch.) traditional Chinese clothes comprising a jacket and pants, often worn by *amahs* or maidservants

Sampan: (Ch.) generic name for any small boat propelled by oars or a scull

Sari: (Hi.) traditional Indian dress comprising a long piece of material elaborately wrapped around the body

Sarong: skirt-like garment wrapped around the lower body, worn by men and women

Songkok: small hat worn by Muslim Malay men

Tabik: formerly a Malay greeting or salutation, usually to a superior (no longer in common usage)

Trishaw: three-wheeled vehicle propelled by a man peddling either in front of or from behind the passenger seat

Ulu: literally upriver, a slang term used by British and Australian military personnel to refer to the jungle

Wallah: (Hi.) combined with a trade, the person who performs or is associated with that trade

PART ONE

1

The bombers were returning. Down at the airstrip, with the drone of the approaching aircraft becoming increasingly louder, a bustle of activity ensued. Crash tenders, fire rescue units and speeding ambulances raced to their designated areas of the runway, and there they stopped, with engines running, ready and waiting for the planes to land. From the control tower at RAF Kuala Lumpur, cutting the blackness of the Malayan night, signals blinked. And from beyond the perimeter of the airfield, gunfire, aimed at the incoming planes by Communist terrorists lurking in the nearby jungle, stabbed the darkness.

The first plane came straight in, the bright beam from her nose searchlight cleaving a passage over the roof of the jungle below. She flew over the railway embankment at the approach end of the runway before her engines were cut. The plane plummeted down and with a screech of tires hit metal, a bounce, more screeching as she hit again, the squeal of brakes, and the twin-engine bomber was running free, heading for the palm grove at the far end of that perilously short runway.

Before that first bomber came to a standstill, a second bomber roared out of the darkness over the jungle, and came in low and slow, her searchlight flashing on only moments before crossing the railway embankment. She, too, hit metal and bounced up the runway until she ran free; to be followed in procession by three more planes, all running the gauntlet as tracers and more stabs of flame from Communist terrorists' gunfire greeted them on that final approach.

The sixth bomber was still out there, in the darkness, with smoke billowing from a dead engine. Blinking lights from the control tower beckoned.

"Hello KL. Hello KL. This is Red Fox Six. Are you receiving me?" The voice flooding into the control tower was clear and calm. "Come in, KL."

"KL control to Red Fox Six. Receiving you. Over."

"Red Fox Six to KL. Starboard engine gone. Losing altitude fast. We're coming in now. Do you read me? Over." Except for a hint of urgency, the voice remained calm.

"KL to Red Fox Six. Read you loud and clear. Come on in, but watch out for the embankment. We're waiting for you. Over."

"Roger, KL."

From out of the darkness the bomber's searchlight suddenly shot a piercing beam of brilliant light at the runway, illuminating brightly the many emergency vehicles lining the perimeter, the short strip of perforated steel plate and tarmac that was the runway, and the forever ominous railway embankment. The plane's alignment was perfect, except she was too low.

"Red Fox. You're too low! Pull up! Pull up!" yelled the voice from the control tower.

"Damn it! Not going to make it," was the only reply that could be heard; it was as if the pilot was speaking those last few words to himself.

Everyone looked anxiously towards the source of the approaching bright light and the loud roar of the plane's one good engine. Suddenly, there was a vivid flash, immediately followed by a thunderous explosion as the twin-engine bomber slammed into the railway embankment and lit up the night sky at the end of the runway.

Red Fox Six, with its crew of three, was no more. Instead, the remains lay scattered in tiny fiery fragments over the end of the airstrip, the railway embankment, and the surrounding mass of jungle beyond.

Leading Aircraftman (LAC) Peter Saunders, dressed in cooks' whites dirtied by working in the camp kitchen, cradled a loaded .303 Enfield rifle in the crook of his right arm, and from a listless left hand there hung a military issue, brown enamel tea mug. Emaciated and weak from his second bout of malaria since being posted to Kuala Lumpur, four and a half months ago, Peter Saunders felt as if he was floating on air. He stood alone, among worn out rubber trees, under a canopy of green and brown in the old plantation on the hillside overlooking the airstrip. He could not see the railway embankment from where he stood, but he had seen the glaring flash and heard the terrible explosion that followed. As if in a trance he stared at the jumping ghost-like shadows among the trees, an eerie show created by the fiery inferno that now engulfed the scattered remains of the bomber. And above the trees, where the plane had gone down, a red and white glow flickered illuminating the night sky over the jungle. LAC Peter Saunders was just too sick to care.

Immediately following the explosion, the night noises were silenced in the jungle-overgrown rubber plantation, but only for a brief few moments. Soon, around him, life resumed again, the screams and shrieks of frightened monkeys in the tree tops, squeaks and squeals from smaller animals, the yelping of camp dogs—all mongrels fed and befriended by lonely RAF personnel—the buzz and twitter of ten billion insects and the throaty bellow of bullfrogs. And, of course, there was the ceaseless high-pitched whine from cicadas and the myriad mosquitoes. LAC Peter Saunders heard only the mosquitoes. These he dreaded, for in such a short time they had brought him debilitating ill health. Sweeping a sweaty arm across his perspiration-drenched face, and smearing his glasses as he did so, he turned and walked dejectedly on. With the flickering glow over the railway embankment behind him, he slowly made his way along the half-mile muddy path which separated the cookhouse from the basha, a mud-floor hut constructed of *lalang* grass and roughly hewn coconut trees in which the RAF catering section personnel lived. The path was lit in places by an occasional light bulb strung up on a rubber tree. These lonesome bulbs created an aura of eerie insect-filled light which dimly illuminated, amid the silver and grey greenery, other huts, shadowy, with some in complete darkness. Originally built to house Malayan rubber tappers, and later, British and Australian prisoners of war during the Japanese occupation, these huts, in primitive and dilapidated condition, now housed British servicemen of the Royal Air Force who were stationed at RAF Kuala Lumpur.

A new RAF station was on the planning board, a modern camp with a much longer airstrip, but that did not help LAC Peter Saunders; he hated RAF Kuala Lumpur. To him the camp had meant only hard and hot work in the primitive kitchen, and ill health; sickness from malaria, from ringworm, skin diseases, foot rot—he could not remember ever feeling so sick in his whole nineteen years of life.

He didn't fear the Communist terrorists who might be lurking nearby as he resumed his walk along the muddy path. He had become used to their presence, for they were everywhere, not only in the jungle, but also in the villages, and even going about their business unnoticed in Kuala Lumpur, the capital itself. If they were out to get him, he knew they would. Anyway, he felt just too sick, too weak and too dispirited to care.

Eventually he arrived at the cooks' basha at the left of the path, on a hillside, and almost hidden in the dense undergrowth. Like the kitchen, it was a mud-floored, bug-infested, part *lalang* grass and part wood hut with four-foot-square openings on one side, which served as glassless windows. There was no mosquito mesh covering these openings, so bugs, winged and wingless made their entry. However, unlike the kitchen, the basha did have a galvanized roof, rusted and with holes in places which let in the rain but it was, at least, rat free.

The crude wooden door was ajar, so Peter pushed it open to enter into another world, where men slept fitfully, sweating, naked and unashamed, some beneath mosquito nets, others with their net thrown aside, but all with their loaded rifles and Sten guns, cold mistresses, in bed beside them.

Needing to urinate, Peter went out the back door of the shack, but did not go as far as the screened in 'desert lily', a two-inch pipe about the height of a man's crotch, with a funnel in the top in which one was expected to pee. There would be too many mosquitoes buzzing around the funnel waiting eagerly to bite any exposed dangling appendage. Nor did he visit the primitive latrine twenty or more paces into the undergrowth. Why bother? The latrine was simply a deep, drilled-out hole in the ground covered by a wooden box with a nine-inch-diameter hole cut in its top, placed invitingly over the hole for patrons to sit on when doing number two. The thunderbox, as it was called, was hidden from view on three sides by chest-high *atap*, the Malay word for dried palm fronds. During the day there were always millions of mosquitoes buzzing around the thunderbox waiting to bite someone's bare ass, but at night trillions of the little bloodsuckers awaited some poor wretch to come and drop his pants. And worse, on rainy nights black spitting cobras often visited that immediate area searching for frogs. Peter hated frequenting that smelly place and did so only during the daytime and out of sheer necessity. This night he peed up against an old rubber tree growing not too far from the basha's doorway. Relieved, he returned to the basha, undressed, and then crawled unsteadily into bed to lie alongside his cold, uncaring rifle.

A party of about eight headhunting Dyak tribesmen, brought in from Borneo by the British government, was returning to the camp when Peter Saunders passed the guardroom on his way to the sick-quarters just before nine the following morning. Clad only in filthy khaki shorts, the short brown men carried no guns, just long knives called *parangs*, and their trophies of that night's hunt: the heads and hands of Communist terrorists waltzing grotesquely from grass belts worn around their waists. Peter Saunders felt sickened by the sight. But it had to be. The hands would be fingerprinted and the heads photographed for identification purposes. The Dyaks grinned at Peter and shook their bodies causing the heads and hands to do a grim dance to their movement. A wave of nausea swept over Peter, but he checked himself from throwing up and turned away from the gruesome spectacle.

He hurried on, towards the overgrown hillside where the sick-quarters, a cluster of three thatch-roofed shacks, was perched. The air was hot and oppressive, but there would be no rain until the afternoon; at RAF Kuala Lumper it rained almost every afternoon. Peter's khaki drill uniform was already sticking with perspiration to his body when he eventually arrived at the doorway leading into the sick-quarters waiting room. There he was greeted by a very young, very white medical orderly who had obviously only recently stepped off the boat from England. A 'moon-man' without a doubt, thought Peter. Bum fluff showed on a face that had never seen a razor and the young airmen had acne too.

"LAC Saunders," was all Peter said.

"Ah, yes. The medical officer is expecting you. I'll let him know you are here. Please take a seat," said the medical orderly, smiling in a friendly manner and speaking in precise English. There was none of this Malay and Chinese jive thrown in, which one was apt to do after a few months of being stationed in Malaya.

"Thank you," said Peter, and he sat down on a well-worn wicker chair, feeling the seat of his pants and the back of his jacket sticking coldly to his clammy body. The medical orderly returned almost immediately, so Peter stood up and was politely ushered into the medical officer's domain, a whitewashed room, surprisingly clean, tidy and efficient looking. Considering that it was difficult, nay impossible, to make any of the dirty old shacks at RAF Kuala Lumpur appear clean, tidy and efficient, Peter Saunders was always impressed by the place; as a patient he had certainly seen it often enough. The only difference was that now there was a new medical officer. The one he had come to know so well had become tour ex (tour expired) and had returned to the UK.

"Good morning, Saunders," greeted the young flight lieutenant, looking up from where he was seated at a desk.

Peter noted that the man's skin was just as lily white as that of the orderly. Another 'moon-man', he decided. He replied, "Good morning, sir."

The medical officer (MO) beckoned the sickly and emaciated airman standing before him to take a seat in front of the desk, and when Peter was seated he asked in a kindly voice, "How old are you, Saunders?"

"Nineteen, sir," Peter replied.

"Ah, yes. I have it here. You're not a national serviceman I see. You're in for five years; hopefully a career man."

Peter did not answer him but instead watched silently as the MO studied the file he held. Finally the MO looked up and said, "So you're the chap with the malaria problem, eh?"

"Yes, sir."

"How are you feeling this morning?"

"A bit shaky, sir."

The MO, studying the file again, said, "Hmm! Quite impressive!" Then, "Quite impressive!"

"What is, sir?"

"Your file. You seem to have had everything in the book during your stay at KL."

"I have been sick an awful lot," acknowledged Peter.

"Yes," said the medical officer.

Peter was not sure what that 'yes' meant, so he remained silent.

A minute or two passed before the MO said, "I see that you broke a few records while at RAF Kai Tak, Hong Kong."

"Sir?"

"Well, there's a notation here about you. Hmm. Let's see now. Yes, almost a year ago, and written by the medical officer at Kai Tak, stating that you were the youngest, shortest and lightest airman at that time in the whole Far Eastern Command. That was in mid-fifty-one. It appears that, probably out of curiosity the MO at Kai Tak took the trouble to check out these statistics. Where you aware of his findings?"

"Yes, sir. He called me to the sick quarters one day and told me."

"Yes." Again silence for a minute or more before the MO continued, "At that time your weight was seven stone, or ninety-eight pounds. But I note that just one week ago you weighed in at just over six and a quarter stone. We can't have that, Saunders. If you keep this up, soon you'll be nothing more than skin and bone, a skeleton on my hands."

"Yes, sir. I'm aware of that," said Peter.

The MO removed his horn-rimmed spectacles and wiped perspiration from them with a clean, very white handkerchief. "Bloody hot, isn't it?" he said.

Peter acknowledged that fact with a simple, "Yes, sir."

Replacing his spectacles and again looking at the file on his desk, the MO suddenly said, "On medical grounds I'm sending you down to Changi in Singapore, where you can take a rest and recuperate. I'm giving you two weeks sick leave before you report for duty there." Still studying the file, he paused for a few moments before looking up and saying, "I've managed to secure you a posting at Changi. Until you are tour ex, Changi will be your permanent posting."

Hardly believing what he had just heard, LAC Peter Saunders let out a deep sigh of relief. It was as if a great weight had suddenly been lifted from his shoulders, and for the first time in the long four and a half months he had been stationed at KL he felt he had something to smile about. "Thank you, sir," he said, almost in a whisper. It was if he was having a beautiful dream listening to the medical officer who had resumed speaking.

"Your replacement should arrive today, so I suggest you report immediately to Station Headquarters, have your clearance chit signed by the end of today, and we'll have you flown out of here tomorrow on the first plane bound for Singapore."

"Thank you very much, sir," said Peter, rising to his feet. "I can't thank you enough, sir."

The medical officer smiled in a kindly manner. "Good luck, Saunders, and good health," he said, rising to his feet and shaking hands with the skinny little airman. And as he ushered Peter to the door, he said, "I hear it's an altogether different life at Changi."

2

A steady hand and a heavy finger had made them; six capital letters carefully grooved into the sand a few feet above the water's edge to form the word 'SHEILA'. Soon, the incoming tide would wash over and erase the word but Sheila herself was still very much a sweet memory, far from being forgotten by the writer of that name in the sand.

Midway between the name written in the sand and where the previous tide's high water had left a thin, ragged line of seaweed twenty feet up the beach, two youths lay on their backs, soaking up the sun, their bodies, clad only in skimpy swimming costumes, facing a cloudless Singapore sky. The two were in quiet conversation, but occasionally one or the other would lift his head to speak to a third youth, LAC Peter Saunders, who was standing a few feet from them, at the water's edge. Peter was paying scant attention to their conversation, however, his thoughts being elsewhere as his eyes roved across the sparkling blue water that stretched away into the distance to where it reached green islands and the hazy coastline of Malaya.

Almost two months had passed since Peter Saunders had arrived at RAF Changi, a period in which his health had improved dramatically. No longer sickly white and emaciated, he was now deeply suntanned, several pounds heavier, and once again fit and full of vitality. Brimming over with newly found energy, he had not felt so well since his posting from RAF Kai Tak, Hong Kong, almost eight months ago.

It was a Saturday afternoon in mid-November 1952. The place: Changi Beach, a popular strip of rather dirty-looking sand separating the sea from the giant air base of Royal Air Force, Changi, situated fourteen miles north-east of the main administrative centre of the island city-state. The temperature was in the eighties, the sun scorching hot. The tidal water of the Johore Strait, separating the British Crown Colony island of Singapore from the vastness of Malaya, was low, but with its swift current was coming in fast. Soon Peter would swim again. He didn't like to swim when the tide was low because then the water was shallow and the bottom was mud in which slimy grasses grew, inhabited by poisonous water snakes. He would wait awhile, to when the water had risen enough to cover the lower slopes of the beach. Like a vast lake, the surface of the water lay shimmering and blue, ruffled only by the wash of a motorized pleasure boat streaking towards the open sea, and a cargo-laden junk plodding along in midstream, its tattered mainsail up, and its dual outboard motors fighting against the fast-moving current. The few narrow and sleek fishing boats made no wake, they were too slow; nor did the many sailing dinghies from Changi's yacht club, dotting the water in a slow race as they tacked towards the islands in a light breeze which barely filled their sails. The only other ruffling of the water was the gentle lapping of tiny waves around Peter's bare feet, caused by the incoming tide.

Faintly, in the far distance, he could see the most southerly state of Malaya, Johore, its coastline just a blur on the horizon, a watery haze hanging motionless over swamplands and tangled masses of jungle wilderness.

In the foreground, opposite Changi Beach and roughly two miles away, lay Peter's favourite island, Pulau Ubin, a long strip of fertile land embraced by thick vegetation, knee-high green grasses and tall coconut palms. On the westerly side of Pulau Ubin, a Chinese fishing village lay nestled in a sheltered bay almost hidden in the greenery. Scattered over the rest of the island were many little homes made from palm planking and thatch, their Chinese and Malay dwellers seemingly happy with their smallholdings of chickens, ducks and goats, and their small plots of land. They could also reap a constant harvest from the bountiful sea.

To the left of Pulau Ubin, plainly visible, looking like green molehills on a shimmering field of blue, were smaller islands basking in quiet tranquillity. To the right lay ghostly Fortress Island, and the ugly nakedness of dismantled and blown-up gun emplacements—an awful reminder of the Japanese invasion of Singapore. During World War II, all the heavy guns on Fortress Island were pointing out to sea from where, logically, an enemy would begin its invasion. But the attacking Japanese army did nothing logically; they came from the north, from Thailand, marching and riding bicycles down jungle paths in the Malay Peninsula, all the way to the Johore Strait. The guns proved useless against them. The British soldiers who had manned those guns and blown them up at the fall of the island were dead, massacred by the invaders; and this happened just ten years back, in 1942. Now, with its tragic memories partially concealed beneath a thick mantle of tropical undergrowth, the island lay as peacefully as it did before any conqueror came to its shores.

Behind Fortress Island lay the much larger island of Pulau Tekong Besar, its towering hills seemingly always shrouded in jungle mist, and blending with the steamy coastline of Johore.

During the past nine weeks, Peter Saunders had often explored the islands off Changi's shores by renting a canoe-like fishing craft from Pop, a short, thick-set, very active middle-aged Chinese fisherman who never wore anything except a pair of dirty old khaki shorts, and a smile on his weather-beaten, good-natured face.

Pop owned and operated a coffee shop on the beach, a crude shack really, made from driftwood and old sailcloth; its roof thatched palm fronds and rusty sheets of galvanized iron. It was situated roughly a hundred feet above a line of dried seaweed and little bits of refuse that had been washed ashore by the last highest tide. Here, Pop rented out four rowing boats and two primitive but very seaworthy native canoes by the hour to the beach-goers, mostly RAF personnel from Changi. His petite wife, Momma, assisted him in running the shack by selling to its patrons Green Spot orange drink, fried rice and other Chinese foods. Momma was about thirty, friendly, smiled a lot and showed off her many gold teeth. Pop and Momma had four very young children. The elder girl and two boys, happily nude and suntanned, were either getting underfoot in the shack, playing in the boats or running around on the beach laughing and making lots of noise. A newborn baby girl spent most of her time sleeping in a crib suspended by a heavy coiled spring attached to a bamboo beam supporting the roof of the shack. The family also had a friendly, skinny, brownish-coloured mongrel dog which rested its chin on the knees of patrons to the shack, and looked up at them with big brown sad eyes imploring them for a handout of whatever was being eaten. Also living in the shack was a flock of chickens, which clucked happily as they ate food dropped to them. And when there was no food being dropped, they pecked at the great variety of insects that emerged from every nook and cranny of that flotsam-built shack. Pop's coffee shop was quite an interesting place and by visiting the beach whenever he had the opportunity, which was almost daily, Peter Saunders had become one of Pop's best customers.

Deep in thought, Peter now gazed across the broad expanse of water separating Singapore from Malaya. His journey from his mother and three brothers in Plymouth, England, had seen him posted first to Hong Kong and later to Kuala Lumpur in Malaya, and remustering from a fighter plotter to a cook. With twenty-eight other fighter plotters straight from the Royal Air Force radar and fighter plotter training school at RAF Bawdsey in Suffolk, he had been en route to Korea from Liverpool on the troopship *Empire Pride* when, on reaching the docks at Kowloon, Hong Kong, he and the other twenty-eight were informed that there was a glut of fighter plotters in Korea. What could be done with them? They were not wanted in Korea. The RAF could not lose face by returning them the ten thousand miles or more to England. Hence, they were dumped at Kowloon docks, taken by military vehicles to RAF Kai Tak airport, and as good as told to get lost until the great minds at the top decided what to do with twenty-nine redundant fighter plotters. Peter thought of the several months he and the others had slept in tents at the edge of a runway, sleeping late, eating the finest food he had ever known, taking daily swims in the camp pool, and freely and happily sightseeing fascinating Hong Kong. He had done guard duty often, and had been given odd jobs to do from time to time. He had painted the sergeants' mess, cleaned aircraft, and shuffled papers at SHQ. But the fun job was when he volunteered to act as a drowning man to help train aircrew on how to save their comrades should they ditch into the sea. Peter at that time was very fit, and a strong swimmer, swimming being the only physical sport at which he excelled. There were perks for being such a cheerful and friendly drowning man too. On numerous occasions pilots had taken him up on flights as supernumerary crew, enabling him to experience the thrills of flying. He had flown in training Harvards, Beaufighters, transport planes, bombers and even in the first military jet bomber assigned to Kai Tak, the two-seater Meteor, loving them all, and with never the slightest fear of flying.

Then fate had stepped in. He had become friendly with LAC Jimmy Phillips, an officers' mess cook, who invited him up to the officers' mess and kitchen at Kai Tak. To the right of the officers' mess, black-clothed Chinese peasants—men, women and children—worked the many paddy fields, which smelled strongly of human excrement, especially at night. To the left were mountains and the narrow harbour entrance. And there, in the kitchen at Kai Tak, and over a period of less than a month, LAC Jimmy Phillips had taught Peter how to ice cakes, bake bread, make soups and sauces; in fact, enough of the art of cooking that he not only enjoyed the work, but also had become quite proficient at the various tasks entrusted to him with, of course, Jimmy keeping a critical eye on him.

It was not long before the catering officer also had his eye on him, and soon he was asked to report to the catering office, which he did.

The catering officer, a man who was liked and respected by everyone in the catering section, had smiled at him in a friendly manner, told him how pleased he was with his work, and of how a promotion in rank would come his way, from airman first class to leading aircraftman if he remustered and became a cook. Thus, Peter Saunders remustered, and the catering officer took him and several of the other cooks in his car to Kowloon where they celebrated his remustering by eating at a swanky restaurant and then getting drunk as lords in a low class bar. It was the catering officer's way of saying 'thank you.' Flight Lieutenant Williams was that sort of officer, a type few and far between. No wonder the men under him, the biggest drinkers and womanizers Peter had ever met, thought so highly of their officer in charge.

Peter's promotion in rank came, and with it, one month later, a posting to RAF Kuala Lumpur where there was a shortage of cooks. And here Peter found himself, on the island of Singapore. Since his arrival at RAF Changi he had felt very much at home with his new posting. At the request of the flight lieutenant in charge of his new section, Peter had chosen to forgo his two weeks recuperation leave in order to secure a permanent position in the sergeants' mess under the exuberant and straight-talking Sergeant Muldoon instead of working in the regular airmens' mess. He and Sergeant Muldoon hit it off together right from their first meeting. Sergeant Muldoon suggested that the two of them work alternate early and late shifts seven days a week. Meaning, Peter would report to the sergeants' mess at noon to work the late shift and to supervise the running of the kitchen until about eight in the evening or until dinner was over. He would then be off duty until six the following morning when he would return to the kitchen and work until lunch was over, or whenever Sergeant Muldoon sped into the kitchen on his ancient bike and relieved him. However, Peter's hours of duty seldom worked out in such a manner as, quite frequently, The Muldoon, (the name the sergeant was generally known by,) would take two or even three days off at a stretch, and Peter would be obliged to work double shifts throughout those days. But when the sergeant finally did show up, Peter was sure of getting at least an equal number of days off. Weekends were also arranged between the sergeant and himself to suit each other's needs. Undoubtedly their working relationship was excellent, even though Peter found himself doing all of Sergeant Muldoon's office work such as making out the three daily menus, keeping a daily inventory of the stores, and checking the ration deliveries. But he liked Sergeant Muldoon and had found him to be a good working partner, fair in his dealings, almost always cheerful and with a good sense of humour. Also, there was no hassle, bullshit or RAF red tape with him. The Muldoon was a sergeant who, providing no problems arose in the kitchen, preferred to live and let live.

Peter thought of the many differences between working at KL and Changi. At KL it was all hard work, whereas at Changi's sergeants' mess he did very little cooking and was there mainly to supervise the running of the kitchen. Actually, the Chinese staff needed little if any supervision as all were skilled at their jobs, hardworking and completely dependable. In truth, Dai Yat, the Chinese number one cook, better known as Charlie, ran the place. Charlie could not read any English, but he could speak pidgin English. On arriving at the kitchen to begin his day's duty, Charlie would first ask the sergeant or Peter to read him the menu. He would give his opinion, and then instruct the other cooks and kitchen hands their work for that shift.

When Sergeant Muldoon did show up for work on his bike, he always rode it at breakneck speed into the kitchen, slamming on the brakes on reaching the door of the combined kitchen store and office, and on dismounting would invariably ask Peter, "Any complaints? Any problems?"

If Peter admitted, "Yes," which was seldom, and then told the sergeant the name of the complaining senior non-commissioned officer and the nature of the complaint, the fiery, ginger-haired Irishman would angrily puff himself up, hunt out the complainer, and tell him in no uncertain manner to 'Inform me of your stupid complaints, but don't bother my cook,' and end by saying, 'Get stuffed!' which Peter found most amusing. However, when Peter answered, "No complaints, Sarge," The Muldoon would happily make some encouraging remark such as "keep the buggers happy, Pete," remount his bike, and sing out as he made his exit, "I'll see you tomorrow, Pete. Then you can take the next two days off." Sergeant Muldoon seemed very happy with his new leading aircraftman cook.

Desiring to return to good health, Peter spent most of his free time on Changi Beach, which was about a one-mile walk from where he lived, Block 128. There he sunbathed and exercised by walking the long sandy beach, swimming for hours in the warm water, playing ball with Pop's kids, and by his new-found hobby, canoeing. His good health had returned surprisingly fast, attributed not only to his almost daily visits to the beach but also to the nourishing food at Changi amid good company and in a healthy environment. Moreover, his work duties were light and almost stress free. Peter knew that all these factors contributed to his restored health. Since leaving Kuala Lumpur, he had experienced only one bad bout of malaria, which knocked him out for a couple of days. On his recovery the medical officer told him that he could expect recurring attacks at any time. At least he was now aware of this fact and would recognize the symptoms. The diagnosis did not particularly bother him; he was only too grateful at being away from that awful kitchen at Kuala Lumpur and from the nightmarish jungle to care about an occasional attack of malaria.

3

Back at Changi Beach, this being a Saturday, there were numerous people enjoying a carefree afternoon: mostly Chinese, a few Malays and Indians, also several Europeans, the majority British service personnel from the military camps scattered across the island. Several people were seated in Pop's coffee shop including a group of young British army lads being chatted up by two Chinese prostitutes. One was Molly who had F.U.C.K. tattooed on the fingers of her left hand and L.O.V.E. tattooed on the fingers of her right. The other was good-natured Lucy, nicknamed 'The Bucket' by those military personnel who had an intimate knowledge of her. Both girls were in their mid-twenties, attractive, well known, well liked and popular with the local servicemen, mainly army lads. The two girls came to the beach on most Saturday afternoons to relax, as well as to unobtrusively advertise and boost their trade. They never caused trouble or embarrassment to anyone; in fact, quite the opposite. They played with the children, talked and laughed a lot with Pop and Momma, and almost always behaved themselves in a perfectly lady-like manner. Pop's coffee shop was a fun place, busy too, especially on weekends and the many religious holidays.

Peter Saunders was listening with scant interest to his two companions, who were discussing the girlfriends they had said goodbye to many months ago in the UK. He was far more interested in observing the futile efforts of a horseshoe crab, which a few moments earlier he had whisked ashore with a bare foot. The greenish-brown crab lay on its hard-shelled back, its armour-plated legs futilely kicking the air, its long spike-like tail prodding the sand in a desperate attempt to right itself.

Peter sighed and turned his eyes from the harmless, helpless crab to where his two companions lay. How like them to be talking, always talking of the same two girls they had dated before leaving England. He himself did not have a girlfriend; in fact he had never had a girlfriend. The girls he had known had always wanted someone bigger and better looking. He looked like a little boy of fourteen wearing glasses when he joined the RAF, instead of being a seventeen-year-old. He'd had a crush on Elsie, a sixteen-year-old girl whom he had worked with at The Vineries, a South Devon horticultural firm, before joining the RAF. Elsie would meet him at the Plymouth motorcycle speedway track every Thursday evening, and there he would be thrilled by the very fact that she was standing at his side as he watched his favourite team, The Devils, captained by Pete Landsdale, and supported by Peter Robinson and Len Reed. That brief boyish romance lasted until the evening he went to meet her at the usual spot only to find her accompanied by a man ten years or more her senior. Puppy love or not, that evening Peter was very hurt, and afterwards gave girls little more thought. However, he did enjoy looking at Chinese girls here in Singapore, finding himself aroused by them, especially when they sat wearing a *cheongsam*, a dress revealing their legs all the way to their thighs.

Turning his attention again to the crab, Peter slid a toe beneath its broad back and with a swing of his foot hurled the creature upward and away from the shore. It plopped with a splash, and quickly sank from sight below the surface of the water, leaving little ringed ripples where it had disappeared.

"I suppose both of you are counting the days," Peter said, turning to his two companions and walking over to where they lay. "Supposing you find your girlfriend knocking around with someone else when you get home, eh?"

"She won't be," assured Leading Aircraftman Jimmy Edwards

sincerely. "Not mine. Not my Sheila. I know her too well."

"I hope so, for your sake," said Peter, who then smiled and said. "You know, I hated KL, but now that I'm here, I'm in no hurry to return home. I like it here. And besides, I've no one to go home to except my mother and my three brothers."

Both Jimmy and his companion, Leading Aircraftman Dylan 'Taffy' Evens, sat up. Jimmy, scooping up fine sand and allowing it to pour between his fingers, said, "I also like it here, but I prefer to be home."

"Why?" asked Peter. "It's always cold and rainy in the UK, and you'll never find a beach over there like Changi."

"Perhaps not," said Jimmy Edwards. "But in Brighton at this time of the year I'd be making a small fortune, what with working with the film company as well as helping my mum run her guesthouse. There's good money in guesthouses, and plenty of tips. You can make a lot on the side. And when I go to the beach, it won't be with a couple of chaps. No, sirree. There'll be no cold nights in bed for me in England either, because I'll have Sheila with me. We plan to get married as soon as I get back."

"Good for you. It's nice to see someone who has such faith and confidence in his girlfriend," Peter said, sitting down between the two. He watched as the water lapped to and fro over the word that had been SHEILA but was now nothing more than smooth wet sand. The tide was coming in fast.

The three young men looked over with considerable interest at a Women's Royal Air Force (WRAF) personnel, one of the few that came to the beach, stripping down to a brief bikini.

"All right," laughed Taffy, sitting up and tossing his chin towards the near nude WRAF, "Which would you prefer, Jimmy, putting a screw into one of your damn Vallettas or screwing her?"

Jimmy ignored the question. Instead, he said, "As I've said before, Sheila and I are getting married as soon as I get back. She's the only one I'm interested in."

Peter lay back on the hot sand, but so close to the water's edge he could feel the incoming tide foaming over and around his feet. He watched the water rush in, stop, and then recede, to trickle away, leaving what had been hot, dry sand, smooth, wet and cooled by its passage.

His thoughts were of his two companions who like himself were serving a full two-and-a-half year overseas tour of duty in the Royal Air Force Far Eastern Command.

Jimmy Edwards, the elder of the three, was twenty, tall and handsome, with a suntanned, muscular body. He spent most of his time outdoors, either at the beach or outside one of the large hangars near the dispersal unit where he was employed as an aero-engine mechanic working on Valletta aircraft. Khaki shorts and a pair of plimsoles was his normal rig-out, even on duty.

Dylan Evans was altogether different. He, too, was suntanned, not brown, but a blotchy red. Short and plump, his sun-bleached blonde hair was a tangled thatch topping a podgy, usually happy face. Born nineteen years ago in a little mining village on the eastern border of Glamorganshire, he was the youngest son from a family of generations of coal miners, yet here he was, a leading aircraftman cook at the officers' mess at RAF Changi in Singapore.

Taffy Evens and Jimmy Edwards were just two of the many RAF friends Peter had made since his arrival at Changi. They had become beach buddies and met almost daily. Now, contentedly lying on his back watching wisps of cloud floating across an otherwise clear blue sky, Peter's attention was suddenly drawn to the arrival of three young Chinese women, clad in colourful *cheongsams*, who were making their way single file along the narrow, much-trodden dirt path which wound snake-like through knee-high grass. The path led all the way from the far end of Changi Village, down past a boat-landing stage, across a narrow concrete bridge, then onto and through this stretch of waste until it reached the beach, to eventually end at Pop's coffee shop.

"Now, to me, those three girls are much more interesting than your prattle," Taffy said, grinning.

"Yeah, a bit of all right," agreed Jimmy.

"But, Jimmy, they are not for you. Remember, you're saving yourself for Sheila," joked Peter.

"And they're not for you either. You'd never get that lucky," replied Jimmy.

"But I can look," said Peter. "I love those *cheongsams*. They really show off a woman's figure. Why don't English girls dress like that?"

"English girls like to keep you guessing. That's their idea of teasing," said Jimmy, grinning. "What you're seeing here is the Chinese method."

"In that case I prefer the Chinese way," said Peter.

"Me, too," agreed Taff. "Hell! Just look at those curves. Boy oh boy, just think what I could do with them! Well, there's three of them and three of us. The question is, how do we get to know them?"

"Perhaps Peter can get you an introduction. He speaks a bit of their lingo," said Jimmy. "Personally, I'm not interested."

"Nor they with us," said Peter. "Nice Chinese girls don't have anything to do with servicemen, especially low-ranking 'erks' like us."

"How bloody true," admitted Taff.

One of Pop's nude children, a two-year-old boy, ran gleefully out to greet the three young women, closely followed by the tail-wagging mongrel dog. They were now only twenty yards from where the three airmen sat 'girl watching'.

Each girl carried a small handbag, and each wore a sexy, tight-fitting *cheongsam*, the timeless and very popular high-collared dress buttoned at the neck, with the skirt slit to well above the knees, cut to reveal shapely legs all the way to the thighs.

"Perhaps they're school teachers," suggested Peter.

"School teachers, my ass! You must be joking!" said Taff. "Not with faces and figures like theirs."

Conversation ceased among the three youths as they watched the army lads get up from their table and leave the shack accompanied by Molly and Lucy, the two Chinese prostitutes. "Hi, gorgeous!" a soldier said to one of the three Chinese girls as they passed each other on the path. The girl ignored him.

Several other people were also leaving the beach; it was time for a late lunch, and afterwards, a siesta.

The leading Chinese girl was met by the mongrel dog, which barked and wagged its tail frantically in a big show of friendliness. Pop's nude little boy greeted her by running to her and raising his arms expectantly. She picked him up and hugged him, all the while laughing and talking to him in Cantonese.

On entering the coffee shop, the three were greeted by a friendly nod from Pop, who got up from the table where he was repairing a fishing net and gestured for them to sit down upon wooden stools provided at one of the half dozen weather-beaten, wood-planked tables. Momma, smiling and showing off her many gold teeth, said, "Hello," in Chinese and asked if she could get them something. One of the girls ordered three cups of coffee.

"It's a pity Chinese girls are not friendlier to us servicemen," Peter said sadly. "I would really like to make friends with one."

"Unfortunately, we don't have much to offer them," said Taff.

"I know," said Peter. "The little one with the nice smile is so lovely. I wish she was my girlfriend."

"There's no chance of that happening," said Jimmy.

The three watched as the girls drank coffee, talked to Pop and Momma, played with the children and laughed a lot. They were now the only customers, the other patrons having taken the path back to Changi Village. The beach was also thinning out, probably because the sun worshippers had seen the ominous black clouds darkening the horizon, which were rapidly rolling in towards Changi.

Hurrying along the path, a class of Chinese school children headed towards the shack, about thirty little boys, each with a neatly rolled-up towel tucked beneath an arm. Onward they came, seemingly as if walking amid waist-high grass, some singing, others shouting happily to one another, their lone teacher, a thin, bookworm of a man, bringing up the rear. Noisily, the procession passed close to where the three young airmen lay on the sand, and then, in a long line, still laughing, singing and shouting, they wound their way in front of the coffee shop, playfully kicking sand into the air and at each other as they headed up the beach. Eventually, on rounding a far bend, they were lost from sound and sight.

Pop's three children came down to the water's edge. The little girl fell in and began to cry. The two boys ignored her, their attention happily focussed on rocking to and fro one of the several rowing boats drawn up on the beach. At a table in a corner of the shack, Momma began nursing her baby; and when the baby began to cry she placed her into the cradle of cloth hanging from the overhead beam and gently rocked her to sleep.

Meanwhile, the three young women had retired to two rickety little huts annexed to the main shack. Constructed of equally rough, weather-beaten wood, these huts were the changing rooms Pop had built for the use of his coffeeshop clients. And on the hot sand above the incoming water's edge, the three young airmen watched expectantly and waited. Within minutes the two rickety doors opened and, clad in one-piece bathing costumes, the three young women stepped cautiously out onto the hot sand and into brilliant sunshine.

"Wow! Get a load of that!" exclaimed Taffy. "They're beautiful."

"Let's wait for them to come down to the beach, then we'll try talking to them. They'll probably ignore us, but it's worth a try," said Peter.

Once away from the changing huts where there was no shade, the sand was a real foot-burner, so the three young women, laughing and shouting, raced down the sloping beach towards the water and did not stop until they were in knee deep. There, less than fifty feet from where the three young airmen were ogling them, they splashed each other, and screamed with laughter.

Watching the girls but saying nothing, Peter wondered how he could become acquainted with them. On an impulse, he said to the others, "I'm going for a dip." Standing up, he waded into the water, then suddenly dove with hardly a splash, to slide from sight beneath the calm surface.

Meandering his way along the bottom through a forest of tall grasses firmly rooted in mud, he eventually reached deep water. He then turned and swam towards the girls. And when he could hold his breath no longer, he rose to the surface quite close to where they were standing waist-high in the shallows.

Suddenly, from Changi airfield, the piercing whine of turbo-jets broke the tranquillity of the afternoon, screaming higher and higher until they had reached their maximum pitch. And then the whine settled down into a fast approaching whisper, until suddenly, from off the main runway, and flying low over their heads, shot a British Overseas Airways Corporation (BOAC) Comet named Yolk Peter, the first-ever commercial passenger jet airliner. Glinting in the dazzling sunlight, her undercarriage already gracefully folding up into huge wings, her vapour trails and hot air flow descending on those below amid a whiff of unburned jet fuel, and with the roar of her mighty jet engines following her passage, that graceful, beautiful aircraft rapidly ascended over the Strait, the nearby islands, and then the mainland of Malaya far in the distance. Within seconds she became nothing more than a dot on the horizon, and then she was gone. Her first stop would be Rangoon in Burma, then on to Calcutta in India, and in a matter of hours she would once again swoop down and land at her home terminal, Heathrow Airport in London, England.

The three RAF boys and the three Chinese girls watched in awe as the jet aircraft passed low overhead and streaked out across the water. But now, out of sight, the aircraft was forgotten, their attention concentrated again on the pleasures of their immediate surroundings. Peter, showing off, swam outward for several yards in a fast crawl and then lay floating on his back. He spat out salt water, hoping he would be noticed by the girls and wondering whether he could speak to them without appearing too forward.

Seemingly oblivious to the young man in the water who had approached so near to them, the three girls, up to their knees in shallow water, were wading along the foreshore, splashing each other and laughing in delight.

They were just a few yards from him. Peter watched as one of the girls slipped and suddenly sat down in the water. This caused considerable amusement among them for they shrieked with laughter. Peter, fascinated, could not take his eyes off them, especially the smaller of the three who had waded out from the beach and who was now standing up to her waist in water. He watched as she plunged forward with her arms outstretched, swam a few strokes, and then, almost immediately, was on her feet again, but now shoulder deep in water, spluttering and laughing, and a little closer to him.

Drifting with the tide, the fibrous husk of a coconut floated towards Peter. Holding out a hand, he caught the water-sodden husk as it drew near and, without a second thought, tossed it towards the girl who, at that moment, had turned her face towards him. The husk dropped with a splash not more than an inch from her nose. Giving a little cry of feigned annoyance, she rebuked him in Chinese, wagged a finger at him, and then catching hold the husk tossed it back at him. He laughed and again plonked the husk near her; then he dived under the water, swimming with the tide, allowing it to carry him towards her. Bobbing up alongside her and laughing, he greeted her, "Hello." She ignored him. He blew out a mouthful of water. "Aren't you going to say hello?" he pleaded, smiling. Then the fast tide carried him away from her.

The girl had an amused smile on her face when she again threw the husk back towards him. But the husk plopped into the water halfway between them. Both hurried towards it, Peter swimming, whilst she waded out into even deeper water. Each reached for the husk and were soon fighting for it, all the while laughing and splashing each other. The Chinese girl took hold of the husk and would not let go, and Peter felt her floating hair sweep across his face. Reaching out a hand he playfully pushed her head under the water, just for a few seconds, then let go but she seemed to lose her balance and was floundering, and the next moment she disappeared below the surface. She came up choking and gasping for air, then with a gurgled scream she sank again. Peter, to his horror, suddenly realized that the girl could not swim. Frantically grabbing her floating hair, he pulled her head to the surface. He then slipped an arm around her to keep her from sinking again. She was coughing and spluttering but she did not struggle as he pulled her towards the shore. Obviously frightened at what had taken place, her two girlfriends waited in the shallows until Peter was close enough for them to help their friend to the safety of the beach. There she lay on the sand, shaking with fright, coughing up water, spluttering, and eventually swearing loudly in Cantonese at Peter.

Embarrassed, Peter was standing over her saying, "I'm sorry. I'm so very sorry. Please forgive me."

The girl swore at him again. Eventually, though, she sat up, still coughing and stared at him angrily.

"I didn't realize you couldn't swim, and I did say I'm sorry," said Peter.

"Go away. You very bad boy," the girl said, glaring at him.

But Peter did not go away.

The two girlfriends began to giggle and appeared to joke about him to each other. Then they left their friend alone with him and returned to the water.

Not knowing what to do next and certainly not wanting to leave her, Peter sat down beside her on the wet sand. At first he looked out to sea, and then he looked at the girl sitting at his side. How beautiful she was, even in anger. A strap of her costume had slipped from her shoulder partially revealing small breasts so appetizing he wanted to bend his head and kiss them. In open admiration he studied her face, her tiny hands, her shapely legs stretched out upon the wet sand. Her skin, the colour of fresh cream, was smooth and without blemish. Reaching out a hand he gently touched her arm. "I am sorry," he repeated, quietly and sincerely.

"Please go away and leave me alone," she answered coldly, pulling her arm away from his touch and looking not at him but instead out across the water.

"You're very beautiful," he said to her. "I'm sorry, but not too sorry. At least I've had this opportunity to meet you. My name is Peter."

She remained silent. He's very young, she thought. Perhaps fourteen or fifteen. He must be a schoolboy, and all schoolboys do silly things. And he didn't look evil. Surely he meant her no harm. He was only a little boy wanting to play. And he seemed to be a gentle boy. Looking up into his sincere eyes, she said, "You are young boy. You make bad because you young."

Peter replied, "Well, that's nonsense. Anyway, I'm older than I look."

"You go school here? Why you live in Singapore? Your daddy is army boy?" she asked.

"Good grief, no! I'm not a schoolboy," Peter said, laughing. "I'm nineteen. I'm in the RAF."

Obviously puzzled, she looked quizzically into his face.

"I'm an airman. I'm stationed here at Changi," he said. He flapped his arms as if he were a bird in flight. Her anger melted and she forced herself not to giggle at the sight of him looking so serious while flapping his arms up and down. Of course she knew what an airman was, but he looked far too young to be a serviceman. "You know, a bird," he was saying. "An airman is like a bird. He flies."

"Do you fly?" she asked, almost unable to control her laughter. Her anger had melted and she was interested in this boy. He looked so innocent, and he made her laugh.

"No, I don't fly. Well, not very often. Only when I'm being posted from one camp to another."

"You are an officer?" she asked. "You are very young to be an officer."

"No. I'm not an officer. I'm just an airman. A tiny cog in the wheel," said Peter, warming more and more to her company.

"A tiny cog in the wheel! I do not understand."

"It's just a saying, meaning I'm someone who helps in a small way."

"Oh! I see," she was saying, when suddenly, rising from the nearby runway with a roar, and slowly gaining altitude as it passed low over their heads, a Handley Page Hastings aircraft, a four-engine aircraft of Transport Command headed north, its course altering due west as it approached the coastline of Malaya. It was probably on its first leg to England, thought Peter.

"What work you do? You fly big one, same as that?" asked the girl at his side.

Peter laughed, "No, I'm not a pilot, nothing so exciting. I'm a cook."

"A cook!" She repeated the two words as if more amazed than if he had said he flew big planes. "You are very young to be RAF cook," she said. "What you say your name is?"

"Peter," he answered.

"Peter," she repeated, and then again, "Peter," as if turning the name over in her mind.

"Yes, Peter," he was saying, loving the way she pronounced his name. He decided to try his Chinese on her. "Now that you know my name, what is your name?" he asked in Cantonese.

A look of intense surprise came upon the girl's face. Astonished, she asked in Cantonese, "You speak Chinese?"

Peter chuckled. "A little," he said, again in Chinese.

"Where did you learn Chinese?" she asked.

"Here and in Hong Kong, and mostly in the kitchens where I work. In the kitchens many of the workers speak no English, so I learn Chinese and speak to them in Chinese. And I can write a few Chinese characters, too," Peter boasted. Eagerly he bent forward and with his index finger drew a short horizontal line in the wet sand. "Yat," he said, "One." Then he drew two horizontal lines, "Yee, two," He followed by writing in the sand all the characters up to ten, reading them in Cantonese as he wrote them. "I can write up to a thousand," he bragged. "And look, I can speak and write 'one cup of tea,'" This he also did in Chinese. "I can speak and write several other kitchen terms in Chinese," he said.

"You are a very clever boy," said the girl in a surprised and delighted voice.

"And look!" said Peter laughing. "See if you can read this." Carefully, and with considerable thought, he moved his index finger through the wet sand until he was satisfied at the characters he had drawn. "Well?" he asked.

The girl studied the characters. She was not sure, but she thought she knew and she began to giggle.

"It means," said Peter seriously, "There's a fly in my soup."

Clapping her hands in delight, the girl exclaimed, "Oh, you are so funny. The kitchen boys teach you all these things?"

Returning to English, Peter said, "Well, not only the kitchen boys but also the cooks and waiters. There is one kitchen boy that I especially like who teaches me Chinese. He's the one I fight with."

"Fight with?" asked the girl, perplexed.

"Yes. He's called 'Chuff Box.' That's his nickname. We fight often. He's smaller than me, but he always wins. He's teaching me to fight Chinese style. Really, though, we are very good friends." And then he said with a grin on his face, "Perhaps you and I could teach each other something," followed by, "Please, won't you tell me your name?"

Amazed by him, she looked into his enquiring face, a little boy's face full of kindness and innocence, she thought, and she suddenly thought of her late husband. He had been just like this boy when they had first met. There were the same characteristics, the same show of caring, the same qualities, the same youthfulness. Her late husband was not European, he was Chinese, yet she could not help but see a likeness. Perhaps it was just her imagination, she thought. "Why?" she asked Peter. "Why you want know my name?"

Imitating her voice, Peter mimicked, "Why you want know my name?" Then he answered her question quietly and affectionately. "It's because I like you," he replied. "I like to be with you." And at that moment he felt something towards her he had never experienced before with a woman. Without knowing it, he was falling in love.

4

Chan Lai Ming was her Chinese name, but she was also called Rose. Living in a British colony, many Singapore Chinese adopted an English name.

"Lai Ming is a lovely name, and you're lovely, too," said Peter. "But I shall call you Rose. It's such a pretty name," and he gave a little laugh, saying, "it's easy for me to remember."

She smiled. "My friends are Ah Ling and Susy Wee," she said. "Susy is my very special friend. She is soon to be married to a business man who owns a beauty parlour close to the Cathay cinema." Then she asked, "Do you come here often?"

"Almost every day," replied Peter.

"To look for girls?" she asked, looking up into his face and smiling mischievously.

"Good Lord, no!" exclaimed Peter. "Well, maybe just to look at them." Then he said, "You're the first Chinese girl I've spoken to here on the beach."

"You are not married. You are too young to be married," she said. They were statements, not questions.

"I'm not too young," said Peter. "But, no, I'm not married," and he wondered why she was so curious.

Accompanied by Jimmy and Taff, her girlfriends had moved a hundred yards or more down the beach. Peter could hear them shouting and laughing, and he watched them for moments as they frolicked together in the shallows. He was glad that he was alone with Lai Ming. Fascinated, he studied her. She had such a beautiful face, even though, as she gazed out to sea she looked so sad. With her jet black hair falling down around bare shoulders, he saw her as a cuddlesome doll and was daring himself just to touch that creamy, porcelain-like skin. He wanted to hold her to him and to kiss that exquisite little mouth, but instead he did nothing except sit and study her, and wait until she spoke again.

Eventually, when she did speak, she caught him by surprise. Turning her face to him, she said, "I was once married. I was very young. I was only sixteen. I was married to a good man, a kind and devoted husband."

"What happened to him?" asked Peter.

He detected tears forming in Lai Ming's eyes, but for the moment she controlled them. A tremor, though, entered her voice when she said, "He is dead. He died in an accident."

"Oh. I'm sorry," said Peter.

"It seems such a long time ago, but many times I still think of him," she said. Now, without a doubt, he could see tears in her eyes, tears that were about to run down her cheeks.

"Perhaps it's best you don't talk about it," suggested Peter, feeling uneasy at seeing her looking so sad.

She smiled through her tears at him. "You are a good boy," she said. But she wondered, why am I thinking of my husband when with this boy, this complete stranger?

After a pause of several seconds, deep in thought, and looking far out across the water, Lai Ming quietly said, "I want to tell you."

Thus, that day, while sitting with Lai Ming on the sands of Changi Beach, Peter listened and learned much of her past. Spellbound by her soft, lyrical voice, he did not interrupt her.

She was born in Palembang, on the island of Sumatra in Indonesia, she said, to Chinese parents who were murdered by the invading Japanese when she was in her early teens. She herself was rescued by a young Chinese ship's engineer who sneaked her aboard his ship, an old tramp steamer bound for Singapore. On the ship's arrival in Singapore, he asked her if she would marry him. She had said 'yes' not only because she had no one else in the world to turn to, but because she found in him so many good qualities and was attracted to him. Shortly afterwards, they were married. He looked after her well, providing her with all she needed, even sending her to a good school in Singapore where she learned to speak English. To her, her husband was the best man in the world. Together, they were both blissfully happy, and even happier when she bore him a son. Somehow they managed to survive the cruel Japanese occupation of Singapore and it was not too long before the British returned and peace came once again to the island. Three years ago her husband was returning from Brunei on the same ship in which he had brought her to Singapore. It was to be the ship's last voyage and was being delivered to a ship-breaker's yard. The ship never arrived at its destination. When miles out at sea a boiler in the engine room exploded killing her husband and the crew working in the engine room. The ship sank in deep water. Only three deck hands and the cook survived to tell what happened to their ship, and of their ordeal swimming in shark-infested waters, before being picked up by a passing freighter.

Lai Ming paused, her eyes searching Peter's face, then, after a few moments, she continued, "I am alone now, to fend for myself and my seven year old son. He is at a boarding school here in Singapore." Sighing wistfully, Lai Ming became silent again, her dreamy eyes gazing at him, her memory flooding back to those happy days when her husband sat at her side looking at her, just as this boy was looking at her now. She shrugged and smiled at him. "I don't know why I have told you so much about myself," she said. "We have not met before, and soon we shall go our separate ways." She placed a tiny hand on his arm. "Peter, I don't know why I tell you my troubles. I have never before told a stranger of my past." Taking her hand from his arm, she ran tiny fingers through the sand that separated them.

Peter saw her lovely, almond-shaped eyes again turn away from him, and he believed she was actually blushing. He lay back on the sand and watched billowing clouds scudding across the sky, black clouds that soon would blot out the sun. White horses were already racing across the wind-swept water of the Johore Strait; water which, only minutes ago, had been calm and still, was already whipped up into a fury. Away to the left palm trees swayed ominously. Peter thought, we're in for a hell of a storm, and it won't be long in coming. But, for the moment, he cast the threat of the approaching storm aside. "I'd like to know you better, Rose. I would like you as a friend," he said sincerely, again sitting up and looking into her face.

She smiled sadly at him, "For me it is a big pleasure meeting you, Peter, and I have forgiven you for nearly drowning me, but our paths must go separate ways." She looked away from him as she continued by saying, "After today we shall not meet again. It is better that way." But she knew she spoke those last words with a heavy heart.

"I don't understand you, Rose. Why shouldn't we meet again?" Peter asked. "Don't you like me?"

She smiled tenderly at him. "I think you are a good boy." She was about to say more when a large drop of rain, and then another, splashed cold upon her bare shoulders. Lifting her face to the sky, she watched as a mass of rolling black clouds finally extinguished the sun, and she felt the warmth of the air turn suddenly cold. The brightness of the day was gone, suddenly it became almost dark.

Peter wanted to say, "Let's get our asses out of here," but instead politely said, "Rose, we must go, and quickly." Jumping to his feet, he stretched out a hand to assist her. "Come," he said, and she grasped his hand and he pulled her up so that she stood facing him. She was not even five feet tall, not by two or three inches. He felt like a giant towering over her, the top of her head did not even reach his chin. A warmth towards her flooded through him as he looked down upon that beautiful little face and into those lovely brown eyes that were gazing up into his. He wanted to crush her to him, to hold her and to feel her snug in his arms, but he just stared down at her in wonderment. A vivid flash of lightning striking close by, immediately followed by a booming crack of thunder directly overhead, brought Peter back to the predicament, even danger, they were in. The skies had opened up, too, for suddenly cold, heavy rain lashed down upon them. With urgency in his voice, Peter shouted, "Let's run to the coffee shop." Then he remembered his clothes lying on the beach several yards away. "Excuse me," he said, and raced away from her. Scooping up the already saturated clothing, he then raced back to Lai Ming who was already hurrying towards Pop's shack.

He heard Taffy shout, "We're heading back to the village, Peter. Are you coming?"

Peter shouted his reply, "No. I'm staying here. You'll get drenched. Stay here."

"No. I've a buffet to do this evening at the officers' mess. Good luck. See you later," Taffy shouted.

Peter watched as his two friends disappeared into the deluge of rain that was now cascading from the heavens, then he raced after Lai Ming who was already halfway between the beach and the coffee shop. In the distance, not far from the beach end of Changi's main runway, a grove of palm trees swayed before a quickly rising wind, and huge green leaves of banana trees growing in the silt near the shack loudly rustled their warning. More vivid flashes of lightning lit up the sky, and the sharp crack and rumbling of thunder grew louder, constant, and more intense. Catching up with Lai Ming, he again grasped her hand, and feeling her fingers entwine in his, they raced to the sanctuary of the coffee shop through sheets of cold, blinding rain.

Running, dripping with water, laughing and still holding hands, Peter and Lai Ming dashed into the palm-thatched shack which provided some shelter from the howling wind and driving rain. In several places, though, the roof leaked like a sieve, the constant dripping of water forming little pools of muddy water in the dirt below. Lai Ming's two girlfriends were already seated at a table.

"Hey, Pop, four hot coffees and a packet of biscuits, please," shouted Peter, as he and Lai Ming joined the two girls at the table.

Pop grinned in his usual friendly manner and replied, "OK, Johnny. One minute." He shuffled away on bare feet to where a blackened water pot stood amid glowing embers within a bucket-shaped charcoal fire, the kitchen's centrepiece. Yellowish-brown smoked fish hung from an overhead beam of bamboo, and in a shallow china basin were several black and white striped eggs that had been buried for months in warm mud and were now ripe and ready for eating. From another bamboo beam a basket of green and yellow Chinese cabbage and lettuce swung in the wind. Beneath these were open boxes containing root vegetables, and in a corner of the kitchen were a number of smoke-blackened pots and pans in which Pop and Momma's gastronomic delights were cooked.

In a far corner of the shack sat Momma, once again lovingly suckling her newborn baby. Around her, still naked, her other three children played, running in and out of the tiny waterfalls flowing through the roof, shrieking with laughter, and making comic faces when the cold rainwater splashed down upon their bronzed bodies.

A flock of scrawny hens braved the storm by scratching in the mud outside the shack, while others pecked insects from the dirty, sandy, wood-planked floor, from the rotted plywood and canvas walls, and from the termite-ridden poles holding up the place.

"Hello again," said Peter to the two seated girls. "This is quite a fun place, isn't it?"

Both Ah Ling and Susy Wee giggled and looked with some curiosity at him, and then at Lai Ming.

"He is just a little boy," teased Ah Ling in Chinese. "You are stealing a little boy from his Momma."

"But you know what they say, 'Big boy, big cock. Little boy, all cock,'" said Susy, also in Chinese. And to Lai Ming's absolute embarrassment both girls exploded into a fit of giggles.

"He speaks some Chinese," snapped Lai Ming at her friends in English, and then she scolded them in Chinese.

Obviously embarrassed, Ah Ling buried her face in her hands, and said, "Me very sorry." Peter, though, detected poorly suppressed giggles.

Sitting across from Peter, and trying to keep a straight face, Susy said to him in Chinese, "What's your name?" But she too could not stifle her giggles.

"They are both very naughty girls," said Lai Ming. "I am ashamed of them."

Peter chuckled. "I think they are both very funny girls," he said. He hadn't understood what was said word for word, but he did get their meaning. "My name is Peter," he answered Susy in Cantonese.

"Me very happy to meet you, Peter," responded Susy, in English, and she held out her hand for him to shake. "Friend of Ming is friend of mine," she said.

"Thank you," said Peter, realizing that neither Susy Wee nor Ah Ling spoke English as well as Lai Ming did.

The conversation was interrupted by Pop, who approached the table saying, "Here, Johnny, four coffees and biscuits," and he set before them four miniature blue-tinted cups of steaming hot coffee and a packet of sweet biscuits. "One dollar eighty cents," he said.

Peter said, "Thanks, Pop," and paid the man.

Now, torrential rain was falling, and as the wind shrieked and howled, lightning streaked through dark skies, and the continuous peals of thunder smote the air like gunfire from a thousand howitzers. In places, the canvas sides of the shack blew apart, the wind whipping the ragged ends so that they flapped violently. The water-logged roof leaked more than ever but Pop, Momma and family remained unperturbed, having experienced countless such storms.

"Peter, can you play mahjong?" asked Lai Ming suddenly.

"A little," he answered. "Why?"

"I would like to play but there must be four players. I have seen that the coffeehouse man has a set of pieces. I think he would loan us the set. It may rain for two or three hours. By playing mahjong we could occupy ourselves until the storm passes over." She turned and spoke to Pop in Cantonese, who grinned and nodded, got up from where he sat, and took from an old tea-chest a long cardboard box.

Approaching the table, he placed the box in front of Peter. "You savvy mahjong, Johnny?" he asked. "Not much English boy can do. This Chinese game. Velly hard game. English boy, no quick. No same Chinese boy. Chinese boy velly quick."

"I know," acknowledged Peter, thinking of the quickness of the Chinese cooks and kitchen boys where he worked. "They are fast at whatever they do," he said.

Pop grinned. He was quite pleased at his knowledge of English. He emptied the box of mahjong pieces onto the table, one hundred and forty-four little oblong tiles, painted green and white, and coated with a shiny lacquer. Engraved into the separate pieces were Chinese characters; on some, dots, on others, Chinese numerals, peacocks, wheels, and some with colourful, brightly painted pictures on them, each piece denoting their place and worth in the game of mahjong, The Four Winds.

The three girls shuffled the tiles, clattering and banging them as they turned the pieces face down. Then they shuffled them until satisfied, and then placed them in four double rows to be dealt out.

The violence of the storm was now unbounded. The screaming wind blowing in from the sea hurled the pouring rain against one side of the swaying shack, where it beat upon the flapping canvas more and threw off showers of cold water.

Pop returned to the repairing of his net, Momma was crooning over the baby who was now asleep in its cradle of cloth, and the children were still chasing gleefully after the wet and ruffled dog. The outdoor chickens had all come in from the rain and were now busily scratching and pecking and clucking in every part of the shack as they enjoyed their luncheon dessert.

The mahjong pieces were dealt out and the game began.

A little over two hours later the rain stopped. The storm had passed over Changi. The black cumulus clouds had rolled away almost as unnoticed as their arrival, and once again the sun shone, no longer hot and fierce, but weak and watery, as it slid with gentle ease towards the edge of the world.

A dewy mist hung thinly in the air, perfumed and sweet, a steamy haze lazily lifting skyward, sucked up by the heat from the sodden earth. In the tall grasses surrounding the shack, bullfrogs honked incessantly and praying mantids jumped from their hiding places to leap joyfully through wet rushes. The dog had crept from its hiding-place beneath a table, and on sniffing the air sprang through a gaping hole in the torn canvas, shook its shaggy hair, gave a woof of delight, bounded away through a covering of tall grasses and headed towards a hut where a Malay fisherman's family lived. The chickens were again busily pecking in the muddy sand outside the shack; now that the rain had ceased, there were plenty of insects for them to feast on.

The game of mahjong was over. Lai Ming was carefully arranging the tiles one by one back into their box, her tiny, delicate fingers toying with each piece as she slowly and methodically fitted it into its place. She said little when Ah Ling and Susy Wee excused themselves to walk along the beach. Her mind was confused but she would not allow her eyes to betray her confusion, so she kept them fixed upon the box. The boy sitting opposite her was eager. There was no want of trying on his part. He had asked her repeatedly during the game for a date—to have dinner with him, to visit the Tiger Balm Gardens, the Tropical Gardens, the zoo over at Johore Bahru, or any place of her choice. But if she said, 'yes,' she knew that it would eventually hurt him, so she had repeatedly said 'no.' She stole a glance at him. He was still a boy, and she an experienced woman. Again she thought to herself, whichever way I go, I will hurt him, but having said 'no,' it will hurt him the least. She did like him though. He was the first boy her heart had warmed to since the death of her husband, yet she had to refuse him. She wondered if she should tell him the truth about herself. That should discourage him. But she could not tell him the truth. He would not understand.

The sun, weak and watery, and sinking quickly, cast its final rays of the day upon the water as it sank down over a horizon streaked with beams of gold, orange and indigo. The glow spread in a wide arc across the heavens in many more colours before the sun finally sank from sight behind the jungle-clad hills of Johore; then the bright colours suddenly faded, and it was already evening.

Together, Peter Saunders and Lai Ming had watched the setting of the sun, and then they turned to face each other.

"I don't know why you keep refusing me, Rose!" Peter persisted. "'The African Queen' starring Katherine Hepburn is showing at the Capitol Theatre. I love Katherine Hepburn, she's always good, and I've heard it's a very good picture. I could take you there this evening! Just for the one occasion. On my word of honour, I'll be a perfect gentleman, and I'll see you safely home in a taxi." Lai Ming was shaking her head, but he continued, "I'd be so very happy to have your company, Rose."

Again Lai Ming shook her head, "No, Peter, I will not go with you, and that is my final word. I am getting cold. I must dress. It is time to go," she snapped. "Why me? Peter, there are many younger girls in Singapore who would love to have you as a boyfriend."

"I've never met any," said Peter.

"That is because nice girls are often shy. They too find it difficult to make friends. The boy must break that shyness barrier, but once broken the boy would have a true friend, maybe for life. Why don't you try to find such a girl, a young girl, but not a widow who is so much older than yourself, a widow with a seven-year-old child. I know you say you want to take me out, just the once, but I don't think so, man is not made that way. You may wish for my company more than once, and although I would probably enjoy your company, I have plans for the life ahead of my son and I, plans that mean everything to me. And Peter, you must not come between my plans and me. You cannot be part of my plans. I cannot allow it. You cannot be in my life," she said vehemently.

"Why? I don't understand you, Rose!"

"I cannot discuss my plans with you, but I do know that no one must interfere with them. Don't I make myself clear to you?" she demanded.

Hurt and confused, Peter said, "Rose, I have no wish to interrupt anything that you have in mind, but I like you so much. I just don't want to lose you now that I have found you. I want your company, your friendship. I have no wish to pry into your private affairs." He paused for a moment, then, shaking his head, said, "I cannot understand why my taking you out just the one time or a hundred times for that matter can upset any plans you may have."

Pop and Momma sat at a table in the far corner of the shack eating their last meal of the day, boiled fish and cabbage, and boiled white rice from shallow bowls. Occasionally they glanced to where the boy and girl sat talking a few tables away, and they threw meaningful looks at each other, but they ate in silence.

He looks so pathetically sad and lonely, Lai Ming thought. "You just don't understand, Peter. You are making it very difficult for me," Lai Ming said quietly, "and difficult for yourself."

Peter remained silent, staring vacantly and fingering an empty coffee cup. He had been so hopeful, so blissfully happy with her company, and so absolutely sure of himself. Now it seemed futile to argue or plead further.

Lai Ming read his thoughts. She felt sorry for him. Her eyes were also sad. She knew how he felt, he was just another of the countless number of young servicemen away from their homes and family. Each and every one of them must experience some pangs of homesickness and loneliness, she thought. Peter, sitting opposite her, was not unique. Here in Singapore, thousands of miles from his home, family and friends, he was just another lonesome boy. Just a short while ago, on the beach and here in the shack, he was filled with exuberance and elated by her company but now he was downcast, his face showing disappointment, almost melancholy. She could end his loneliness, she knew, but at what cost, to him as well as to herself? She was lonely, too. Perhaps, in a sense, lonelier than he. She needed a good friend, a good boyfriend, someone who would love her as she so desperately wanted to be loved, and someone to whom she could give her love.

Pop came to the table and said to Peter, "You want something, Johnny?"

Peter answered, "No, nothing else, Pop, thanks."

Pop nodded. He liked this boy who came almost daily to his shack. He remembered how Peter had recently said to him, "Some day in the near future, you could build a beautiful restaurant right on this spot. You and your wife would have others to work for you, and you would make lots of money. And as there's a lovely view of the islands from here, you could call your new place the Island View Cafe." And Pop had smiled at the eager, enterprising youth, nodded his agreement, but had said nothing. Time will tell, he thought. He took the box of mahjong pieces from Lai Ming's hands. "He comes often," he said to her in Cantonese, nodding his head towards Peter. "He is a good boy. He is honourable."

"Thank you," she said to him, and suddenly she felt confused no longer; Pop had made her mind up for her, just through those few words. Why not, she thought. She needed someone kind, someone she could trust.

She was about to speak when Peter got up from the table, and in a sad voice said to her, "Rose. I'm going to change," and he gathered up his clothes from where he had left them on a nearby stool and disappeared into one of the changing rooms.

Ah Ling and Susy, having kept at a respectable distance by walking the beach during the long conversation, entered the shack moments after seeing Peter get up from the table.

"Well?" asked Ah Ling, intense curiosity plainly written on her face. "Is he going home with you?"

"No, I have no wish to take him to my home. He is a good boy," said Lai Ming, " but he is very young."

"If you don't want him, I will take him," teased Ah Ling. "I will teach him fucky-fuck," and she giggled and looked at Susy for her to say something.

She did. "Ming, he is young, but you need a boy to call your own. And he looks to be a good boy."

"I am sure he is," Lai Ming said, almost in a whisper.

"Well, why not enjoy him? I can see by his face that he will respect you as a friend, as well as be a good lover," said Ah Ling.

"You are right, Ah Ling, and you are a good friend. You are both good friends," she said, startled by her own admission. "I will speak to him, and I will surprise him," she said.

Her heart was pounding when Peter, looking sad and rejected, emerged from the changing room and joined the three girls at the table. Lai Ming waited for him to sit down, which he did, opposite her. Then, taking his hand in hers she stroked the back of it with her fingers. "Peter, I have changed my mind," she said softly. "I would like to go to the cinema to see that picture with you. What is the name of the picture? I forget."

Speechless, Peter could only stare at her in disbelief.

"Well?" she asked, a gentle smile playing on her face as she looked into his bewildered eyes.

"'The African Queen'!" Peter spluttered. And now, suddenly filled with relief and happiness, he exclaimed, "I don't believe you, Rose. What happened?"

"I told you, I changed my mind," Lai Ming answered quietly, her soft eyes not moving from his.

"Oh, God!" Peter gasped, "Rose, I just don't know what to say. Suddenly you've made me the happiest man in the world."

"I am glad for you," Lai Ming answered, again very quietly, and she gave his hand a gentle squeeze.

"Shall we go this evening?" asked Peter.

"Why not?" A lock of black hair fell across her brow. Lifting a hand she deftly swept it back over her head. "Yes, I would like to go to the pictures with you this evening," she said.

"That's fantastic!" Peter exclaimed. Elated, he said, "And after the pictures, I'll take you to dinner, and we'll have cocktails together, and maybe we'll dance."

Lai Ming smiled at his enthusiasm. "You make me laugh, Peter," she answered. "You make everything sound so wonderful. I know we shall enjoy spending this evening together."

Susy, listening to the conversation, said in Chinese to Lai Ming, "Now that you two love birds have decided what you are going to do, we must go because it's getting late, and soon it will be dark. We must return to the city."

"Yes, you are right, it is time for us to change and go," said Lai Ming. She got up from the table and, accompanied by her two friends, walked towards the changing rooms.

5

Changi Village had only the one road running through it, a tarmacked road bordered on both sides by a strip of unpaved land, stony and dusty when the weather was dry but full of muddy potholes and wide pools of water when it rained, which was often. On these strips of unpaved land huge shade trees grew. Their main purpose, though, were as parking places for vans owned by local merchants and the few cars which visited the village; the public generally used the frequent and excellent bus service to and from Changi and the main city of Singapore. Planked boardwalks, about eight feet wide and raised a few inches from the ground, ran much the length of the street. These provided pedestrians protection from the mud and the dirt beneath, and upon which they could walk and browse at leisure the varied open shopfronts lining both sides of the street. There was much to see: the Indian emporiums, Chinese clothing and tailoring shops, china and glassware shops, and those which sold ivory artefacts, animals carved from mahogany, leather suitcases, picturesque wall mats, chess sets and music boxes. There was something to suit everyone's taste.

On one side of the street were several bars and eating places, some catering to the palates of the local population, the others to the many military personnel and their families visiting the village. Those which catered to the locals were mostly out of bounds to all British military personnel, but Peter Saunders could not understand why this was so, especially as they appeared to be clean and well-run establishments. Perhaps, he thought, it was a leftover from the old colonial days when the white man considered himself superior; it was just 'not done' to mingle and fraternize with the 'natives'.

On this evening, although the tarmacked road had already steamed itself dry, the parking places were muddy and filled with pools of rainwater. Saturday evening, early yet, but in an hour or so the boardwalks would be alive with throngs of people wandering up and down that two-hundred yards of shopfronts, enjoying the vibrant noises, gaudiness and exotic smells. Changi Village was not a residential area but simply a district where people of many ethnic backgrounds— Chinese, Indians, Malays and Caucasians—came for pleasure and to shop. Everyone, or so it appeared, coexisted with easygoing tolerance for one another.

At the seaward end of the village, Peter Saunders, accompanied by Lai Ming and her two girlfriends, left the already darkened beach path and stepped into the brilliantly lit area surrounding the police compound and customs offices. Across the street was the Changi bus terminal and taxi rank. Peter had already decided that he would take the three girls by taxi the fourteen miles to the city, but first he had to return to camp to shower and change his clothes. He would wear his brown slacks and a sharkskin shirt, both painstakingly ironed to perfection by him, the same style of clothing worn by most military other-rank personnel when off camp in the Far East.

While he went off to change, Lai Ming and her two friends would wait for him at Changi Eating House. Next door was Jong Fatt's provisions store situated directly opposite the taxi rank. Peter made sure the three were comfortably seated at a table overlooking the street, ordered them coffee and from there took a taxi the mile or so back to the catering block where he instructed the Chinese driver to wait. Dashing madly up the four flights of stone steps to the third storey, he threw off his beach clothes, hurriedly washed, and then quickly donned his walking-out clothes.

"Hey! Saunders! Where are you off to in such a bloody hurry?" shouted one of the cooks from halfway down the billet.

"I've got a date with a lovely Chinese girl," Peter shouted back breathlessly. "I'm taking her to the pictures."

"Not one of the Saturday afternoon whores who frequent the beach is she?" shouted back the other.

"No. She's a real lady," Peter answered.

"Well, watch out she doesn't give you the clap," the other sang out as Peter dashed from the billet. In his eagerness he almost flew down the four flights of steps and into the open door of the waiting taxi. In less than half an hour from when he had left the three girls, he had rejoined them, finding them completely at their ease, talking and laughing among themselves and still sipping coffee at Changi Eating House.

"Shall we go?" Peter asked Lai Ming.

"Yes," she replied. Her two girlfriends giggled and joked, speaking Chinese words that Peter did not understand. He was not sure whether Lai Ming was amused or annoyed by their remarks. She said to him, "Come! It is late," and together the four left the coffee shop and clambered into the waiting taxi. Peter found himself snugly squeezed into the back seat between Lai Ming and Ah Ling. Susy sat up front.

"Singapore," Peter instructed the driver, indicating that he intended to be taken to the main town on the island.

His face expressionless, the driver mumbled his acknowledgement, the taxi moved forward and soon was speeding rapidly away from Changi Village.

On arriving at the outskirts of the city, Lai Ming gave instructions to the driver, who nodded, slowed and weaved in and out among the dense traffic. Ah Ling was the first to alight. The taxi stopped at the entrance to a brightly-lit amusement park blasting out Chinese music from giant amplifiers. Ah Ling giggled when she said, "Goodbye, Peter. Have a good time." And he watched as she got out of the car and entered the place through a garishly lit turnstile. Minutes later the taxi entered a street where foreboding red, white and black 'OUT OF BOUNDS TO

HIS MAJESTIES FORCES' signs were clearly visible. Peter had no idea as to which part of the city he was in, knowing that never before had he ventured into this street, and he became slightly nervous at being in an 'out of bounds' area.

Two streets further on, Susy said it was time for her to also leave their company. She smiled sweetly at Peter and held out a dainty hand for him to shake. Instead, he kissed it. She giggled and said that he and Lai Ming would surely enjoy each other's company. Saying, "Goodbye," she alighted from the taxi and disappeared among the multitude of people thronging the sidewalk.

Finally Peter was alone with Lai Ming. Smiling to her, he gave her hand a gentle squeeze.

At a junction in the road there was another 'OUT OF BOUNDS' sign, and above it, a street sign which read Lavender Street. The taxi turned into Lavender Street and sped along for some considerable distance before turning right into a narrower, less busy street where a sign read Bendemeer Road. Less than a hundred yards farther, Lai Ming requested the driver to stop.

Peter looked out the taxi window to view a dilapidated, wood and stone, two-storey block of flats. Long bamboo poles alive with fluttering laundry reached out from windows on the two upper floors. The building looked very old.

"Is this where you live, Rose?" Peter asked, apprehensively.

"Yes," Lai Ming replied flatly. "Please. You must come quickly. Many military police patrol here."

"At this time of the day?"

"Yes. You must be careful not be seen by them. I will take you to my apartment where you'll be safe and can remain while I ready myself for the cinema."

Paying the driver, Peter then looked in all directions, but seeing no sign of the feared military police, he alighted. Hastily he followed Lai Ming through a short, narrow alleyway until they reached a green painted door in a red brick wall. "This is the side door," said Lai Ming to Peter. "It is safer for you to come this way." She knocked on the door and called out a name in Chinese. The door creaked open, and confronting them was a grey-haired, gaunt, sickly faced woman who was no more than four-feet in height, clad in a pajama-type costume of black cotton trousers and jacket, a *samfoo*.

"This is Wan Ze, my *amah*," said Lai Ming to Peter. "She is a servant of the building, but I pay her extra to take care of my needs."

"Oh," said Peter, mystified but less nervous of the situation. However, he said nothing more and followed her into the building.

Once inside, Lai Ming led the way up a short flight of narrow linoleum-covered stairs to the next floor, where there was a bamboo door, which she unlocked and slid to one side. "Please, come in," she said. And when he thanked her, she said, "Welcome to my home," and ushered him into a small but surprisingly clean and tidy bed-sitting room. Obviously, the inside of the building is better maintained than the outside, thought Peter.

"Please, sit down. I will make tea," Lai Ming was saying, a wisp of a smile hovering on her face.

"Thank you," said Peter, sitting down upon a wicker chair, one of a matching pair at two sides of a small glass-topped wicker table. He was no longer nervous, just curious, so that when Lai Ming left him he looked at all that was around him. Dominating the room was a king-sized bed with two clean, very white sheets on it, the top one neatly turned back, and without a wrinkle to be seen on either. At the head of the bed, stretching its whole width, were two white pillows with the words 'GOOD MORNING' embroidered across each in pink and green silk; and in a corner of each pillow was embroidered a blue and yellow bird which resembled a swallow in flight. A glass-covered bedside table stood at the head of each side of the bed. And against the wall at the far side of the room was a large, crescent-shaped mirror overlooking a glass-topped dressing table on which lay an assortment of make-up paraphernalia. The only other piece of furniture in the room was a lacquered wardrobe with its door ajar, a Chinese calendar hanging on the inside of it. Peter could see many colourful articles of ladies clothing hanging from a rail inside the wardrobe, and many pairs of dainty shoes in two tidy rows covering its whole floor. All the furniture appeared to be fairly new and modern, and spotlessly clean floral-patterned linoleum covered the floor. I like it here, it's cosy, Peter decided, already feeling at ease and completely at home.

He heard water running and the clink of china coming from below as Lai Ming prepared tea in the downstairs kitchen. Also, he could hear Chinese voices, Chinese music, and the rattle of pots and pans, sounds filtering in through thin walls. It must be the neighbours, thought Peter. He could also hear the sounds of traffic passing along the street below, outside the bedroom's one window. Peter picked up a Chinese magazine from the table and thumbed through it, looking at the pictures and studying the Chinese characters of which he recognized few. He looked up, relieved when Lai Ming returned to the room and came to where he sat. She was carrying a round wicker tray, which she placed near him, on the table. On it was a floral bone china teapot, matching teacups, a sugar bowl, a plate of assorted biscuits, dainty cloth napkins, and two silver teaspoons. Lai Ming smiled graciously at Peter. "You are my honoured guest," she said, almost in a whisper. "I will pour you tea."

"Thank you. But aren't you having any?" enquired Peter.

"I shall take tea with you after I have washed and changed," replied Lai Ming.

"Then I shall wait for you," said Peter.

"No, please don't. You must be thirsty," she said, delicately pouring him tea from the pot. "Do you take sugar?" she asked. And when he replied," Yes, one spoon," she laughed and said, "Only little squares," and she dropped a cube of sugar from a spoon into the tea. "Now I must wash. I will not take long," she said. Peter did not notice the longing look in her eyes as she turned and disappeared into the adjoining bathroom.

Moments later he heard the splashing of falling water coming from the bathroom, and he wondered how Lai Ming must look naked beneath the shower she was now taking. He wished he could take a peek at her. Smiling at his own mischievous thoughts, he wondered just how angry she would become if he went to her and asked could he share the shower with her. But only a few minutes elapsed before the sound of splashing water ceased, and he was sipping hot tea and fantasizing on how she must look stepping from the shower, when suddenly the bathroom door opened and out stepped Lai Ming into the room where he sat. She was wearing a multi-coloured *sarong* wound around her body and held in place by a fold in the cloth tucked into the cleavage of her bosom, and nothing else. She had not dried herself so that where the *sarong* did not cover her bareness droplets of water glistened like a million tiny jewels.

Putting down the teacup, Peter said, "That was quick." His remark was quite innocent, even in an enquiring voice, but he suddenly felt a surge of sexual excitement within him. Entranced, he could only stare at her.

Slowly, seductively, she walked to where he sat, and when near him she stopped and stood before him, a gentle smile hovering ever so faintly upon her beautiful face. Lifting a dainty hand, she loosened the fold in the *sarong* and pulled it free, so that the *sarong*, with nothing to hold it up, fell from her and dropped in a colourful pile at her feet. Thus she stood before Peter, naked, her hands hanging loosely at her sides as if in complete surrender. "Peter, do you like me?" she asked, quietly, her eyes looking into his.

Peter, who had never before seen a naked girl in the flesh, could only stare at her in disbelief. He had some idea of what a woman's body looked like, having seen pictures of them in blurred outlines in the 'men only' magazines, but those photographs showed only the women's breasts, nothing else. He had never seen a woman's vagina, not even in a photograph. Magazines did not show that part of the female anatomy in 1952, nor had there been forms of pornography from which to learn, not with his upbringing. And promiscuity, especially among younger people, was rare. Peter knew nothing, or next to nothing, about sex.

Astounded by her nakedness, his mouth sagged open and his eyes stared at her in amazed disbelief. He was shocked at the sight of the triangular mass of black, curly hair which reached upward from between the top of those lovely legs. He loved, though, the sight of her small firm breasts reaching out to him so invitingly, their surprisingly large nipples erect, all but asking to be fondled and kissed. Still in disbelief at what he was seeing, he shook his head and closed and opened his eyes a few times to make sure he was not dreaming. But he heard her voice saying, "Well, Peter?" And he saw that she really was there, naked, smiling lovingly at him and reaching out her arms to him. "Do you like me?" she repeated.

"Oh, God! Yes, Rose!" he answered, almost inaudibly. "You are beautiful." And as if in a trance he stood up and went to her, wrapped his arms around her, and held her gently to him. In a daze, he was unsure as to what to do next.

"Take off your clothes," she whispered, smiling up into his bewildered face. Then she freed herself from him, went to the bed, lay down upon it, on her back, and gazed up at him. "Hurry!" she insisted.

Kicking off his shoes, Peter quickly unbuttoned and took off his shirt, then slid his slacks, underpants and socks off in one downward sweep so that all lay in a heap on the floor. Never before had he known himself to have such an erection as that which he now had.

Holding out her arms to him, Lai Ming pulled him down upon her. She, too, was surprised at his erection, at its very largeness. She put out a hand to stroke his erect penis. And as her fingers daintily touched and encircled the throbbing shaft, she heard Peter gasp and saw and felt his hot sperm pulsating from him in quick, long spurts onto her hand and over her body where, in tiny rivulets, it ran down over her breasts and over her belly. She was not surprised at the quickness of his ejaculation, he being so extremely nervous and excited; it had taken only the touch of her fingertips for him to lose control and allow the floodgates to open.

Thrilled and without thinking, she exclaimed, "Peter! You are a virgin! You are a boy-virgin! I am your very first woman!" and she clasped her hands in delight, her face fully showing her joy.

Peter, never before feeling so embarrassed, said unhappily, almost sullenly, "I've had lots of women before you," and he got up from her bed. He wanted to dress and be gone from her. He felt foolish, and so humiliated.

Lai Ming smiled and nodded knowingly but said nothing, regretting deeply what she had already said to him and wishing she could retract her words but it was too late. Now, she must not embarrass him further. But she was sure he was a virgin and that he was completely naive about sex, and she was aroused by the thought. He was such a good boy, so well spoken and gentle. Her mind was already made up, he was going to be her boy. She would teach him the art of love, and how to make love the way she wanted to be loved. For the first time since her husband's death she felt deliriously happy.

Getting up from the bed and standing before him, she put her arms around him and looked lovingly up into his eyes. Softly, almost in a whisper, she said, "Peter, let's take a shower together." And she hugged him to her, then stepped back so that he could see her, and caught hold his hand and led him to the bathroom.

There was no bathtub, only a showerstall with a pink curtain draped around it. Still holding his hand, she went ahead of him, and when they were both inside the showerstall she turned the two taps to where she knew the water would come out warm. And when the water was splashing down upon them she took a washcloth, and said, "I will wash you, Peter."

He felt her hand gently stroking his body, caressing him, fondling him, and he felt the warm washcloth she held in her other hand washing his belly, the tops of his legs, and then, carefully and gently, that which she held. He felt himself getting a second erection, and with her holding it and washing it with warm water, it felt good.

"Now it's my turn," he said, taking the cloth from her. And with the water cascading down upon them, he washed her and explored her body; first her shoulders, her supple arms and her tiny hands. Then, taking his time and studying every part of her, he caressed as he washed her firm little breasts, her thighs, her tummy, her smooth little bottom, and finally that fascinating place between her legs. He felt her flinch, and heard her gasp and say, "Oh!" very quietly, as his fingers slid in between the pubic hair to penetrate and examine the little place that felt so soft, so warm and so inviting; and he again became fully erect and wanting to be inside her. But on looking down between their two naked bodies, he could not help but chuckle, for he found the sight amusing, almost comical. Lai Ming was so short, the head of his shaft reached higher than her belly button and lay almost between her breasts. She was looking up at him with a quizzical smile on her face, as if to say, 'Well, Peter! What are you going to do with it?' He shrugged, smiled down at her upturned face, and bent his head and kissed her lightly on the nose. She giggled and allowed his fingers to explore her more.

Suddenly, Peter said what she so eagerly wanted to hear him say, "Let's go to bed, Rose." Turning off the water, he pulled the shower curtain aside and stepped from the stall, ready to have sex, the thoughts of his premature ejaculation erased from his mind.

Lai Ming followed him into the bedroom. Standing in front of the mirror so that he could fully see her reflection in it, she quickly wiped him dry and then patted herself with the same bathtowel. And when most of the wetness was gone from her, she dropped the towel and held out her arms to him, and for moments they hugged and kissed each other. Then she fell backwards onto the bed, pulling Peter with her, still in her arms and on top of her.

Placing her arms around his neck, she pulled him to her. "Oh, Peter, I want you so much," she whispered. Their lips met and they kissed passionately. Intrigued, Peter began again to explore her, caressing and fondling her breasts and gently rolling erect nipples between his forefinger and thumb. She was sighing, it felt so good. With urgency in her voice, she whispered to him, "Peter! Kiss me here!" and she pushed her small body upward until her breasts reached his mouth. "Kiss me," she repeated. Her breasts were so soft and beautiful, so close to him, the nipples so inviting. Lowering his lips, he took a nipple in his mouth and gently sucked upon it, her hand reaching up and holding the breast to him like a mother would her baby.

"Oh, Peter," she whispered, "you're a good boy." And now her fingers were sliding through his hair, her lips passionately kissing the side of his neck. And as she clung tightly to him, he could feel sharp little teeth nipping at his skin. "Be good to me, Peter," she was saying in a hasty whisper. "Be good to me."

He gazed down upon her tense face and desiring body. "I'll always be good to you, Rose, always."

"Don't talk, Peter," she was saying, "Not now," and she cuddled up tightly beneath him, her arms encircling him, pulling him down and holding him to her, so tight both could feel the heat and the dampness of perspiration between their bodies. His hand slipped down between her legs and found what it sought. He allowed his fingers again to explore beyond those lips that were so soft and inviting; inside it was wet and warm and slippery and everything was so soft, like velvet. He withdrew his fingers, feeling warm sticky moisture on them. He felt her hand slide down over his body and catch hold his manliness, felt it being positioned so that as he eased himself against her and pressed his body forward, it slid with ease into her. She was gazing with misty eyes into his; now there was love and want in them, and the smile had gone from her face. He felt her muscles growing taunt within her, and her stretched out legs quivering beneath him. Her eyes closed. He could feel the movement of her body quickening under him, and those muscles growing even taunter. Now she was biting him, holding onto him with sharp teeth as she allowed him to have his way with her. His lips roved over her eyes, her nose, her cheeks, her hair and on her lips. He wanted so badly to kiss her breasts, but she being so short they were out of his reach. Thus they held each other, she pulling him into her, closer, deeper. She felt in heaven, lost in a seething sea of ecstasy, a mist engulfing her whilst she lay gasping, moaning and softly crying out to him.

Peter gazed at the contorted face beneath him. Was he too big for her, he wondered. Was he hurting her? Was she in pain? "Rose, am I hurting you?" he whispered.

"No! No! Don't stop now," she pleaded.

Pressing his lips to hers, he slid his hands beneath her buttocks and pulled her even more firmly to him, pushing harder and faster into her, and as deeply as he could penetrate. Now she was gasping and crying out to him. He wanted to let her rest for a moment, but she didn't want to rest, and their movements continued in frenzied haste until he could hold himself no longer, almost blacking out as he ejaculated into her. And she, at the same time, gave a few quick, short gasps, and cried out to him, "Oh! Oh! Peter! Peter! Ohhhhhh," and then her gasps died away and she suddenly went limp beneath him, her body relaxed, her face composed.

Several seconds passed before she smiled up at him and gave him a quick kiss and a hug. She was satisfied, not only physically but also with the knowledge that it was she who had broken him in; he was a boy-virgin no longer. She kissed him again, the tips of her tiny fingers gently stroking his back. "You OK, Peter?" she asked.

"Yes, Rose," he answered. "Are you?"

"I'm finished, Peter."

"So am I."

"You feel good?"

"Yes. And you?"

"It was wonderful. You are a good lover."

"I thought I was hurting you," he said. "Did I hurt you?"

"No, silly boy. I enjoyed everything you did to me." Then she said, "Peter, I have no wish to embarrass you, but you were a boy-virgin. Is it correct to call it that?"

Peter's cheeks flushed hot. "I told you, I've had lots of girlfriends before you."

"Maybe, but not as you have had me." She then said, "We did not take tea. By now you must be very hungry."

"I am. I've not eaten since breakfast," replied Peter. "We've not gone to the pictures so please allow me to take you out to dinner," he offered.

"No, but thank you, Peter. We shall eat here. The *amah* can fetch us dinner from a nearby coffeehouse. I will call her, then we must wash. Go under the sheet," she bade him, and wrapping herself in the *sarong*, she called out to the *amah*, who hurried up the stairs, knocked on the door, and was asked to enter. She grinned at Peter, and said, "Hello," in Chinese.

"Wan Ze speaks no English," said Lai Ming to Peter. "So you can practice your knowledge of Chinese on her," and she smiled at the *amah* who, not knowing what was said, shrugged her shoulders and grinned even more.

"Peter said, "How are you?" in Cantonese. To which the *amah* replied, "Very well. And you?"

Peter wanted to say, 'Quite fucked, actually,' but instead said in Cantonese, "Rose has treated me well."

Lai Ming smiled graciously and then spoke to the *amah* who nodded her head in acknowledgement, and said, "Yes, yes, I can get. I go now."

Turning to Peter, Lai Ming asked, "Peter, what would you like to drink?"

"A bottle of beer if it's possible, please," he replied.

"Chinese beer?" Lai Ming asked.

"I don't care," he said, laughing. "Any beer."

Turning again to the *amah*, Lai Ming said, "One large Tiger beer."

The *amah*, still grinning and nodding towards Peter, jokingly asked, "Is he old enough to drink beer? *Wah!* Tsh! Tsh! He looks very young, like a little boy."

"He is old enough," replied Lai Ming, "And we are both hungry."

"I wonder why," teased the *amah*, and without more conversation she left the room. Lai Ming waited until the *amah*'s footsteps could be heard descending the stairs before saying to Peter, "Come, we must wash."

With an enquiring look on his face, Peter slid from between the sheets. 'God! What a hard bed,' he thought, 'and the mattress is so thin.' He felt underneath the mattress. Instead of bedsprings his hand contacted a layer of wooden boards. Shaking his head in wonderment, he followed Lai Ming into the bathroom.

There, Lai Ming said to him, "I will wash you," and she took from under the sink a wide enamel bowl and filled it three-quarters full with cold water from a tap in the shower stall. Turning, she carefully placed the bowl down on the floor. Then, taking a bottle of Dettol disinfectant from beneath the sink, she poured a little of its contents into the bowl, which immediately turned the water to a cloudy, milky white. She then squatted down, almost over the bowl, and beckoned Peter to squat down likewise, to face her, over the bowl.

She smiled what could have been a motherly smile. "I must make you a nice clean boy," she said, dipping the face cloth into the water. Peter, unable to resist the temptation of the closeness of her breasts, reached out, took one in each hand and felt for the nipples. "Naughty boy. Be serious," she admonished, pushing his hands away. "There is plenty of time to play, later." Then, taking his genitals in one hand and the washcloth in the other, she gently and carefully washed them. Peter flinched at the coldness of the water, and her touch tickled. "You don't like to be washed?" asked Lai Ming.

"It's rather different from what I've been used to," said Peter, "but it feels nice."

Lai Ming smiled a reply. And when satisfied that he was clean again, she dropped the wash cloth into the bowl, got to her feet and handed Peter a towel. "Now, you wipe," she said. "My turn to wash," and she again squat herself down over the bowl. Standing over her, Peter watched fascinated as the little Chinese lady performed her own ablutions, first by washing her stomach, then the whole area where her pubic hair grew. Then, with one hand she splashed water up into her vagina, and cleansed herself. Unconcerned, she smiled up at him. She did not mind him watching her. "You make much," she said.

"It was all your fault," Peter said, laughing, "but I enjoyed it."

"Me, too," she said.

They were still drying themselves in the bathroom, and hugging and kissing each other when the *amah* returned carrying a wicker basket containing the dinner. Placing the basket upon the table, she called out, "Ming, I have your food and drink, and beer for the little boy. *Wah!* Tsh! Tsh!"

"Thank you. We shall be right out," shouted Lai Ming, laughing at the words of her *amah*. Reaching into a small locker, she took from it a brown and gold coloured *sarong*. "For you, Peter," she said, handing the cloth to him. She then showed him how to put it on, and how to keep it in place without fear of it falling down around his feet. She then put on the *sarong* she had previously worn, winding it around her, but taking it higher than her waist so that it also covered her bosom. There she tucked a corner snugly into her cleavage. "We go eat," she said to Peter, and he followed her into the room where the *amah* awaited them, and where the food smelled good.

With the basket came plates, dinner napkins, sauces, and even a knife and fork. "I use chopsticks or a spoon," apologized Lai Ming. "I have no use for a knife and fork. The eating house has loaned us these." She made a mental note to buy a knife, fork and spoon for Peter. "And see, the *amah* has brought you beer," she said, taking from the basket a large bottle of Tiger beer and a glass tumbler. "It is much to drink. I hope you don't get drunk," she said. Next, she took from the basket a bottle of Green Spot orangeade which she placed on the table and put a straw beside it. "For me," she said. "I seldom drink alcohol. Ah! Here is our dinner. I hope you will like it." She took from the basket three covered containers held together by a wire frame with a carrying handle. Unlatching the frame and placing the containers to form a triangle on the table, she lifted the three lids. "There! A Chinese dinner!" she exclaimed smiling at Peter who had sat himself at the table.

"Oh, it looks delicious," said Peter enthusiastically. "And I'm so hungry. Everything looks so appetizing."

"I am glad," said Lai Ming. "Let me explain each dish."

"These are fried prawns, aren't they?" interrupted Peter. "They really are a jumbo size."

"We call them Cantonese fried scampi," said Lai Ming. "The sliced cucumber among the scampi makes the dish more pleasant to the eye, and in this hot weather it gives the hot food a cool and appetizing appearance."

"You should be a cook," laughed Peter.

"I like to cook. Some day I shall cook for you," replied Lai Ming. "And I like to look at cookbook pictures." Pointing with a chopstick, she continued, "Here we have pork fried rice, which I like very much. And in this third dish we have Chinese vegetables. These are snow peas, fresh water chestnuts and bamboo shoots in a soybean paste." She turned to the *amah*. "Everything is good," she said. Reaching for her handbag which lay on the dressing table, she took from it money and paid the *amah*, who wished them, 'Good eating,' left the room, and loudly clip-clopped on wooden shoes down the stairs.

Peter was in a quandary. Should he offer to pay for the dinner, or would the offer insult his lovely hostess? He decided to simply say 'thank you,' which he did. Lai Ming, bowing her head, said, "It is an honour to have you as my guest, and it is a pleasure to share a meal with you. Come. Eat before it gets cold. I will open and pour your beer."

What service! This is really living, thought Peter, as he again thanked Lai Ming whilst helping himself to the fried scampi.

When the three containers were almost empty and they had eaten their fill, Lai Ming suddenly asked, "Peter, when must you return to camp?"

"I'm due to report for duty midday on Monday," Peter replied. Then he thought a moment and remembered that Sergeant Muldoon had mentioned eleven or sooner on the Monday morning as he wanted to take his wife to an afternoon show. "I must report for work at or before eleven on Monday," he said.

"And today is only Saturday, so you have all day free tomorrow, and also a little of Monday morning?"

"Yes, that's right," answered Peter.

With the chopsticks she held, Lai Ming prodded the one remaining snow pea on her plate as if studying it. "Would you like to stay here, stay with me, sleep with me? I would enjoy your stay," she said, without looking up.

"Oh, Rose, I'd love to," Peter replied. "We could do such a lot together. Go to the cinema or even visit the zoo."

She looked across the table with an impish smile on her face. "Or we could stay here and make much love," she said coyly.

"Oh, Rose, I don't think I shall ever really understand you," said Peter, and getting up from his chair and going to her side, he bent over her and kissed the top of her head. "I'll love you always, Rose. Always," he murmured. "I know I shall." And he put his arm around her, and placed a hand upon her breast.

She did not push his hand away from her. Instead, she placed a hand upon his and pressed it to her bosom. "Thank you, Peter. I hope I never cause you problems. I never want to hurt you," and she got up from her seat and put her arms around him. "You stay until Monday. I will make sure you catch a bus or taxi back to camp in time for your work. You stay with me, Peter, and we'll be very greedy. I will give you all of me, all that you can possibly want, and in return, I want all of you, everything that you can make with me. I want you to be my boyfriend, my lover, and I will be everything you need of me."

Peter cuddled her in his arms. She was so soft, so warm, so lovely. "You're a darling," he said. "I'll always treasure you," and again he felt himself getting an erection.

"Peter! Look! You are being naughty again," exclaimed Lai Ming, laughing and sliding her hand down to that which stuck forth beneath Peter's *sarong*; they both looked down and laughed.

"I can't help it," said Peter, almost apologetically though grinning boyishly.

"I think he needs me," said Lai Ming. "Let me relax him. Let's go back to bed."

6

Sergeant Muldoon, the non-commissioned officer (NCO) in charge of the sergeants' mess kitchen at RAF Changi, was having a bad Monday morning. His troubles began the moment he awoke with his wife complaining of a severe sore throat. Next, his bike's front tire was flat with a nail in it, forcing him to walk the mile from the married quarters to the sergeants' mess. On his arrival at the kitchen, he saw that the plate-wash boy had ringworm, so sent him to the medical officer, who sent him home. Two hours later Muldoon was asked to report to the hospital where he was informed by a medical officer that his number three cook had been diagnosed as having leprosy. LAC Saunders, his cook and right-hand man had still not shown up for work and it was already past eleven o'clock. To make matters worse, he had been told that Saunders had not been seen on camp since the previous Saturday afternoon. Now, to top it all, Lou Fook, the number two cook, had burned the roast beef that was to have been served for lunch that day.

Sergeant Muldoon shook his head in resignation. "Lou Fook," he said icily, "When it's brown it's cooked, but when it's black it's fucked. Can't you get that into your daft head?" It was not in Sergeant Muldoon's nature to lose his temper or get angry, but today everything had gone wrong causing him to be in a foul mood. "You call yourself a cook. You're not fit to be a kitchen coolie. I want a cook working here, not a damned charcoal-burner," he shouted, prodding the still smoking joint of beef with a long-handled kitchen fork. "Look at this mess! Just look at it! Sixty mens' rations gone up in smoke," moaned the exasperated sergeant, shaking his head in despair.

A very dejected Lou Fook stared solemnly at his toes, muttering, "Me very sorry, sergeant. Me very sorry me forget meat."

"Sorry! Sorry!" fumed the sergeant. "Sorry won't bring back the damned meat ration. Hey! Chuff Box! Fetch a swill-bin." And when Chuff Box, the young kitchen boy, brought the swill-bin from the kitchen yard and placed it near the table, the sergeant angrily lunged at the blackened beef with the fork, lifted it from the burned-out roasting pan of still smoking fat and hurled it into the swill-bin.

At that moment, Peter Saunders, clad in clean cooks' whites, brown shoes, and with his RAF blue beret at a jaunty angle, strolled into the kitchen. In brown shoes he was improperly dressed but, since remustering to become a cook, such RAF rules and regulations meant little to him. Nor did his improper dress bother the sergeant. But then, few in the catering section bothered with rules and regulations or took any notice of Station Standing Orders and Station Routine Orders. The cooks simply didn't bother to read them. "Sorry I'm a bit late, Sarge," he sang out, and was about to explain how the bus had broken down this side of Geylang when he realized the sergeant was angry, but not at him.

"What's the matter, Sarge?" he asked. Then, eyeing the still smoking roasting pan, said, "Ah ha! And what have we here? Have we cremated a corpse, Sarge?"

"Damn it, Pete, it's not funny," fumed the sergeant, nodding his head towards the swill-bin. "It's in there, the roast beef that we should be having for today's lunch."

Peter peered into the bin, then at the burned-out roasting pan, and finally at the wretched Lou Fook. "Oh! I see! It's like that, is it? Well, in that case, there won't be a need to make Yorkshire pudding today," he said jokingly, grinning and winking at Lou Fook.

Lou Fook remained silent, his eyes fixed upon his toes.

"This idiot burned it," said the sergeant.

"Anyone can forget once in a while, Sarge. We'll just have to make do with something else. We can use the tinned spam. Make fritters out of them."

"The spam's for this evening's salad."

"Oh! Well in that case I can nip down to the airmens' mess and nick something for this evening's meal. What else is on for lunch?"

"Braised rabbit and Lancashire hot pot."

"So, what's wrong with spam fritter as a third choice?"

"I suppose it's OK," the sergeant answered wearily, accustomed these last few weeks to allowing his new RAF cook to sort out these nagging problems. "All right, spam fritters it is," he said with some reluctance. He picked up the telephone and called through to Percy, the corporal in charge of the sergeants' mess dining room staff. By the look that came on the sergeant's face it was obvious that Percy was not happy at having to change all twenty luncheon menus, especially at having to substitute spam fritters for roast beef and Yorkshire pudding. "I'll stick them up your bloody ass if you don't watch it," Sergeant Muldoon growled, banging down the receiver. "What a nerve! Stick 'em up my ass, he said, and he's queer. He should stick 'em up his own ass," he said testily.

Peter chuckled. "Oh, he's just miffed at having to change the menus at the last moment," he said, knowing full well that the sergeant cook and the overweight messing corporal seldom saw anything eye to eye. "So what else is new, Sarge?"

The sergeant sighed. "Not only has Lou Fook burned the meat but this morning the fool served cold sausages to the Chairman of the Messing Committee (CMC) for breakfast. The CMC came into the kitchen about an hour ago and blew his stack at me. Me! Sergeant Muldoon! The other mess staffs will be laughing their heads off, and Christ knows what the catering officer will think if he hears about it." The irate sergeant finished by saying, "If I had my way, I'd wring this blasted fool's neck."

"Aw, come on, Sarge," laughed Peter. "He's not as bad as all that!"

"Oh no! Is that what you think? Well, yesterday he put curry powder in the steamed fruit duff, the spotted dick as you call it, that was supposed to be served with custard as one of the luncheon desserts."

"It was just a little mistake, Sarge. He must have thought the jar contained mixed spice. Anyway, what did you do with Lou Fook's curried spotted dick?"

"I served it as a savory pudding with the roast pork."

Peter, still laughing, said, "You really did?"

The sergeant eyed Peter suspiciously. "What are you so damned chirpy about today?" he asked.

"I met a girl on the beach last Saturday, a Chinese girl," Peter replied. "She took me to her home and I spent the weekend with her."

"You did what?" spat out the astounded sergeant.

"I met a Chinese girl on Changi Beach and spent the weekend with her. I'm sorry I'm late, Sarge. It's because the bloody bus broke down after it left Geylang," he apologized. "Christ! I'm absolutely fucked. But what a weekend I had!"

"Nice Chinese girls don't mess about with servicemen," growled the sergeant. "And most certainly not with other ranks. Is she one of the whores that hang out at the beach?"

"Certainly not, Sarge. She's a lovely little lady. And you've got to remember, Sarge, times are changing."

"Maybe they are, and maybe they're not, but I don't like the sound of it. Don't come to me when you've a blob on your knob, or worse. You're better off staying in camp overnight."

"Aw, come on, Sarge," and Peter laughed, "we only live once."

"I know. But just be bloody careful. Anyway, changing the subject, I've something to tell you, something important. Come into the office. I don't want this getting around."

Peter silently followed the sergeant into the combined office and food store, waited until the sergeant was seated on the lone chair behind a small table which also served as a desk, then perched himself on a corner edge of the table. "What's up, Sarge?" he asked.

"I'll tell you what's up, Pete, and it's not pleasant. Remember those bumps which appeared on Wee Lim two or three weeks ago?"

"What about them? At first I thought he had a bad heat rash from standing over the stove."

Wee Lim was the very dependable, hardworking number three cook who, though young, was excellent at his profession. Only a year older than Peter, he was of the same slight stature and of a gentle and friendly disposition. He and Peter had hit it off as friends right from the start. Also, during Peter's first weeks at the sergeants' mess, Wee Lim had taught him many cookery tips, as well as many words and phrases in Cantonese; and Wee Lim, who had known only a smattering of English, had constantly improved his knowledge of the language through conversing with Peter.

Unusually grim of face, the sergeant said, "Get ready for a shock, Pete."

"Well, come on! Let's hear it."

"Leprosy," answered the grim-faced sergeant.

"Leprosy?" said Peter incredulously.

"Yes. He's got leprosy."

"My God. I can't believe it! So what happen's now?"

"I don't know. I intended sacking old Lou Fook and making Wee Lim number two."

"He would have been a good replacement, but that's out of the question now. Where is he?"

"He's at a leper colony in Singapore. I've written down the name of the place." Sergeant Muldoon looked at a scratchpad on his desk. "The hospital is on Yio Chu Kang Road," he said, reading off the name from the pad. "It's an isolation hospital, for lepers only."

Peter shook his head in disbelief. "There's no cure for leprosy is there, Sarge?"

"I believe there is," answered the sergeant. "It's a long job though. The MO said that Wee Lim must remain at the colony for at least nine months. But he also said he expects it will be for a much longer period."

"I'd like to go and see him, Sarge."

"No, Pete. It's probably not allowed, and it wouldn't be wise. Do you understand me?"

"Gosh, Sarge, I wish we could do something for him. Poor bugger, he must be in an awful state."

"That's for sure. I don't know what we can do though. I'll ask Charlie. He's Wee Lim's uncle. We could send him packets of biscuits and boiled sweets from the K ration boxes. We could even send him some tinned fruit."

"How would we get the stuff to him?" asked Peter.

"Charlie could take it. He'll want to visit his nephew."

"It's a good idea, but it's taking a big risk. It's stealing as far as the RAF is concerned."

"I know. But I'm sure Charlie's too smart to get caught. And if the police stop him, I'll sort them out."

For the first time since arriving in the kitchen that morning, Peter almost felt like laughing. God help anyone who got in the way of the fiery little sergeant. He'd sort out anyone who crossed him. "It's good of you, Sarge," Peter said. "Wee Lim's a good fellow and a damned good cook."

Then, thinking of the awful illness, he shivered with a chill of sudden fear. "Christ, Sarge, he's been in close contact with everyone in the kitchen, and all the while he's been cooking for the mess members. Is leprosy contagious?"

"I don't know," the sergeant replied, but by his troubled looks, he too was fearful.

"I bet there'll be a hell of a panic if the mess members get wind of this. The sickquarters will be swamped with enquiries."

"The less said the better," said the sergeant.

"The less said the better about what?" boomed a man's voice from the kitchen. The next moment the office doorway was blocked by a huge hulk of a man wearing an RAF police uniform, a service revolver in a white holster slung at his hip, and on each sleeve of his khaki drill (KD) jacket a grey armband with the letters SP written on it in big white letters. Flight Sergeant Cameron was a man to be reckoned with. Not only was he a tough rugby player, a judo expert and the station boxing champion, he was also the chief of the RAF provost police in Singapore; a twenty-two year man serving his last five. His only health problem was that he suffered from ulcers. Instead of eating in the dining room, he often frequented the cooks' domain in the kitchen where he enjoyed a meal of lightly boiled eggs or milk pudding before going on duty patrolling the red-light districts of the city. "About what?" he repeated, propping himself up in the doorframe and pushing his square, granite-like face menacingly forward as if ready to tackle the first person who opposed him.

With no more than a glance in his direction, Sergeant Muldoon answered, "Oh, nothing important, Jock."

"G'morning, Flight," greeted Peter Saunders, momentarily putting Wee Lim from his mind.

"What's so good about it?" asked the flight sergeant.

"What's the matter? Your ulcer playing up again?" asked Sergeant Muldoon.

"No, touch wood," answered the flight sergeant. He entered the office and tapped the wooden desk with giant, vice-like fingers. "But having the wife and kids out here gives me more headaches than I need," he said.

"Oh! Come on, Jock! You don't mean that. How are they, anyway?" asked the sergeant.

"Oh, they're all fine," replied the flight sergeant. "Flossy is settling down to the life out here. Slowly, mind you. She's still a wee bit scared when I'm on nights. And she's still complaining of the smells."

"She'll get over that," said Sergeant Muldoon. "How about the kids?"

"Oh, they love it here," the flight sergeant answered. "The heat doesn't bother them like it does their mum, and there's lots for them to do." Then turning to Peter Saunders, he said, "That reminds me, Cookie, there's something I want to ask you."

"Don't try pinning anything on me, Flight," laughed Peter. "I ain't done nuffink," he joked.

The flight sergeant's stony face lost some of its hardness to actually crease into a smile when he said, "I probably could pin something on you if I wanted to, but this is something personal I want to ask you."

"You want me to cook you something special."

"No. It's nothing about food."

Puzzled, Peter said, "Then what?"

"I'd like you to do me a favour."

More puzzled than ever, Peter said, "Me do you a favour? A favour for the provost police chief? What is this, Flight? What are you getting me into?"

"I'll ask you later. It's nothing so dreadful, nothing to do with police work, and nothing to do with the RAF. So don't look so concerned." He turned to the catering sergeant. "Changing the subject, did your leave pass go through, Paddy? Or did the old man turn it down?" he asked.

"It's still down at the catering office. The Warrant Officer (WO) in charge of catering turned it down. He's got a bee in his bonnet. The Command Catering Officer is coming to inspect all messes at Changi next month. The WO said he didn't think he could spare me until after the inspection."

"That's tough. So there'll be a lot of bullshit going on around here for awhile, eh?"

"You can bet on that," answered Sergeant Muldoon. "By the way, how's the banana situation with you? Do you need any? An issue arrived yesterday."

"That's what I came in for, Paddy. There's nothing like eating a banana or two when I'm touring the city at night."

"I'll get you a bunch," said Peter, who was still perplexed as to what the flight sergeant wanted to ask him. "How is that stomach of yours these days, Flight? Still playing you up?" he asked.

"Thankfully, it's been quite settled this last week or so, but if I eat pastries or fatty foods, I pay for it." The flight sergeant gave a gruff laugh, "Cookie, the lightly boiled eggs and egg custards you serve me in this office are my life-savers."

"Would you care for a couple of eggs now?" volunteered Peter. "I'll have them ready in a jiffy. It's no trouble."

"No, but thanks all the same. I'll just take some bananas. I'm in rather a hurry."

And as Peter disappeared into the fruit store, he shouted, "Flight, what was it you wanted to ask me?"

The flight sergeant waited until Peter emerged from the fruit store before saying, "I'd like you to babysit my two kids."

"What?" shouted Peter, completely taken aback. "Am I hearing you right, Flight? Did you say babysit?" he asked. In one hand he held a brown paper bag containing a big bunch of bananas.

"Yes, babysit. What's so mind-boggling about that?" asked the flight sergeant. "There's nothing new in the job. I'd like to take the missus to a show in town. All I'm asking is for you to babysit my two kids for a few hours whilst we're away. The *amah* won't stay evenings, and it would just be for the one evening. I'd pay you, of course, and there are perks. All you have to do is come around to my home this Thursday evening, say around six, and look after the kids until about ten or until we get back. The favour I'm asking you is nothing more than that."

"Christ! Some favour," said Peter scornfully. "Thanks, but no thanks, Flight. Can you imagine what everyone in the catering section would say if they hear I'm babysitting for the chief of the provost police? They'll call me an arse-kisser. I can just see Ginger Rundle lying on his bed laughing his fat head off. And Mike Chalmers calling me a little sissy and a creep, bumming around the police chief."

"Don't you think you're making too big a deal of this? It would only be for those few hours," said the flight sergeant.

"No thanks, Flight. I'd consider most anything else, but not babysitting."

"Too bad. You'd enjoy it. You'd have a lot of fun playing with my kids, and there's always plenty of beer in the fridge. It would get you out of the block for awhile," said the flight sergeant seriously. Then he said, "I think you'd like my kids. They're easy to get along with. Anyway, I'll ask you again tomorrow."

"Thanks, Flight, but no thanks. The answer will still be, 'No.'"

"Perhaps, but think about it."

"I have thought about it. Anyway, did you say Thursday?"

"Yes, Thursday."

"Well, that's put the lid on that."

"Why?"

"I've a date on Thursday."

"You've a date!" exclaimed the flight sergeant, frowning. "Who with?"

"A Chinese girl I met down on the beach last Saturday."

"Really! Not Molly or Lilly or The Bucket, I hope, or one of the other prostitutes that hang out down there," said a now serious Flight Sergeant Cameron.

Proudly Peter said, "Nope, she's not one of them. She's a real lady and the most beautiful woman in the whole world. I was down on the beach swimming with her. I asked her for a date, she accepted, and she took me home."

"Just like that?" asked a challenging Sergeant Muldoon.

"Yep, just like that. Well, more or less."

"What do you mean, more or less?" asked the sergeant.

The flight sergeant interrupted the conversation. "What does she do for a living?" he asked.

Suspicion, Peter thought, was already in the flight sergeant's tone of voice. "She not a 'pro' if that's what you're thinking," he said indignantly.

"I didn't say she was," said the flight sergeant, a hint of a smile creasing his rugged face.

"But you're thinking she is, aren't you?" said Peter, becoming more ruffled.

The flight sergeant placed a heavy hand good-naturedly on Peter's shoulder. "Look, lad, I think on many things, but I don't always say what I think. But what does she do for a living? She must do something."

"I don't know. I didn't ask her," answered Peter, feeling interrogated and already cornered. "I think she's a school teacher. She speaks better English than any one of us."

The provost police flight sergeant was not impressed. "Where does she live?" he asked.

"I don't know. I didn't ask her," answered Peter.

"But surely you must know which area she lives in. You must have seen street signs."

Peter had seen several street signs. He had seen the sign which had Lavender Street written on it and another at the intersection, which read Bendemeer Road. He had also seen at least three of the dreaded 'OUT OF BOUNDS' signs, meaning out of bounds to all military personnel. In fact, he had passed by them, both to and from Lai Ming's home.

"I didn't take much notice," lied Peter uncomfortably. He never liked to lie, especially to the flight sergeant, not only because the man was head of the provost police and might easily suspect that he was lying but also because during the short time he had been at the sergeants' mess, he and the big Scotsman had become quite friendly. But how could he tell him that Lai Ming lived on a road just off the infamous Lavender Street, knowing that the whole area was out of bounds to service personnel. Weakly, he said, "It was in the centre of the city somewhere. Where the streets and buildings all look the same. You know, little Chinatown."

"And you're going to visit her again on Thursday. You'll be going to her home, so if that's the case you must know her address."

"No, I don't know her address, Flight. I'm meeting her at the Green Line bus station. We've made plans to go over to Johore to visit the zoo."

"Hmm, you'd never make a policeman, that's for sure."

"And you'd never make a cook, Flight. That's for sure," answered Peter, considerably cockier than he felt.

The flight sergeant laughed. "I just don't want to see you getting into any trouble, Cookie. However, I can only presume that the woman is not a bad type if she's going to the zoo with you. All right Saunders, skip the babysitting for now. I'll ask you again at a later date."

"You'll be wasting your time, Flight."

"We'll see. I'm still a wee bit curious about this woman you met at the beach, where she lives and what she does for a living."

"Don't be nosey, Flight," replied Peter, now laughing and feeling more at ease. "You can leave my girlfriend out of your detective work. You do enough snooping as it is."

"Once a policeman, always a policeman," replied the flight sergeant. "By the way, changing the subject, when do you sit for your senior aircraftman's trade test?"

"I don't know. I've passed the education test. As for the practical and theory, I'll have to wait until the catering officer puts me down for those."

"Isn't it about time he did?"

"Not really. I've been an LAC for less than eight months. I'm in no hurry to be promoted to an SAC. I've still got more than three years to do."

"It will mean more money and put you in line for your corporal's tapes."

Sergeant Muldoon interrupted them by saying, "I'm expecting him to be sent to the aircrew mess here at Changi in a month or two. The Far Eastern Command has decided to open a school of cookery there. There'll be a cook chosen to represent every RAF station in FEAF (Far Eastern Air Force). I'm expecting Pete to be the chosen cook from Changi."

"Only one from Changi?" asked the interested flight sergeant.

"Yes. There'll be just the one LAC selected from every catering section in the Far Eastern Command. The two other RAF camps on the island, Tengah and Seletar, although short of cooks, will probably each send one. And Kai Tak, KL, Penang and Colombo will also send a man to make up a seven-man course. It's supposed to be a ten-week advanced training cookery course."

"It sounds good," said the flight sergeant. Turning to Peter, he asked, "Are you hoping you'll be the chosen cook from Changi?"

Peter shrugged. "I don't care so long as I get back to the sergeants' mess after the ten weeks are up."

"Who'll be the instructor?" asked the flight sergeant.

"There'll be two, both chosen from Changi," answered the catering sergeant.

"Oh! Who?"

"Flight Sergeant Bates, the Cornishman, and Warrant Officer White. God knows what Bates can teach anybody other than how to make Cornish pasties but the WO knows his stuff. A good skive that's what I think it'll be and a waste of public funds."

"Not if it improves their catering ability and knowledge," argued the flight sergeant.

"But will it? I bet Charlie, my number one, and Wee Lim have taught Pete here more in the few weeks he's been with me than what any instructor can teach him in ten weeks. And he will be a great loss to me. I doubt if the old man will send a replacement."

Peter, ready to head off to the airmens' mess pantry to pilfer something for dinner, said, "OK, I'm away then. Cheerio, Flight."

"So long, Cookie. Watch your step with that lady on Thursday."

Peter laughed and said, "Thanks for the fatherly advice, Flight. I'll be back in a jiffy, Sarge."

"OK Pete," the sergeant replied. "Don't be long. I want to get home."

"Don't forget your bananas, Flight," Peter sang out as he departed. He walked through the small, square courtyard surrounded by a high wall and out onto the hot, shimmering, sun-drenched road. Taking a short cut, he walked across grassy banks where tall palm trees stood and huge poincianas decorated in great clusters of red blossom shaded the area. The airmens' mess was only a couple of hundred yards away, perhaps less, but it was a long, hot walk in the heat of the midday sun.

"Has he told you anything about this woman he met at the beach, Paddy?" asked the flight sergeant.

"He hadn't mentioned her until a minute or two before you came in," replied the sergeant.

"Maybe I can find out something about her. I'm curious, for his sake," said the flight sergeant.

"You're a nosey bugger, aren't you?" said the sergeant, laughing.

"Perhaps I am. But if she is of bad character, I'd hate to see Cookie get mixed up with her. He's so damned naive."

"He's just young," said Sergeant Muldoon. "We all learn by our experiences, good and bad."

"You're right, Paddy. Anyway, I must be off. I'll see you tomorrow." Striding out of the kitchen office the giant flight sergeant departed, heading for the guardroom which was just over the hill. He was still wondering about the Chinese girl. Who was she? Where did she live? How did she earn her livelihood? He liked Saunders and thought him to be very clean-cut and honest. He could trust him. That's why he had asked him to babysit. He arrived at the guardroom with Saunders and the Chinese girl still on his mind. He would, he decided, have a couple of his SPs keep an eye on the lad.

7

Later that evening, the lovely Chan Lai Ming, the popular Chinese prostitute known locally as Rose of Singapore, was at home, the home so many men knew as a place to gratify their sexual appetites. The majority of these men departed satisfied; many were repeat customers.

Lai Ming was in her bedroom, a cozy room kept clean and tidy by her *amah* Wan Ze. After a two-hour nap, she had risen from her bed, bathed, put on her make-up, combed her hair, and was now standing in front of the shuttered window meditating, a frown on her face, thinking about him; not of any of the many other men who visited her but only of him, the young British airman she had met on the beach and brought to her home. What a wonderful time they had spent together, she mused. Now, already ten hours had gone by since he had given her a final kiss goodbye and had departed, to return to his work at the sergeants' mess kitchen at RAF Changi, exhausted but very happy.

Standing at Lai Ming's side was Wan Ze, a thin, sickly faced, diminutive woman clad in a black *samfoo* of cotton trousers and matching jacket. Her grey hair was brushed straight back, flat across the top of her head and hanging down her back to her waist in a single plait. Wan Ze had been a loving and caring nurse to Lai Ming's son from birth and had watched him grow through good times and bad. Now, she remained with Lai Ming as her faithful *amah* and loyal friend.

"What is the matter, Ming?" asked Wan Ze, a concerned look on her parchment-like face.

"It is nothing," replied Lai Ming, turning for a moment to face her *amah*. She gave a weak smile. "It is nothing," she repeated. Again she turned to stare at the closed shutters, and to think of the young airman who had spent the weekend with her.

Wan Ze said nothing more. She knew when to remain silent. But she was puzzled. Never before had she seen her mistress in this mood.

With some apprehension she watched her mistress walk without a word across the green and brown coloured canvas floor to her dressing table, to pose nude before the tall mirror fixed to the wall. The mirror reflected fully an artistic picture of oriental beauty at its finest.

Lai Ming studied herself, her eyes caressing her naked body. She remembered how Peter had reacted at seeing her naked that first time, and she smiled at the memory as, with a pink powder puff, she patted the nipples of her breasts. Then, as her thoughts changed, a frown came upon her face and she turned sadly away from the mirror. What should she do? What future lay ahead for both her and her son? How could she alter her way of life? And now she had Peter, the young Englishman. Would he turn out to be just another, like the rest of them, wanting her only to satisfy his sexual desires? No, of course not, she told herself. He was different from all the others. But why did she think he was so different, she wondered. Why had she felt so completely happy and relaxed when with him? Why had he made her feel like a real woman again? The hours they had spent together were mutually exquisitely pleasurable hours. She thought of those two dreamy nights together when she would awake to find him snuggled up behind her, an arm thrown across her and his hand upon her breast, always her breasts as if they were his comforters. She would slide a leg back over his and push herself gently against him. He would awaken, and they would make love, silently and sweetly, and then fall back into a deep, blissful sleep. Frowning and shaking her confused head, she told herself that time alone would tell. She walked to her dressing table and from a drawer chose a set of red, flimsy underwear. First slipping into the tiny panties, she then covered her small breasts with the lacy bra. Next, from the mahogany wardrobe, she selected a blood-red *cheongsam*. The *amah* watched her every move but said not a word.

Sliding into the clinging, sexy-looking dress, Lai Ming again posed in front of the mirror. Satisfied, she sat down at the dressing table and again combed her hair, which flowed in black, silk-like waves down around her shoulders. She had a thoughtful expression on her face. Was it correct for her to lead him on in such a manner, she wondered. When at Changi Beach, should she have persisted with a firm "No"? She had repeatedly said "No" but he had looked so sad and lonely and she had felt sorry for him. And she, too, was lonely. She needed a real boyfriend. She liked him, but would it be right to encourage him further, she wondered. And how would their relationship end, this beautiful love affair they had so suddenly created? Would it end in jealousy, anger, despair, or even violence? He was so very young, so trusting and naive, yet so eager for her companionship and desiring so much to love her and be loved. His honest eyes so reminded her of her late husband. Behind those eyes was surely the same understanding and caring, she told herself. And his habits, too, were reminiscent. Even the way he had fidgeted with his cup in Pop's coffee shop on the beach, and more so, the way he had spoken to her in a kind, gentle voice and reassuring manner. He brought back memories sweet and dear to her, of life that was so full of happiness when with her husband, especially those last few short years with him after the Japanese no longer ruled the island.

And his body, it was so youthful and full of vitality, of love and passion. She had wanted so much to be properly loved, and he had satisfied those wants. She hated the kind of love asked and paid for by the men to whom she sold herself at the Butterfly Club—to the aloof British military officers, the prosperous businessmen and government officials, and the many other men who visited the club where she worked as a 'butterfly girl'. She thought of how many of those men were so pompous and so high and mighty when at their office desk yet crude and ignorant in the art of lovemaking. Many clients whom she took to her bed were British civil servants and colonial administrators of Singapore. Also, there were the rubber planters, tin-mine owners and managers, high-ranking police officers and other British officials from the mainland of Malaya, down for a few days rest and relaxation on the island. Those from Malaya, having spent lonely months up north, were generally nicer and more generous to her than the officials on the island. They never objected to paying the high prices she asked.

She was just one of the more than thirty girls who worked without salary at the Butterfly Club, persuading the customers at the all-male club to spend their money on expensive drinks. In return, the girls were allowed to use the club as an ideal place to solicit free from harassment. The owner of the club did not mind the girls taking home a club member providing enough drinks had been bought and paid for by him beforehand. As for Lai Ming, she was so popular with the men at the Butterfly Club, they had given her the name, Rose of Singapore. Many of the other girls at the club were much younger than she, and possibly more beautiful, but Lai Ming had such a lovely smile and a gentle, charming manner which enticed to her a continuous clientele.

When business was bad at the Butterfly Club, she roamed Lavender Street soliciting military men of the Australian and British army, navy and airforce, American sailors, too, when the US fleet visited Singapore, and men from the many merchant ships which put in to Singapore's vast harbour. The majority of the military men she approached were young, sex-starved and eager and willing to pay as much as twenty Malay dollars for a short time. For a couple of hours she charged a few dollars extra, and if they could afford her price, they could enjoy her favours in an all-night session. She brought them to this upstairs room, fulfilled their sexual needs and sent them on their way satisfied and happy—from the lowest-ranking soldier to the men in high positions. She charged them accordingly, depending on their wealth and status, also depending on how much she liked or disliked the man. She had often liked a client but had never fallen in love with one. But Peter was different from all the other men she'd had sex with. He was not a client. He was and would remain someone special, her boyfriend and lover. But, she repeatedly told herself, she must keep him in ignorance as to how she earned her livelihood. She could not afford to allow him or anyone else to disrupt her plans for the future. Also, there were always the many bills that had to be paid. Yes, of course she would see him again. She would keep her promise and meet him at the bus terminal on Thursday, and together they would visit the zoo. After, and she smiled, she would again take him to her bed. Already she was eagerly looking forward to Thursday afternoon. She would not tell him of her dirty business. And if he should find out! She shrugged. It would be up to him. She would never ask him for money and would readily give herself to him knowing that she needed his friendship, love and affection as much as he needed hers.

She chilled as she thought of another serious problem that might arise. Supposing she gave him a sickness. I must be much more careful, she thought. From now on I must always examine the penis of the man before he enters me, and from now on I must always make the man wear a contraceptive. Also, I must make sure to visit the social welfare department for my monthly checkup. I cannot allow Peter to get sick. She picked up her watch and looked at it as she slipped it onto her wrist.

Giving her hair a few final strokes before placing the comb down upon the dressing table, she gathered up her red handbag from a nearby chair, opened it, checked the contents and then snapped the catch shut. She lifted a hand mirror from the dressing table and peered into it, studying her face awhile before patting her cheeks with the powder puff. 'I must go,' she told herself. 'Already men at the club will have consumed several drinks and should be ready to have a woman.' She gave a final reddening touch to her lips. Satisfied, she replaced the lipstick on the dressing table, then turning, gave Wan Ze a faint smile.

"You are different tonight. You are troubled, Ming," ventured the apprehensive *amah*. "What is the matter with you? Are you sick?" She stood her ground, awaiting an answer.

"It's nothing," replied Lai Ming. "Perhaps I am a little tired tonight.

Do not be concerned."

The devoted old *amah* nodded, cracking the millions of lines in her wizened face as she attempted a smile. Ming would tell her if something were wrong, she told herself. Ming always did. But she was different tonight—not at all talkative, but quiet, even moody. It was not like Ming to be moody, and she wondered why, but said nothing.

"I am going to the Butterfly Club," said Lai Ming. "I hope to return within the hour, so stay awake to unlock the door for me."

The *amah* nodded gravely and said, "Yes, I shall stay awake and await your return."

Then Lai Ming, Rose of Singapore, left the room and quietly made her way down the narrow staircase to her tiny kitchen and the apartment's rear entrance. There she unlocked and opened the heavy outer door and, with dainty steps in her red high-heeled shoes, she quickly walked the deserted alleyway into a moonlit street. It was already late, with few pedestrians and little traffic to be seen. She walked as far as the intersection of Bendemeer Road and Lavender Street. There, she hailed a cruising trishaw.

8

Having completed his morning shift at the sergeants' mess, Peter Saunders rushed back to his quarters to prepare for his date with Rose that afternoon. When he reached his bedspace at one o'clock, the many cooks and other members of the catering section who had worked the early shift had already returned from duty. Several had immediately flopped down upon their beds and were already sound asleep.

LAC David Simmons, an airmens' mess admin' orderly, was seated on a folding chair in the shade of the wide verandah, an open book hiding the high-powered binoculars focussed on the open three-storey WRAF block situated directly across from the catering block.

Five other young airmen sat around a bed playing blackjack, the favourite pastime for quite a few members of the catering section. Two cooks, still in their cooks' whites, were watching.

Peter Saunders was soon taking a cold shower and, in his strong Devonshire dialect lustily singing, "Jan Pierce, Jan Pierce, lend me yer grey mare. All along, down along, out a long lee. Fer I want ta go-o to Widdicombe Fair."

Suddenly, from a bed near the ablution area, a voice shouted, "Hey! Saunders! Rap up that bloody noise! I wanna get some sleep."

"Yeah, shut your gob," someone else shouted.

Finishing the song, Peter ended with a loud, "Tra la la! Tra la la!" He then began to loudly sing, "Rose, Rose, I love you, with an aching heart."

"Hey! Saunders! For Christ's sake, shut up!" the first voice shouted.

"Don't you like my singing?" shouted back Peter Saunders, chuckling to himself as he washed soapsuds from his body beneath a shower of ice-cold water.

"That's not singing. That's one 'orrible row," shouted the second voice. "What d'you do with the money, mate?"

"What money?" shouted back Peter, turning off the flow of water.

"The money your mother gave you for singing lessons, idiot," the voice answered.

Peter Saunders laughed and stepped out of the shower, letting the louvered door swing shut behind him. Naked and bronzed by the sun, his sinewy body dripped water onto the concrete floor that separated the ablutions from the sleeping quarters. Reaching for a towel that hung from a hook on the outside of the shower door, he wound this around his midriff, slipped his wet feet into a pair of Chinese flip-flops, and then entered the spacious living quarters of the three-storey block.

"The trouble with you chaps is that you don't appreciate good bathroom singing," he said, grinning at his critics. "You ought to be glad there's such talent in your midst."

Milton Smith, an airmens mess cook, replied, "Talent! My ass!"

Peter was about to comment when the man lying on the other bed said, "What are you so happy about, Saunders?"

"I've a date."

"Who with?" asked Milton, who, except for a sheet covering a small part of his mid-section, lay on his bed naked.

"With a Chinese girl."

"Wheredya meet her?" asked the other airman.

"On the beach," replied Peter.

"One of the whores?" asked Milton.

"No! Of course she's not a whore," replied Peter indignantly.

Milton sat up and rearranged the sheet so that it covered a little more of his body. He shrugged white shoulders. He never went out into the sunlight unless he really had to. "Well, watch yourself, or you might end up with what I caught. It was no Far Eastern chill, the MO assured me of that."

Peter shrugged. He was well aware that the majority of the cooks were great womanizers, especially after a gut full of local beer, and most of them were heavy drinkers. "It could happen to anyone. The girl I met on the beach, though, she's different. She's decent. She's a regular nice girl."

Another cook, Airman Blondie Phillips, rolled his naked body over, farted, then pushing his pillow behind his head, propped himself up into a sitting position, and said, "Women are all the same, Peter. Great deceivers." Farting again, he exclaimed, "God, those shirt-lifters have really got to me," and his fat face broke into a big grin.

Peter smiled but said nothing. Blondie Phillips wasn't really a bad sort although he was uncouth at times. Peter looked down over the two rows of beds on his side of the floor, several now occupied by sleeping off-duty cooks and others in the catering section. Flip-flopping towards his own bedspace, Peter reached the card-playing group who were too intent on the game, and on the growing pile of Malayan dollars stashed in the centre of the service blanket covering the bed, to give him more than a fleeting glance.

For these five airmen, playing blackjack was definitely their favourite pastime when off duty. It was either that, sleeping, or consuming large quantities of Tiger beer in the NAAFI or the Malcolm Club on the camp. And as gambling was strictly forbidden in the camp institutions and a military offense, members of the catering section took their bottles of beer to the block where there was little likelihood of being disturbed. A couple of the card players smoked cigarettes, others were drinking beer, but all were engrossed in the card game. The bedspace around them was littered with fag ends, dead beer bottles and glasses in various stages of fullness. Stored in a bedside locker were more bottles of beer, warm, of course, but no one in the card-playing group ever thought of drinking beer other than at room temperature.

Peter stopped at the foot of the bed and waited until the players had finished the hand before saying, "Hi, Rick," to the dealer.

LAC Gerald Rickie, or Rick, as he preferred to be called, was Peter's best friend, and certainly the friend he had known the longest since joining the RAF. He was one of the surplus fighter plotters who had been dumped off the MV *Empire Pride* at Hong Kong and had helped Peter at many and varied odd jobs before he eventually remustered into the Signals Section at Kai Tak. Shortly thereafter he was posted, first to Kuala Lumpur, where he and Peter met again, and then to Changi, Singapore, where they resumed their friendship. Except in physique, they had much in common. Both were excellent swimmers who had often swam together in the waters surrounding Hong Kong and now in the sea off Changi Beach. Both loved and respected the sea. They enjoyed boating, too, venturing out together across the Strait of Johore in one of Pop's fishing canoes. Also, both were marksmen with a rifle, though neither discussed the latter nor gave it thought.

Rick's billet was approximately a hundred yards from the catering section block, and next to the senior non-commissioned officers quarters. Rick, however, spent very little of his free time at the signals section block, preferring to visit the catering section block to see if Peter was off duty and wanting to go for a swim, or to enjoy an excursion to the islands offshore in one of Pop's two canoes. When Peter was not around, Rick sometimes played blackjack with the card players. He'd also joined the catering section's dart team.

"Hi, Rick," Peter repeated.

"Hello there, Pete," Rick answered. "Going to meet Rose?"

"Yep."

"Lucky you!"

"Yeah. We're going to the zoo over at Johore Bahru."

"Good for you!"

"She's nice, Rick."

"So you've told me, ten thousand times since last Monday. And I believe you. Taffy Evens told me he was with you when you met her. He said she's a good-looking bit of crumpet. You're a lucky bugger, Pete. I wish I could find someone nice."

"You might if you stop wasting time playing bloody cards."

"Is she sexy?" asked LAC Jimmy Brown, another airmens' mess cook and one of the card players.

"She's beautiful." said Peter.

"In other words, she's got one on each side and still breathing," said Jimmy Brown. "Come on, Rick, deal the damn cards."

Rick said, "You're just jealous, Jim. Perhaps we're all a bit jealous." He quickly dealt another hand and without looking up from the game asked, "Pete, what if she doesn't turn up?"

"She'll turn up, Rick," Peter answered. "What makes you think she won't?"

Rick shrugged his broad, deeply suntanned shoulders. "I don't know. I'm surprised you've got as far as you have with her. You know these Chinese bibbies, the respectable ones, they're seldom interested in servicemen."

"I suppose she's taken a fancy to me. I don't know. But she'll be there. I know she'll be there," said Peter with certainty in his voice.

Scooping up a pile of paper money, Rick turned to Peter, grinned and said, "My luck's in today, the first time in ages. I suppose it's because I'm banker for a change."

Peter, who was not a gambler, said, "Perhaps."

"I think you're in love," laughed Rick, shaking his head.

Peter chuckled, suddenly remembering what his mother had told him when he became so despondent at knowing Elsie was seeing someone else. "Love is like a mutton chop, sometimes cold and sometimes hot. Love is heavenly. Love is strong. And so is a mutton chop if kept too long." Peter chuckled at his own words. He still thought the verse silly, but nevertheless, funny.

"Oh! For crying out loud," said Rick, shaking his head.

Other card players shook their heads as if in despair, but faces brightened, some laughed, pillows were thrown at Peter, and someone threw his socks up into the whirling blades of the overhead fan where they spun for moments before being whisked away into the unknown.

"Well, I'd better get my finger out or I'll be late," Peter said, turning his back on the card players.

"Good luck," said Rick, who was already dealing the cards again.

"Don't come back with the clap," shouted Bertie Brown.

Peter hastened towards the main road where he could catch one of the frequent buses which would take him into the city centre. The meandering camp road was sizzling hot, so in places he left the road and hurried across slopes of cool, well-tended grassy lawns overhung by tall coconut palms and blooming poinciana trees full of scarlet and orange flowers. Eventually, he arrived at a little used path almost buried in overhanging tall grasses, took it and continued onward, passing the rifle range, until he finally arrived at the almost deserted, two-lane road which ran parallel with Changi's main runway. On crossing the road, he stopped beneath a concrete shelter which had a sign with 'Bus Stop' written on it in red letters.

Seating himself upon a wooden bench inside the shelter, he peered through a heat haze, down the long, straight road leading into Changi Village for signs of the bus. There were none. God, it was hot in that bus shelter, and on contemplating its merits, Peter thought how useless the shelter really was. It gave little or no protection from the sun and certainly none from the monsoon rains which so often lashed down in fury upon the island.

To him, the most interesting aspect of the bus stop was that it overlooked the main runway, where, from that lonely stand, one had a clear view of the planes taking off and landing. Peter watched as an RAF Viking aircraft of Transport Command raced down the runway and lifted lazily into the sky long before it reached the coconut palm-lined perimeter at the far end of the airfield. In the far distance, beyond the runway's end, Peter could see the waters of the Johore Strait twinkling like a million diamonds in the bright sunlight. A shimmering heat haze rose from one end of the runway to the other.

Peter was watching a four-engine transport plane making its final approach when a woman's shrill voice startled him. "Bananas, Johnny. Only ten cents. Pineapples. Pomelos." Turning, Peter faced a diminutive, hunchbacked old Chinese woman pulling her fruit cart. Everyone at Changi knew this little Chinese woman and her fruit cart. She was a permanent fixture, never going further than between Changi Village and the bus stop she now stood at. In a small, wrinkled hand she held a bunch of very ripe finger bananas. "Very cheap, Johnny," she said. "Only five cents for one."

"Oh! Hello, Momma. No, I'm sorry, I don't want any fruit today," Peter answered.

The little woman's parchment-like, suntanned face managed a sad smile. "Very cheap for you, Johnny," she repeated, pleadingly.

Peter looked at the diminutive figure holding up the bananas, and at the pathetic little handcart she pushed all day and every day. Hell, he thought, a dollar doesn't mean much to me, but to her a dollar meant a lot. "OK Momma, I'll have a banana," he said. From his wallet he took a green, one dollar note, the equivalent of two shillings and fourpence in Sterling. He handed her the note and chose a banana from the bunch offered. And as the old woman counted out the change, he said. "That's OK Momma. You keep it." She seemed not to understand him, so he took the coins from her and dropped them into her apron pocket.

"Thank you! Thank you!" she exclaimed, her tired eyes lighting up and her weather-beaten face creasing into a big smile. First examining the bunch of bananas she held in her hand, she then held them out to him, saying, "For you, Johnny. You good boy."

"Thanks, Momma, but I don't want them, really I don't," Peter said, shaking his head and gently pushing away the hand holding the bananas.

"You take," she insisted.

Thinking he might offend her if he kept refusing, he said, "All right, Momma. I'll take them. Thank you very much."

The woman grinned her pleasure. "You, very good. You *ding ho* boy. Bye-bye," and with that the little old lady picked up the shafts of her fruit cart, gave one heave, and was once again heading down the sloping, half a mile or so of road to Changi Village. She would rest only the once along the way. She always rested at the same spot beneath a huge poinciana tree in bloom with scarlet flowers, which grew at the roadside. Her husband was hanged from a limb of that tree by the Japanese during their brutal occupation. Now, she always rested beneath its heavy boughs, but what she thought about as she rested, nobody knew. She spoke neither of her dead husband nor of the Japanese. Peter's eyes followed her down the seemingly endless road. When she passes on to the next world, he thought, Changi Village will be that much smaller. But for now, she was a fixture.

A cream and red bus with a blunt nose raced from the village towards him. Fearing it would not stop, Peter held up his hand. The bus slowed then squealed to a stop alongside him. A Chinese conductor, dressed in a sweat-drenched, fawn-coloured uniform, stood impatiently on the slotted wooden platform at the doorway. Peter climbed aboard and sat facing inward, next to the door. He paid the twenty cents fare. The bus, drawing away, rapidly increased its speed along the deserted two-lane highway. There was never much traffic along that stretch of road except on weekends and holidays.

From his seat Peter studied the other passengers, a pastime he always found interesting, for without fail there would be a mixture of races riding the bus.

Across from him, a middle-aged Chinese couple sat bolt upright, looking straight ahead, their faces devoid of expression and seemingly oblivious to their surroundings or to the other occupants of the bus. Two Malay boys, probably not yet in their teens, each wearing a black *songkok* clamped securely to black wavy hair, sat giggling and whispering to each other. A white woman in her mid-thirties, obviously

British and probably from the married quarters at Changi, sat staring out of the window, totally absorbed in the passing scenery. She was dressed completely in white. A new arrival from Britain, thought Peter.

An exquisitely beautiful Malay girl of about seventeen years, wearing a hint of lipstick and whose face was subtlety powdered white, sat directly opposite. Peter noticed the lipstick because it was so uncommon for Malay girls to use such make-up. He also noticed that her hands were dainty and that she wore tiny gold chains on delicate ankles. Fastened to her hair by colourful, shiny pins, she wore a purple and gold silk scarf, which fell lightly about her shoulders all the way to her slim waist almost concealing the brown and gold silk *baju* she wore. A multi-coloured *sarong* reached almost to her ankles.

Peter, fascinated by the girl's beauty, stared admiringly at her. Their eyes met, only for seconds, but long enough for him to see her blush and shyly turn her head as if to look out the window. Peter smiled to himself. This Malay girl was so lovely, he thought. But, he told himself, Rose was even lovelier. Thinking of Rose, he sank deeper into the leather upholstery. It was a forty-five minute journey to the city centre, so he must be patient.

Now, some distance to his left but clearly visible from the road, the grim-looking, grey stone walls of notorious Changi Gaol came in sight. Less than seven years ago, thousands of British and Australian prisoners of war had died within those walls, from starvation, neglect, brutality and torture at the hands of the conquering Imperial Japanese Army. And there, too, many hundreds of other servicemen and civilians, both men and boys, were shot, bayoneted, or beheaded by the ceremonial swords of the invaders. What awful secrets Changi Gaol held within its grim, grey walls! Now, it housed the island's criminals.

With no time for memories, the bus sped onward, passing through low-lying fertile farmland where fields were alive with young green shoots, white turnip tops, yellow heads of Chinese cabbage and carpets of blossoming multicoloured flowers. Farmers worked knee-deep in mud in some of the fields, bent low about their tasks, their brown, sinewy bodies glistening with sweat as they toiled in the torrid heat of the early afternoon. An ox, splashing in the mire, grunted and heaved between the shafts of a wooden plough, followed by the ploughman fighting his way against the slippery, sucking mud.

The bus roared onward through rustic, noisy little villages, through palm groves and worn-out rubber plantations, to eventually climb a twisting, treacherous hill to a hair-pin bend at the top. Once around this bend and over the brow, one could look down upon the outskirts of the Lion City, the main city of Singapore.

By now the traffic had increased in density making the going slow. The speed of the bus was reduced to a crawl at times as slow-moving trishaws crossed its path and crowds of people swarmed, not only on the wide pavements, but also out onto the wide road. The bus arrived at Geylang, where it stopped for a few minutes near the market to fill up with passengers until there was only standing room left. The bus then proceeded onward, but only for a short distance before it stopped again, at a road junction, this time greeted by the crash and clatter of gongs and cymbals. A Chinese funeral procession was crossing in front of the bus, the cortege preceded by a brass band playing a lively air. The highly decorated and picturesque hearse, drawn by umbrella-covered pallbearers, displayed a huge portrait of the deceased. This was followed by barefooted, loud-wailing mourners, some of them paid to drive evil spirits away from the deceased and to send him on his way with a free and easy passage. Several minutes passed before the procession came to an end, allowing the bus to resume its journey. But now it was at a faster speed, along Kallang Road, passing the civil airport. Then a traffic light turned red which held the bus up for a minute or so more; and when the light turned green, a motorist ahead stalled the engine of his car.

Peter swore softly to himself. He hadn't as much time to spare as he had thought. He wished he had hurried more when getting ready in the block. He should have caught an earlier bus. He had less than thirty minutes now to reach the Green Line bus station. Impatient now, he swore again. Finally, the engine of the car ahead started, and the car began a turn to the right. But now a trishaw blocked the path of the bus, and an elderly Chinese male passenger slowly dismounted from it, fumbled for money and then casually paid the fare. "For goodness sake, get a move on," Peter murmured to himself. Every minute counted now. Supposing Rose was on time and he was late? Would she become angry with him and leave? No, he told himself, she wouldn't leave. She would wait for him.

Finally, with a sudden jerk, the bus drew up outside the Capital Theatre. The door slid open and almost everyone in the bus made the usual mad dash to get out first. Peter allowed himself to go with the flow of humanity, exiting the bus and finding himself between a deep monsoon drain and the pavement. He was well aware of that monsoon drain having had the misfortune of falling into it one dark night when it was flooded and raining, and he was hurrying to catch the last bus back to camp. Being new to Singapore and unaware of the monsoon drain running parallel with the rain-drenched street, he had fallen into it, breaking his Box Brownie camera and bruising just about every part of his body, plus getting soaked by filthy water. Now, he was always cautious when near monsoon drains.

He walked around the rear of the bus and out into the street. A cruising taxi slowed and the driver looked enquiringly at him. Peter nodded a reply and the taxi drew alongside him. The driver reached back and opened a rear door for Peter to get in.

"Green Line bus station," Peter shouted, followed by, "*Fai di ah*, Johnny! *Fai di ah!*" (Hurry, Johnny! Hurry.)

"OK Johnny," was the man's response. The taxi cautiously eased into the flow of traffic, accelerated and within minutes drew up outside the Green Line bus station. Peter alighted and handed the driver a couple of dollars.

With a pounding heart he anxiously looked for Rose among the waiting crowd, but he could not see her.

Moments later the Green Line bus arrived on schedule, made a U-turn and came to a stop at the Singapore/Johore Bahru bus shelter. Again

Peter scanned the people who were waiting to get on that bus but Rose was not among them. Looking at his watch he noted that he was not late for their date, in fact the bus was not due to depart for another ten minutes. He watched as the few passengers who had arrived on the bus alighted.

The first off, and in a great hurry, was a Malay boy of about ten years, dressed in a multicoloured *sarong* and wearing a black *songkok* clamped over a mop of greasy-looking hair. He sprang from the doorway of the bus with such force that when his feet hit concrete the black *songkok* fell from his head and, caught by the wind, it began rolling towards a water-filled monsoon drain. The boy ran to retrieve the *songkok*, but in vain. The wind took it and deposited it in the middle of the monsoon drain, where it was swiftly carried away, bobbing along on the surface of the fast-flowing water. With a forlorn look on his face the boy gave up the hopeless chase and disappeared among the crowd.

A skinny, gaunt-faced Chinese woman with a baby strapped to her back was the next passenger off the bus. Carefully, she stepped down the two steps. How poor, ill and undernourished she looked, thought Peter. However, she was no worse off than so many other people on this island paradise where the population is vast but where there is much poverty and unemployment. The woman with her baby disappeared among the crowds milling on the sidewalk.

The next two people to alight had to be American tourists, Peter decided. Perhaps a rich businessman and his wife slumming it, travelling by bus while sightseeing in Singapore. The man, fat and in his fifties, had an expensive looking camera hanging from his shoulder and a big, unlit cigar clamped between his teeth. The woman wore expensive looking clothes, and God, what a hat! And she talked too much and too loud; 'yak yak yak,' she carried on to her male companion, who didn't seem to be the slightest bit interested in what she was yakking on about. Indeed, he began to study a map and ignored her completely.

Dropping the two tourists from his mind, Peter began worrying about Rose. Why was she not here? A sinking feeling of disappointment was coming over him. Surely she was not going to let him down, not after they had so intimately enjoyed each other's company just days before. Perhaps she was sick or perhaps she had decided not to see him again. He recalled how, when they had first met, she had repeatedly told him he was too young for her. Or could she have forgotten the date with him? But he found that too difficult to accept, especially after the way she had acted towards him during that sex-saturated weekend together.

Frustrated, Peter looked at his watch again and said, "Damn it." Any minute now the bus would be leaving. The driver was standing outside his cab smoking a cigarette and talking to the conductor. Both were khaki-uniformed Chinese males in their mid-thirties. Their conversation was coming to a close. The driver spat the cigarette end into a waste-bin and, laughing over a final joke, the two parted. The driver climbed into his cab and the conductor gave Peter a questioning look as if asking, 'Well! Are you coming or not?' When Peter stared forlornly back at him and made no move to get on the bus, the conductor shrugged as if to say, 'No! Very well then, stay there,' and he stepped onto the platform of the bus the same moment as the driver started the engine.

Dismayed, Peter groaned and said, "Damn! Damn! Damn!" Rick was right. Rose was not going to turn up. A feeling of disappointment swept over him the like of which he had never experienced before.

9

"Hurry, driver," Lai Ming urged. "I'm late. It's already time for the bus to depart."

"I drive as fast as I can. It is not my fault that we are late. If that son of a coolie had not pedalled his trishaw in front of my car, we would have been at the bus stop ten minutes ago," replied the taxi driver. "He cost me a day's pay."

"Precious money for you, precious time for me," said Lai Ming. She made no mention that it was the taxi driver's fault, that it was he who had run a red light, had collided with the trishaw crossing the road on green, and had crushed the trishaw's right rear wheel. It had taken a whole ten minutes for the two angry drivers to settle the dispute. Eventually, however, the taxi driver, knowing he was at fault, had sullenly given in rather than have the police called, and had paid the trishaw driver not only the price of a new wheel and tyre but also compensation for the man's lost earnings.

The taxi rounded a bend and squealed into the bus terminal.

"Your bus is still in its bay but about to depart," reassured the taxi driver. "I will drive in front of it so that it cannot leave without you."

"Thank you," said Lai Ming, sighing with relief and looking towards the already closed door of the bus. She saw Peter standing outside the bus looking crestfallen. The taxi swung into the bay blocking any forward movement of the bus. "You have done well," she said to the driver, handing him ten dollars instead of the two dollar fare. "That will help pay for the wheel," she said.

"Thank you. You have a big heart, Ming. All the taxi drivers know that you have a big heart. We shall meet again." The driver leaned back and opened the door for her.

"Most probably," replied Lai Ming as she stepped out and into the shade of the covered bus bay.

Peter had seen the uncommon sight of the taxi drawing up in front of the departing bus and was looking in that direction when Lai Ming suddenly appeared from around the front of the bus. All fear of rejection immediately left him, and his disappointment was replaced by a big smile of happiness. It was her, every lovely little inch of her. She had kept her promise and was walking to where he stood.

Uplifted at the sight of her in her blood-red *cheongsam*, Peter heard himself saying, "Oh, Rose! I'm so very happy to see you again."

Lai Ming gave him a reassuring smile. "I'm late," she whispered to him as she boarded the bus.

Lightheartedly, Peter followed her on and sat down in the seat next to her. The taxi had sped away. The conductor rang the bell and the bus pulled away from the shelter.

"Hello, Peter. How are you?" Lai Ming's eyes twinkled mischievously as she spoke.

"Gosh, Rose, I'm all right! But you had me worried. I was beginning to think you wouldn't show up, that you didn't want to see me again."

"You thought that?" Lai Ming asked as if surprised.

"Yes," he answered. "I did."

"Silly boy. When Rose make promise, me keep promise. Me go zoo. You go zoo." She was laughing, knowing that she was speaking pidgin English, but not caring. She purposely lapsed into pidgin English at times. It was easier for her. She didn't have to think so hard for the correct words.

"I'm sorry for doubting you, Rose," Peter said apologetically.

"That's OK, Peter. You happy to see me?" she asked.

"Oh, yes! You've made my day, just by being here beside me," he answered.

"Thank you. I happy for you," said Lai Ming, and then asked, "You wait for me long time?"

"Just a few minutes, but it seemed like ages. I suppose I did get a little anxious."

"You funny boy," she said, and taking his hand in hers she gently squeezed it and placed it so that their two hands rested in her lap. Smiling lovingly up into his face, she said, "Today we make happy times together, yes?"

"I'm sure we shall," said Peter. "I've been looking forward to seeing you again."

Lai Ming gave his hand another reassuring squeeze, then turned and looked out of the open window. "You know this road, Peter?" she asked. "We now travel on Singapore's main highway."

"I don't remember it," said Peter. "Is this Bukit Timah?"

"Yes, Bukit Timah Road. We go from the city, then straight through the centre of the island until we reach the northern coast. There we shall arrive at the causeway, which will take us across to the mainland of Malaya. I shall point out and try to explain to you the places of interest."

Peter gazed upon her lovely face with the cute dimples. Her jet-black hair smelled faintly of gardenia perfume. Her lips were a dark shade of red, and a hint of powder showed upon her cheeks, dabbed lightly over rouge. Her dress, sleeveless, was buttoned at the front of the high collar so that it hid her neck, and her shapely body was as if cocooned in a sheath of silk, which accentuated her curvaceous figure.

"We are approaching Bukit Timah Racetrack, Peter," Lai Ming said, breaking the silence. "Soon you will be able to see where the horses run, and if we are lucky, maybe we shall see them practicing on the track. Do you ever bet on horses, Peter?" she asked.

"I think any form of gambling is a mug's game," he said, looking out of the window at the passing scenery. "You don't bet on horses, do you?" he asked.

"Yes," she answered. "At times."

"You do?" he asked, surprised.

"Yes. I am a member of the Turf Club."

Peter was even more surprised, and showed it.

"Why are you surprised?" she asked.

Peter shrugged his shoulders. "I don't know," he said. "You don't look the gambling type."

"I don't know what a gambler should look like, but I like to gamble occasionally. Most Chinese people gamble. Anyway, Peter, to gamble is not the only reason I go to the race meetings. There are other reasons."

"Such as?"

"Well, I like the excitement that goes with horse racing, the glamour and the colour. I love horses and I love to watch them race. There! See! That's the entrance to the track," and she pointed a dainty finger towards a wide gravel pathway leading through green parkland. "That's the gateway to great wealth or to the gutter."

Again surprised by her words, Peter now faced a serious Lai Ming. "I suppose you are just one of the countless unlucky ones," he said.

"Yes. I have lost money at the track. But one day," and her eyes sparkled as she paused for breath. "One day I shall win, and I shall win big, a fortune. I shall win either on the horses or the Chinese lottery."

Peter did not interrupt her. Instead, he listened.

"And when I do win, do you know how I shall spend my money? I shall buy a villa here on the outskirts of the city. And, oh, it will be such a nice house, and it will be mine. I see it often in my dreams, a red brick house, with frilly, white lace curtains at the windows. There will be a green lawn at the front with borders of pretty flowers, red, pink, yellow and blue flowers, all growing happily together. And at the back of the house there will be a vegetable garden and fruit trees, and an ever-flowing fountain in the middle of a tiny lake full of silver and gold fishes hiding beneath lily pads. Ducks will splash in its cool water. And there will be a little stone bridge spanning the lake." Suddenly, she stopped talking and smiled wistfully at Peter. "I talk too much," she said. "Please forgive me. It is only my dream. Nothing more."

"It's a beautiful dream," said Peter. "I sincerely hope that one day it will come true."

"Thank you," she said quietly.

The bus sped onward, along the miles of Bukit Timah Road, with the new housing projects left behind and the countryside now all around them. They were heading towards the almost mile-long stone and cement causeway that not only carries the highway but also railway tracks and a fresh-water pipeline, and which reaches out like a long arm, linking the island of Singapore with Johore in Malaya.

The sun was way past its zenith when the Green Line bus pulled in and halted at the customs shed at the Johore Bahru end of the causeway. After carefully adjusting his tie, Peter followed Lai Ming out of the bus onto the scorching hot roadway.

At the customs shed they stood with the other passengers who had stepped off the bus, but it seemed that people of European origin were treated differently. An official waved Peter on, and then realizing the Chinese woman at his side was in his company, he also waved her on. The other local passengers were lined up, questioned, and some of them searched.

A canvas-canopied trishaw pulled up alongside Peter and Lai Ming, its bronzed, skinny driver clad in an old pair of sun-bleached khaki shorts, a very wide-brimmed straw hat secured by string to his head, and on his feet he wore old canvas shoes. "Where to, Johnny?" he asked, with a friendly smile.

Lai Ming answered him in Cantonese. The journey, being some considerable distance, caused the trishaw owner's smile to broaden in anticipation of receiving a big tip. He gestured in a friendly manner for the two to get in. Peter assisted Lai Ming to her seat and then sat down beside her. The conveyance was no more than a light sidecar attached to a bicycle, similar to many thousands of others plying their trade, both on the island of Singapore and throughout Malaya, where transportation by trishaw was popular. Unlike in Hong Kong, there were very few coolie-drawn rickshaws for hire.

For the next several hundred yards the rider slowly pedalled the trishaw along the coastal road, between avenues of coconut palms, lianas and loquat trees. To the right could be seen expensive homes surrounded by well-tended green lawns and, to the left, lay the Strait of Johore in placid tranquillity. Only the wash from the bows of small craft disturbed its calmness, leaving little wakes of sparkling white and silver astern of them. And, in the far distance, slowly heading towards Singapore's naval base, the British Royal Navy aircraft carrier HMS *Unicorn* stood out against the horizon. Nearer the coastline, two escort vessels, a destroyer and a frigate, overtook an ancient looking Chinese junk whose patchwork of a mainsail was hauled in tight to catch what little wind there was.

The driver stopped the trishaw beneath a giant rubber tree where, within its shade, there was a hint of coolness. Here his two passengers alighted. Peter handed the man a Malay dollar and told him to keep the change. Smiling happily, the driver thanked him in Chinese, took to the pedals again and rode slowly away to seek another fare.

"Well, Rose, where do we go from here?" asked Peter.

She laughed. "Come. I show you," she said as she led the way up a twisting gravel path, which brought them to the zoo gates. The entrance fee was fifty cents each; Peter handed the gatekeeper a dollar. A crowd of small children immediately gathered around them, offering peanuts, still in their shells, at twenty cents a packet.

Hand in hand, the two lovers walked the many gravel paths that wound through the tropical growth and banks of spongy grasses. It was as if they were alone for they did not notice the other visitors, mostly Singaporeans enjoying an afternoon away from the jostling crowds of the city. At one of the garden benches they stopped and sat down. Lai Ming nestled against Peter just enough so that it was not too obvious to those who passed along the path, that she held his hand in her lap and stroked it with the tips of her tiny fingernails. "It is so very peaceful here," she said. "I love to see all the different animals and birds. And I like to see fish, too. I love to see all these creatures among this greenness. It is so much nicer here than in crowded, noisy Singapore."

"Have you been here often?"

"The first time was the only time. My husband brought me here." She looked at him, and again he saw much sadness in her eyes, just as he had seen sadness in them when she had talked about her husband the day they had met on Changi Beach. "I fed the monkeys then, under the same tree, and we sat on this very same seat together. We had only been married a few months. It does not seem such a long time ago, yet a number of years have come and gone since his death."

"I am sure he was a good man," said Peter, in a sincere voice.

"He was! Believe me he was. I could not have wished for a better husband."

Peter was unsure what to say next, and there was silence between them for several moments. Eventually, he said, "The good die young, Rose."

"Unfortunately, that seems to be true," she answered.

"It must have been heartbreaking for you, hearing the news that he had been killed."

"It was. It was a bitterly cruel blow, especially after all we had been through during the Japanese occupation. Finally, with the war ended, I never thought anything like that could happen to my husband. It was terrible for me. I cried for months after his death. I could not eat. I could not sleep. I wanted to die. I hoped I could kill myself and be with him, but I had to care for my baby. Only because of my boy did I live. He was all I had, and all that I have now. All my family lived in Sumatra, but now they are dead, all killed by the Japanese.

"They were murderous swine, weren't they?"

"They were sent by the devil," answered Lai Ming venomously. "Peter, after they conquered Singapore, I saw the heads of people chopped off by them like chickens' heads. At the naval base I saw the heads of white men impaled on the iron spikes of the gateway, with notices pinned to

110

those heads informing the public just what the Japanese could do to the all-powerful, invincible white men who had ruled Singapore. The heads remained on the spikes for many days, blackened by the sun and half-eaten by birds and maggots. I saw the Japanese kill many people with their swords and bayonets—men, women and children, mostly Chinese. It did not matter to the Japanese who they killed, or for what reason. Human life meant nothing to them." She paused for moments in thought, then continued, "I remember an awful day being forced to witness a group of about twenty Australian soldiers, prisoners of war, being shot to death outside the doors of St Andrews Cathedral. We were forced to watch the executions. It was supposed to show us that the Japanese are a superior race."

"We are getting terribly morbid. It's time we changed the subject."

Lai Ming smiled at him, "Yes, you are right," she said. "I am sure that you are not a man of violence."

"I like peace and tranquillity. I hate anything to do with war," Peter replied adamantly.

"You remind me so much of my late husband," said Lai Ming. "You have his good qualities and the same principles."

Shrugging his shoulders, Peter replied, "Really?"

"Yes. I realized this very shortly after we met on the beach." Lai Ming chuckled, "When at my apartment, you were so completely occupied with me and my body, you said very little about yourself and your family. I would like to know something about them."

"What would you like to know?" asked Peter.

"I'd like you to tell me about your father and mother. Do you have brothers or sisters? Just little questions," said Lai Ming.

"My mother is alive and well, and I have three brothers, two older and one younger. We were still very young when my father was killed."

"Oh! Your mother also must have a sad story. How was your father killed? In the war?"

"Yes, in the war, by the Germans."

"I'm sorry. Was he also in the RAF?"

"No. He was a private in the army, just an ordinary soldier. He was called up at the beginning of the war and killed shortly after, in France, at a place called Dunkirk."

"Your mother must have had a terrible time, to lose her husband and to have four hungry little boys to feed."

"Yes, I'm sure those were bad times for our family, but I didn't think much about it at the time. I was too young to understand. I must have been about seven when we had news of my father's death."

Hand in hand, a young Chinese couple walked past them along the gravel path, not looking twice at the European boy with the Chinese girl. They were too preoccupied with each other. They too were in love.

Another half-hour slipped quickly by.

Chattering monkeys still swung to and fro in the treetops but the birds were quieter, snoozing now on boughs and among the tall grasses growing around the pond. In the pond, silver and gold coloured fish swam lazily in placid water, not even disturbing the bullfrogs that were silent and asleep beneath great green lilypads. And Lai Ming and Peter Saunders laughed together, talked on many things, and enjoyed feelings of blissful closeness to one another in the little world they had created and shared only by themselves.

Eventually, Lai Ming said, "Peter, let's go home. We shall eat and drink at my house. There, *amah* get you one Carlsberg. You drink, then we make something. After, *amah* get dinner. After we eat, we make something all night. We go taxi home. You pay taxi. I pay dinner. OK?"

Peter, laughing at her sudden change to pidgin English, teasingly asked, "What is the something we make, Rose?"

"You know what something. Something you like make with me."

"Something I like make with you, but something you no like make with me?" Peter teased.

"You know what I speak. I show you later how much I like."

Minutes later a taxi sped the two southward, seemingly the whole length of Bukit Timah Road, then through a labyrinth of minor roads foreign to Peter until it arrived at the junction of Bendemeer Road and Lavender Street. The driver, following Lai Ming's instructions, eventually pulled up outside the alleyway leading to her apartment. Peter paid the previously negotiated fare, as well as tipping the driver handsomely, and was about to get out when Lai Ming hissed the one word, "Wait," and she grabbed hold of his arm. "No move," she whispered. "RAF police car behind."

Peter froze in his seat, then nervously sank lower, to be out of view through the rear window. In the out-of-bounds areas he was safe while in a vehicle but the moment he got out the military police could arrest him. "No look up," whispered Lai Ming in a surprisingly frightened voice. Suddenly, he heard an engine rev up, and he saw a white jeep with two RAF military police in it pull alongside him. He tried to look away but he was sure their eyes were on him. This is it, he thought. He was about to tell the driver to move on and out of the out-of-bounds zone, when to his surprise and relief the jeep pulled away. He watched until it disappeared, far ahead, among the traffic.

"Phew! That was damned close," he exclaimed. "I could have sworn they saw me."

"You must always be very careful when you come to my home," said an obviously frightened Lai Ming. "Always look before you step from car."

"Yes, I'll remember that," said Peter, still unnerved by such a close call. He looked around him, at the people on each side of the street, at the traffic flow coming from ahead, then turning, he made sure there was not another military police jeep behind him.

Once in the alleyway and approaching the door, Lai Ming gave a nervous laugh, and said, "Peter, please, in future, when you come to my house you must ask the *amah* in Chinese to let us in. I have my key, but it is good practice for you. Do you remember the words I taught you?"

"Yes, of course I remember them," said Peter. He knocked on the door, and when he heard movement behind it, in not much more than a whisper, he said, "*amah, hoi mun ah, fai di ah.*"

"Who is it?" he heard the old *amah* ask in Chinese.

"Ming and Chicko," he replied, laughing, recalling how the old *amah* had referred to him as Chicko, a boy, during that last visit.

He heard the *amah* muttering and swearing behind the locked door, but after working with the many Chinese help in Hong Kong, and among the kitchen staff at the sergeants' mess, he believed that although the majority of Chinese people swore a lot, it rarely meant anything to them.

"Ming. Is it you?" he finally heard the *amah* ask.

"Yes. It's me. Open the door." And when the door opened and the two had stepped inside, Lai Ming said to her *amah*, "It is good. From now on, when you hear Peter's voice, you will know to open the door."

The *amah*'s toothy grin greeted Peter, and she replied, "*Wah!* He is a good boy for you, Ming, that I can see. If he is not a good boy," and she wagged a skinny finger at Peter, and said, "*Tsam koi ge tau!*" (I'll cut off his head.)

"She is a good watchdog for me. She would protect me with her life," said Lai Ming in English to Peter.

"Yes, I think she would," he acknowledged. "But I am sure that you are very good to her."

Lai Ming smiled at this remark but made no comment. Instead, she said, "Now that she knows you are my boyfriend, she will also protect and obey you." Thus saying, Lai Ming again turned to her trusted friend and maidservant. "I need you to visit Wang's shop to buy a bottle of Green Spot and a bottle of Carlsberg beer. No, make that two Carlsberg beers." Turning to Peter, she said to him, "Today, I make special for you, two beers. After fright from police, I think you have great need. But remember, it is special. I no like boyfriend drink too much." Lai Ming took money from her handbag and gave it to the *amah*, saying, "Please, you go now. Hurry."

"Tsh! Tsh! Ming, I wonder why you are so impatient," teased the *amah*, and she laughed, saying, "but I go and come back quickly."

Without another word the *amah* took to the alleyway, the loud clip clopping of her wooden-soled clogs audible on the concrete until she reached the street. Lai Ming smiled at Peter, and said, "Come," and he followed her up the narrow stairway.

The moment they were in the bedroom, and with the sliding door closed behind them, she came to him, put her arms around his neck and drew him close so that her face nestled against his chest, and his face became pillowed in the waves of her silky hair. She held him thus without a word between them for several moments, then her face uplifted to his, and smiling lovingly, she said, "I love you, Peter. I love you very much." Then, in almost a whisper, she said, "You are my boy. I want always to make you happy and content." Her hand slid down and felt his manliness. "He is very big and hot," she whispered to him. "He needs me. I make something special for him. You undress, Peter, and lie on bed."

"I think we should first wait for the *amah* to return," said Peter matter-of-factly.

"No. The *amah* will not enter my bedroom without my permission. Come! I undress you. I shall take good care of you."

Peter laughed, "You are a funny lady. I've never met anyone quite like you before," he said, realizing that she had already taken off his tie and was now unbuttoning his shirt. He helped her take it off, and then she undid the belt to his slacks and unbuttoned his fly. "I'll do the rest," he said, kicking off his shoes, but she, giggling happily, persisted by pulling both his slacks and underpants down around his ankles.

When he was naked and lying on his back upon her bed, she crooned over him, her lips running over his body and her hands feeling and exploring his private parts. "Oh! Peter. You are so ready for me," she whispered. "And I am in much need of you."

With rapt admiration, he watched as she undressed just feet from where he lay. Sensuously, she slid the *cheongsam* from her body and dropped it to the floor. She was so lovely standing there in the half-light of early evening. She undid the little red bra and dropped it across the back of the chair. Her breasts were small but they were firm, round and so deliciously inviting he was tempted to grab her, pull her to him, and kiss and suck upon them. She saw that he might get up from the bed and come to her, so she held up both hands as if to ward him off. "No! Wait!" she said. "Watch me, but no touch." Her eyes were on him as she slipped her tiny red panties with white lace fringes down about her legs and stepped from them. As if a statue, she stood there, knowing that his eyes were feasting on that triangular-shaped black fleece shrouding that little place which so intrigued him. "You still like me, Peter?" she was saying in a quiet, almost inaudible voice.

"Oh, yes, Rose, you're beautiful."

"Everything is for you," she said, and she came to him and sprawled her naked body upon his. "And all that you have is for me," she whispered, and she put her arms around him and hugged him.

10

From six that Sunday evening until nearly one the following Monday morning, a constant rain had drenched the streets of Singapore. But the rain had finally stopped and the streets, now glistening wet, silver-streaked and grey-shadowed by the moonlit night, were almost deserted; a far cry from the previous afternoon when the city had bustled with an anthill-like multitude of people. A great majority of the people had sought the dryness of shelter when the rains began, a sudden heavy downpour which quickly turned into a street-flooding torrent. Thus it rained unabated for almost seven hours, and when, after midnight, it finally did stop, most of the populace slept, as did Peter back with his unit at RAF Changi.

Already it was almost two in the morning. Back in the city, a few people still roamed Lavender Street: those seeking pleasure and those supplying pleasure. The in-betweens were the trouble-shooting police, both military and civil, who vigilantly cruised the almost deserted streets in their jeeps and patrol wagons. Also, there were cruising taxicabs driven by weary, overworked drivers scanning the doorways of the many bars, nightclubs and brothels for likely fares because it was in this street that they could expect to find them, this being the centre of the red-light district. Here, at this time of night, there was sure to be more customers than in any other part of the city.

At Lavender Street, near the junction of Serangoon Road, an old

Indian hawker, swathed in a filthy, tattered white robe, sat asleep cross-legged on the wet pavement, his basket of fruits, nuts and sweetmeats at his side. He catered mainly to the late night revellers coming and going from the noisy, garishly lit, all-night hotel bar facing where he sat. But tonight he was just too tired; his eyes would not remain open, and he had fallen asleep.

A drunken German sailor, on shore leave from his ship out of Hamburg—now lying at anchor in Singapore's vast harbour—crashed through the swing doors of the bar, tripped over the old hawker's basket, staggered a few feet, then fell face down on the wet road. Moaning, he rolled over onto his back, cursed loudly, lay awhile, then slowly regaining his feet he tottered a few yards, groping as he did so for some support but there was none. He slipped and fell again, and rolled with a splash into the filthy water of a flooded monsoon drain running parallel with the sidewalk.

The old Indian hawker, awake now and cursing for all to hear, scuttled about the sidewalk gathering up the scattered contents of his basket. A rather old and fat Chinese woman ran from the bar and in her haste almost fell over the hawker. Recovering, she ran to the German sailor's aid and pulled him by his hair from the fast-flowing water. Wet, dirty and drunk as he was, she would take him home, as up until now business had been bad that night. Surely this man would not complain after being rescued from the monsoon drain, taken home and given a good time, she told herself—at least not until he was sober. Previously, she had seen him flashing money around at the bar for all to see, and he had bought drinks for several of the barmaids whilst bragging to them about his ship and how he had come ashore at Clifford Pier by launch. Now, the fat Chinese woman was ready to relieve him of some more money. But she would be fair. Like the majority of Singapore's Chinese prostitutes, Fatty Fanny had certain scruples and was always fair. He would stay the night with her. She would attend his needs and entertain him as best she could, then she would take from his wallet the amount of money she thought due her, and no more. And in the morning, when he was in a fit state to leave her, she would call a taxi and send him back to Clifford Pier. Stopping a passing taxi, Fatty Fanny and the cab driver wrestled the drunken sailor upright and helped him into the back of the taxi. Moments later the taxi disappeared down a moonlit alley.

Further along the street, seemingly oblivious to the fact that they were in a red-light district and that they might be seized at any moment by the military police, a group of rowdy British soldiers returning to their unit split the night air with their hollering. One of the soldiers, following in an unsteady gait some distance behind the others, began a bawdy song about a girl who sold her ass in Piccadilly, but his comrades drowned out his feeble efforts with their own rowdiness. A taxi glided alongside them and with a lot of shouting and coarse language they all bundled into it, and the taxi sped away.

Nearby, another British soldier, tall, broad-shouldered and clad in a jungle-green uniform, stood outside the bar chatting up a vivacious and petite Chinese girl of less than five feet in height, dwarfing her. He had consumed a few Tiger beers, but not enough to make him drunk, just a little tipsy. And why shouldn't he be a little tipsy? This was his first night of R and R on the island after spending eight months with his tank regiment up in the northern part of Malaya. He had done his share of killing, and he had seen several fellow British soldiers in his regiment killed. Now, he just wanted to forget the war and have a woman. Those were his regiment mates who had bundled themselves so noisily into the taxi. They were looking for a rowdier bar and more beer but he needed a woman, not more booze. Bareheaded, his khaki beret loosely rolled in his hand, he stood looking down at the lovely almond eyes beneath silky black hair which reached no higher than his navel. He liked the smiling little face that peered mischievously up at him. He also liked the way she was dressed; her light blue *cheongsam* hugged her smooth and tightly, accentuating the curves of her petite body. Admiringly, he looked her up and down, at the little mounds that were her breasts beneath the tight-fitting dress, and at the creamy-coloured thighs displayed provocatively between the splits in her dress. Her hands, too, he noticed, were delicate and tiny, and her arms soft and creamy-coloured in the moonlight. Under her arm she carried a small handbag that matched the colour of her dress. He looked into the uplifted face again. She had a lovely face, he thought, not a hard face that one might expect of a prostitute; and he liked the way her shining, jet black hair fell in waves down around her shoulders. He wanted her, and he wondered how much she charged.

She, in turn, was studying him. Could he be more than just a little drunk? Was he a mean or nasty type, or violent, or an abuser of women? Almost always these thoughts went through her mind during the initial encounter and bargaining time which normally followed. But whatever her feelings towards him, he had money, and she needed money. Obviously he had consumed alcohol but he was steady on his feet and his voice was not slurred. He seemed all right, so she hoped to make him a customer.

So far that night business had not been good, she had had only the one customer. At the Butterfly Club the competition had been fierce. There had been too few men and far too many younger girls than she, so she had left there unescorted. The Long Bar at the Raffles Hotel was surprisingly quiet and lacking in men, too, so, disappointed, she departed from there also without a client. And on catching a taxi to the Lucky World amusement park she found that the open-air coffeeshops, where at times she solicited her business, had been drowned out by the many hours of rain. Most people, on coming out of the theatres, night clubs, bars and dance halls, finding a deluge of rain pouring from the heavens, had done the sensible thing, they had gone home, or back to their unit, or had returned to their ship. Because of the rain most men had not made that planned excursion to have a quickie or an all-night session with one of the girls; that venture could wait until a drier night. So now, this prostitute, as well as the majority of the other girls who worked the streets, had had very little, if any, business. They cursed the rain, even though it had ceased over an hour ago. Now, a bright full moon shone overhead in a cloudless sky full of stars.

The Chinese girl talking to the soldier had been lucky enough to have already entertained an Australian sailor that evening, but it had only been for a 'short time'. The sailor had, however, made a date to spend Saturday night with her. Financially, Saturday night was usually her busiest and best night of the week, so the price agreed upon was high; it had to be high, as generally she could earn far more money on 'short times' than by men paying her for an all-night session. But her price had not appeared to daunt the Australian sailor, for on leaving her home his last words to her were that he was prepared to pay any amount she asked, and that he looked forward to seeing her again on Saturday night. He had spent a little more than half an hour in her bed, had paid her well, departed satisfied, and ten minutes later she was back on Lavender Street.

Her thoughts returned to Peter, and she winced at the thought of him finding out what she was doing. He would be asleep now, in the cooks' billet at the camp, unsuspecting, trusting and completely ignorant of the life she led. What would happen if he found out the truth about how she earned her livelihood, she wondered. But how could she keep it from him? She had thought of him often and she was thinking of him when, at the entrance to the bar, she had met the soldier who now stood towering over her. Almost angrily she had shaken Peter from her mind. She needed money, and the only way she could get money was to earn it—the old-fashioned way.

"Hello, soldier," she said. "You like go my house for good fucky-fucky? I give good 'short time'."

The soldier winced, momentarily taken aback by the crudeness of this lovely little woman. But he asked her, "How much?"

Without hesitation, she replied, "Twenty dollars."

"Aw! Come on, luv! I want to borrow it, not buy the damned thing," he said.

The girl shrugged, laughed, and she again thought of the funny little Frenchman who had visited her some nights ago and who, while in bed with her, had jokingly said that Parisian prostitutes had the saying, "Beesness is ze beesness, and love is ze bullsheet." The saying and the way the Frenchman had said it had amused her; she had remembered it and now wanted to repeat it to this potential customer balking at her price.

Stifling a giggle, she said, "My price is twenty dollars."

"That's too fucking much," said the soldier.

"Have you spent all your money on beer?" asked the girl.

"So what if I have?" the soldier replied irritably. "Today's my mate's birthday, and we've just come down from up north. We've been on a bit of a piss-up."

The girl ignored his remarks. "My price is still twenty dollars," she said, and she gave him a big smile, "Come on, Johnny, you look a nice boy. I give to nice boy very good short time for only twenty dollars. Don't you think me worth twenty dollars?"

"Hell, I don't know! But I can't afford that much."

"Then I suggest you go back to camp and do what other boys do," she said indifferently. "You know, wanky wanky, money in the banky."

Annoyed, the soldier said, "Go to hell!"

Also ignoring this remark, the girl turned from him. She was disappointed. For a Sunday night, customers were few and far between. Still, it was not yet two o'clock. She might find someone yet, especially as it looked as if the rain would keep off for the remainder of the night. She would walk Lavender Street for another hour, then, with or without a client, she would return to her apartment, go to bed and sleep. She had walked only a few yards when she heard heavy footsteps following her. Turning, she saw that it was the soldier, who with long strides was catching up to her.

"I thought you were on your way back to camp," she said.

"Look 'ere," he replied. "Stop a minute. Let's talk."

"Well, you heard my price," she said.

"Look! I'm not a bloody officer, and I'm not a rubber planter. I'm a squaddy. I can't afford twenty bucks, but I'll give you ten."

"Make it fifteen and I'm yours," she said. "Because I like your looks."

"Atta girl. Now we're getting somewhere," said the soldier. "You make it twelve and you've got yourself a deal."

She studied his face for moments before replying. He was very young, probably not yet twenty. It was a pity he had been drinking, she thought. She never trusted men who had had too much to drink. They could be dangerous. However, a client was a client, drunk or sober, and she thought of the money. Twelve dollars wasn't much, but it was better than nothing. She knew that it was a lot of money to this young soldier on his lowly pay; not like that of many of her customers. Low ranking servicemen were the lowest paid white men in the colony, which made her feel some empathy towards him. Agreeing, she said, "OK Johnny, twelve dollars. But you pay taxi driver."

"What taxi driver? We'll walk!" said the soldier.

"OK! But it would be safer if you go my home in taxi."

"Why?"

"Don't you know what street you are in? This is Lavender Street. You're out of bounds."

"Christ! Am I? Well, who gives a fuck?"

"You should. So far you have been lucky. If you get picked up by the military police you will be in big trouble, and there will be no fucky-fucky for you tonight."

The soldier began to laugh. "I don't give a damn about the military police, but I'd hate to miss the fucky-fucky. All right, twelve bucks it is. Get a taxi." Then he said to her, "I hope you're clean."

"I'm clean, Johnny. I can show you my card. It's stamped and signed up to date."

"I believe you," the soldier said.

Having watched and awaited the outcome of the bargaining from his cruising taxi, the driver, seeing his services were now required, drew level with the odd-looking couple standing talking together on the sidewalk. He reached back and flipped open a rear door. "Where to, Johnny?" he asked quite pleasantly. Business had been brisk for him while it was raining, but for the last hour fares were few and far between. Now, he did not mind going short distances, even a street or two.

"Wherever she wants to go," answered the soldier.

"OK Johnny," said the driver, smiling a hello to the girl. She used his cab often. He watched as the soldier followed the girl into the back seat, and when they were seated he spoke to her in Chinese. She nodded. He knew where to take them.

The taxi sped along notorious Lavender Street, a street where brothels, opium dens and gambling houses flourished. But for those who were unaware, it was just another street where dilapidated living quarters overhung shopfronts, the stone walls and woodwork a mass of blistering, dirty paintwork. In the daytime when sunny, laundry, like flags of many nations, hung from long bamboo poles stretched from window ledges out across the street. And where there were no shopfronts and tenements there were shoddy garages, scrap metal dumps, boiler repair works and other eyesores.

Passing a ship's boiler repair shop where several huge boilers lay grotesquely shapeless in the shadows of the moonlit yard, the taxi left Lavender Street and turned into Bendemeer Road. Soon the girl's home was reached, a building typical of the Chinese architecture common in that area—a house within a row of houses, the second floor overhanging the sidewalk and supported on stone pillars. Laundry hanging from poles sticking out of windows normally festooned this street, too, but not on this rainy night.

The taxi stopped. "Is this it?" asked the soldier.

"Yes," replied the girl. "Give the driver two dollars."

The soldier did as bid and, on alighting, he followed the girl into a narrow alleyway. A mongrel dog sniffed at his ankles, and chickens in a wire enclosure clucked nearby, annoyed at having been disturbed at such a late hour.

On their arrival at a green painted door near the end of the alley, the girl took a key from her handbag, unlocked the door, pushed it open and stepped inside. She beckoned the soldier to follow her. Locking the door behind them, she led the way through a small kitchen where a wok sat on a fire that had long gone out, and where there were blackened cooking pans hanging from a whitewashed wall. Watched by the eyes of a wrinkled-faced old Chinese woman, she ushered him up a flight of canvas-covered stairs where, at the top, she pushed open a sliding door made of wallpapered bamboo. Drawing aside a heavy curtain covering the entrance, she said, "Come, step inside, soldierboy. Don't be bashful."

Again the soldier did as he was told by stepping into a room that was a living room and bedroom combined. The bed was the main feature of the room, its headboard backed up against the far wall. The soldier looked at the inviting bed, at the two pillows and he smiled ruefully as he read, 'Good morning,' that was embroidered on both pillows in letters of silk. In a corner of each pillow, also in embroidered silk, was a pair of blue and yellow swallows in flight.

Casually, the young soldier looked about him, at whatever else furnished the room. This wasn't the first whorehouse he had been in, not by a long chalk, but he was curious; unless drunk he was always curious when visiting a whorehouse. The canvas on the floor was freshly polished he noted and the room was clean and tidy. But the majority of whorehouses were clean and tidy, those that he had visited these past two years since his arrival in the Far East.

"Do you like my room?" the girl asked.

The soldier shrugged his shoulders, "I've seen better, but I've seen a lot worse," he answered. He walked to the door of the bathroom and looked inside. A look of surprise came upon his face. "Wow! Now that's different! That's the first modern bathroom I've seen in any Chinese whorehouse. Real plumbing, eh?"

"It was specially put in and paid for by me," said the girl. "It's better for business."

"You must be the queen around these parts to be able to afford a shithouse like that. Here's my twelve dollars. It'll help pay the water bill."

"Thank you," the girl said, accepting the paper money and putting it into the middle drawer of her dressing table.

Taking a packet of twenty Players cigarettes from his shirt pocket, the soldier opened the pack and with a flick of his fingers flipped a cigarette to where it could be easily accepted. He offered the cigarette to the girl. "Care for a fag, Mag?" he asked.

She smiled up at him. "I don't smoke," she said. "And my name is not Mag, It's Rose. What's your name?"

The soldier lay the cigarettes down on a glass-covered bedside table and began stripping off his jungle-green jacket. "Bill," he said, "Bill Eldridge. I'll have a fag later."

Unfastening her *cheongsam*, the girl slipped it down over her body. "Bill is a nice name," she said. She told every man that came to her room that he had a nice name. She carefully folded the *cheongsam* and placed it over the back of a chair. Next, she unclipped her dainty bra and placed that over the *cheongsam*. Finally, she slipped her tiny panties down around her legs and stepped out of them. She had repeated this undressing act far too many times now for her to be embarrassed or ashamed.

"OK Bill, hurry up. I make for you good time," she said.

She lay on the bed on her back, watching him take his pants off, and awaited the encounter.

Less than an hour later, and not more than ten minutes after the soldier had made his exit, the girl, already douched and dressed, again picked up her little blue handbag and placed it under her arm. As soon as she left the house her *amah* would make the bed and clean up the place, making sure the bedroom would be inviting and ready to be used by her next client. Slipping into her shoes at the bedroom doorway, she quietly made her way down the stairway. And as she passed through the tiny kitchen, she spoke a few words to the old woman sitting half asleep near the dead charcoal fire, opened the door that led into the alleyway, and then again stepped out into the moonlit night. Locking the door behind her, she walked through the narrow alleyway until she reached the road.

A trishaw took her back to her pitch at the hotel doorway where she had met the soldier. There she would seek a new client. She had not long to wait. Two US sailors, dressed immaculately in white uniforms, on shore leave from a US submarine visiting Singapore on a good-will mission, came out of the hotel bar and walked towards her. One was tall and skinny, the other short and fat. They appeared to be friendly and perfectly sober. She approached them and said to the one who looked the nicer, "Hello, sailor. You and your friend like good time, good fucky-fucky?"

The two American sailors stopped and smiled at the cheeky, diminutive and beautiful Chinese woman confronting them.

"Why not?" the short one said.

"Sure, why not? She's cute!" his companion exclaimed. Both then began bargaining with her. She knew she would get a good price from these well-paid US navy men, and they were sober as well as friendly. Good fortune certainly seemed to be with her this night after all.

PART TWO

11

In the year 1952, Singapore, the Lion City, the gateway to the Orient, was a tropical garden-like island paradise and a very cosmopolitan city. Chinese were by far in the majority but there were also Malays, Indians, British, and minorities from many other parts of the world. Here lived the very rich, the poor, the honest men and rogues, students intent on an education, barebacked coolies and prostitutes galore. And on every part of this small island—twenty-six miles east to west and fourteen miles north to south—British soldiers and members of the Royal Air Force and sailors of all ranks from His Majesty's Ships could be seen. Also enjoying the island's many amenities were seamen from every part of the globe. Mostly, these men were on shore leave off modern, luxury cruise liners, old and rusty tramp steamers, huge oiltankers and merchant ships, as well as junks, dhows and other such small craft loading and unloading cargo in the world's second largest seaport. The thirty-six-square-mile harbour boasted the best facilities in Southeast Asia, with giant warehouses and many long concrete docks lining the port. The city of Singapore was itself built around the harbour. Local fishermen and boat builders rubbed shoulders with adventurers, airline crews and pearl divers. And there were the tin-mine managers and rubber planters who journeyed down from Malaya to enjoy a spell of rest and relaxation on the island. Added to these was the gradually increasing number of tourists, mostly wealthy Americans, sight-seeing the Far East. Chinese women with babies strapped to their backs were numerous, as were the peanut, sweetmeats and fruit vendors, trishaw *wallahs* and taxi drivers. They mingled jostling each other, shouting, cursing, singing and laughing, each and every individual seemingly talking in a different language in this grossly overpopulated city. But what a city! So beautiful, so richly colourful, surprisingly clean in many parts, though ugly and drab in others, especially in the poorer Chinese tenement sections of which there are many. A strangely exciting, almost intoxicating aura captivates the visitor. The exotic smells, and the bright fluorescent lighting of advertising signs flashing rainbows of colours at night. The many and varied colourful costumes of the populace, the multicoloured *sarong*, the slinky *cheongsam*, the pajama-like *samfoo*, the graceful *sari* and the *baju kebaya*, to name but a few. The steady roar of traffic, and the constant blaring of horns from impatient drivers, mostly taxi drivers. The spirited bargaining with the trishaw riders, the orangeade and fruit carts which are like little islands on the overcrowded sidewalks, the clothes-lines of bamboo, like flag-bedecked yardarms, stretching from windows often halfway across the street. There's the drying of fish, with only a layer of newspaper separating it from the unsanitary pavement. The fish lies there baking under the torrid sun, smelling to high heaven, until it turns a rich yellowish-brown and becomes a delicacy. Street urchins and beggars clutch at the arms of passers-by, and ragged shoeshine boys grope at the legs and feet of potential customers to attract their attention. One could hear the quick talk of the street-traders selling a fantastic assortment of goods, their voices mingling with the loud clatter of mahjong tiles coming from doorways and open windows where games were being played.

Leading Aircraftman Peter Saunders loved Singapore. To him it was a gay city, full of excitement and adventure. Even the gaudy black, red and gold Chinese characters splashed on walls and pillars along the sidewalks stirred an awakening within him, making him feel completely at home and at ease with the environment.

Now, around and above him, neon advertising signs winked

incessantly, their bright lights illuminating in multiple colours traffic, shopfronts, and the million and one people who crowded within their glaring light. Mingling with the seething mass of humanity, he threaded his way expectantly among the milling crowds, knowing that Rose would not fail him; she would be there, waiting for him at their agreed-upon meeting place at the Capitol Theatre. By now Peter worshipped Rose. She meant everything to him.

Five weeks had already slipped by since he had had the good fortune of meeting his lovely Chinese girlfriend on Changi Beach. Five whole weeks, during which time they had spent many, many happy hours together—at theatres, dining at good but inexpensive restaurants, taking strolls along the sea front, visiting the zoo, the beaches and, on one occasion, dancing at an all-night cabaret. Regardless of where they visited, their afternoons or evenings always ended with the two of them in Lai Ming's bed, where she taught him the art of loving a woman. Also, and with great patience and repetition, she taught him her dialect, Cantonese. In her bed they kissed, talked, touched, caressed one another and had wonderful sex, and the hours flew by, and at times whole days passed without them leaving her home.

This evening, though, as Peter made his way among the masses, he did not feel well, and he was becoming increasingly apprehensive. Early that morning he had reported to the camp medical officer to receive his annual TABT injection prescribed to all British servicemen on a tour of duty in the Far East. And after the injection was given to him in his right arm, he read with grim humour 'Wellcome' the name of the vaccine maker printed on the medical form lying on the MO's office table. But to Peter, the shot had not been at all welcome, as he knew he would suffer terribly from the effects of the injection for days. He was already feeling sick, as if he was suffering from a bad bout of influenza and his arm had become painfully stiff. On the bus which had brought him from Changi into the city, he had experienced feelings of nausea, but had paid little heed, repeatedly telling himself that it must be the effects of the injection. Now, though, he felt feverish.

A sudden chill went through him and he shivered and belched foul air. Stopping for a moment, he looked at the lights and noticed that his vision was blurred. The air was hot and humid, and although he was sweating, he shivered again. He took a handkerchief from his pocket and mopped his clammy, fiery hot brow. Suddenly, a dreaded thought came to him. Supposing the way he felt was not caused by the injection but instead by another bout of malaria. These first tell-tale symptoms were certainly similar to those he had experienced during previous attacks of the dreaded disease.

On legs that felt like jelly, he arrived at Capitol Theatre, entered the crowded foyer and made his way to the corner where he knew Lai Ming would be awaiting him. She was there, greeting him as always with her lovely smile and a "Hello Peter."

"Hello, Rose. How are you this evening?"

"Very well," she answered. "And you?"

"Oh. All right I suppose." He felt like saying, "Bloody lousy," but there was no point in causing her concern.

She was smiling up at him, a smile that he now knew so well, a sweet, tender smile in a lovely little face. Her eyes, too, betrayed her feelings for him. Always they were so full of love and kindness towards him.

On this rare occasion she wore a European style pale turquoise dress which reached an inch or so below her knees. In one hand she held a little handbag of a matching colour, and in the other, two theatre tickets.

"I arrived a little early so have already purchased the tickets," she said. "The crowd grew quickly and I thought, if I wait, we may fail to get a seat. Here, you take them, Peter."

Accepting the two buff-coloured tickets, Peter said, "Thank you. I'll pay you later."

"No, Peter, I pay this time," said Lai Ming. "You are always generous and good to me, and I am happy with your company. I shall pay, just this one time. It is my way to say, thank you."

"But Rose …!"

"Don't argue, Peter, or I shall get angry."

Rose turned and headed towards the marble stairway that led to the circle. Peter caught up with her, and at the upper foyer he opened the felt-clad swing door so that together they entered into the magnificent, air-conditioned auditorium.

A petite Chinese usherette dressed in a smart brown uniform inspected their two tickets before escorting the pair up the centre aisle to the rear row of seats. "Please. Sit here," she said, smiling and giving them an 'I know what you have in mind' look. She then returned to the exit doorway where she whispered and giggled with another brown uniformed and equally petite usherette while awaiting other patrons to arrive.

Looking at Rose seated beside him, Peter felt very happy. How different to have her company than to go out on the beer with the boys, he thought. Taking her hand in his, he said, "Thanks, Rose. Not only for buying the tickets but also for your good company." He placed an arm around her and drew her close, wincing as pain surged through his arm. "Oh, bloody hell!" he exclaimed.

Turning an enquiring face towards him, Lai Ming asked, "What is the matter?"

"Nothing," Peter replied.

"Nothing? You are OK?"

"I'm all right," Peter said, drawing her closer to him.

"No! Please, Peter, don't put your arm around me," she rebuked him. "Not yet. Wait until the lights are out," she said, pulling herself away from his encircling arm.

"Oh! Oh! Don't!" Peter groaned as she put pressure on his arm.

"There is something wrong with you, Peter," Lai Ming said, becoming alarmed. "What is it?"

Feeling sick and shivery, Peter slowly and gingerly took his hurting arm from around her. "I had an injection in my arm today," he said. "Once a year all British servicemen get this injection. It's to stop them getting certain diseases." He did not mention his having had malaria.

"Oh! I am sorry to have caused you pain," Lai Ming said as the first advertising slide splashed itself colourfully across the screen.

More patrons arrived and sat down, and more slides were shown. Soon, the auditorium was full, the news began, and the lights gradually dimmed until the cinema was left in darkness except for the glow from cigarettes, and from the one bright beam of light shot down from the projection box.

Suddenly, another feverish spasm surged through Peter's body, and he shivered and shook violently, just for seconds, and then it was gone again. Settling back in his seat he closed his eyes as if in sleep.

Slowly, it seemed, time passed. Eventually Peter opened his eyes. The huge screen was now one big blur. Waves of nausea hit him again and he began to shiver violently. With his handkerchief he mopped wetness from his perspiring brow, yet he felt very cold and shivery.

"Damn the malaria. Damn the injection," he silently cursed. Both seemed to be attacking him simultaneously, as if the injection had brought on the malaria. What a time to have an attack, he thought. Why couldn't it have happened while he was in camp, safe in his own bed. He lay back against the soft cushioned seat shivering and shaking helplessly. How futile now to wish that he had used the mosquito net more often when at KL. But even then, the mosquitoes would eventually have got him; they had been everywhere, night and day, whining, and dining on him. Feeling as if he was suffering from a bout of flu, he could not stop shivering, his hands were shaking, his head felt hot and clammy, his mouth parched and his tongue felt like a strip of dry leather. He badly wanted something cool to drink.

On the screen a love scene was in progress, but Peter neither cared nor saw it.

Lai Ming leaned her head towards his so that he felt her soft hair brushing his face. She turned and smiled at him. "Good picture, eh, Peter?" she said, pressing her lips to his cheek. Only then did she realize that he was not well. His face was too hot, much too hot. She lifted a hand to his forehead. Dismayed, she gasped, "Peter! You are sick!"

"It's the injection."

136

"No! It cannot be! It is something else, something worse!"

For brief moments Peter ceased to shiver, but he felt weak and very thirsty. "It's nothing to worry about," he whispered to Lai Ming, giving her arm a reassuring squeeze. She again lifted a hand to his forehead.

"Peter, you are ill. Tell me, do you know the sickness that now attacks you?"

"It's malaria," Peter answered flatly.

"Malaria!" said Lai Ming, momentarily lost for words.

His eyes streaming, his body feeling weak and brittle, racked with cold painful shivers, and drenched in perspiration, Peter tightened his grip on Lai Ming's cool hands. Frightened, she took a handkerchief from her handbag and with it wiped his brow. Even in the dimness of the theatre she could see he looked terribly ill. What should she do, she wondered. Should she send him back to the RAF station in a taxi, where he would receive treatment? But once he was out of her sight she would worry, and she would not be able to see him or be with him, and she did want to care for him. Therefore, there was only one alternative. "Peter, I take you home," she said.

Rising from her seat, Lai Ming beckoned him to follow her, which he did, as if in a trance. She took hold his good arm and guided him down the red-carpeted marble steps and out into the noisy, neon-lit street. A cruising taxi drew near. She waved it down. The young Chinese driver jerked open the rear door.

"Ah! Your boyfriend drink too much," he said, grinning. "Where do you wish to take him, Lavender Street? If not, I know a very good hotel in Serangoon Road."

As if unhearing the taxi driver's remarks, Lai Ming pushed Peter into the back seat of the taxi and spat out her address. "Hurry," she shouted.

The driver stared at her but said nothing more.

A single beam of silvery moonlight pierced the room, infiltrating the closed, rough wooden window shutters. Except for that one ray of moonlight the room was in shadowy darkness. The air was hot and humid and, but for the occasional whine of a marauding mosquito, strangely silent. A sweet smell of incense from smouldering incense sticks, combined with the smell from a perfume-laced anti-mosquito coil burning beneath the bed, filled the room.

At one in the morning there was little traffic in the street below to disturb the silence of the night in that upstairs room. Inside, there were just soothing whispers from Lai Ming comforting Peter who lay at her side. She had heard that malaria is treated by quinine, so she had sent Wan Ze to a nearby bar to buy a case of quinine water. The barman himself had brought the case of quinine water to her door, and had willingly carried it into the kitchen for the *amah* who gave him a sizeable tip. Already Peter had thirstily drank two bottles of the quinine water but he was now in a far worse state than before, so much so Lai Ming wondered whether or not she had done the right thing in bringing him to her home. Perhaps he needed medical care, which he would have received had she taken him back to Changi. Anxiously she watched as he rolled and twisted his shaking body in fitful sleep.

With increasing frequency, he moaned and talked loudly to himself, obviously in a state of delirium as the flames of fever burned within him. When he lay quiet and still for several minutes, Lai Ming gave a sigh of relief believing him to have gone into a deep sleep and she settled herself down beside him, ready too for sleep. But then he stirred and suddenly sat up, and looked with frightened unseeing eyes at the low ceiling above, and into the dark shadows all around him. He moaned again, fell back upon the bed, and became still.

Unsure as to whether Peter was in a deep sleep or had lost consciousness, Lai Ming again placed the cool, damp cloth to his feverish brow. She then bent her face and kissed a feverish cheek. "The devil must soon go from you," she whispered to him. "Now, you sleep." Sighing audibly she sank wearily back upon the thin mattress of her bed. "My poor sick boy," she whispered as tears flowed freely down her cheeks.

And except for the whine of that lone mosquito, all became silent in that little upstairs room.

The din of passing traffic and the shouts of hawkers lustily advertising their wares in the street below the shuttered window awakened Peter. Already mid-morning, a single ray of brilliant sunlight beamed through the chink in the closed shutters, just enough to light the room. Peter felt incredibly weak, his vitality completely drained, his mouth dry, but the fever had left him, leaving him cool and able to think clearly. He lay on his back staring up at the low, whitewashed ceiling, not yet quite realizing where he was, although the ceiling looked familiar. He knew that he had had a very bad night, feverish and full of bad dreams. He remembered meeting Lai Ming at the Capitol Theatre and sitting next to her in the back row. He could recall nothing of the film though, just a faint recollection of its beginning, Lai Ming laughing, and he himself feeling miserably ill. Looking towards the foot of the bed, he saw that a multi-coloured *sarong* covered him from the waist down. His head rested on a soft white pillow, but the mattress felt ungiving, as if he were lying on a wooden floor.

Slowly lifting himself on his good arm and turning his head, he read 'Good Morning' and saw two swallows in flight in the corner of his embroidered pillow. He tried to sit up, but couldn't, so rested himself upon an elbow and looked about him. A little face plainly showing weariness and worry rested upon the pillow next to his. Lai Ming lay at his side curled up in a feotal position. Quiet and still, and breathing gently, she was naked except for her legs, which were partially covered by a corner of the *sarong*. Peter managed a smile. "I am home. Thank you, Rose," he whispered. But she did not hear him.

Telling himself that he must not wake her, Peter carefully lowered himself to his former position on the hard bed. God, he felt weak, and he badly needed a cool drink. He was hungry, too. Slowly he pieced together what had happened. The arm that had received the injection had stiffened so much that now he could not bend it, and it was sore, but not nearly as painful as it had been yesterday. Faintly he recalled the taxi ride here, the grinning Chinese driver, and Lai Ming seated at his side in the back seat. He had faint recollections of the old *amah* assisting Lai Ming in helping him up the narrow stairway, and of Lai Ming undressing him. Afterwards there was blackness, fever, and terrible nightmares, which he could not remember.

Outside, in the street, it would be very hot, but in that little room it was surprisingly cool. A sweet smell of smouldering incense sticks hung in the air, a pleasant smell, soothing, so much so that Peter inhaled deeply whilst listening to Chinese voices, a radio playing Cantonese music, and the rattle of pots and pans coming from next door. The crying of a baby came through the thin walls from the opposite side of the apartment. All were familiar sounds. "I am home," Peter again whispered to himself.

Lai Ming remained asleep, on her side, a worn-out look on her face, and her hands clasped loosely together between her knees. The whiteness of her pillow looked even whiter against the blackness of her hair.

At his side, on the glass-topped wicker table, a large bunch of green grapes lay temptingly in a white china dish. Next to the dish was an already opened full bottle of Green Spot orange drink and a half empty bottle of quinine water covered by a plain glass tumbler. Carefully, Peter eased himself into a sitting position, noting that he wore only his underpants. He looked towards the open wardrobe and saw his shirt and trousers hanging among womens' clothing. His vest, socks and tie lay neatly on a chair at the foot of the bed. Famished and thirsty, having not eaten since lunchtime yesterday, he reached for the bowl and ravenously ate large oval-shaped seedless grapes, finding them sweet and juicy and very refreshing. Next, he reached for the bottle of Green Spot, and filling the tumbler with its contents, drank greedily. The sugar in both the grapes and the orange drink soon began to revive him. With gusto, he continued eating more grapes, and then drank a little more Green Spot. He refilled the glass with the remainder of the quinine water and drank that, too. Already he felt much better.

Lai Ming, sighing in her sleep, rolled over onto her back. The *sarong* fell from her legs exposing her nakedness. Peter gazed down at her in

140

wonderment. Her beautiful little body always fascinated him, and he was forever intrigued by that little hairy place between her legs. Now, it looked so inviting, he was tempted to bend down and give it a kiss. But he knew to kiss her would instantly awaken her. Instead, he drank more orange until he had emptied the bottle, his eyes all the while roving over and devouring the beauty of his nude girlfriend.

Peter ate the last of the grapes and returned the bowl to the bedside table. Now, sexually aroused by Lai Ming lying there naked on the bed beside him, he eagerly wanted to kiss and caress her, and to possess her. Should he wake her, he wondered. No, he mustn't, he told himself, because she might become angry with him. He looked at his watch. Ten minutes past ten. He wondered why she was still sleeping. Normally, when he awakened, she also awakened and they made love.

Moving closer to Lai Ming, Peter placed an arm next to hers and compared the colour and texture of their skin. He noted that hers was smooth and a creamy colour, whilst his was hairy, tanned by the sun, and considerably darker than hers. Suddenly, Lai Ming's eyes flickered open and she flinched in her alarm at his nearness, her hands flying up to protect herself.

Peter gazed down into her bewildered face. "It's me, Peter," he said.

"Oh!" she said with a sigh of relief. "Are you all right?" she asked, surprised to see him looking so well.

"I think so," answered Peter. "Thank you, Rose. I'm glad you brought me home. I love you so much."

"And I love you, too, Peter. I want no harm to come to you, only happy things." She smiled up at him, put her arms around his neck and pulled him down to her so that their lips met and she held him to her in a gentle embrace. Then, suddenly, with all anxieties drained from her, Lai Ming began to sob beneath him. "I was so frightened, Peter. You were so sick. I should have sent you back to your camp for proper care, but I was selfish. My need was to look after you myself, and now I am glad that I brought you home."

"So am I," Peter whispered in her ear. "So don't cry."

Through tears she smiled up at him, and still crying said, "I am happy now, Peter. The devil sleeps. When he rises he can find others to torment."

Only one event occurred the previous evening that now bothered Lai Ming. Whilst she was helping Peter out of the taxi, and without her usual caution, a military jeep with two RAF special police in it had pulled up behind them. She knew that they were RAF police because they were dressed in KDs, and wore white gaiters, white webbing and white covered caps. Too late, Peter was already out of the taxi and half way across the gap that separated him from the somewhat sanctuary of the alleyway. Being too sick to see or care about anything, he could not have seen the two men in the jeep but they must have seen him. At any moment she had expected them to challenge him and to ask to see some form of identification. If he showed them his 1250—his RAF identification card, which he carried in his wallet at all times—they would surely arrest him for being out of bounds. Hurriedly she had helped Peter into the alleyway. Then, looking back, she was astonished to see the two military policemen grin and nod to one another; and one of them actually gave her a smile and a friendly wave of his hand, and a "Good night, Rose". And then, surprisingly, the jeep moved away, and she had watched it until its rear lights disappeared at the junction of Lavender Street. The brief encounter had startled her, but the night that followed frightened her so much so that she had forgotten about the RAF military police. Now, remembering them, she was puzzled. Why had they not challenged Peter? And how did they know her name, and why were they so friendly towards her? She decided not to mention the incident to Peter. It would only worry him.

12

Speaking in Cantonese, Betty Chong said, "Ming, I hear you have a boyfriend." She spoke inquisitively, without looking up as she toyed with an emery board, delicately manicuring in short curving strokes her long, red-lacquered fingernails. "Molly Chen told me he's very young, and that you met him on the beach at Changi."

Lai Ming had never been really friendly with Betty, though not unfriendly. It didn't pay to be unfriendly with others of her profession, especially those who worked with her at the Butterfly Club, she never knew who might procure her a client. She considered Betty to be vulgar, lacking refinement and having a foul mouth; also, she was well aware of the reputation the other had for giving clients quick and cheap oral sex in a back room of the club.

"Yes, I do have a boyfriend," Lai Ming said to the nineteen-year-old beauty sitting next to her, who seemed so completely preoccupied with the careful manicuring of her long, clawlike fingernails. "He's a good friend," she said, deciding to have no further conversation on her personal affairs.

Stretching out her hand, Betty surveyed her handiwork. Seemingly satisfied, she yawned, crossed her legs and hitched up her *cheongsam*, making sure that she showed off a goodly portion of her creamy white thighs. "I'm surprised that you have not chosen an older man, a man of high position and much wealth," she said with a sneer.

"My boyfriend has finer qualities, Betty," replied Lai Ming, iciness creeping into her voice. "He is of gentle breeding and good character, qualities superior to wealth and high position, if those are all a man possesses."

"Speak for yourself. My man has money and a good business," said Betty.

"So what are you doing here?" asked Lai Ming coldly. "I thought your pimp is your boyfriend. It is because of you that he has money. My boyfriend is not a pimp."

"And he does not know that you are a whore, I suppose," smirked Betty.

Before Lai Ming could answer, a fat man with a codfish-like face, thinning grey hair, perhaps in his late sixties, and dressed in a white tropical business suit and a gaudy red tie, waddled from the crowded bar and flowed his flabby body onto the small circular dance floor. As if surveying cattle at an auction, his leering eyes quickly scanned the ring of about thirty girls seated at little tables surrounding the dance floor of the Butterfly Club. Spotting Betty, he lurched over to where she sat and said in a drunken voice, "Hi, baby. How's my little girl tonight?"

"Walter!" shrieked a suddenly very much alive Betty. "Where the fuck have you been?" she shouted in English. "I didn't know you were in town. Come and sit down. Buy me a drink. Have one yourself," and she reached up and grabbed the fat man by the arm and pulled him down into the vacant seat between her and Lai Ming. For the clients' benefit, the girls were not allowed to sit next to each other. They had to leave every other seat vacant for the guests. That was the club policy.

A dainty Chinese waitress immediately swooped down on the trio with a tray at the ready.

"Canadian Club and ginger for me, and a drink each for these two girls," the fat man wheezed.

"Thanks, Walter. Two champagnes," ordered Betty.

The waitress smiled, sashayed back to the bar, and within minutes returned with the Canadian Club and ginger, and two glasses of very weak carbonated tea.

Walter, an import-export agent, whether drunk or sober, was always generous to the ladies. "Put it on my tab, Lilly, and the usual twenty percent for you, honey," he said, making an unsuccessful grab at Lilly's firm little ass.

Slipping away from his groping hand, the waitress gave him an even bigger smile as she lilted in pidgin English, "Tank you. You make velly good time at Butterfly Cub."

"I always have a good time at the Butterfly Club," said Walter, and raising his glass, he sang out, "All the breast. Hey! Talking about breasts, Betty, I'd like to go suck on yours. How about you and me shacking up tonight?"

"Whenever you're ready," replied Betty. In Chinese she said to Lai Ming, "I told you it's the ones who have money that count. Not a penniless boy with a hard-on."

Lai Ming ignored her remarks.

Walter downed his Canadian Club and ginger in a couple of gulps, then turning to Lai Ming, he said, "Please excuse us, lady. Betty's the best piece of ass between here and Houston. So I'm gonna enjoy another piece of it. Always do when I'm in town."

Lai Ming smiled but made no reply. Her thoughts and her eyes were on a blond-haired, bean-pole of a man who had at that moment entered the club entrance. She recognized him immediately as one of her frequent and better-paying clients. She got up from her seat, nodded a goodbye to Walter and Betty who were about to leave, left her drink on the table, and hurried over to where Maxwell, an American sailor, stood eyeing the girls.

"Hello, Maxel," she said in a demure voice. She could never pronounce Maxwell. It never came out right.

"Rose! How are you? Christ! Was I hoping to see you here. I lost your home address. How's my lovely little Butterfly girl?"

"I am well, Maxel," Lai Ming replied, a radiant smile on her face. "And now I am happy because I see you again. Please, come, sit down with me." She led the man to a vacant table that was furthest away from the now crowded dance floor.

The same waitress as before pounced on them. "You like drinky?" she asked.

"I'll have a Ding, Ding and Dong," laughed Maxwell. "What's your poison, Rose? Your usual watered down tea?"

"No Ding, Ding and Dong," the waitress apologized. "Ding, Ding and Dong Hong Kong beer. No Three Bells beer in Singapore. Here, Tiger beer."

"Oh, shucks, I forgot. Yeah, I'll have a Tiger beer. And get a drink for the lady. God, it's good to see you again, Rose," said Maxwell, catching hold her hands, looking longingly into her eyes and laughing. "You're as beautiful as ever."

"Thank you," said Lai Ming. She liked Maxwell. He was a bit loud but he was a kind and generous man. He had often talked to her about a wife and two children somewhere miles away in America. But he was a sailor, often far from home and needing female companionship. "When did your ship arrive in Singapore?" Lai Ming asked.

"Yesterday morning. I looked for you last night but couldn't find you. I thought I'd find you here. God, it sure is great to see you again, Rose."

"Thank you," said Lai Ming. "I am happy to see you, too, Maxel."

Maxwell Clinton, the radio officer aboard the general cargo carrier, the MV Southern Star, flying the flag of Panama, but owned by an American company, had been to sea almost all his adult life. When ashore he appreciated the niceties taken for granted by landlubbers; for example, a good woman. He knew a good woman when he found one, and Rose happened to be one of them. During the past two years he had paid several visits to her home, generally for a two- or three-day period. He was never drunk, always a gentleman and also very generous with his money. Lai Ming wished all the men she took to her home were like Maxwell.

She smiled. "How much time will your ship stay in Singapore?" she asked.

"She's out of the water. We're having a paint job done on her from stem to stern. Yesterday they hauled her, scraped her bottom and cleaned all the rust and barnacles off her. Today they'll finish cleaning her, then they'll be painting her with antifouling paint. The job won't be finished for at least another three days, so how about I stay with you until she's ready to be put back into the water? I could stay until Monday evening, or perhaps even until Tuesday morning."

The waitress brought their drinks. Maxwell paid for them while Lai Ming gave thought to his suggestion. Two weeks had passed since Peter had been so ill. Since then she had enjoyed his almost daily visits and his passionate, insatiable lovemaking. She delighted in every minute he spent with her and she begrudged him nothing, but because of his frequent visits she was losing a considerable amount of business, and that meant loss of money. It was now eleven in the evening; Peter had returned to camp at midday. She had told him she would be entertaining her son for a few days, Friday, Saturday and Sunday nights being her busiest times of the week. Monday was her slowest, therefore she had asked him not to visit her until Monday afternoon. Peter, however, had told her that he was on late shift on Monday, so would not be able to visit her until Tuesday afternoon. It would work out perfectly, she decided. Maxwell could stay with her until Monday, or even until Tuesday morning if he so wished, and the money he paid her would make up for much that she had failed to earn because of Peter's visits.

"You stay at my home how much time you like. We go when you ready, Maxel," she said. "I want make you happy when you come Singapore."

"Attagirl," said Maxwell, getting to his feet and towering over her. Stretching forth his big hands, he took her dainty hands in his and pulled her to her feet. "Screw the beer," he said. "Come on doll-baby. Let's go." And hand in hand they walked out of the Butterfly Club and climbed into a waiting taxi.

Later, up in Lai Ming's room, Maxwell kicked off his shoes. "That's better," he said, smiling to Lai Ming. "It's great to be back."

Lai Ming acknowledged his remarks with smiles and an approving nod of her head. And when Maxwell removed his jacket, she took it from him and hung it on a hanger in the wardrobe. He then took off his perspiration soaked shirt, which she took and draped over the back of a chair. The *amah* would wash the shirt and his socks and underwear in the morning.

Although Maxwell had not visited Lai Ming in almost six months, he felt quite at home in her little apartment. Everything looked the same, just as he remembered it, even the pillows with 'Good Morning' embroidered on the snow-white cloth, and the dressing table, with the family photograph of Lai Ming, her late husband and the sleeping baby, as well as others of shots of Lai Ming, under the glass top. All appeared to be the same as before. No, there was a difference, an addition. Another photograph had been slipped under the glass and was now the centrepiece, a photograph of a smiling young white youth with a protective arm lovingly around the waist of a happily smiling Lai Ming. Maxwell studied the photo for some moments. Obviously the pair knew each other intimately, as both appeared to be so blissfully happy.

Reaching even lower than Maxwell's navel now that she had taken off her high-heeled shoes, Lai Ming looked up and into the other's face with inquiring interest.

"Your boyfriend?" he asked, tapping on the glass top above the photograph.

"Yes," Lai Ming replied.

"Gee! He sure is a lucky guy," said Maxwell. He then said, "He looks very young."

"He's almost twenty."

"A British serviceman?"

"Yes. He is in the RAF."

"The Royal Air Force, eh. A pilot?"

"No. A cook."

"Oh!" exclaimed Maxwell, as if surprised. "I've never thought of cooks in the Royal Air Force. Pilots come to my mind, and navigators and gunners, but not cooks."

"Someone has to cook," smiled Lai Ming patiently.

"Sure. Of course. I hope he treats you right."

"He does."

"Rose, I'm just curious, so don't get mad at me. Does he pay you? Or is he happy to have a business woman like yourself as his girlfriend?"

"He does not know of my business," said Lai Ming flatly.

"He doesn't. He sure must be goddamned naive, Rose."

"He is, Maxel. That is just one of the many reasons why I like him."

"He's gonna be in for a helluva shock when he eventually finds out. And he will. He can't be that dumb."

"I know," replied Lai Ming sadly. Then she brightened. "But, please, no more talk. *Amah* bring you beer. Then we make something."

"OK, honey. But I'd hate to see you get hurt in any way."

Lai Ming shrugged. "I'm sorry, because I think he will get hurt the most," she said. "Ah! Here is my *amah* with your beer." Taking the bottle, she thanked the old *amah* who, nodding a reply, clip-clopped back down the stairs on wooden-soled shoes. Lai Ming took an opener from the drawer, flipped the cap of the bottle off, and handed Maxwell the bottle and a glass. "Now I go wash," she said, and she disappeared into the bathroom.

Maxwell poured himself a glass of beer, murmuring, "Christ, it's warm. Won't they ever learn?" He stripped off the remainder of his clothes and stretched himself out upon the hard bed. His head touched the headboard and his feet overhung the rail at the bottom. Why did the Chinese always make beds that were too short for his lanky six-foot, six-inch frame, he wondered. Surely there must be some tall Chinese people. He sat up and took a drink of warm beer, grimaced, then reached for his trousers which lay on the floor. Rummaging through the pockets, he pulled out a pack of Chesterfield cigarettes and a silver lighter. He flipped a cigarette from the pack, lit it, then lay back on the bed and blew smoke rings towards the ceiling.

A few minutes later Lai Ming emerged from the bathroom wearing a *sarong*. She smiled at Maxwell. He was a good customer, very easy to please and always one of her best payers. She had learned long ago never to even think of quoting him a price, because at the end of his stay he always paid her much more than the amount she normally charged her clients.

Reaching between her dresses, and to the rear of the tall wardrobe, Lai Ming's hand contacted what she sought, a box of Durex contraceptives. Always she bought a gross at a time and hid them away at the rear of the wardrobe so that Peter wouldn't find them. Peter never used contraceptives. Both he and she preferred it that way. But with Maxwell, he was different. From the time of his first visit to her home he had insisted on using a contraceptive.

She sat down on the edge of the bed, grasped Maxwell's penis and gently squeezed it towards its tip. She performed this simple task on every man she took to her bed, every man that is except Peter. She had to be so careful; she dreaded even the thought of giving Peter any form of venereal disease. Satisfied that no creamy coloured pus appeared at the opening of Maxwell's penis, she broke open the contraceptive packet and skillfully rolled the rubber down over it.

"You, OK Maxel?" she asked.

"Fine," Maxwell answered, blowing yet another smoke ring towards the ceiling. Sitting up, he stubbed out the cigarette in the ashtray provided on the little table next to the bed. He then reached out, slipped the *sarong* from Lai Ming so that it fell to the floor, and pulled her onto the bed so that she lay flat on her back.

13

The long, curving strip of brownish sand at Changi Beach lay shimmering in the sunlight of mid-morning. The beach was strangely quiet. Gone was Sunday's ringing laughter, the shouts from splashing swimmers, the shrieks of children and the babble of voices in many tongues from the hundreds of sunbathers.

On this Monday morning Changi Beach was deserted. Well, almost. Three Chinese fishermen could be seen repairing a nearby bamboo and chicken-wire *kelong*, a fish trap, which had suffered some damage during a recent storm. Primitive yet effective, the *kelong* comprised a line of bamboo poles pushed into the seabed, with wire netting interwoven between the poles. Radiating from the coastline at ninety degrees and stretching from the low-water mark of the beach to more than a hundred yards out into the tidal strait, the *kelong*, from the air, looked somewhat like a long arrow, the arrowhead being the actual trap. On reaching the impenetrable bamboo poles and wire mesh, fish swimming parallel with the beach were forced to swerve seaward where they were funnelled into the arrowhead of the trap. There, a huge net of forty feet or more across sagged a few inches off the bottom. And there the fish remained, alive and swimming freely above the net but unable to escape, awaiting the fishermen to haul up the net and empty the trap of its sea-harvest. Usually, the larger fish were immediately taken to markets, whereas the smaller fish were soused in brine, sun-dried and eventually sold as *ikan bilis*, a very popular snack and flavouring ingredient in local dishes. The three fishermen were repairing a crude thatched hut built above the arrowhead, the only shelter that protected them from the elements.

Less than a hundred yards to the east of the fish trap and a short distance along the coast from Pop's coffee shack, eight more Chinese fishermen stood waist-deep in the murky water. Slowly, they were hauling in the two ends of a net stretched crescent-like one hundred yards out across the water. Only the murmuring of the still receding tide on the sand and the occasional loud, "*Aiyah*," from these fishermen could be heard as their glistening brown bodies heaved in unison, hauling in the heavy net yard by yard to where a *sampan* wallowed at anchor in the shallows. The *sampan* was tended by its owner who skillfully shook the incoming net over the gunwale, emptying a flashing silvery harvest of fish into the bilges of his narrow craft.

It was almost low tide. The water had long receded from the sand, exposing a muddy coastline. Reeds and several species of sea-grasses, unseen when the tide was in, now rose several inches above the surface of the water where they swayed to and fro in the gentle breeze.

Left stranded high and dry on the burning-hot sand and far from the water's edge, the coffee shop owner's boats lay overturned and unneeded, their green and white paintwork blistering in the intense heat.

Clad only in brief swimming costumes and seated on rough wooden stools at an equally rough table in Pop's shack, LAC Peter Saunders and LAC Gerald Rickie, Pop's only customers, sipped on cooling orange drinks while they studied a road map of Singapore. Twenty minutes prior, whilst waking through Changi Village, Peter had purchased the map at Jong Fat's Emporium.

"See, Rick, that's where she lives," Peter was saying, tapping an index finger on the map where Bendemeer Road met Lavender Street. "I'm sure I could find her home easily enough by taxi, or even by walking from the bus stop at Geylang. It doesn't look too far to walk from Geylang to Lavender Street, then to the junction at Kallang Bahru, and finally to Bendemeer Road."

"Aren't you scared walking in that part of Singapore alone?" asked Rick.

"No, not at all. The people there won't harm me. In fact, Rose's neighbours are quite friendly towards me."

"I'm not thinking of the people, I'm thinking of the bloody military police! Her home's in the middle of the red-light district."

"I know," said Peter, "I'm certainly nervous of the patrols there. But I'd keep a watchful eye open for them, Rick. Anyway, perhaps I still don't look old enough to pass for a serviceman. They probably wouldn't take a second look at me. If they should try to stop me, I'd run like hell."

"Well, if you're caught, it's your funeral."

"I won't get caught. Anyway, what shall we do now? The tide's too low for swimming."

"Let's sit here awhile and take life easy," said Rick. "We'll think of something."

The mongrel dog came to where Rick sat, placed his furry chin on a bare knee, looked up into Rick's face with sad-looking eyes, and as Rick patted and stroked the nuzzling head, the happy dog wagged its brown stump of a tail contentedly. Two of Pop's children, naked as usual, came and petted the dog, and then began to tease him, so that he lost interest in Rick and ran away, scattering chickens that had been busily scratching for insects in the sandy dirt behind the shack.

Peter Saunders scanned the calm Johore Strait, the palm-studded green islands blurred by a heat-haze, and the almost indistinguishable coastline of Malaya in the far distance. He watched as an old Chinese junk with its tattered squaresail hanging limp and idle, chugged laboriously upstream, powered by two huge outboard motors, its great hull low in the water, and its decks heaped high with an assortment of cargo; but there were no crew members to be seen.

Shifting his gaze from the junk, Peter's eyes swept past Changi buoy to where a much smaller vessel, a motor cargo launch, cut a swift passage through the calm water. Silver spray swished and leapt from her narrow bow and white foaming water churned around her stern. She was but one of many vessels which plied the waters between the islands and the mainland during the course of a day. Peter watched as the craft slowed, turned from the main channel and entered the short and narrow channel leading into Changi Creek and a little harbour where many small cargo boats docked; a safe haven from storms. The cargo boat navigated a sandbar before disappearing round a bend at the entrance to the inlet.

Pop, wearing just a pair of dirty shorts, came and collected the two now empty glasses. "Two more, Johnny?" he asked Rick.

"Yes please, Pop. Green Spots."

The coffee shop owner gave the pair a friendly smile and went to where he kept his supply of soft drinks in an ice-filled chest. These two boys were his most frequent customers. He was aware that Peter was having a love affair with the pretty Chinese girl who had played mahjong weeks ago during that stormy afternoon. At times he would ask of her, and Peter would smile and reply, "*Ding ho*, Pop." Pop liked both Rick and Peter. They were good boys who spoke kindly to both him and to his wife, and often they played on the beach and in the water with his children. He returned with the drinks and set them down in front of the boys.

"Thanks Pop," said Peter.

Having finished hauling in their long net, the fishermen were now seated in the *sampan* sorting out the fish and placing them on ice in boxes in the bilges. Soon they would depart to drift down the shoreline in search of another likely fishing spot in which to cast their net.

The sun, higher now and almost overhead, cast few shadows. Newcomers had arrived on the beach, mostly off-duty RAF and WRAF personnel. None were in the water yet, the tide being so low. At least another hour must pass before the water would be deep enough to swim in without tangling with the sea-grasses. Now was the time to sunbathe in idleness, beachcomb, play ball on the sand or, preferably, to relax in Pop's shack.

Rick, sipping on his orange drink, gazed out across the water. It looked so lovely out there, the water was calm, blue and sparkling.

He looked at the boats drawn up on the beach; half a dozen up-turned rowing boats and two fishing canoes, one of the latter slightly larger than the other. It was just the day for a few hours on the water, he thought. Turning to Peter Saunders, he asked, "Feel like going for a trip in one of the boats?"

"Do you?"

"Why not? Let's take the big canoe over to Johore, or pay a visit to a couple of the islands."

"OK. It's better than sitting around here."

"Right, then. I'll speak to Pop. By the way, Pete, do you have any money with you?"

"Just about enough to pay for the drinks. Haven't you any?"

"About a dollar."

"That's a fat lot of good."

"Well, what shall we do? Put it on the book?"

"No. I think I can make a deal with Pop. The next time I come to the beach, I'll bring him some more tins of sardines and herrings from the sergeants' mess."

"Would Pop be agreeable?"

"I'm sure he will. It saves wasting his time fishing. And it saves his wife's time cleaning and cooking the fish. He was as chuffed as a pig in shit when I gave his wife a few cans as a gift a few days ago. And so was she. She told me the kids loved fish in tomato sauce. They never cook theirs in tomato sauce."

"Pete, you've got one helluva nerve. Don't you know that you're stealing RAF supplies? You'll do time over the wall if you're caught."

"If I'm caught, then it's just too bad. The mess members rarely eat tinned fish, but the Chinese staff love them. To them it's a luxury. But the damn tins keep piling up every time the ration truck arrives, so I have to get rid of them one way or the other. I'm doing the sergeants' mess a favour by trading them away."

"Doesn't Sergeant Muldoon keep a check on the stores?"

"No. That's left to me. Anyway, he'd never check tinned fish. I'm sure he's only too glad to get rid of them. Just watch me sign out a few dozen tins from the stock sheet during the next few days and put on the menu sardines on toast and marinated herrings as appetizers a few times. The mess members rarely eat tinned fish, but as far as I'm concerned, they're going to love them for awhile."

"Well, it's your funeral. If you think it's OK, I'll call Pop over. Shall we return to camp for tea?"

"Definitely. I think we should be back by four or four-thirty."

"You've a date with Rose this evening, I suppose," said Rick.

"Not really. I'm supposed to see her tomorrow afternoon. But as Sergeant Muldoon has given me the day off, I thought I might as well surprise her this evening. I'd like to arrive at her home, say at six, and take her out for dinner. It'll be the first time that I've made my way alone to her apartment. She'll be thrilled."

Calling Pop over to where they sat, Peter explained to him their financial problem, and could they borrow a canoe in exchange for tins of fish.

"You take boat, Johnny, anytime," the good-natured shack owner said. "You good friend. We always make good bargain."

"Seems like you've fixed it, then," said Rick. "I'll pay for the drinks."

"Thanks. That suits me," Peter said, laughing. He then jokingly said, "But remember, it's my turn to sit in the stern, where the action is."

Out in mid-stream, between Changi and the island of Pulau Ubin, a Chinese motor junk passed closely across the stern of their canoe, its high bows cleaving a curling passage, and its huge bulk and surprisingly high speed ploughing up the smooth surface of the Johore Strait.

Seated in the stern, Peter skillfully spun the canoe around to head into the junk's wake. For a few moments, as the canoe turned, the little craft rolled drunkenly over a dangerously high swell. Laughing lightheartedly and without a care in the world, Peter shouted to Rick, who was sitting amidships, "I bet that bloody great thing is making at least ten knots. Here we go!" and with ease, he stroked the double-bladed paddle into the water until he brought the bow around so that, although slapping noisily and bouncing hard, the waves created by the passing junk rolled harmlessly beneath the little craft. Such waves, if taken on the low, square stern of the canoe, could easily have swamped it. The square stern accommodated a small outboard motor used by Pop during those rare occasions when he did go fishing. The little craft itself was seaworthy and could safely ride big waves like a cork in a bathtub if handled properly.

A brown-skinned Chinese seaman dressed in khaki shorts appeared on the raised poop deck of the junk, looked with disinterest as the canoe bobbed up and down in the wake astern, and then turned and disappeared down a hatchway. The two boys in the canoe watched as the fast receding hulk, with its two huge outboard motors thumping, moved farther and farther away, heading towards the RAF seaplane base at Seletar. The swell passed and soon the water became still again, allowing the canoe to ride a calm surface. Only the gentle lapping of water against the bulwarks could be heard as Peter plunged the paddle into the water bringing the canoe back on course, to head for Pulau Ubin.

Porpoises rolled and played some distance up the channel, and there were flurries of sparkling silver as shoals of small fish leapt from the water in an attempt to escape from them. A seahorse skipped across the water on its tail in front of the canoe, and transparent jellyfish could be seen floating lazily by as the canoe made fast headway among them.

From his position sitting amidships, Rick stretched himself out full-length on his back in the shell of the canoe. First brushing powdery salt from his body, he relaxed, his face turned skyward to watch little puffs and patches of white wispy cloud lazily sailing across an otherwise clear blue sky. Knowing the tide was coming in, taking them on its strong current steadily towards the far shore, he was content to allow Peter to paddle alone for awhile. He knew it was easy paddling. Of more importance was keeping the craft on its course so that the tide would take them close to Pulau Ubin, and not out to sea. But Peter, he had found, was an expert at handling the canoe, thus did not need help.

When the canoe was almost at the shores of Pulau Ubin, Peter woke up his now sleeping companion by singing out, "Rick, wake up. We're almost there."

Rick yawned, then studying the land ahead, said, "It looks so peaceful. Just a few huts among palm trees."

The canoe passed a long reef of brown sand and grey coral on its port side, a tiny islet about two hundred yards from the main island of Ubin. Guided by Peter, the canoe drifted silently into a wide, shallow bay of calm, clear water, lined by a green, palm-lined shore. Below the surface of the water the seabed showed off many of nature's wonders; minute fish, their scales glittering silver and gold, and blues and reds, swam lazily just inches below the surface, while others glided cautiously over the sandy bed or meandered among submerged rocks and aquatic plants. A young barracuda, not more than a foot long, with cold beady eyes, lay motionless in the water. It was in no hurry to go anywhere. Its swiftness, when needed, could catch it a meal in a moment. A purple and brown jellyfish, the size of a dinner plate, and tinted with orange spots, drifted upward alongside the canoe. On making contact with the huge foreign object, the jellyfish changed its colour to blue, then to a deep green as it sank from sight amid the sanctuary of seaweed growing on rocks. Seahorses leapt from the water, their long, pointed heads poised alert as they skipped on their tails across the calm surface, away from the intruders.

The two boys had arrived at the luxuriant and fertile Pulau Ubin, where tall coconut palms grew on the foreshore in abundance, their crowns heavy with ripening nuts. Further inland, knee-high green grasses rustled and swayed in the gentle breeze. Here, at this part of the island, all was peacefully silent and deserted. The two boys knew from a previous expedition that a Chinese fishing village of a dozen huts built on stilts lay further along the coast. Also, they had seen a number of Malay *atap* huts, made from coconut palms and grasses, scattered over the island, some close enough together to form a small *kampung*, or village. Generally, though, there were individual huts, with a small vegetable and fruit garden, and a clearing where chickens scratched for bugs and worms and where goats chewed on rank grass.

Peter allowed the canoe to drift along the shoreline to where the palm trees and beaches ended and mangrove swamps took over.

"Let's turn around," said Rick. "It's more interesting at the other end of the island."

"OK. But we'll be fighting the current. It's going to be slow going."

"I know. But it won't be too strong here in the channel between the island and the reef. I've never known a strong current here."

"I have," answered Peter. "But that was when the tide was going out. Believe me, one person has little chance of canoeing against a receding tide. I was caught once by it when alone."

"What happened?" asked Rick.

"I couldn't fight the current, so I paddled until I got to the shore, then waded through the mud dragging the canoe behind me in about four inches of water until I reached the other end of this island. Then I got back in and paddled like hell for Changi Beach, with the bows pointed almost towards Seletar. Even then I was almost carried out to sea. When I finally reached shore, I was far from Changi."

The bow swung to starboard and for some moments the canoe was caught and carried by the tide broadside on. But the bows quickly came around until they faced the incoming tide, and the two boys dug their paddles in, fast and deep, and the little craft slowly gathered speed.

Returning to where the coconut palms came down to the beach, they followed the coastline until they reached an outcrop of rocks. Further along, they could see a narrow stone jetty jutting out across mudflats, where a boat landing stage reached out across shallow water. The water was still very low, even though the tide was coming in.

"Let's head for that jetty, Peter," said Rick. "We'll secure the canoe there and go ashore for an hour or so."

"And do some exploring," said Peter, "like Robinson Crusoe." Both laughed. It was such a happy, carefree day.

The jetty, just a narrow, concrete walkway built upon iron girders, was about thirty yards long. From the water, one could see that the walkway was spider-webbed with cracks and broken in places, and that the girders were eaten away by rust and encrusted with barnacles and slimy green muck.

Peter swung the bow of the canoe around and drew the frail craft alongside the jetty. Clutching at an iron strut, he quickly let go his hold on it. "Hell! That's damned sharp!" he exclaimed, holding up his hand and seeing blood running from cut fingers. Cursing, he sucked the wounds and spat blood and saliva over the side, noticing now that the rusted strut and lower parts of the jetty were thickly coated in shellfish and jagged coral. "I should have known better," he said to Rick as he nursed his hand. "Christ! That coral's bloody sharp. Let's move on and find a better place to go ashore."

After allowing the canoe to drift away from the jetty, the two boys resumed paddling. Minutes later, on rounding a headland, they arrived at a sandy beach half hidden by grey coral rocks alive with penny-size black crabs, sea-lice and masses of clinging barnacles and limpets.

Suddenly, a ringing peal of a girl's laughter broke the silence. Both boys immediately stopped paddling and listened as more laughter followed. It seemed to be coming from behind a headland of rocks a short distance ahead.

"Shh," whispered Rick, motioning Peter to be quiet. "There's at least two of them. I bet they're Malay girls. Let's go and take a peek."

"OK. But be quiet. If they're Malay girls they won't hang around once they know we're here."

"I know."

Again they allowed the canoe to drift, this time away from the rocky shallows in which they had found themselves. They then lifted their paddles, and as quietly as they knew how, brought the canoe around another spur of rocks and a low headland to find themselves wallowing in a picturesque, palm-lined bay. There, carefully and quietly, Peter eased the stern of the canoe between two concealing rocks. More laughter came from behind those rocks. Obviously they hadn't been seen. In silence they crouched behind the rocks and peeped over the top.

Playing in shallow water were two Malay girls wearing *sarongs*, and both were bare from the waist up. Totally unaware of the intrusion on their privacy and place of bathing, they sat in the water playfully splashing each other and shrieking with laughter.

Without making a sound the two boys watched the girls with amused interest.

"I'd say they're both are about eighteen," whispered Peter.

"Yes," agreed Rick. "Let's paddle over and give them a surprise. You can ask them in your best Malay if they'd like a ride in our boat."

"I doubt if I know enough Malay to hold a conversation," said Peter. "I only know phrases such as 'what's your name?' and 'will you give me a cigarette?'"

Rick laughed. "You can forget about asking those girls for a cigarette. But you're the linguist around here. I don't speak any of their lingo."

Using their hands, the pair eased the canoe carefully and quietly around the rocks, drawing it slowly closer to the unsuspecting girls who were too engrossed in their frolicking to notice the approach of their captivated audience. A *sarong* fell from one of the girls and drifted away on the tide. The girl, now nude, her mood gay and uncaring, laughed and chatted happily as she lay on her back splashing with her legs in the shallow water.

"Excuse the much-used cliché, Pete, but you've as much chance as a snowball in hell of getting close to those two," whispered Rick.

"I know, but it's fun watching them," Peter replied.

"As soon as they spot us, they'll be gone," said Rick.

He was right. The nude girl suddenly pointed a finger in their direction, and shouting, "*Aiyah! Aiyah!*" she sprang after her *sarong*, which by now had been carried several yards away from her. The other girl, immediately on spotting the two boys, turned and raced through the shallow water and headed towards the beach. There, she disappeared behind a great clump of bananas growing just yards above the high water mark.

"What did I tell you? I knew they wouldn't like our company," said Rick. Then, looking towards the girl who was still in the water, he commented, "She's lost her *sarong*, Peter. Let's be perfect gentlemen and help her retrieve it. Grab your paddle."

No sooner had Rick said those words, he froze in horror, aghast at what he was seeing. Quite close to the canoe, nostrils and a pair of eyes had risen to the surface of the water, followed by a brownish-coloured flat head and a scaly back that was moving silently and swiftly towards the girl chasing after her *sarong*.

"My God, Pete! That's a crocodile!" Rick cried out. "And the girl's still in the water!"

Peter Saunders glanced at his friend. Rick was good at jesting, but this was the first time Peter had ever seen Rick look scared. He looked towards whatever Rick found so horrifying and saw unblinking eyes in a grotesque head that had a long and narrow snout, gliding rapidly towards the girl in the water. The girl had already spotted the dangerous reptile and appeared to be paralyzed with fright. She stood waist-deep in the water watching the approach of the crocodile in horrified amazement.

Rick was shouting, "She hasn't got a chance."

Peter thought fast. Rick seemed to be right. The brute was quickly closing in on its intended victim. They must do something, and fast. They were the girl's only hope of survival.

"Rick! Hurry! Grab a paddle," he found himself shouting. "No! Throw something at the bloody thing. Anything. I'll head for the girl."

In feverish haste, Peter desperately drove the paddle deep into the water, sweeping his arms down and back again and again; the canoe surged forward, gaining speed with his every frantic stroke. Rick was shouting at the crocodile hoping to distract it from its prey. He had already thrown the bailing can, empty bottles, and even his pair of tennis shoes at the brute, but to no avail; it was quickly closing in on the

162

terrified girl. Now, her screams echoed across the water as she watched the horrifying head come between her and the sanctuary of the shore. Her screams suddenly ceased. Gasping and whimpering with fright, she began splashing and floundering towards rocks jutting up from the water. But the crocodile was much faster than her.

Immediately behind the crocodile raced the canoe, with both Rick and Peter paddling furiously. And they were gaining on the huge reptile, drawing alongside it and almost riding on top of the huge, scaly back. That damned thing is even longer than the canoe, Peter agonized, and he paddled harder.

A few yards from the sanctuary of the rocks, the terrified girl tripped and fell. Whimpering, she lay kicking and thrashing her arms, her body sinking into gooey mud.

The crocodile, now almost on top of its prey, seemed sure of its meal. Long, tapering jaws opened to display a gaping, vicious mouth surrounded by wicked-looking teeth. Then, as if the beast seemed unsure from which angle to make its attack, the jaws snapped shut. For moments the huge body swirled right over the fallen girl; then again those awesome jaws opened. Momentarily Peter stared into a cavernous throat, the upper and lower jaws of the mouth surrounded by ragged-looking, yellowish teeth. And then Peter struck. Standing up and balancing himself in the rolling canoe, with all his strength he rammed the double-bladed paddle into that seemingly endless cavern. Savagely twisting the paddle and pushing all the while, he forced the wooden blade further down the reptile's throat. There was a sickening crunch, followed by just one terrified scream from the girl as the crocodile hit her with its huge, writhing body. Losing his grip on the paddle, Peter fell backward on top of Rick, almost capsizing the canoe. In a frenzy, the crocodile, with half the paddle jammed down its throat and the other half sticking out from its jaws, churned and thrashed the water furiously as it tried to rid itself of the inedible object. Smashing itself against the canoe, it jarred every plank, almost throwing the two boys into the water. Then it slid beneath the canoe, and for an awful moment

Peter thought the brute would capsize their frail craft. But the crocodile, sliding into deeper water, sank from sight. Moments later a splintered half of the double-bladed paddle bobbed to the surface and floated on muddied swirling water.

Peter turned a wan face to Rick, who looked sick with fear, not for himself, but for the safety of the girl still in the water.

"I say, old chap, do you think we've given that old meanie indigestion?" Peter asked, trying to sound calm.

"Oh, for Christ's sake, Pete!" answered his shaken friend. "Let's see if the girl's all right." Rick got up and cautiously clambered over the side of the canoe into knee-deep mud and water to where the girl lay face down and very still. "We must get her ashore." He was surprisingly calm now. All fear had left him, his thoughts preoccupied in getting the girl safely out of the water. "If you see that big bastard, try to keep him occupied," he heard himself shouting. "If it gets close enough, hit it with my paddle, but don't let it get near us."

However, there was no sign of the crocodile.

Grasping the girl under her armpits, Rick lifted her head clear of the water. She sagged limply. Was she dead, he wondered. But no, he saw that she was breathing. Hearing a splashing of water behind him, he turned to see the girl's companion wading through the shallows towards him. Sighing with relief, he greeted her by saying "Hello. Come to give me a hand, eh?"

Without saying a word, and with her big brown eyes wide with fright, she assisted Rick in pulling her friend, first out of the water, and then over a sheet of mud alive with scurrying tiny crabs and sea lice. Rick sighed with relief when his feet touched warm sand, and he was even more relieved when the three of them were a dozen paces up the beach. There, in the shade of a young coconut palm, they lay down the unconscious girl.

"Thank God!" Rick muttered, as he sank wearily down beside the girl. Then he wished he knew how to give mouth to mouth resuscitation or artificial respiration. He checked to make sure the girl was still breathing. She was, and seemed to be coming around. "Wow! You're beautiful," he murmured, and gazing down upon her lovely face partially hidden beneath long, jet-black hair, he bent over her and kissed her wet, sandy forehead. The girl opened her eyes and stared up at him in puzzlement, whimpering a little but without uttering a word.

"See! I can perform miracles," said Rick, laughing to the other girl, who, seeing her friend's recovery, stroked her hair and comforted her by speaking softly in Malay. Blushing now, perhaps because of her friend's nakedness, she gazed at Rick in amazement but said nothing.

Peter, meanwhile, had retrieved the remains of the double-bladed paddle and now triumphantly waded ashore carrying a chewed-up and splintered one-bladed paddle. "I managed to save this," he said proudly. "Anything I can do to help?"

"No. I don't think she's hurt," answered Rick. "Just swallowed a lot of water and had the living daylights scared out of her. She fainted, that's all."

"I was scared shitless," said Peter, tossing the busted paddle down onto the sand and joining the group.

"I've never seen anything so frightening in my whole life," said Rick. "She's had a very narrow escape."

As the tension eased, both boys relaxed and were now smiling at the two girls, and eyeing them in open admiration.

"Well, Rick, what now?" asked Peter.

"I don't know. But let's hang around to make sure they're both all right."

"You mean you want to ogle them," laughed Peter, squatting Chinese style. Picking up a small stick, he doodled in the fine sand and studied the two girls.

"Why don't you try out your knowledge of Malay on them?" suggested Rick.

"OK. Why not?" Turning to the two girls, Peter said, "*Tabik.*" He was not sure whether *tabik* meant 'hello' or 'goodbye', but it was worth a shot.

Both girls responded by giving coy smiles, and for moments they spoke quietly among themselves. Eventually, the girl draped in the *sarong* murmured, "*Terima kasih, tuan. Terima kasih.*"

"She's thanking us, Rick. She said, 'Thank you, sir. Thank you.' Now isn't that cute?"

"What's her name? How old is she? Good job that nasty old croc didn't have you for his dinner, isn't it, sweetie pie?" teased Rick.

The poor girl didn't understand a word he said, and a tear suddenly rolled down her face. She held out a hand and touched each boy lightly on the cheek. "*Terima kasih,*" she whispered shyly. "*Terima kasih.*"

Both boys grinned at the naked girl.

She glanced down at her nakedness, then up into their admiring faces. Blushing more and smiling shyly, almost in a whisper, she again said, "*Terima kasih.*"

"Pete, can you ask their names?" asked Rick.

"Yes, that's easy," replied Peter, and turning to the girls, he asked, "*Nama siapa?*"

The girl wearing the *sarong* answered by pointing to herself and saying, "Siti." Then, pointing to her naked companion, she said, "Faridah."

"Well, those are nice names," said Peter. "Siti and Faridah, eh?"

Both girls shyly nodded their heads.

"Miss Siti and Miss Faridah, that's their names, Rick."

"Well, it's a pleasure to meet you both," said Rick.

Unperturbed by their own nakedness, both girls looked at Rick in wonderment, at his muscular physique and handsome face.

Walking over to the canoe, which he had pulled up onto the beach, Peter took from it a wet, white RAF towel. Returning to the group, he offered the towel to the naked girl. "Later, we'll try to find your *sarong*, love," he said.

Taking the towel from him, Faridah giggled as she slipped the towel around her waist, and demurely said, "*Terima kasih.*"

"Oh, please don't mention it. Anything to oblige a lady," laughed

Peter. He sat down again. There was no point in hurrying away now. "Sit down, Rick," he said, and to the girls, "*Mari sini, duduk.*" And they all sat down except for Rick, who lay down, on his back in the warm dry sand. "Right. Now that we're all comfortable, we can have a chat."

The girls blushed and giggled.

Gazing at their loveliness, Peter tried to remember words in Malay, those he had learnt whilst stationed at RAF Kuala Lumpur. Eventually, he asked, "*Awak tahu cakap Inggeris?*"

There were more blushes from the girls, giggles and shakes of their heads.

"They don't speak a word of English, Rick," Peter said.

"I didn't think they would. But talk to them, Pete. Ask them something. Ask how old they are."

"OK, I'll try." Thus, with considerable thought, Peter translated words in his mind before saying slowly to the girls, "*Berapa umur awak?*"

Faridah, still blushing, pointed a finger at herself. "*Lapan belas,*" she murmured coyly, and nodding towards her companion, said, "*Tujuh belas,*" whereupon both girls fell into fits of giggles.

"Faridah is eighteen and Siti is seventeen," said Peter to Rick. "I'll try to tell them that they're really beautiful."

"Yes. Count me in on that one," agreed Rick.

"*Awak banyak cantik,*" Peter told the girls, pleased with himself at remembering so many words of Malay, and smiling at their obvious embarrassment.

"*Terima kasih, tuan,*" said Faridah, hiding her blushing face in the palms of her hands.

Suddenly, from behind banana clumps sprang three angry, tough-looking, young Malay men wearing only *sarongs*, two brandishing big sticks, the third armed with a *parang*. Menacingly, they advanced on the four sitting in the shade of the palm tree, and glared angrily down at the two intruders to their island. Fortunately the angry looks of two of them turned to that of bewilderment at seeing the two girls sitting at their ease unharmed. One of the three youths, however, as if jealous of the situation, hovered over Rick, threatened him with the stick, and spoke angrily in Malay to both him and to Peter.

"Hey, wait a minute," snapped Peter. "We aren't bothering your women." Turning to Rick, he said, "He thinks we've molested the girls. They must have heard the girls screaming."

Getting to his feet, Rick breezily said to the Malay youth menacing him with the stick, "I say, old chap, it's not what you think. So you can put that damned thing down. We're not hurting your women."

The Malay man, not understanding a word, simply stared back in puzzlement at Rick but he did lower his weapon.

Siti now spoke a fast flow of words to the three Malay men, all the while pointing to Faridah. Then Faridah had her say. Within moments, the faces of the three men turned from bewilderment to smiles of relief as the two girls related to them the near fatal encounter with the crocodile, and of how the two boys had saved Faridah from certain death. This was followed by giggles from the girls, and by utterances in Malay of "Oh! Good men!" as the now suddenly very friendly locals vigorously shook the hands of the two young adventurers, slapped them on their backs and invited both to return with them to their *kampung*.

"Do come," the girls were saying. "Allow us to show you our hospitality."

"We thank you, but we must go now," answered Peter. "We shall return and call on you another day."

"You promise?" said Faridah.

All the while she had been speaking in Malay, and Peter was quite chuffed with himself at being able to converse with her. "Yes, I promise," he replied.

A short while later, the two boys, now seated in the canoe, were preparing to depart the island. The canoe, however, was not yet completely afloat, its stern being stuck in the mud. The two boys waited for the next wave to come rolling in, and when it did the canoe lifted, and both boys used their paddles to clear the little craft away from the beach. But then another wave came and sped them back onto the mud. Rick and Peter were laughing hilariously at their predicament. "It looks as though we're not going to leave the island after all, not just yet," said Rick.

As for the two girls, they stood nearby, ankle-deep in mud, plus there were now several other villagers clustered around them, and still more were arriving on the scene. All were in a festive mood, laughing and calling 'Selamat jalan' (goodbye) to the pair in the canoe but the two girls, though laughing, had tears in their eyes. Faridah approached Peter, touched him lightly on the arm and murmured, "Terima kasih, tuan. Terima kasih. Jangan lupa datang lagi, ya?" (Thank you, sir. Thank you. Don't forget to come back again, OK?)

"Goodbye!" said Peter.

Grasping the canoe's blunt stern, the two girls pushed, and the canoe, caught on a receding wave, slid from the mudflat into shallow but deep enough water, where it was immediately caught in the flow of the current and carried away from the land.

"Selamat jalan," the two girls shouted, waving their arms above their heads. "Terima kasih. Jangan lupa, ya? Jangan lupa!"

Rick and Peter dug their paddles in deep, sending the canoe quickly away from the island. And when a goodly distance from the shore, they put down their paddles and waved and shouted their final farewells. The two girls and the crowd on the shore waved back. Taking to their paddles again, they heard a last, 'selamat jalan' and watched as the two girls and the crowd, still waving, passed from sight as the canoe rounded a headland.

Now, all was silent except for the paddles slipping into the water, the lapping of waves beneath the bow, and the gentle splashing of water against the gunwales. There were no gulls wheeling in the sky, crying in their search for food, nor were there motorcrafts chugging noisily up the channel, and from the distant Changi airfield all was quiet. This tiny portion of the world was at peace, if only for the moment.

"I bet that old croc is still gnashing its teeth and spitting out splinters!" joked Rick.

"I wonder what Pop will say when we return this busted paddle to him. I'll offer to pay for it, of course."

"We'll split the cost," said Rick. "Anyway, he's bloody lucky to get the canoe back in one piece."

Both boys resumed paddling, dipping their blades in deep, which sent the canoe shooting forward to steadily close the distant between it and the beach at Changi.

With a powerful forward stroke of the paddle, Rick said wistfully, "You must be looking forward to seeing Rose tonight. You're lucky, Pete."

"She's better than tea and crumpets, Rick. Just think, I'll be seeing her in a few hours from now. That's if I'm able to find where she lives."

14

The sun was quickly sliding down over the horizon, casting its last golden rays over Singapore, to end another day of scorching heat. The moon was already riding the heavens, pale and full, drifting lazily higher to take its majestic stand in the sky. And as the sun sank from sight and the sky began to darken, a few stars appeared, faintly at first, mere twinkles of light flickering in the dusk of evening. Gradually, though, more stars appeared until galaxies of shining fairy lights and the full moon drove all darkness from the sky.

What could be more picturesque and peaceful than the moon over Malaya thought Peter Saunders as he happily hurried along the crowded pavement. Carefree though he was, he kept a wary eye on the slow-moving traffic approaching him from both directions. He knew that come early evening the dreaded military provost police in their jeeps and patrol wagons vigilantly cruised the red-light district; and he was a lone European on foot, out of bounds, and in the very heart of that district.

In the monsoon drains, ditches, and amid patches of grass growing near the roadway, bullfrogs had awakened and were setting up a chorus of never-ending din. A few black bats flitted through the still air in search of their first meal of the night; the setting of the sun had ended their slumber. But Peter Saunders paid no heed to the little creatures. Instead, he concentrated on following the route he had memorized from the road map bought that morning at Jong Fatt's. He was also thinking of how he would surprise Rose and how pleased she would be at seeing him a day earlier than planned. Also he was still wondering whether or not he should tell her about the exciting afternoon he had spent with Rick, of how they had rescued a Malay girl from the jaws of a crocodile at Pulau Ubin.

Walking north on Lavender Street, he had already passed the junction of Kallang Bahru. Soon, he would arrive at Bendemeer Road, where a turn to the right would bring him to Rose's home. He knew he was walking in the right direction because he remembered many of the places he passed, having seen them on numerous occasions from taxi windows.

As he walked onward, hoards of people flowed in all directions around him. Chinese were by far in the majority. But mingling among the Chinese were Indians, mostly Sikhs wearing white turbans, white flowing smocks of cotton, and sandals on their feet. Malays, the gentlemen of the Far East, all wore the traditional *songkok*; their women, dainty and coy, were swathed in colourful *sarongs* and tight-fitting *kebayas* glittering with gold and silver threads.

The roofs above him here in this neighborhood were as uneven as a rough sea, living quarters overhung shopfronts, the streets littered with junk and refuse. There were shacks, too, in places, built from plywood and rusted corrugated iron, many supported by sagging bamboo poles. This was where many of the coolies dwelt, a playground for the city's many mongrel dogs and semi-wild cats, a breeding place for rats, and a home for a multitude of poor. Strangely enough there was next to no crime in this wretched area, hence Peter felt no fear.

He should have taken a taxi from the bus terminal, he told himself, but he liked to walk and had wanted to see this part of the city. He passed through a somewhat better area, where there were cheap hotels and boarding houses, most of these with tea rooms and some with gambling rooms where mahjong ruled.

Peter hurried on through little Chinatown, as it was known to differentiate it from the main Chinatown surrounding Boat Quay. Upper stories of tenements, supported by stone pillars, protruded over crowded sidewalks running parallel with deep monsoon drains. As if from a million radios the clash of gongs and cymbals of Chinese music and the loud singing in both Mandarin and Cantonese drowned out even the traffic noises, the babble of a million voices, and the loud clickety-clack of mahjong tiles being slammed down by players intent on their game in open doorways and windows. A Chinese tailor attempted to entice Peter into his shop by saying, "I make good suit for you, Johnny, very cheap. For you, very special."

"No thanks," said Peter. He passed dispensing herbalists displaying strange wares in huge jars, cotton sacks and raffia baskets. Eating houses were plentiful, with black and white striped eggs and great bowls of Chinese fried rice on display. Crisp-looking, reddish-brown Peking ducks and barbecued chicken and pork ribs hung from hooks in open windows. A windowless fishmonger's shop displayed the catch of the day, also several kinds of yellowish-brown, sun-dried fish called *ikan bilis*. All the fish were spotted with flies. The fishmonger's day had not ended at sundown. He would work far into the evening, for although his fish looked unappetizing to Peter, customers were plentiful and the trade brisk.

Above the street, as if flags of celebration, hung part of the city's washing. These colourful arrays of clothing were suspended from bamboo poles reaching out across the street from open windows, the far ends sagging towards passing traffic below. And in that street, as in numerous others in the city, trishaw *wallahs*, shoeshine boys, beggars, hawkers, tourists, and ordinary citizens going about their business, mingled and jostled.

In his hand Peter carried a paper bag containing a tin of fifty Players cigarettes, a part of his free bi-weekly RAF issue. These he would give to Wan Ze, the *amah*. Rarely did he fail to bring the old woman a small gift such as a tin of cigarettes, a packet of tea, or a few tins of herrings or sardines from the sergeants' mess kitchen, or even a box of chocolates bought at Jong Fatt's. Also, on those frequent occasions when she washed and ironed his shirts or ironed his trousers, he gave her a couple of dollars.

Thinking of the *amah*, and anticipating her surprised reaction at opening the door to his unexpected knock, he smiled to himself. "*Aiyah!* It's the child! *Wah!* Come in, child," she would most likely cackle. Once inside the house, with the door closed behind him, he would hand her the cigarettes. She would show off her gold teeth as she grinned and thanked him by saying "*Do tze*, Chicko." She would then shout up the stairs, "*Aiyah!* Ming-ah! Your little boy is here. He has come to play with you. *Wah!* Tst! Tst!" and she would chortle and grin mischievously at Peter.

Rose would step out onto the landing at the top of the stairs, smile sweetly down at them, and say, "Hush, Wan Ze! You are being very naughty. Peter, what a lovely surprise. Please come up. Take no notice of my naughty *amah*."

Eventually Peter turned into the smaller, less noisy and less populated Bendemeer Road, and shortly after arrived at the alleyway he sought. He walked to the green door at the end of the alleyway and knocked upon it, the knock Rose had instructed him to use should he visit her. He felt a little nervous, but not unusually so. He always felt apprehensive whilst awaiting the *amah* to open the door. He didn't mind being out of bounds when in the open street because, if seen by the provost police, he could outrun them and hide. But if passing provost police should happen to look down the alleyway and see him there, he had little chance of escaping from them. And even if he did escape them, he knew the house would be marked and kept under surveillance. He didn't like to remain standing in the doorway for any length of time, and now that the door was not being opened, he was growing more nervous with every passing moment.

Again he looked nervously down the alleyway to where he could see the road traffic and people crossing its entrance. Why wasn't the *amah* opening the door, he wondered. He knocked again, louder than before, and shouted, "*amah, hoi mun ah*," and then in English, "Rose, are you at home? Please open the door."

Impatiently he waited. Then he heard agitated, muffled voices from within. He thought he could hear Rose speaking in a quietly pleading voice, but he could not hear well enough the words being said. Seconds passed into minutes and the door had still not been opened. He banged on the door, shouting, "Rose, are you OK? Why don't you open the door?" A scuffling noise from within was his only answer, and then he heard hurried heavy footsteps on the wooden stairway leading up to Rose's apartment. He heard the same heavy footsteps on the concrete floor behind the door he now stood at, just for moments before they retreated towards the back door. Then he heard the rasping sound of the iron bolt on the back door being drawn, and the squeal of the door being opened. That door always squealed on opening. With a sudden sickening feeling, Peter immediately realized that someone, a much heavier person than either Rose or the *amah*, had just exited through that back door.

Silence now, and with the green door remaining shut to him, Peter was filled with fearful uncertainty. His mind began to whirl. Had someone harmed Rose and had already run from the house? The heavy footsteps he had heard were neither Rose's nor those of the *amah*. Who could it have been, he worried. It sounded like a man's footsteps. Lifting a clenched fist, he hammered upon the door, shouting all the while, "*amah*. Lai Ming. *Hoi mun ah, fai di ah. Fai di, Fai di ah. Ngo hai* Peter," (Open the door, quickly. It's Peter here!)

He heard the familiar grating noise as the door's heavy bolt was slid back. The door swung ajar a few inches, just wide enough for Peter to see the face of the wizened old *amah* peering fearfully at him through the narrow opening. Annoyed and now suspicious, Peter stared back at the old woman. Saying not a word, he sensed that something was terribly wrong. One push and he shoved the door open. He roughly pushed the old woman aside. She slipped, fell, and gave a short scream as she landed on her back among the few pots and pans of the kitchen. Peter, usually kind and generous towards the *amah*, now didn't give her a thought. Nothing mattered except that he had to see and speak to Rose. Shaking

175

the flimsy framework of the stairs, he bounded up them three at a time, to halt and listen for a brief moment on the landing. From Lai Ming's room an ominous silence prevailed. Coming from below, he could hear the loud whimpering of the frightened *amah*.

Fingering the door catch, Peter slid the door open, threw back the curtain, and stepped suspiciously and with mounting dread into the apartment.

Lai Ming sat preening herself in front of the mirror, seemingly oblivious of his presence and quite unconcerned. She neither smiled nor turned to face him but sat watching him in the mirror, her face expressionless and without emotion. Never before had she acted in such a manner towards him. Choosing a comb from the dressing table, she slid it calmly and slowly through her long hair. She wore only a *sarong*.

"Hello, Rose," said Peter, feeling a dryness in his mouth, and not able to say more.

"Hello, Peter. I did not expect you today. Our arrangement was for tomorrow afternoon," Lai Ming replied coldly, her face without its usual smile of welcome.

Peter irritably replied, "Of course you didn't expect me today. I thought I'd give you a happy surprise, so I came a day early."

"It is better to be a day early than a day late," Lai Ming said in a monotone and unfeeling voice. "Why do you not sit down? I am very happy to see you, Peter."

"Are you? You don't sound it. And you don't look happy," said Peter. "What's happening?"

Lai Ming shrugged. "I do not feel well today," she answered calmly, still stroking the comb through her hair.

"Who was here? Who just left and went out the back door?" Peter asked.

"A girlfriend," Lai Ming answered in the same flat and toneless voice.

"She left surprisingly fast. In fact, she left as soon as she heard me knocking on the door."

Turning to face him, Lai Ming did not reply. Instead, she had a look on her face as if appealing to him, beseeching him, saying, 'Don't ask me more, Peter. Please, don't ask me.' Peter detected fear in those eyes, or was it sadness? He was not sure. But he was too young and immature, and too much in love with her to understand her silent pleadings.

"So, it was a girlfriend," he said.

"Yes, a girlfriend," she replied slowly, evenly. "I do have friends other than you."

"Hefty girlfriends?"

Lai Ming remained silent, not understanding the word 'hefty.'

"You have big girlfriends," Peter said.

"Yes. She is a big girl."

Peter, saying no more, looked around the room. It became obvious to him what had taken place there; yet he could not bring himself to believe that, just minutes ago, his girlfriend had been entertaining another man. He stared at Lai Ming in utter disbelief, his whole world crashing around him. He stared down at a large glass ashtray, one he had never seen before, full of cigarette stubs. "I thought you didn't smoke, Rose," he said, his voice thick and heavy.

"I do occasionally. Do you object?" Lai Ming asked, her eyes settling on the ashtray full of cigarette ends. "The *amah* has been cleaning the room, and she too has been smoking," she lied.

"Those are from Lucky Strike cigarettes, American ones," said Peter. He saw the empty beer bottle standing where his bottle normally stood. "I see that she also drinks Carlsberg beer. She certainly has good taste. No, I don't think so, Rose. You are not telling me the truth," Peter said, shaking his head in disbelief. "Nobody likes to be lied to."

Lai Ming did not answer. What could she say? Sadly she gazed into his tormented eyes. Oh, how terribly unhappy and distressed she knew he must feel. This would surely be the end of his love for her. She should have told him the truth at the beginning of their relationship. But that was not possible. Their love affair would not have begun, not existed if he had known the truth. Now, the less she said the better. She could see that he was bitterly hurt already without her making matters worse. She swallowed hard, trying to remain calm, though her heart felt sick and heavy within her.

"Well! Did the *amah* drink the beer?" Peter demanded.

"No. My girlfriend drank the beer."

"Rose, why must you lie to me? I've never met a Chinese girl who drinks beer."

Peter's eyes darted around that little room he had come to know so well. Hers followed his, but she said nothing. From where he stood he could look into the bathroom, and she knew it was of no use pretending or lying further. Both could see the shaving brush and razor forgotten and left on the sink.

"She shaves, too, eh?" Peter said, with cold anger creeping into his voice.

Lai Ming neither answered him nor moved from where she sat.

Walking into the bathroom, Peter picked up the shaving brush and felt the bristles. "Still wet," he said. A discarded blade lay near the razor. In the toilet bowl he saw a used contraceptive floating in the water. Sickened, the blood drained from his face, and he felt that he must spew his guts up at any moment. He spotted a torn and empty contraceptive packet lying on the floor of the bathroom. Picking it up, he rolled it into a tiny ball, tossed it in Rose's direction, and stood staring at her with anguish and despair in his eyes. Completely devastated, anger and jealousy consumed him. On stone feet he managed to walk to the bed, where he sat down and stared with unseeing eyes. Thus, he remained for several minutes. Eventually, he looked up and shaking his head sadly, said in a grief-stricken voice. "Rose, please don't lie to me any more."

Saying nothing, Lai Ming sat and watched him. Again Peter looked at the crumpled empty packet lying on the floor. He then turned his head and looked to the far corner of the room near the tall mirror. There, he could see Dettol-laced, murky water in the same bowl that Rose had used so often to wash his genitals after he had had sex with her. Next to the bowl stood the bottle of Dettol, a roll of cotton wool and a bar of wet soap in a saucer, all very recently used. Peter looked at Lai Ming incredulously. He didn't know what to say. He still couldn't believe what he was seeing. When his friends at Changi had kept asking him, "Was she a prostitute?", his reply had always been, "She's a lady." Now, he felt betrayed, humiliated and angry that his girlfriend Rose was indeed a prostitute.

Lai Ming read his thoughts. "I'm sorry, Peter. I should have told you the day we met. I made a big mistake bringing you home without telling you first." She spoke softly, composed and in a very sad voice.

"Sorry! Just like that! My God, I can't believe it. You're a prostitute. I've been loving a whore and living in a brothel these past months," said Peter, almost breaking into tears.

Lai Ming did not answer him.

"Rose, I loved you, and I do love you with all my heart. I trusted and respected you. You were my little angel." Peter paused. Suddenly he felt so silly at being made such a fool of and knew that he was about to burst into tears. "And now I find that you are nothing more than a common prostitute." Grief-stricken at hearing himself repeat that last word, he buried his face in his hands and wept. "A prostitute," he again repeated, as if unable still to believe himself.

Lai Ming rose from her dressing table and walked over to where Peter sat. She sat down at his side but didn't touch him. She knew that to touch him now would only make matters worse.

"You leave me with no words to say, Peter. Please, I get you glass of brandy."

Without an answer from him she hurried downstairs. He could hear the tinkle of glass and the slamming of a cupboard door. Next, she was again at his side with a bottle in one hand and a glass in the other. Pouring brandy into the glass, she offered it to him. "Come, Peter, drink," he heard her saying. In shock, he took the glass, and putting it to his lips drained it in one gulp. The brandy flowed fiery hot, warming but not soothing him. He still loved Rose. She was so kind, so good-hearted. "Thank you," he said.

She looked at him with pity and great sadness. "I'm so sorry, Peter. I should have told you. I know how badly you are hurting, and I never wanted to hurt you. I should have told you the day we first met, but I couldn't. And afterwards, I still couldn't. I didn't want to lose you." She took a silk handkerchief from a drawer of her bedside table and with it dabbed her eyes. Then she, too, began to weep. Peter had never seen Rose cry before. Always there had been gentle smiles on that lovely little face, never tears. "I just didn't want to lose you," she sobbed.

Peter's emotions clashed. Crazed with jealousy and anger, and knowing that very soon he would be leaving her for the last time, he now took an almost sadistic pleasure in saying, "So you're a prostitute who'll fuck any man for a few bucks. I bet I've followed in the footsteps of others many times, or as the chaps back at the camp say, 'batted on a sticky wicket'. Perhaps you had one, perhaps two, maybe three or even more men before letting me screw you. But what does it matter if there was one, ten, a hundred or even a thousand others?"

Knowing that he must release his anger, Lai Ming, with tears rolling down her cheeks, remained silent.

"Tell me, Rose. How many men do you take to your bed and ask for no payment? Is it a game with you? Do you fuck for the fun of it?" He knew those words hurt; he saw her wince, but he meant to hurt her. He wanted to hurt her as much as she was hurting him.

"I have no boyfriend other than you, Peter. You must know that. You must believe me."

"Why should I?"

"Peter, I wanted you, and I still want you. You, with the love and affection that you have always given me. You are kind and good, and I need you. Never have I asked you for money. I want you! You! You! Don't you understand, Peter? Yes, I admit I'm a prostitute. But you are my boyfriend. I need you. Other men mean nothing to me."

"Is that what you tell all of them?" asked Peter cruelly.

"Please, don't talk like that, Peter. I kept my secret from you believing that it would be for the best, for both our sakes. But now that you know my lifestyle, you are hurt and angry with me. Give us both a chance, Peter." Lai Ming's face suddenly brightened. "You sit where you are, Peter. Don't think on bad thoughts but think of all the happy times we have enjoyed together, and think of the happy times ahead of us. I shall pour you more brandy. You drink it, and while you drink I shall take my *sarong* off, and you must watch me take it off. I want you to look at my body, everything of my body, all of me, and think of what you want and need of me. But don't think of my body only. Think of my companionship, my friendship, my love for you. Always there is a home here for you," Lai Ming cried. "You can still be happy if you don't think too much. Always you think too much. You need me, Peter, as I need you, so I shall pour you a drink, and then I shall undress."

"You can pour me a drink, but I don't want you to take your *sarong* off, Rose. I don't want what thousands of other men use." Peter, completely stunned by events and in an ever growing black depression, didn't seem to know what he was saying or doing. Pushing Lai Ming from him, he stood up, only to find the room swirling round and round, and his vision blurred. Even Lai Ming, standing so close to him, was just a blur. Feeling as if he were about to faint and fall, he steadied himself by holding on to the edge of the bed. There was no reason to remain longer, he decided. "I must go, Rose," he said. "I don't want to see you again. You have your life to live, and I have mine. We are from two different worlds. Goodbye, Rose," and he turned to leave.

"Wait, Peter, wait!" Lai Ming screamed, springing after him. "You cannot go. You must not go. You haven't given me a chance," she pleaded.

"A chance! What do you mean? A prostitute won't give up her way of life. You won't."

"I cannot give it up. I need the money. But you must give me a chance even if I must explain everything to you."

"If you tried to explain, you'd only hurt me more," said Peter. "No, Rose, our love cannot be. Everything is finished between us. I cannot love a whore. I'm going."

"You have not loved a whore, Peter. You have loved a prostitute. I love you, Peter. You know that. Now you want to hurt me."

"Is that possible?"

"I have a heart. I am the same as any other woman. I have the same feelings. Peter, you must not go," she implored, going to him and clinging to his legs. "Don't go. Say you won't go. Sleep here with me tonight. Tomorrow we will talk and decide. But please! Please don't leave me! You must not leave me!"

Peter felt as if his whole world had been shattered. His life had revolved around Lai Ming, and now there was nothing. Ripping her clenched hands from his legs, he pushed her savagely from him so that she fell sobbing bitterly against the headboard of the bed. Feeling sorry for her, he desperately wanted to go to her, lift her up in his arms and kiss and caress her. But he was too hurt, and his pride would not allow him to do so. He felt very small and silly. He must not look at her more or he would go to her. He must do something. He must leave her be, and be gone.

"Goodbye, Rose. I wish you all the best," he said, his voice choking with emotion. "I'm going now. It's better this way." He so badly wanted to stay with her but he could not.

Turning his back on her, he pulled the curtain aside and left the room, leaving the woman he loved sobbing where she had fallen. He could still hear her crying as he descended the stairs. As if in a trance, he passed the old *amah* cowering in a corner of the kitchen. He did not speak to her, nor she to him. Opening the door, he stepped out into the alleyway and walked towards the moonlit street. So this was the end of his beautiful friendship with the girl he loved, he thought bitterly. Everything was finished. He didn't want it to end, but he didn't know what to think or do. With his mind in turmoil, he decided there was only the one thing to do, get drunk, as drunk as could be. He was angry with himself and angry with her. But what was the use? His whole world had collapsed. The woman he loved, trusted and idolized was nothing more than a common prostitute.

He stopped a passing taxi and got in.

"The New World," he snapped.

"OK Johnny," acknowledged the driver.

"And hurry! *Fai di, fai di!*"

"OK Johnny. I go quick quick."

Two hours and several rum and cokes later, Peter Saunders still sat at the same little table in the dance cabaret of the New World Amusement Park. No matter what, he could not have been more emotionally distraught. The cabaret had not yet livened up. The twenty-cents-a-dance girls, the New World's hostesses, were still arriving, some alone, some in twos and threes, and some accompanied by talkative *amah* scurrying along behind their mistresses on tiny feet, like faithful dogs.

A sexy-looking Chinese dance hostess sitting alone at a table near Peter's made come-hither eyes at him, and turning her body in his direction, crossed her slender legs, hooked her skirt up a few inches and showed all she dared in public view. Angry and depressed and already semi-intoxicated, and with his mind furiously revolving around Rose, Peter ignored her obvious advances. Through his torment, however, he could at least see that the woman was not nearly as young as she would undoubtably like to appear. Wrinkles showed in a face almost hidden beneath a thick coating of creams and rouge, and she wore a dark vermilion coloured lipstick, which did not help her looks. She must be at least forty, Peter decided. He looked away from the woman and took another drink, and she, realizing there would be no business with him, turned her attention towards a couple of jungle-green uniform-clad British soldiers sitting at a nearby table contentedly consuming bottle after bottle of Tiger beer.

With his emotions in turmoil, and becoming more depressed and angry, Peter sat tense, clasping a glass in shaking hands, his brain whirling, his nerves near breaking point and his mind returning to and frantically churning over the events of the past few hours. What now? What should he do? Repeatedly he asked himself these same questions. The wonderful romance between him and his lovely Chinese girlfriend had come to an abrupt end. Yet, how could it end, just like that, after all the wonderful times they'd spent together? He realized that he still loved Rose and that he would always love her regardless of what she did for a living. And now, with the girl he loved living so very near him, just fifteen miles away, it would be impossible for him to remain in Singapore without wanting to see her. Not seeing her would drive him crazy. On the other hand, how could he love her as he had the past months knowing that she was having sex with other men, and God only knows how many? It would be impossible, unthinkable, to carry on a relationship as they had done so blissfully until now. Yet, he must have her. He could not lose her. He must think of something. Perhaps he should have waited and listened to her explanation. But listening to her, hearing the lurid details would surely have made matters worse.

Damn her! Why did she have to be a prostitute, he angrily asked himself. Not bothering to pour coke into his glass, he gulped back neat rum, coughing as the fiery syrup slid down his throat. He looked with blurred eyes to where the Chinese dance hostess sat looking bored. The soldiers had gotten up from their table and left without giving her a second glance. Soon, though, she was giving the eye and showing off her shapely legs to a group of Chinese youths who had recently arrived and seated themselves at a table close to hers. They were ordering their first drink of the evening.

Deciding that this was not the place in which to get drunk, Peter Saunders got to his feet then, swaying slightly, he walked out of the cabaret, mingled with the jostling crowd of night-time revellers for awhile, and eventually pushed his way through a turnstile at the New World's exit.

The Red Lantern Club situated on a corner a hundred yards further down Jalan Besar and not far from the junction of Rochor Canal Road, was his next stop. Having visited the place on a couple of occasions with Rick long before he met Rose, Peter knew that it was a vile den of iniquity frequented by low-class whores. But it had atmosphere, the chow served there had been good and the beer ice-cold.

Brushing through the swinging red half-doors, he gazed about him to see what other customers the place had drawn. A US navy ship must have arrived in port because the place was crowded with American sailors dressed immaculately in white uniforms, their little round hats tucked neatly in the waistbands of their trousers. Ashore for the evening, they were expecting a good time. Some sat on high stools drinking at the bar, others stood about drinking in small groups, while yet more, who had been latched onto by the club's girls, were openly necking. Quite a number were waiting their turn to enjoy a quickie, and others oral sex, from fast-working girls in curtained-off cubicles in the rear. The American sailors called these girls 'fucking machines', which was a reasonable description seeing as how these girls could service an average of eight men an hour. It certainly is some club, thought Peter. The place hadn't changed a bit since he was there last; the waitresses were the same girls, always smiling, always joking, and forever hopeful of getting big tips out of their customers, which they often did. The barmaids were the same three, all very efficient and quick at pouring drinks and mixing their customers' cocktails. The band, such as it was, comprised the same three Chinese lads who played their instruments just as badly as when he had first heard them months ago. Peter, however, was not interested in the merits of the band. He needed a drink. He noticed that the same manager ruled the joint, a jolly-faced, grotesquely overweight Chinese man who smiled congenially at everyone while repeatedly checking the takings in the till.

Peter sat down on a stool at a corner of the bar, the only stool vacant. Except for the numerous American sailors, the only other customers were young chaps in civvies, quite obviously British servicemen out for a good time getting boozed up, and perhaps hoping to shack up with one of the girls after the Yanks had left at midnight to return to their ship. The British servicemen could not compete financially with the American sailors' wads of dollars.

The waitresses were young, attractive girls, but the prostitute hostesses were not so young or as attractive. All had seen at least forty years, and most looked those forty years, like hens made up to look like spring chickens. But, oldish or not, these ladies of the night persisted in their quest, and often got their man, for a quickie in a cubicle, or for an all-night session at their home.

"Rum and coke," said Peter to the barmaid.

The girl smiled at him in a friendly manner and reached behind her for a bottle of rum.

Sick at heart, Peter could not get the happenings of a couple of hours ago out of his mind. He could clearly see the contraceptive lying limp and used in the toilet bowl, the empty beer bottle on the table and the cigarette ends in the ashtray. He could hear the heavy footsteps on the stairs and on the concrete floor leading to the back door. Very depressed, in despair, and lost in jealous anger, a black depression and agonizing thoughts, he was brought back to his surroundings by a feminine voice cooing in his ear, "Hello, darling."

"Hi," replied Peter, swivelling around on his seat and expecting to see one of the club's girls attempting to latch on to him. He would have bought her a drink, just to have someone to talk to. But it was not one of the club's girls. Peter stared at the owner of the voice for some moments before suddenly realizing that the person was not a female, but a Chinese boy dressed in woman's clothing. Disgusted, Peter snarled, "Scram! Sod off!" and turning his back on the uninvited transvestite, he picked up a newspaper lying on the bar hoping that it would occupy his mind and help rid him of the newcomer.

"May I sit and talk with you?" the other asked in a sexually enticing voice.

Peter angrily faced the Chinese boy. "No. Bugger off. I want to be alone," he said. He had no time for queers, especially those who bothered him. However, Peter could not help but study the boy who appeared to be about the same age as he. I don't believe it, he thought. This boy would do any girl proud the way he presents himself. A neat and well-pressed black skirt fitted snugly around a slim waist, and a frilly white bra peeped out from beneath a pink silk jacket with tiny red buttons. The boy's legs were covered in sheer nylon stockings and on his feet he wore dainty high-heeled shoes, also pink. It was obvious to Peter that the boy wore a wig of wavy black curls that fell around narrow shoulders, and little bangs that almost reached his pencilled-in eyebrows. His skillful application of rouge and lipstick would put many women to shame. Nothing had been spared, it seemed, in the boy's attempt to present himself as a woman. Even the perfume he used was delicate. It was lavender.

The boy, ignoring Peter's negative answer, sat down next to him on a recently vacated stool.

"Many men prefer my company to that of one of those bitches," he said, nodding towards the ten-dollars-a-quickie girls fluttering around the room. "Many welcome me into their company with rapture. Isn't it strange that a few boys, boys just like you, young and handsome, just simply cannot welcome me. Why, I wonder?" He sighed, looking down over himself. "And I, so young and fresh," and he began to feel sorry for himself, or so it seemed. Then he looked up and smiled and winked at Peter. "You're camp," he said, waving a hand effeminately in front of Peter's face. "I think you're gay, just waiting for the right boy to come your way. I'd like to be that boy."

"Please go away," said Peter, more bewildered than disgusted by what he was seeing and hearing.

Seeing the look on Peter's face, the youth asked, "Do I look that bad that you cannot like me just a little?"

"Please, go away," answered Peter. "I'm in no mood for company."

"Oh, my dear boy, don't be such a bore. We could be such good friends."

Peter remained silent. A transvestite was something new to him. He had heard and read about them but this boy was the first he had come across in his travels. A few gays had crossed his path since his enlistment in the Royal Air Force but certainly not in drag.

As for this boy perched on the high stool next to him, Peter decided to ignore him, so discreetly turned his attention to the paper he had picked up from off the bar. It was in Chinese. Disgusted, Peter returned it to the bar.

"I'll buy you a drink," the young transvestite offered, smiling and beckoning the barmaid to him with an effeminate wave of his manicured hand.

"I don't want a drink from you. I've no wish to drink with you, so please go away. Leave me alone," said Peter.

"Oh, my dear boy, please be sociable. Yours is a whisky, isn't it?"

"It's rum. But you're not paying for anything that I drink."

"Oh! Excuse me! I'm sorry I asked," and the other looked hurt and disappointed.

The barmaid, placing the rum and coke on a paper napkin in front of Peter, looked at the two enquiringly as if asking, 'Who's paying for this?'

Peter read her thoughts. "Please get him a glass of peppermint and ask him to leave me alone. The drinks are on me," he said.

"Oh! That is sweet of you," suddenly smiled the young transvestite. "But please, if you don't mind, I'd prefer a gin and orange. I have a real taste for gin. It really sends me."

"Give him a double shot of gin. Maybe it'll send him over the hills and far away," said Peter dryly to the barmaid.

The barmaid smiled. She understood and was obviously amused at what she was seeing. "I'll make a gin and orange," she said, and turned to where several American sailors were demanding drinks. "OK guys. I come quick," she sang out. For her, this would be a good night tip-wise. American sailors always tipped well, especially those who thought they stood a chance of getting a piece of her ass.

"Now, please," the young transvestite implored Peter. "Let's not quarrel. I want boys to like me. Many do you know. Many simply adore me. It's my good company, I suppose. My name is Ruby. May I ask yours?"

"No, you may not," answered Peter, still annoyed.

"Why not?"

"I've no wish to tell you."

"Why?"

"Why don't you find yourself a nice girlfriend and enjoy her company, instead of acting so daft?" said Peter.

"A girlfriend! But I don't want a woman," blurted out the boy angrily. "I abhor women!" and spreading his hands out palms upward towards Peter as if in despair, he exclaimed. "Oh! Please! My dear boy, how can you speak of women to me? I like men! But women, never!"

Peter sighed and downed half the rum and coke. On any other occasion he might have been more tolerant, and might have found some interest in this boy dressed in girl's clothing seated next to him. But tonight he was in no mood for such unusual company. Standing up, he said, "Here, Ruby. Here's two dollars. Pay for the drinks and look for someone else." With these words spoken, Peter pushed his way through the crowd, through the swing doors, and strode out into the night, leaving the transvestite awaiting his gin and orange, and a boyfriend.

Bugis Street was Peter's next place of call. Bugis Street lit by the white glare of a hundred kerosene lamps swinging from the overhanging eaves of the many chow stalls criss-crossing the dusty square. Bugis Street was infamous, an ingress to hell, a paradise for pickpockets, prostitutes and the young thugs and hoodlums of the city. To the taxi drivers, trishaw *wallahs*, stall owners, the cheap musicians and the shoeshine boys, Bugis Street was a goldmine.

As for the needs of society, Bugis Street, though an ugly place contaminated by the filth of the city, had its merits. Society often paid visits to the street, many to have a good time feasting on delicious meals from the chow stalls, drinking and making merry with friends, as well as with the many prostitutes sitting at the tables hoping to sell their wares. Yet, many such visitors would rue the day they paid that call on Bugis Street, as wallets departed from one's person in less than a blink of the eye. There, many vicious fights broke out, injuring the innocent more often than the perpetrators. As for picking up a woman for a short time or for an all night's entertainment, several of the prostitutes who plied their trade there did not report monthly at the Social Welfare Department for a check-up, or receive shots of penicillin if needed. Hence, quite a number of these women carried venereal diseases.

Bugis Street, as far as Peter Saunders was concerned, was a lively, interesting place to visit, where the beer was cold, and a place that never closed. At night Bugis Street was packed, and even during the day the Chinese stall owners were kept busy stirring and tossing fried rice and other tasty foods in giant woks heated over open charcoal braziers. They were also kept busy warding off the many pariah dogs and numerous rats. The swarms of flies pitching on the food didn't matter, they didn't eat much. Peter had visited Bugis Street twice before, but again, that was before he met Lai Ming. On those two pleasurable occasions, he had found himself fascinated by the noisy, garish street, with its exotic smells filling the air and the blaring Chinese music, so vibrant and alive. But tonight, there was nothing that could fascinate him or cause him pleasure.

Elbowing his way through the milling crowds and meandering between rickety tables, square-topped stools, the cheap-jack stalls and the chow stalls, Peter eventually found a vacant table at the far side of the street. He sat down on one of the four stools provided at each table and awaited service.

"Shoeshine, Johnny? Very good shoeshine! Best shoeshine in Bugis Street, Johnny. Fifty cents, Johnny. For you very cheap."

Peter gazed down upon a shaven-headed, ragged urchin pawing at his shoes whilst grovelling on bare feet in the dirt. About eight years of age, covered in grime and festering sores, the skinny little boy looked up at him with pleading, big brown eyes, beseeching him in grim silence an opportunity to earn a few cents. He held the brush, polish and cloth in eager hands; a wooden shoe box and foot rest lay in the dust between his dirty feet.

"Shoeshine, Johnny? Best in Singapore. Only fifty cents, Johnny," the boy pleaded.

"I don't want a shoeshine," said Peter, shaking his head.

190

The boy's eyes sparkled. He was not going to be outdone by mere words. Again he clutched at the foot nearest him, and dragging the filled shoe a few inches towards himself, attempted to slide the shoe box beneath it.

Peter drew his foot away, the boy grimly hanging onto it. Just like the previous occasion when out with Rick, thought Peter. He had ignored the pleading, persistent shoeshine boy, and had turned his back on him and returned to his beer. He had felt hands pulling at his feet, supposedly towards the shoe box, but he had paid no heed. Then, when the boy departed, and when Peter went to pay for his beer, he couldn't. His wallet was gone. The seam in his trouser pocket had been slit open by an expert hand, and his wallet had fallen into that hand. But, this being Bugis Street, what else could one expect, for no angels worked in Bugis Street, that was for sure. Peter knew all shoeshine boys were not pickpockets, perhaps far from it, but he had become extremely wary of them.

"I don't want a shoeshine," he repeated firmly.

"Thirty cents, Johnny. For you, only thirty cents. You, very good friend. *Ding ho* friend. Me very cheap. Thirty cents, Johnny." Again the boy heaved and dragged at the shoe nearest him.

"No," hissed Peter, even angrier now than when he had first arrived. "Leave me alone. Go on! Scram! Get away from me! Beat it!"

The boy, falling backwards, away from this sudden verbal attack, sat down in the dirt swearing in Chinese and making ugly faces at Peter. Soon, though, the boy turned his attention upon a young Chinese couple who had just sat down at the next table. At first, both ignored the shoeshine boy, and laughed and whispered to one another in soft talk. Finally, tired of being pestered further and angered at seeing his ladyfriend's ankles touched by such grimy hands, the young man clouted the boy about the head, sending him sprawling in the dirt. Whereupon the boy sprang lightly to his feet, grabbed a wok full of fried noodles from a nearby chow stall, and splattered the whole hot mess over the unfortunate couple. Screeching with laughter, he then ran as fast as his young legs would carry him away from the messy scene.

"Hello, Peter."

The Chinese couple was forgotten as Peter heard his name spoken. He spun around on the stool to see who knew him. A tallish, ginger-haired girl stood smiling down at him. In every way she looked Chinese, but she may have been Eurasian. A ginger-haired Chinese girl, he knew, would be unique, but this girl had a brilliant shock of reddish hair. Peter was sure it was not dyed. How could it be dyed hair, especially after seeing this same girl nude, just last week on Changi Beach, flaunting her wares to a couple of British soldiers. Peter observed then that she also had red pubic hair, plus the tattoo of a naked woman standing astride that same area.

"Oh! Hello, Molly! Fancy meeting you here. How are you? Please sit down," Peter invited, waving the girl to the seat across from him.

"I'm OK" the girl answered, sitting down "Going to buy me a beer?" she asked.

"I thought nice Chinese girls didn't drink beer," he said. "Sure. Of course I'll buy you a beer."

"You're Rose's boyfriend, aren't you?"

"I was," Peter replied.

A stallholder in a dirty vest and shorts took Peter's order and returned minutes later carrying a tray on which were two bottles of Tiger beer and two glasses. Peter paid the man, then poured the beer.

"Cheers, Molly," he said, raising his glass.

"Cheers," Molly answered. They watched a fight that had broken out on the far side of the street. There was a lot of shouting, tables and stools were being overturned, bottles and glasses smashed, and many bowls of noodles thrown.

Molly broke the silence between them. "You said you were Rose's boyfriend, as though it's finished between you. What's the matter? Had a fight?"

"A fight? No, but we are finished. Everything's finished."

"Don't you like her anymore?"

192

"Molly, don't ask questions about our affairs. Please, don't speak to me about Rose."

"OK! OK! I was only trying to help."

"I don't want help. I just want to forget her, everything about her."

"Would you like to come home with me?" asked Molly. "Stay all night. If you are in a bad mood, I can make it a good mood. We can have a good time together."

"I'm not going home with you, Molly. But thanks all the same."

"Are you broke? If you are, it doesn't matter. You can come to my home even if you have no money. You can pay me what you like when you see me sometime on Changi Beach. It's OK, I trust you. The RAF boys who know me know that I'm not hard-hearted."

"I'm not broke, Molly. But thanks all the same. I know that you're a good girl, and I like you, but I don't want to go with you."

Molly laughed scornfully. "What's the matter? You're not scared, are you? If you wish to see my health card, I have it here in my handbag. Don't worry, it's stamped up to date."

Peter smiled at the beautiful girl sitting seductively next to him. He felt sure that she must be absolute dynamite in bed. If he had not known Rose, he might have been tempted, he thought, especially now that he felt so low. "I don't wish to see your card, Molly," he said gently." I don't even wish to discuss your business with you."

"My business is good business," said Molly.

Peter's face froze as he kept his sudden anger in check. "Your business. I don't like it," he said.

"Perhaps you are a hypocrite," Molly ventured.

"I don't think so."

"I bet I make much more money than you."

"I'm sure you do. But let's not discuss the matter further." Peter forced a smile.

"You said you and Rose are finished. I don't believe you," persisted Molly. "You've had a row with her, a big row, and now you're on the beer like a silly schoolboy."

"Please, Molly, if you're going to talk like that, I'd rather drink alone."

"OK, suit yourself. But Rose won't like it." Molly stood up. "Thanks for the beer, Peter. Sorry I can't be of more help."

"That's all right. Thank you for your company, Molly. I needed someone to talk to."

Molly gave him a friendly smile. "For you, anytime," she said. "Don't drink too much. Remember, Rose won't like it." She turned and espied a group of half-drunk American sailors who had just arrived at Bugis Street. Again turning to face Peter, she winked an eye and gave him a sly grin. "They will pay," she said. "Be seeing you," and she walked away, towards the table where the sailors were being seated.

Suddenly, a mist descended over Peter's eyes. One moment Molly was standing there beside him, the next she was gone. Now there were loud noises all around him throbbing through his brain, and then this mist that had suddenly enveloped him. "Rose won't like it. Rose won't like it," he repeated to himself. "They will pay. They will pay." His mind, scarred and tortured by what he had learned, seemed to burst asunder. Suddenly, he became like a madman frenzied with great anger. Leaping from the stool, he smashed the bottles and glasses to the ground. "And I don't like it," he savagely hissed. "I hate it. But I'll stop her. She will have one boyfriend or none."

He staggered drunkenly to the line of waiting taxis, and as a door was thrown open for him, he flopped in and fell behind the grinning driver.

"Lavender Street, Johnny. And for God's sake hurry. Lavender Street. I'll direct you from there."

The taxi driver had seen it all before. "OK, Johnny," he said. The taxi shot forward and Bugis Street was left behind.

15

Grief-stricken, Lai Ming had sobbed herself to sleep, but she awoke as Peter entered the room and sat down on the edge of her bed. Her eyes, dulled by crying, looked up into his, but she did not smile.

"I knew you would return to me, Peter," she said.

"What made you so sure?"

"I just knew you would."

"Tell me who was here when I arrived this evening. I want to know."

Lai Ming sat up but refrained from touching him. "You will be angry if I tell you," she said quietly.

"I want to know."

"It can only hurt you, Peter."

"I want to know who was here."

Lai Ming sighed. "Very well, but I have warned you. You will get hurt."

"You can't hurt me anymore, Rose. Not more than you already have."

"I'm so sorry, Peter," Lai Ming said, almost in a whisper. "I am truly sorry. Now, please remember, I prefer to tell you nothing about who was here, but you insist, so I will tell you," she said sadly, her cheeks putty-grey and stained through weeping. "An American man, a friend, an officer from off a ship was here," she whispered. Reaching for her handbag, which lay on the dressing table, she took from it a wad of American dollars and showing them to Peter, said, "Look! He gave me these."

Mute in his increasingly seething anger, Peter stared wild-eyed and in disbelief at the American money. Suddenly, he snatched the wad of dollars from her and threw them across the room. "So, for those bits of paper you sold your body," he said, clenching his fists. He felt as if he was about to throw up. "You sold your body for those," he repeated. "Another man lay with you, and before him, hundreds I suppose, probably thousands."

"You asked me to tell you, Peter."

"You are nothing more than a dirty prostitute," he hissed, a savage tone in his voice. "I've been living in a brothel. Why did you bring me here in the first place? Why did you want to hurt me?"

"I did not want to hurt you. I have never wanted to hurt you. I love you, Peter."

"Love me! How can you love me yet allow other men to fuck you?" He was crying in his anger, his tears running down over his bewildered and grief-stricken face.

"You do not understand or you would not speak to me in such a manner," Lai Ming said sadly. "You just do not understand."

"I understand only too well. You're a prostitute, a fucking whore who fucks anybody. I loved and treasured you, Rose, and now I find that you're nothing but a whore. I can't believe it. I just can't believe it," he moaned in seething anger. Then, his voice rising, he said, "So that is the reason why I could never spend Saturday evenings with you. Because Saturday night is the best night of your week, the night you are sure of customers for your filthy business. You would lose money if I were with you, wouldn't you?"

"It is my business, Peter. Why should I have told you of my business? We have been very happy together, why should I spoil it? You have been happy with me, Peter?"

"Happy! Of course I've been happy. I loved you. But you tricked me into loving you, and now you've killed all that."

"No, Peter, I no trick you. Our love is natural. We love each other. Don't say tricked."

"Tricked! Of course it was a trick. You made me believe you to be the perfect little lady. The Miss Proper. I trusted you. I believed everything you told me. What a fool I've been. Now you can laugh and think what a stupid person I am."

Suddenly staggering to his feet and swaying over her, drunk no longer but stricken with jealousy and intense rage, he grasped her by an arm and tightened his grip on it. Her face expressionless, she did not move or attempt to draw away from him; only her tear-filled eyes spoke, pleading with him.

"I loved you, Rose. I trusted and worshipped you as if you were an angel. I gave you all that I could give, and thought you were giving me the same in return. But you've been giving yourself to other men. You've been cheating on me. But you will give yourself to no other man. I would rather see you die."

Tightening his grip on her arm, he wrenched her off the bed, feeling a sudden sadistic pleasure in hurting her. She'd hurt him. Now he would hurt her, and he would hurt her more, much more than she'd hurt him. With his free hand he slapped her hard across the face sending her head reeling backward. Then, with the back of his hand, he slapped her face again. Never before had he struck anyone, and most certainly he would never have struck a defenseless woman. But now, shocked and consumed by jealousy and anger, he wanted to punish this woman who'd hurt him so badly. "Take that you stinking bitch," he shouted, slapping her face one more time. Then, wanting to hurt her even more, with all his strength he lifted her off the bed, violently shook her, and then threw her from him, so that she hurtled across the bed and crashed against the stone wall on the far side of the room. There, without even a whimper, she sank as if unconscious into a motionless heap within the narrow space between the wall and the bed. Her face was turned towards him, but her eyes were closed and she was not moving. Eventually her eyes flickered open. Silently she watched him standing, towering over her, on the other side of the bed. She whimpered, but didn't speak, just stared up at him in horrified amazement. Then tears began to roll down her cheeks.

"Peter, what are you doing to me?" was all she said.

"I, I don't know, Rose," Peter said in a frightened voice. "I don't know." Suddenly the awful realism of his cowardly act hit him, and he gasped in horrified amazement, his hands covering his face. "My God! What have I done to you? What have I done?" he moaned.

Scrambling frantically across the bed, he reached down and carefully lifted Lai Ming, and tenderly placed her upon the bed, dreading what harm he might have caused his lovely girlfriend. Gently, quickly, his hand roved over her body, caressing her hands and arms, her legs and feet, and then her ribs, all the while fearful that she would cry out as he pressed upon broken bones. Her face was already swollen and there was an ugly purple bruise spreading where he had so tightly gripped her arm.

"My God. What have I done to you, Rose? I had no right to hit you. No right at all." He held her in his arms and gently kissed her swollen cheeks. "Rose, please forgive me," he said in an anguished voice. "I swear to you and to God that I'm sorry. How could I have done such a cowardly thing?" Feeling wretched, he knew not what to do or say. Eventually, he said, "I'm sorry, Rose. God help me, I'm sorry. I must be crazy. I've never hit a woman before, I swear. How could I have meant to harm you? You know I love you."

For several moments they looked intently into each other's eyes. Yes, he loved her. Now she knew for sure that he loved her. Pitying him, Lai Ming lifted a hand and drew his head down to where it could rest upon her breast. Gently she caressed his face and slid her fingers through his hair. "Don't speak," she whispered. "Lie still."

He lay for some moments before wriggling free. "I can't lie still after what I've done to you, Rose. Can I do anything for you?"

"I'm all right, Peter. Don't worry," she whispered, a trace of a smile upon her face.

"Thank God," Peter murmured. "I feel so mean and cruel. I wish that it had never happened."

"Don't think of it, Peter. It is best forgotten."

"I'll never forget as long as I live. I swear to you that I'll never ever strike you again."

"I believe you, Peter."

"I must have gone crazy. Can you ever forgive me, Rose? I'm so very sorry, and I feel terrible." Pressing his face to her breasts, he burst into tears and openly wept.

"Don't cry, Peter," Lai Ming implored. "I don't like to see you cry. Please, don't cry, Peter. I forgive you for everything. You are in shock, and it's my fault. I should have told you. I love you, Peter. I want you. I'll always want you. You are my boy."

Again and again she slid her fingers through his hair as she pressed her body tightly against his. Then, quickly unclipping the tiny cloth buttons to the little top she wore, she drew it aside revealing her breasts. Placing her hand beneath one, she led the nipple to Peter's lips. "Kiss me there," she whispered. She felt the nipple slip into his mouth, he sucking on it eagerly, she holding her breast to him as she would her baby. Soon, she could feel his body relaxing on top of her, like a slowly deflating balloon. She sighed her relief. That is what she wanted, for him to relax. She sighed again as she too relaxed, happy to again enjoy the feeling of being wanted by the boy she loved.

Several hours later, relaxed and completely composed, they lay in one another's arms, the fires of their emotions extinguished, leaving them drained and in a dreamy state of restful, relieved tranquility. Neither moved nor spoke but lay gazing into the eyes of the other, not wishing to break the spell of the moment.

Street noises from passing traffic had subsided. Only cruising taxi-cabs hunting for late fares, the whining of military police jeeps, and the coarser engines of the naval patrol wagons making their rounds of vigilance, broke the silence of the night. The city, moonlit, awaited the coming of dawn.

Lai Ming finally broke the silence. Placing a hand on Peter's shoulder, her face became serious as she said, "Peter, don't go to sleep, not yet. I have been thinking on many things. Let's talk."

"About what?"

"About you and about me. About us, but mainly about me."

"That should be interesting."

"I'd like to tell you everything of my past, Peter. Much more than you already know."

"You've already told me quite a bit about yourself. But you didn't tell me the bad part."

"What I wish to tell you is not meant to hurt you, Peter, but it may. I never wish to hurt you again. But I think you should know of my past, and then you can decide."

"Decide! Decide what?"

"Decide on whether or not we can have a future together, now that you know who I am. As I told you on the beach at Changi, my husband was taken from me, killed at sea. I was left broken-hearted, with little money, and with a baby to fend for. I sought employment, but you have seen for yourself the working conditions here. There is much unemployment. And to labour at unskilled work, if you are fortunate to find work, you cannot expect more than a pittance in pay. In fact it would have been impossible to feed and clothe my child as I have, as well as pay for his medical bills which are forever piling up."

Sitting up, Peter asked, "What do you mean? Why are there medical bills?"

Also sitting up, Lai Ming reached for her handbag. Opening it, she drew out a card and handed it to Peter. "This is the illness my son came down with shortly after my husband's death."

It was still too dark for Peter to read the printed words on the card, so climbing out of bed, he went into the bathroom and switched on the light. In big black letters the heading on the card was KANDANG

KERBAU HOSPITAL.

In smaller letters the second line read, Poliomyelitis Ward. Peter read on, comprehending with dismay what Lai Ming was telling him. He was holding a visiting card stating the time of day patients were allowed visitors. "Oh, my God!" he whispered to himself.

Returning to the bed, he said just the one word to Lai Ming. "Polio?"

"Yes," she answered softly, fighting back tears. "His doctors tell me that his is a relatively mild case, that they are experimenting with new treatments and new medicines so that, given time, he might walk again, and possibly recover completely. Now, with every visit I make to him, the doctors appear even more hopeful."

"Thank God for that," said Peter. "But the treatment must cost you lots of money."

"Yes, it does, for his treatment and medicines, for the doctors, as well as for the hospital."

"I'm beginning to understand. I wish you had told me sooner."

"Would it have made a difference?"

"I don't know."

"But now you know the reason why I need lots of money, to pay my son's hospital bills. Thankfully, I do see improvement in him. But, please, allow me to carry on with my story."

"No, Rose, I've heard enough. I understand what you're going through. There's no need to say more."

"But it is my wish, Peter. I want you to know everything about me, because sooner or later you must decide."

"I know. But it's not necessary to tell me everything."

"Yes, it is necessary, and I shall tell you everything, so please remain silent, OK?"

"OK. If that's your wish."

"It is my wish. Now, I continue. I was devastated at learning the nature of my son's illness, and by almost losing him. But now that I had big bills to pay, I found employment as a dance hostess in the cabaret of the New World. I didn't like the job but I couldn't be choosy. At first I was treated well and my wages were reasonable, but not nearly enough to cover my expenses. I could have earned much more but I always became disgusted with the men, and disgusted at the thought of selling my body. I couldn't do it. But I needed money. Lots of money. I became frustrated. Sometimes I liked a man almost enough to give in to temptation, but I didn't have the nerve so refused all offers. I remained as a dance hostess earning a minimum wage.

"Then, one day, the house manager, a big fat pompous man who I could not possibly like, took me to his room and attempted to seduce me. When that failed, he attempted to rape me, and when I fought back, he fired me. I even had to get out of the room he had rented for me. I roamed the streets seeking work and begging for money. Have you ever tried begging for money, Peter? You would soon learn that without money you are nothing. I have no relatives in Singapore, and my so-called friends deserted me. I was alone, with a very sick child in the hospital, and with money demands coming in daily. Have you ever roamed the streets, Peter, hungry, without money, and sick at heart? I don't think so. You wouldn't know what it is like to plead, to beg with a starving belly, and to be ignored. But I know, Peter. I know. Never again shall I beg. I would rather sell my body a million times over than ever beg again.

"For a while I lived in a stinking shack full of rats, big brown rats that were not afraid of me; and after some time, I was not afraid of them. They became almost like pets. At least I could talk to them without a foul answer. The rain came in through the roof, the floor was muddy, and I had nothing except the clothes I stood up in. I had sold everything else to pay my bills. If my husband could have seen me, he would have taken me to heaven to join him there.

"Finally, through providence, I gave in to temptation. It was absolutely necessary. If I hadn't, my baby most probably would be dead by now.

"My life changed completely one day when, whilst begging outside the Raffles Hotel, a giant of a man came to my rescue and took pity on me. He gave me money and said I must buy food. When I thanked the man in English, he was surprised, and said, "You speak English?" and I answered, "Yes." He then said that I might be of use to him as an interpreter, and that he was a businessman farmer from Australia. He asked if I would accompany him into the Raffles Hotel where he was staying. He bought me clothes and took me to dinner. What a great experience it was for me, to be treated so kindly by this foreigner. Over dinner he told me that he was a collector of tropical seeds and plants, rare orchids, even coconut plants. These he planned to take to Australia where he managed a botanical garden. He said he would like me as a companion whilst in Singapore and would pay me money to be his interpreter. I jumped at the offer. I stayed with him at the Raffles Hotel for a whole month, during which time we visited many places in Malaya; also I acted as his guide and interpreter here in Singapore. The man was very generous. One day, on learning of my son's illness, he gave me a cheque, which covered all of my son's outstanding hospital bills. In return, I gave him companionship and the sex he wanted. I gave it to him, as best I knew how, for I had never before been with anyone other than my husband. Believe me, if that kind Australian had not asked me to have sex with him, I would have offered myself to him. That man saved both of us, my child and me. He was a married man, unfortunately, so I knew there could be no future for us. However, when he left Singapore, he gave me a generous gift of money, also enough to pay the rent at the Raffles for another month. He returned to Australia with a ship loaded with coconuts, plants and seeds. He was a fine young gentleman. But I never saw or heard from him again."

Lai Ming saw that Peter was about to interrupt her. "No. Say nothing. Let me finish," she said and continued with her narrative. "From that time on, I had to sell myself if my child and I was to survive. I gave the matter thought, but not too much thought. It had to be that way. I rented this place and immediately began bringing men here. It was easy, so many men wanted me, I had my pick. And those I take pay well.

Really, Peter, you are lucky to have me for free." Immediately she wished she had not made that last remark, but it was too late.

"I shan't come here again, Rose. If I do you'll only lose money."

"Nonsense, Peter. Don't be silly. I want you and I need you. You are very special to me. If I didn't want you, you know that I would tell you so. But let me finish my story, although there is little else to tell. I hope my son will eventually be well again. Then, I shall have to rethink my plans. But for now, providing the man is clean, treats me well, pays me what I ask and is not drunk, I must carry on my business. It's as simple as that. I have become used to this lifestyle."

Sickened and not knowing what to say, Peter remained quiet, his eyes closed.

"Believe me, I do have a goal," continued Lai Ming. "My aim is to earn as much money as possible in the shortest period of time. To succeed, I must work for many more months, perhaps two or three years more, but I shall eventually succeed in my goal. Then, Peter, my dreams will come true. Have you any idea of my intentions? Don't you remember me telling you of the house in my dreams? I am saving money until I can buy not only one villa, but two, or even three villas away from the noisy city. I shall live with my son in one of those houses. It will be our very special home. The others I shall rent out as a means of livelihood. Those are my plans, and I cannot afford anyone to get in my way. I doubt if I shall marry again, but if I can become a mistress to someone good and kind like you, then I shall. If you stay with me now, Peter, and if you return to me after the RAF, I will be your mistress, always. We would be very happy together, you know that."

"Yes, but it's too far ahead, Rose. It's the present that I'm thinking of. You and me, now."

"Do you have questions for me?"

"No. You've explained enough. I try to understand but it's very difficult."

"I am well aware of your feelings, Peter."

"Why didn't you tell me all this when we first met?"

"I was afraid to tell you. I didn't want to lose you."

"You should have explained everything to me. Perhaps I could have helped you."

"No. I don't think so. Money is the only thing that can help my baby and me. Financially, you cannot help me."

Peter remained silent, fully aware that she was speaking the truth. On his meager RAF pay he could not possibly help her. Eventually, he asked, "Why didn't you ask me for money, Rose, when you first brought me here? I am no different, neither better nor worse than other men who visit you."

"Aren't you?" Lai Ming said softly, running a hand down over his body. "Aren't you?" she repeated. "You are different, Peter. You see, when we first met, you had no idea about me. You didn't know that I sold my body. You respected me. You thought I was just a nice Chinese girl whom you'd like to befriend and make happy. Perhaps you did have thoughts of sex when we first met, which is normal. I could not read your thoughts, but I could see by your actions and speech to know that you liked my company. You liked me. You were not thinking, as most men do, about what I have between my legs.

"You did not realize that I'm a business woman. You were not like the men I meet in nightclubs, cabarets, or on the streets. They know that I'm a prostitute. They ask how much I charge." Lai Ming shrugged her shoulders, then brushed a long lock of hair aside that had fallen across her face. "They offer, and I refuse or accept. They may like me, but not love me. When their sexual desires are satisfied, I am no longer required. I don't give them love and affection as I give to you. My only interest is their money."

"So I'm just a prostitute's boy, not living on your earnings, but enjoying you while others pay?"

"Don't be silly, Peter. It is wrong for you to speak in such a manner."

"What else can you call it?" asked Peter, bitterness in his voice.

"Call it nothing. I can love as well as any other woman," Lai Ming replied fiercely.

Outside, in the street, all was quiet. The street vendors had long gone home and the street-women had returned to their beds, with or without a customer. The military police had returned to Changi, to Seletar, the naval base, and to the several army camps. Now would be a waste of time for them to patrol the red-light districts, because the military boys who were out of bounds in those areas would have already found girlfriends and would be safely shacked up for the night in the girls' rooms. In the immediate area where Lai Ming lived, only a few mongrel dogs roamed the streets. At long last Singapore slept.

PART THREE

16

"And now, to conclude, I would like to propose a toast," and lifting his glass of neat Scotch whisky, Flight Lieutenant Fordham shouted above the din, "To the catering officer, NCOs, cooks and to all the other members of the catering staff who have worked so hard to help make this day so memorable, I wish you a Merry Christmas and a very Happy New Year for 1953. Thank you, everyone, for a job well done."

With those words, Flight Lieutenant Fordham, the duty officer of the day, downed his Scotch, shook hands with the catering officer, exited the crowded ration store situated behind the airmens' mess kitchen and immediately headed for the crowded officers' mess bar where, undoubtably, he would imbibe further in celebrating this festive day.

In the huge ration store, the majority of the RAF airmens' mess cooks and other members of the catering section had congregated to relax and celebrate. Their work was indeed well done; fatigued but satisfied and happy, all were thankful that their busiest day of the year had ended. The great feast of Christmas luncheon, or tiffin as it is called in Singapore, was over. The tea meal starting at five would be a light meal consisting of cold meats, salads and fruits, prepared and served by the Chinese staff. Thus, the RAF cooks could finally relax, unwind, and drink lots of beer.

Luncheon had gone smoothly, every airman and airwoman who dined that day at RAF Changi was given a quart bottle of beer and a

211

Christmas cracker to pull. Following Christmas tradition, officers and senior NCOs acted as waiters during the meal. First up was an appetizer of steamed fresh salmon on a bed of lettuce and cucumber. This was followed by tomato soup, rich, creamy and smooth to the palate. Then came the main course with a choice of three entrées: roast Norfolk turkey with chestnut stuffing and cranberry sauce; roast goose with plum or apple sauce; and sizzling hot whole loins of pork with sage and onion stuffing. There were four different kinds of potatoes to choose from: chateaux, duchess, croquette and plain boiled new potatoes imported from Australia. Buttered Brussels sprouts, garden peas, Vichy carrots and cauliflower Polonaise were offered as vegetables; and diners could help themselves from the pans of steaming hot, rich brown gravy. And after the main course there was much more to come: piping hot Christmas pudding liberally doused in brandied custard sauce, mince pies, glazed fruits, fresh fruits and nuts.

The whole meal had been cooked in time to meet the jubilant and hungry demands of more than two thousand airmen and over two hundred WRAFs, who, with knives, forks, and spoons at the ready, had queued up noisily outside the gateway leading into the serving area. Once served, they proceeded to the two dining halls to enjoy the festive occasion. Everyone who dined at Changi that day ate and drank their fill, so much so that there was little food left over in the hot plates, and most certainly no full bottles of beer remaining on the tables.

Eventually, though, with the luncheon over, the dining halls quietened down. The diners, in various stages of intoxication, had dispersed, many to their blocks, some to the NAAFI, and others to the Malcolm Club, to celebrate further. A few, the sun-worshippers and swimmers, had gone to Changi beach. The dining halls were again empty save for the Chinese clean-up staff, picking up and sweeping away the debris of empty bottles and dirty glasses, nutshells and orange peel, paper hats, menu cards and pulled crackers.

SAC Tom Bates of the fire section became so drunk he thought he could fly. "I'm a bird. I'm a bird. I can fly," he shouted as he sprang with arms flapping from the upper balcony of the Malcolm Club. He was transported to Changi Hospital with two broken legs.

A squadron leader's car was stolen. With it went a case containing bottles of port, sherry, gin and fine Scottish whisky, also a case of Bass pale ale and a cooked stuffed turkey. The car was eventually found minus its contents, a scrawled thank-you note attached to the steering wheel.

With the main meal of the day over, a number of cooks and other members of the catering section were returning from their respective work places to block 128, many to enjoy a well-earned siesta, others to play cards and to drink more beer.

Playing cards at one bedside was Ginger Brent, the fat airmens' mess cook, Cleaver Jennings, the butcher, and two leading aircraftmen, drivers from the motor transport section. All four studied their cards and laughed and talked a lot whilst steadily consuming a whole case of Tiger beer. More cases of beer were stacked under the bed, compliments of the officers', aircrew and sergeants' messes.

WRAFs had come into the card players' conversation, when suddenly Ginger Brent got to his feet and announced, "I think I'll go over and wish them all a Merry Christmas."

"Don't be daft! Sit down!" said Cleaver.

"Yeah! Sit down, shut up and drink your beer. You'll get thrown in gaol if you put one step inside that bird cage," said one of the motor transport drivers.

"Rubbish! I'll bet you ten dollars apiece that I can walk right through their block and get away with it." Whereupon, Ginger Brent put on his shorts, and before anyone could stop him he left the catering block and was next seen walking across the road, towards the WRAF block.

By now, several members of the catering section had gone to the verandah and were watching with bated breath as Ginger entered the WRAF block. Within moments, loud, high-pitched screams could be heard coming from the building.

Ginger Brent wished a "Merry Christmas" to the surprised young

WRAF on guard duty at the entrance to the block, and then climbed a flight of stone steps that led to the second floor dormitory. Once there, he proceeded to saunter down between two rows of beds, many occupied by young women in various stages of undress.

"Merry Christmas, Jean. Merry Christmas, Joan. Merry Christmas, Mary. Happy New Year everybody," Ginger sang out as he passed between the double row of astounded WRAFs. When he reached the end of the block, having wished at least twenty young ladies a Merry Christmas, he almost collided with the fat and jolly Flight Sergeant Maggy Smith, who had stepped out of the shower, naked and dripping wet.

"A Merry Christmas and a very Happy New Year to you, Flight," sang out Ginger Brent cheerfully to the surprised flight sergeant. Grinning, he handed her a bath towel, which, with an astonished look on her face, she accepted. "Don't catch a chill, Flight," he cheekily said as he skirted around her. He then began a leisurely walk down the flight of stone stairs at the far end of the block and calmly exited the building.

On his return to the catering block he hastily took off his shorts, filled his glass with beer, lit a fag, and said, "OK, fellas, let's play cards. Remember, we've all been here for at least the past hour."

Within five minutes three RAF police corporals arrived and towered over the card players.

"OK, Brent! Get your clothes on! You're coming with us to the guardroom," said one of the police corporals officiously. He was a newcomer to Changi, putty-white and obviously just off the boat.

Everyone in the card party looked up in feigned surprise at the intrusion by the three military police, and at Christmas time too.

"Why? What for, Corp?" asked Ginger Brent.

"You know what for. For being in the WRAF block."

"Me? In the WRAF block? What are you talking about?"

"You were seen in the WRAF block just minutes ago."

"Are you serious? I've been playing cards here for over an hour. I haven't left the game, have I, chaps? Well, I did go for a quick piss, but only as far as the latrine."

"He's been playing cards with us," said Cleaver Jennings.

"He has."

"That's true."

"He's never left the game," chirped up others.

"It's Christmas, so would any of you chaps fancy a beer?" asked Cleaver, looking innocently up at the three uniform-clad policemen.

"Just get your clothes on, Brent" repeated the unsmiling police corporal. The other two police corporals were standing aside, aloof and saying nothing. They knew Brent only too well, and they knew better than to mess around with any member of the catering section; that's if they wished to eat well. At this moment they preferred to allow the newcomer to Changi to handle this tricky situation by himself.

Eventually Ginger Brent, still adamantly denying having been anywhere near the WRAF block, accompanied the three police corporals to the guardroom, where he was ordered into a cell and promptly interrogated by an SIB sergeant. Again Ginger Brent swore blind that he had never once left the catering block that afternoon.

Soon, dozens of WRAFs reported to the guardroom and identified Ginger Brent as being the intruder. But an equal number of WRAFs also showed up, who, for various reasons, didn't wish to see Ginger Brent get into serious trouble and denied having seen him.

Finally, Maggy Smith, the fat and jovial flight sergeant, arrived panting and puffing at the guardroom to have her say. "Yes, the airman that I saw in the WRAF block most certainly looked like Brent. He was ginger-haired, fat, a real slob," she admitted. "But, no, it was not Brent. Brent doesn't have the other airman's good looks." She didn't mention that on those occasions when she was orderly sergeant and making her rounds of the airmens' mess, Brent or one of the other cooks usually fixed her a grilled steak, eggs and chips, and allowed her to enjoy her meal in the privacy of the little dining room adjacent to the kitchen, that was reserved for members of the catering section.

On his release from the guardroom, with no charges preferred against him, Airman Ginger Brent returned to his card game and his Tiger beer. He didn't collect his ten dollar winnings from those who had bet against him because to a man they had stood behind him.

As for Flight Sergeant Maggy Smith, whenever she passed the servery when Ginger Brent was on duty, he would yell out, "Hey! Flight! I've seen yours!" And she would laugh and wag a disapproving finger at him.

Further west, in the city of Singapore, the Yuletide spirit was no less in evidence.

"O come, all ye faithful,
Joyful and triumphant,
O come ye, O come ye to Bethlehem."

On hearing the carol singers, Peter Saunders, on a sudden impulse, alighted from the over-crowded bus at Geylang Road. He hadn't heard carol singers for such a long time, not since celebrating Christmas two years ago at his home in Plymouth. After listening to the carol singers, he would take a taxi to Rose's home. The fare would be the same two dollars whether he took the taxi from the bus terminal at the Capitol Theatre in North Bridge Road or from here in the market square at Geylang, the last stop before the bus continued into the city centre.

Milling crowds surrounded the group of young carol singers, teenage Chinese boys and girls smartly dressed in blue neatly-pressed school uniforms. Most likely they were students from the nearby Catholic College, thought Peter. Alone, he stood among a vast crowd of happy people of mixed ages and many races, listening to the young voices of the choir. How sweetly and sincerely they sang, their open carol sheets held high in front of uplifted, joyous faces.

Half the population of Singapore appeared to be here in this market square, although, in fact, the same crowded conditions prevailed throughout much of the city. Europeans, Malays, Indians, Eurasians and Chinese jostled one another good-humouredly, shaking one another's hand while wishing each other, 'Merry Christmas.'

Goodwill towards men, thought Peter Saunders, with considerable reservation. Just two days ago he had received a letter from his mother in which she had written that Percy Savage, his best friend at Plymstock Modern Secondary School, had recently sailed with the Dorsetshire Regiment to Korea. Peter wondered how all those other unfortunates, the soldiers of the United Nations fighting at that moment on the bloody battlefields of Korea, were faring.

On this Christmas Day evening, Geylang was a tumult of noise—of shouting, laughing and singing, the blare and shriek of cardboard toy horns and trumpets, brass cymbals crashing and gongs sounding and Chinese fire-crackers exploding among the crowd. And wherever Peter Saunders turned, he heard the same joyous greeting, 'A Merry Christmas to you.' The choir was now lustily singing, 'God rest you merry, gentlemen.'

When the choir finished the carol, Peter hailed a cab, and moments later he was speeding away from Geylang towards Kallang airport and Kallang Road, a route illuminated by a million flashing, neon-lit advertising signs. The cab hooted a passage through masses of people gathered around the entrance to the Happy World Amusement Park. Then, with screeching tyres, it raced up Kallang Road, only to be stopped by traffic lights at the crossroads where the city gasworks stood. When the light changed to green, the cab immediately pulled away at a fast speed. Swerving around a stationary trolley bus, it turned sharply to the left into Crawford Street, the homes and work places of the city's ship builders. Turning to the right, it entered the beginning of long North Bridge Road, then made a left into Sumbawa Road, returned to Kallang Road, and finally entered Lavender Street. Every time Peter journeyed by taxi to Lavender Street the driver seemed to take a different route, but he didn't mind, he liked the change of scenery, and the fare was always two dollars.

As they had been all day, Peter's anxious thoughts were on Rose. A month had passed since Peter had last seen Rose and for a month he had agonized over whether to see her again or not. Part of him felt repulsed at the very thought of sharing Rose with other men but he couldn't hide from the fact that he was still very much in love with her. What would she be doing at this moment, he wondered. Would she be putting on her make-up, preparing herself for an evening soliciting at the Butterfly Club. Had she missed him?

The cab swerved violently to avoid hitting a trishaw, which without warning had turned and slowly cruised across its path. The taxi driver cursed the trishaw *wallah* in Chinese, bringing damnation upon the head of the unfortunate wretch, and shouting out the window that the man was the illegitimate son of a loused-up whore. Peter smiled to himself, thinking how strange it was that these people swore so much at one another, vulgar words that meant little to them, yet, as with this driver, their usage appeared to sooth aggravated nerves.

A provost military police jeep approached from the opposite direction, a British army patrol, with a couple of watchful, stern and unfriendly-looking redcaps seated behind the windshield. Not taking any chances, Peter slid lower in the back seat of the cab. He'd already passed a black signboard with 'OUT OF BOUNDS TO HIS MAJESTIES FORCES' written on it big red letters. Peter knew that the police could neither arrest a serviceman when in a moving vehicle nor legally raid the dwelling of a prostitute or any other abode in an out-of-bounds area without a search warrant. Nevertheless, Peter tried never to take unnecessary risks.

The redcaps in their jeep passed him by just as another military police patrol approached, this time a wagon manned by a naval shore patrol, the occupants clad completely in white—obviously they were sailors from Singapore's British Royal Naval Base. Peter sank even lower in his seat, sliding down directly behind the driver's back, noticing as he did so a boil on the man's neck that had turned septic. Pitying the man,

Peter forgot the patrol, which passed without loss of speed.

It had just turned eight o'clock; it wasn't yet dark, but dimming. Here there were neither additional bright lights nor unusually big crowds, the Christmas spirit in Lavender Street being at a minimum. The car's tyres squealed alarmingly as the taxi swerved into Bendemeer Road at a frighteningly high speed, sped a very short distance then skidded to a stop.

Another crazy Chinese taxi driver, thought Peter.

"OK Johnny?" beamed the driver, turning his head and showing off a mouthful of gold teeth.

"Yes, thanks." It being Christmas, and Peter feeling like the last of the big spenders, he pushed three dollars into the man's hand. "Merry Christmas," he said. He was now only steps away from the alley which led to Lai Ming's home.

"Thanks. You have girlfriend here, Johnny?" the taxi driver asked.

"Yes."

The driver grinned in a friendly manner. "Many boys have girlfriend here. This house make plenty good business for me," he said.

Sucking in his breath, Peter looked at the man with thoughts incommunicable raging in his mind, perceiving lucidly the many callers to this house. A knot seemed to pull taut within him, and pulsating through his muddled brain he repeatedly heard the words, 'Many boys come here. Plenty good business.' Peter's eyes, icy cold in a suddenly angry face, clashed with those of the driver's.

Startled, the driver averted his gaze from those angry eyes, wondering how his few words spoken merely as idle conversation to his passenger could bring forth such enmity.

However, just as suddenly as Peter had felt anger he relaxed and sighed. "Thanks for the ride, Johnny," he found himself good-humouredly saying in Chinese.

The driver, noting the sudden change and surprised by his passenger's knowledge of Chinese, quickly took a philosophical view of the situation. Now he could make amends for anything wrong he had said. "A good girl, that one, Johnny. All taxi boys are friend of Ming. She has a big heart and a true smile. We know her well," he said, in Cantonese.

Peter, nodding his head in agreement, replied, "Yes, she is a good girl." He gave the serious-faced driver a wry grin. "Perhaps you and I will meet again one day," he said, lifting a hand in a salute of friendship as he stepped from the cab. "Cheers, Johnny. Merry Christmas."

The driver's head nodded in the affirmative, answering the salute by a wave of his hand and a parting farewell grin which displayed again his mouthful of gold teeth, Peter counted six but felt sure there were more. The cab moved away, quickly gathering speed as it headed towards the junction of Boon Keng Road. "Good boy for Ming," the driver muttered to himself. "Bit crazy but good boy."

Peter Saunders looked down the length of the short alleyway, and then up at the shuttered window on the upper floor, the third window on the left above the sidewalk pillar. Up there was her room, quiet, in darkness, and strangely fascinating and mysterious. Suddenly he became keyed up and nervous. Supposing a man was with her! What would he do and what would he say, he wondered. Anxiously, he walked down the alleyway until he reached the green door at the far end. Softly he knocked his usual knock, the knock Rose had taught him. Then he waited, nervously and with a pounding heart.

Creaking on rusty hinges, the big door swung slowly ajar, just enough for Peter to see the wizened face of Wan Ze, the old *amah*, peering at him through the gloom of the kitchen darkness. At first she appeared as if puzzled. Then, on realizing that it was Peter standing outside the door, she opened it fully, a big smile suddenly appearing on her wrinkled face. She looked just the same as when he had last seen her a month ago. Her greying long hair was done up in a bun on the crown of her head, and she was wearing her usual garb, a black *samfoo*, the pajama-type costume comprising loose black cotton trousers and a jacket with a collar buttoned at the neck.

"Hello, Momma. How's tricks?" Peter greeted the old woman in English. He then said in Chinese. "Good evening, Momma. How are you?"

Surprised at seeing him, the old *amah*'s face cracked into so many wrinkles it became one mass of tiny creases. She had liked Peter from the very first moment she met him. He had always spoken nicely to her, in English that she did not understand, but also in Chinese, which he seemed to have no difficulty in learning. Always respectful to her, he was never rude in his speech, nor did he make rude gestures at her like so many of Ming's clients. And he was never drunk or rough. Well, except for that one occasion but that was understandable under the circumstances, she had decided. What she infinitely more appreciated, and what was more beneficial to her, was this boy's thoughtful generosity, his gifts of money to buy food for her and for her ailing, bedridden son who had tuberculosis. In addition, this boy had regularly given him his twice-monthly ration of free cigarettes, plus perfumed soap, chocolates and many other little gifts that were far beyond her financial means. Sardines in tins he had often brought her, and tins of herrings too, some in oil and others in tomato sauce; delicacies shared by her and her dying son, luxuries she could never afford. He had also brought her eggs, packets of tea and tinned fruit. Seldom had he missed bringing her a gift of some sort on his frequent visits to Ming, her mistress.

"*Wah!* Chicko! How are you?" She spoke slowly through creased smiles. "*Aiyah!* Come in!" she invited. And when he had entered the kitchen, she said, "Very pleased to see you again, Chicko," and nodding her head towards the stairway, and clasping her hands over her flat tummy, she bowed to him as if in reverence.

So Rose was up there, the *amah* was telling him to go to her. "Thank you, Momma," Peter murmured. Slipping off his shoes, he crept noiselessly up the narrow stairway until he reached the small landing at the top. Peter felt sure that Lai Ming would be alone in her room. The *amah* would never have allowed him entry into the house, much less so graciously invite him up those stairs had there been a customer with her mistress. Furthermore, if Lai Ming had departed for the evening, the *amah* would have told him so. Lai Ming just had to be in her room.

His heart pounding, his nerves on edge, he paused for a moment before knocking softly on the fragile wicker door. As there was no answer, he slid the unlocked door to one side and drew back the heavy curtain.

Inside, the shutters and the drawn cotton blinds had darkened the room, so much so that Peter had to wait awhile until his eyes adjusted to the gloom. He sniffed the air. Her perfume greeted him. How well he had come to know that exotic, exciting fragrance. He walked to the window and opened one of the two shutters, just enough to allow the moon to filter in its silvery rays.

Lai Ming lay asleep and alone on her bed. A deep sigh of relief escaped Peter, his nervousness left him and he suddenly felt relaxed. He smiled to himself as he gazed lovingly down upon her. She lay in sleep as would a playful kitten exhausted by its frolicking; curled up, her black hair flowing over one of the two pillows which had 'Good Morning' embroidered on them. She slept peacefully in the centre of the big bed, her body naked except for a multi-coloured *sarong* of browns, greens and gold, which covered her buttocks and waist in a single swathe. Peter was sorely tempted to bend over her and kiss those small breasts, which rhythmically rose and fell to her peaceful breathing. But no, he ought not to disturb her. Feeling much sadness, he gazed down upon the girl he loved. Here, lying so still and unprotected was the first and only woman he had ever really known. How small and frail she appeared to be, lying so quiet and without movement upon that bed. To think that fate had brought such grief and misery upon her. Peter leaned over the sleeping little figure and pressed his lips to a warm cheek. "Hello, Rose," he whispered in her ear.

At first she must have thought she was dreaming because she smiled in her sleep but did not open her eyes, not for several moments. Then puzzlement appeared on her face and her eyelids flickered open.

"Hello, Rose," Peter repeated softly, smiling down at the surprised face. "It's me, Peter."

Now she was rolling over onto her back, but not taking her eyes from his.

"Is it really you, Peter?" she asked.

"Yes, it's me. Were you expecting someone else?"

She didn't answer, but instead said, "So you have come back to me."

"I have given the whole matter thought, Rose, much thought." Peter became silent, not knowing what else to say.

"You think too much. You always think too much," Lai Ming said, a touch of annoyance in her voice.

"I know, Rose. I can't help it."

"Well! No think!"

"I'll try not to," Peter said, sitting down on the edge of the bed. "I've missed you."

"Have you, Peter?"

"Yes. Very much."

"I have missed you, too."

"You have?" He sat gazing down at his stockinged feet as if they held all the answers. "Rose, shall we begin again?" he finally asked.

"No, Peter. We cannot begin again."

"No! Why not?" He was genuinely surprised and taken aback by her abrupt answer.

He felt her arm encircle his waist. "Peter, we cannot begin again something never finished."

The realization of her words sank in causing Peter to give a big sigh with relief.

"I expected you to return to me sometime today," she said matter-of-factly. "That is why I am not ready to go out."

Surprised by her words, Peter said, "I don't understand you, Rose. Why today?"

"Because today is Kissmus, a happy time for you," replied Lai Ming, her face serious for the moment. "But I had much feelings you would not be happy not loving me today. You have many friends at the camp but you still feel lonely and in need of me. Holiday times can be lonely times especially at Kissmus. I knew you would be lonely for me. I expected you

223

to come back today. It was today or never. Lie down by my side, Peter," she commanded him, and Peter lay, even more surprised, for he saw that she had begun to cry. "I knew you would return to me. It has been a long, long wait, but I knew you would come back to me someday," she sobbed, laughing through her tears.

With his hands on her bare bottom pressing her naked body tightly to him, he kissed her on the nose, laughed and said, "Where would you like to go?"

"Oh! Any place you like. First go see Kissmus lights, then go some place nice to eat big feast."

"There's a brand new club open for servicemen directly opposite the Raffles Hotel," said Peter. "I've heard it's a first class place—good food, dancing, bars, a swimming pool, everything. Let's spend the evening there."

"Yes, that I would like," assured Lai Ming, but still preferring to spend the evening at home. "What is the name of the club? I have seen it, a great red brick building, but I don't know its name."

"It's called The Britannia Club."

"The Britannia Club," Lai Ming repeated.

"Yes. It's really a NAAFI."

"What is a 'naafi'?

Peter laughed and cuddled her. He was so very happy at being with her again. "Oh, you're a little dope, Rose. NAAFI is the abbreviation for Navy, Army and Air Force Institutes. It's for the convenience of rabble like me. It's a club for servicemen and their guests. I've not been in the Britannia Club yet."

"Then we spend our Kissmus evening in NAAFI, Peter. I like everything you like. But it is necessary to spend good time here first," she laughed, her face aglow. "First I make tea and bring biscuits."

"No! After!"

"After what?" Lai Ming teased.

"You know what after."

"Oh, Peter, you're so impatient," and Lai Ming giggled, knowing that she wanted him as much as he wanted her.

Thus they remained, in sheer bliss, locked together, having beautiful sex and reunited.

Seeping from a neighbor's radio through the thin walls into the quietness of that little room could be heard a Christmas carol sung by a female choir, softly sweetly and full of sincerity of devotion.

"Silent night! Holy night!
Where was dark all is light.
Angels to the shepherd sing.
Glory to the new born King.
Peace. Goodwill to men.
Peace. Goodwill to men."

Listening, each with their own thoughts, Lai Ming and Peter remained silent, not wishing to break the spell of that moment.

"Silent night! Holy night!
Guiding star shine ever bright.
While the eastern Magi bring
Gifts and homage to our King.
Peace. Goodwill to men.
Peace. Goodwill to men."

"Girls from Shanghai," whispered Lai Ming, so quietly as if not wishing to interrupt those angelic voices infiltrating into that darkened room.

"I know," Peter whispered. "They sing beautifully. I love listening to them." When stationed at Kai Tak in Hong Kong, while lying in his bed at night, he would often listen to the singing of these same girls. Originally members of a Catholic choir in Shanghai, they had been expelled from their homeland when the Communist regime came to power. Now they were spending Christmas singing in Singapore, on tour from Hong Kong.

How sweetly and clearly these girls now sang, like mocking birds singing out of sheer joy after a fall of rain. Yet, when Peter concentrated on those uplifted voices praising God and the newborn King, he detected sadness in them. He closed his eyes to enjoy listening to the last verse. It was as if a host of angels were singing to just the two of them.

> "Silent night! Holy night.
> May we know thy delight.
> And with angels may we sing
> Glory to the new born King.
> Peace. Goodwill to men.
> Peace. Goodwill to men."

The girls' voices faded softly away and quietness stole a place in the room again. Rose knew several of the words she had heard but had no understanding of the meaning of the carol. She was Buddhist and did not know the Christian story. "Peace," she whispered to Peter. "Peace for everybody."

"Yes. Peace and goodwill to all men." And Peter sighed. "Peace, yes, but goodwill is first required from us all," he said.

The high pitched whine of a lone mosquito came close to Peter's ear. He put an arm around Lai Ming so that again she lay snuggled in his arms. He would not go out this night. The Britannia Club could wait. He would spend his Christmas at home, with Rose.

17

The weeks following the reunion between Peter Saunders and Lai Ming slipped quickly by. Christmas 1952 and the New Year's Day of 1953 were but memories and already the calendar had turned to February, with Singapore's Chinese population preparing to celebrate Lunar New Year.

Crashing cymbals, clanging gongs, blaring trumpets and shrieks from reed pipes heralded in that joyous occasion. The Chinese population feasted and made merry, drank each other's health and slipped into one another's hands 'hong bao', small red envelopes containing a lucky coin representing wealth and good luck throughout the New Year.

When Peter arrived at Lai Ming's home that day, she was dressed in a new, bright-red *cheongsam* and greeted him with a hug and a kiss and pressed a hong bao into his hand. "*Gung Hee Fatt Choy,*" she said in Cantonese, smiling up at him lovingly. "Happy New Year, Peter."

"Thank you," Peter answered. "*Gung Hee Fatt Choy*. Here's wishing you a very healthy, happy and prosperous New Year, Rose, and the same to both of us." Shyly, he handed her a similar gift of red paper. His hong bao, however, did not enclose a Malayan coin within its folds. Instead, it contained a lucky English silver threepenny piece; like one of those his mother always included in her Christmas puddings. Having explained in a letter home that the coin was needed as a gift to Rose, his mother had sent him a silver coin, a threepenny bit in mint condition.

Delighted with the little silver coin that now lay in the palm of her hand, Lai Ming exclaimed, "Thank you, Peter, I shall always treasure this hong bao," and, leaning forward, she kissed him on the lips.

Their gifts exchanged, Lai Ming poured rice wine into two tiny glasses and thus, together, they toasted the Chinese New Year, celebrating the festive occasion at home. Consequently, the Chinese New Year also came and went, to become yet another happy memory.

Lai Ming took great delight in showing Peter the sights of Singapore, the whole island having much to offer. Lai Ming loved the picture houses, and these they visited often; occasionally they visited one of the three amusement parks—Happy World, Great World, or New World in the eastern part of the city. Peter was not too keen on these places of pleasure because they were generally crowded and always noisy. Being an outdoor person he preferred quieter entertainment, such as visiting the spacious Botanical Gardens, where he loved to wander among the many acres of plant life and in a jungle where monkeys played.

At the Padang they spent happy hours watching cricket matches and football games. Amused, Peter would watch Lai Ming clap her hands as she screamed encouragement to her favourite football team.

Excursions to Bedok, where they would picnic on the beach and swim in the warm open sea, was yet another pastime they enjoyed.

On one occasion Lai Ming asked Peter to take her inside St Andrew's Cathedral, saying that she had often been tempted to enter the big Christian House, or 'big Kisstian House' as she pronounced it, but had not dared. Peter was delighted by her suggestion. He had often seen the Cathedral from the outside but had also never ventured in. So together, on a quiet weekday afternoon, along a gravel path which crunched under their feet, they strolled hand in hand through beautifully kept grounds surrounding that impressive white building standing amid a setting of age-old trees. They entered the Cathedral through a heavy wooden door and walked up the long, carpeted aisle towards the altar. With his back to them, a Chinese youth was playing a cheerful hymn on the organ, perhaps rehearsing for a wedding, and far too absorbed in his music to notice their approach. Interested and curious of all she saw around her, questions flowed from Lai Ming. Peter answered her as best he could.

On yet another day they visited the Hindu Temple in South Bridge Road, a typical South Indian temple, its archways and roof profusely decorated with groups of animals and human figures carved in miniature and painted in vivid colours. From there they took a trishaw to the mosque in North Bridge Road close by Arab Street, its lofty minarets and majestic domes rising and towering above the flotsam of its surroundings. Then on to Tiong Bahru to an interesting little temple on a hillside, standing next to boat-building yards and sail-maker shops. The homes of the craftsmen who worked in the area were built close by, picturesque *atap* and wooden houses set on stilts on the side of a waterway.

One day, while passing through Race Course Road, they came upon another temple. "I like show you," said Lai Ming. So they dismounted from their trishaw and stepped inside the building. Peter, amazed at all he saw there, wished he had brought his camera. An enormous Buddha, crowned by a halo studded with hundreds of brilliant white lights, sat as if in contemplation on an altar. Majestically he sat, still and silent, with vacant unseeing eyes, yet eyes which seemed to look right through him. For several moments Peter was awestruck and unable to take his eyes from that calm, inscrutable ivory face.

In this house of worship, Peter asked the questions, many of which Lai Ming could not answer.

They visited Clifford Pier, Raffles Place, Collyer Quay—all places Peter might not have visited had he not had Lai Ming as his knowledgeable and charming guide. They took walks together along the wide and long Esplanade situated next to the Padang. There they listened to the lapping of the waves on the foreshore below, and watched sleek liners, a variety of merchant ships, huge oil tankers and many other vessels, big and small, lying at anchor beyond the detached harbour. Inside the harbour, smaller vessels—the water carriers, tramps, tugs, junks, *sampans* and the many customs gunboats—maneuvered in the Inner Roads, weaving crazy patterns upon the surface of the water.

One interesting afternoon was spent in that fine, historical building, the Raffles Museum and Library, standing mightily in a picturesque setting enriched by the avenue of swaying palms, recently mown lawns, thick-trunked trees at the entrance, and a host of green bushes festooned in sweet-scented pink blossoms ringing the building. Lai Ming chatted and laughed happily at Peter's side, pointing at the stuffed monkeys, then passing on to where the bear with its family of cubs were at play.

Another afternoon, Lai Ming suggested a visit to Haw Par Villa, or as it is more commonly called, the Tiger Balm Gardens. These famous gardens, situated on the west of the island, consist of seven acres of wonderland known the world over. Equally well-known are its owners, Mr Aw Boon Haw and Mr Aw Boon Par, whose names when translated into English literally mean 'tiger' and 'leopard' respectively. These two well-loved and respected men financed the building of Haw Par Villa.

Peter readily agreed to Lai Ming's suggestion, especially as he had already enjoyed a visit to another of the three Tiger Balm Gardens in the Far East, the one in Hong Kong.

Shortly after Peter had finished an enjoyable lunch of shrimp salad and a Carlsberg beer, Wan Ze shouted up the stairs that she had hailed a cab and that it was waiting for them at the end of the alleyway. It was always safer for the *amah* to hail the cab than for Peter to wait in full view on the corner of Lavender Street and Bendemeer Road.

From Lavender Street the taxi turned right into Kallang, sped down Victoria Street and New Bridge Road, then turned left into Keppel Road with the Empire Docks and West Wharf on the left and the railway station to the right. A few minutes later they were at Pasir Panjang where the narrow road ran between the beach and the sloping entrance leading up to the well-tended Tiger Balm Gardens.

On exiting the taxi a mob of unofficial guides approached them. Lai Ming, waving them aside, purchased a guide leaflet from a stall at the entrance. Hand in hand they walked up a concrete path beneath an elaborately decorated archway built over the incline at the entrance leading up to the villa. There was no entrance fee. They had only to pass the guard at the gate, a ferocious tiger about to spring, fortunately lifeless, man-made and harmless. As they passed the tiger, Lai Ming laughed and said, "Here is the guardian big cat. He looks at us with anger but allows us to pass unharmed."

Thus, the two stepped into another world, a world of fantasy and make-believe, the work of specially engaged artisans brought from China who had created scenes depicting ancient Chinese stories in many forms—of statues and shrines, flowers, shrubs and trees, animals, birds and reptiles of many varied species.

"Almost every scene you will see here in this garden depicts an ancient Chinese story, also our history," said Lai Ming. "I shall do my best to explain, but also you must read the paper. I think you will find the Tiger Balm Gardens interesting."

Peter laughed light-heartedly. "I'm sure I shall," he said.

Once inside, they worked their way upward along a path flanked by porcelain dragons, sculptured rocks and shapely trees, all hand-carved. Soon they came upon gigantic, life-size, as well as miniature, carvings of men, beasts and reptiles, some in forms of unnatural life of which Peter couldn't grasp a meaning. Lai Ming did her best to explain.

Branching away from the main path, off to the right and walking on flagstones, they worked their way further upward amid squatting, giant brown and green bullfrogs with big, bulging eyes, and with monstrous lizards crawling all over them. Also, there were huge turtles, enormous pythons about to strike, open-jawed crocodiles, monkeys at play, rats at war, birds upon boughs, fish in ponds, swans amid lily pads, all life-like, artificial and man-made. There were mermaids combing flowing tresses while basking in the sunshine on rocks, while above them, nude little boys cast fishing lines hopefully into the water. Then they came upon a gorilla, huge and ferocious-looking, with eyes filled with hate, sitting upon the fallen trunk of a tree.

Peter, puzzled by a scene even more so than by others, stopped, stared and studied it. A huge white sow lay on her side suckling not piglets but instead a variety of young animals, though not one of the same species: a bear cub, a kitten, a tiger cub, a baby rat and a puppy.

"How strange, Rose!" Peter exclaimed, puzzled. "Can you explain this to me?"

"Oh, yes! I can," Lai Ming answered, laughing. "Mother pig is feeding what represents all the animals of the forest."

"Why?"

"Because it is a Buddhist symbol. It means much. The best I can describe this scene is that it depicts being charitable to the needy, to be patient and tolerant to all."

"Hmm. Perhaps an animal can be so inclined, but I doubt whether humans will ever attain such merit. Many are too selfish."

"Yes. It is sad, but you speak the truth," said Lai Ming.

Next, they stopped where a fierce battle raged between white rats and black rats. "Here, for example," said Lai Ming, "the moral of this scene is to show how senseless it is to fight because the other is of a different colour."

Resuming their walk, with Lai Ming leading the way, they reached a narrow entrance to a man-made cavern. Lai Ming turned and beckoned Peter to follow her into the cavern, which he did. "Here, in these works of art, is the story of the soul being judged after the death of the body," she said. "I think you will find it interesting."

"The whole place looks like a torture chamber to me," said Peter as he looked about him.

"Yes, you are correct. It is a torture chamber, a place where those who committed sins in life are punished."

"Hey! Don't rush me," Peter exclaimed, laughing. "I must fathom this out."

A plaque on the wall proclaimed in both Chinese and English, "The Purgatory, where punishment in torture form is allotted out to the souls of the dead for the sins committed when with life. The souls of the sinners are judged by ten courts."

Together, Lai Ming and Peter Saunders visited each of the ten courts and ten punishment cells.

In one, a monk who had paid visits to brothels was being sawn in half for his sins. In another, a habitual liar was having his tongue cut out. Adulterers were being thrown into a vat of boiling oil, a devil standing by fanning the flames. A woman procurer of young girls into a life of prostitution against their will was being disembowelled while strapped to a stake. Corrupt officials were being pounded in a pit of nails. A woman who ill-treated her stepdaughter was suffering her fate in Hades by having her heart and liver cut out. Males who frequented gambling houses were either thrown into an inferno or grilled to a crisp on a hollow bronze pillar with a great fire inside it.

As the couple approached the tenth judge, Peter chuckled, wondering which of the ten fates would finally befall him.

All punishments having been meted out, the souls were lined up to await their turn to be fed a great spoonful of 'the tea of oblivion' proffered by an old woman. Once taken, the world they had recently passed through is forgotten, and their souls are spun out of the so-called 'spinning wheel of life'. But now they are in the form of some other living matter; perhaps as a human being, or maybe this time as a bird, or a fish, an animal, an insect, anything that is living, depending on the life led in the last world and sins committed.

The afternoon being hot and humid, they paused for a while to sit and relax in the shade of a great green breadfruit tree, enjoying orange drinks bought from a stall at the side of the winding path. When rested they continued their sightseeing tour of the gardens.

Birds, beasts, idols, they were everywhere. A phoenix, the legendary 'bird of fire' stood proudly on a rock with wings outstretched. There were foxes and wild boar in typical fauna of the Malayan jungle, all man-made. Lai Ming and Peter stopped to study a miniature Chinese garden with tiny figures of man and animals, flowers and trees, and palaces and tiny temples of worship; all beautiful works of art. Peter marvelled at everything he saw at the Tiger Balm Gardens.

Finally, the two climbed to the highest point in the gardens and from there looked down upon all that they had seen, a fantasy land perhaps, but everything in that garden, and almost every scene depicted there had a story and a moral behind it, stories going back thousands of years in Chinese history.

Peter would never forget that enjoyable afternoon with Rose chatting so carefree and happily at his side.

18

"When the March winds doth blow, we shall have snow. Or shall we?" said LAC Peter Saunders looking up at a cloudless blue sky. "I don't think so, eh, Charlie?"

"No. That's for damned sure. At times I've wished that it would snow. I'm sick of this bloody heat," said Peter's lanky companion, Corporal Charlie Brown, an RAF military police dog-handler, as they left the airmens' mess together and walked along the concrete path that led to the road.

"This climate suits me," said Peter Saunders. "I feel like a monkey with its balls frozen off when in cold weather. You know, Charlie, I'm dreading returning to sunny Devon where it rains six days out of seven, and on the seventh it pisses down. Rain! That's just about all we get, there's seldom sunshine."

"You can give me rain anytime instead of this blasted heat. It gives me such a headache. I've got a headache now, throbbing as though I've been belted by a sledge-hammer, and my whole body feels as if it's burning up."

"Christ! No wonder, Charlie. You've really caught the sun. You're as red as a beetroot. What happened?"

"It's my own fault, Pete. After I came off duty this morning, I went to the beach for a dip and then fell asleep on the sand. I must have lain there for two or three hours. I caught far too much sun."

"You can say that again, Charlie. You're baked. You should go to the sick quarters and get something for that sunburn, and for your headache."

"You think I should?"

"Of course you should. One of the medical orderlies will put you right."

"I doubt it," said dog-handler Corporal Charlie Brown. "Not the way I bloody-well feel."

What a difference in size there was between the two airmen walking side by side along that concrete path. Five foot four and slight of build, LAC Peter Saunders barely reached Corporal Charlie Brown's shoulders who, at nineteen, was extremely tall, six foot six and still growing. Corporal Brown, with his tea mug and eating irons in hand, having just eaten at the airmens' mess, was wearing his KD uniform, white webbing, white gaiters, a white police hat with the RAF badge fixed to the front of it, and very shiny black boots. He was not wearing his revolver, and would not be wearing it until he reported for his next duty and signed for it and his dog at the guardroom.

Peter, dressed in his civvies, was walking to the bus stop overlooking the main runway on Changi Road. He was going to Lai Ming's home and would not be returning to camp until lunchtime the next day. That morning he had worked the early shift at the sergeants' mess until Sergeant Muldoon showed up, which was well after two in the afternoon. He had then returned to the catering block where he showered and changed his clothes, and as it was already five o'clock and tea time at the airmens' mess, he had stopped awhile to eat a light meal of bread and jam and drink a cup of tea. Now, on leaving the airmens' mess, he had met Corporal Charlie Brown, who had just finished his tea, and together they walked towards the road.

Just three months ago, Corporal Charlie Brown completed his RAF police training in England and was immediately posted together with his police dog, Wicked Witch, to RAF Changi. A happy-go-lucky type, Charlie made friends easily, including Peter Saunders and several other members of the catering section. He was always ready to indulge in a good yarn-spinning hour in the airmens' mess at night with the duty cooks, over a mug of tea and slabs of buttered toast.

Still discussing Charlie's sunburn, the two reached the road. Good-naturedly, Peter said, "You moon-men will never learn. You come out here thinking you can play around with Mister Sun. Well, you can't! You've got to take it easy, Charlie. Work up to it. First get acclimatized and then eventually you'll be able to safely lie around all day. This sun is hell."

"Don't I know it. Got a match on you, Pete?"

"Nope. You know I don't smoke, Charlie."

"Aw, that's right. I forgot. Perhaps a smoke will clear this lousy head of mine. I feel as dizzy as hell and as sick as a dog."

"Well, I've given you my advice. Go up to sickquarters and get something for it. Then go to bed and get some kip."

"I wish I could get some kip, but I'm on duty at nine over at the signals section. I won't see my bed until six or seven tomorrow morning. Going to visit your girlfriend?"

"Yep."

"Lucky bugger. I wish I had a girlfriend out here."

"What about your girlfriend at home?"

"She's not here. And I've still more than a year to do before I return to good old Blighty and get demobbed. This two years of National Service has really screwed me up. It seems a lifetime."

"Time passes quickly. Too quickly."

"Maybe for you but I count the months, the weeks, even the days, and I mark them off on a calendar. Tour ex seems an eternity away."

"The way you're going about it, it will seem that way. Don't look at the calendar. You'll be surprised at how time flies."

"For you but not for me."

The two were now walking along the road, had already passed the WRAF block and were approaching the Malcolm Club, when Charlie Brown said, "I'm going into the club, Pete, to buy a box of matches and get a cold drink. It may do this head of mine some good. Christ! I was crazy to fall asleep on the beach."

The two parted company, Corporal Charlie Brown branching off to the left and striding towards the Malcolm Club, while LAC Peter Saunders followed the road which led to the bus stop.

His conversation with the police dog-handler already gone from his mind, Peter was now considering how to spend the afternoon and where to take Rose. The weather was perfect, neither too hot nor too humid, just the right day to enjoy a visit to someplace outside the city. He remembered Rose had mentioned how much she enjoyed their visit to the Botanical Gardens. However, on looking at his watch, he realized it was far too late for such an excursion. By now he had almost reached the bus stop.

Meanwhile, Corporal Brown had entered the Malcolm Club, bought a box of matches and an orangeade at the bar, then had settled back in an easy chair and relaxed his burning body. He was thinking how foolish he had been to fall asleep on the hot sand at the beach, with the sun blazing down upon his body and him wearing nothing but shorts. His throbbing headache had worsened and now he felt strangely light-headed, and his eyes were not focussing properly. Everything around him was blurred. He wiped his eyes with his fingers in an attempt to clear them. Suddenly feeling cold and shivery, as if he had a fever, he wiped sweat from his brow, noticing as he did this that his hand was trembling uncontrollably.

Gulping down the ice-cold orangeade, he lit a cigarette, drew on it and closed his eyes. The cigarette might steady his nerves, he thought. But now he felt another sensation, like pins and needles creeping into the throbbing headache. He noticed the Chinese barman staring at him. Perhaps the barman was thinking he had a bad hangover. Charlie forced a grin and the barman turned away and went about his business.

An hour later, Corporal Brown lifted himself with difficulty from the chair, and stood holding onto the table, swaying slightly, and feeling as if he was about to vomit. He decided to return to the police block, take a shower, a couple of aspirin, and try to sleep for a few hours before reporting for duty.

The RAF Malay Regiment motor transport (MT) driver stroked his chin and looked enquiringly across the clearing to where Corporal Charlie Brown, the police guard, sat as if in deep meditation, alone, except for Wicked Witch, who lay quietly at his feet. A full Malayan moon shone down upon Charlie Brown, glittering on his highly polished brasses and causing his white military police hat to resemble a big white plate upon his bowed head.

"Corporal Brown sure has a cob on tonight," said the Malay driver, turning his head and speaking to the airman who sat with legs outstretched upon an empty crate outside the signals hut. "He was acting kind of strange when I drove him here. Said he had a bad headache."

"He told me the same," said his companion, LAC Roberts of the Signals Section. "Looks to me as if he's had too much sun. He looks ill."

"Yeah. He looks bad. He shouldn't be on duty."

"I'm thinking the same. He's never acted like this before."

"No, he hasn't. He's usually the most cheerful of the bunch. Normally I'm glad when it's his turn to keep watch down here."

"Me too. But he hasn't said a dickybird tonight though, except to tell me he has a headache."

The Malay MT driver said, "Perhaps he's got woman trouble. Maybe he hasn't heard from his girlfriend lately."

"This is not woman trouble. Charlie's definitely ill," said LAC Roberts. "I think I'll call the guardroom and explain the situation. Maybe they'll send a replacement."

"If they do send a replacement, Charlie could be charged with self-inflicted injuries for getting so badly sunburned."

"True. I'd hate to get him into trouble. But he's in a bloody bad state," said Roberts.

"Why don't we wait until the orderly officer makes his rounds?" suggested the MT driver. "He should be here within the hour. Let him decide what's best to do."

The three men—LAC Roberts, the duty signaler, AC Hamid, RAF Malay Regiment duty MT driver, and Corporal Brown, RAF police dog-handler—were on duty at the little signals hut which stood in a clearing half-way between the far end of the number two runway and a row of tall coconut palms fronting the beach. To the right of the Signals Section hut were swamps. Corporal Brown and Wicked Witch's duty was to guard the signals hut and its radio operator LAC Roberts. It was considered a cushy number, especially at night, a tea-drinking job where one could relax, talk, play cards and await incoming radio signals. That was a normal night's work. Tonight, however, an uneasy atmosphere hung over the section, all because the police dog-handler was not his usual friendly self.

Corporal Charlie Brown sat silently several yards away from the other two, holding his head in his hands. At his feet lay Wicked Witch, a vicious, black and grey Alsatian trained to kill, her long tongue dripping saliva and hanging loose from gaping jaws. She looked up intermittently and with uneasy eyes at her master, seemingly aware that all was not well with him. Eventually she gave a great yawn, rested her head upon a highly polished boot and studied her master with savage eyes, yet Corporal Brown saw in them only tenderness. He dropped a hand and gently stroked the great head that lay across his feet and breaking his silence said, "Witch, you're a faithful bastard. You know when I'm down, don't you, even when nobody else cares."

The dog yawned her agreement.

"Well, you're the master tonight, not me," said Charlie Brown.

At one o'clock in the morning, a full moon and a galaxy of stars shone their brilliance down upon that two-acre clearing, lighting up the signals hut as if it were already daytime, and all was quiet except for the occasional loud croaking of bullfrogs coming from the nearby swamps.

With no signals coming through, it had been a quiet night so far for

LAC Reggy Roberts. Having taken off his earphones, he now sat on an empty, upturned electrical cable crate in the doorway of the wireless cabin, holding a mug of tea in one hand and in the other an open book, which rested on his knees. It was an interesting book, in his opinion one of the greatest sea stories of all time, *Mutiny on the Bounty* written by Charles Nordhoff and James Norman Hall. But, although halfway through the book, Reggy Roberts could not concentrate on reading it further—tonight he was too concerned about Charlie Brown's unusual behaviour.

Aircraftman Hamid, the young RAF Malay Regiment duty driver, had been with Roberts these past two hours. His job was to shuttle guards and other military personnel to and from outlying posts. Not needed for at least another hour, he was killing time at the quietest location of his detailed route. He now stood leaning with his back against a window ledge of the hut, his handsome brown face catching the full light of the moon.

"He simply said he wished to be left alone," said AC Hamid. "I can't understand the fellow at all. I'll be glad when the orderly officer shows up."

"You and me both," agreed LAC Roberts.

Suddenly, Corporal Brown's head ceased to ache, and with the same suddenness his vision returned to normal and everything around him became clear. He was his usual happy and healthy self again, relaxed and able to enjoy the tranquillity of this beautiful moonlit night. Yet, in his seemingly clear mind, something nagged at him, something he could not grasp. His mind churned. What was it, he wondered. Was it something he must do, or something he would like to do? Then it dawned on him. He had promised his dog a visit to the city. Now would be the time to keep his promise, to walk the lighted streets of the city with Wicked Witch at his side. He'd show her people hurrying to and fro, flashing neon signs, open shops, cars, everything. But it was late, much too late. Or was it, he wondered. He rubbed a sweaty hand across a hot, perspiring brow. Was it too late? Suddenly his mind was made up. No, he decided, it was not too late. Why shouldn't Wicked Witch visit the city and see the lights? "Good old Wicked Witch. Faithful bastard. Good dog," he muttered to himself, bending and patting the dog's back. "You're going to see the lights of Singapore, old girl, and no one's going to stop us. And if they try?" and on his face there was now the look of a madman. "But no one will stop us. Tonight we shall see the lights." Corporal Brown rose slowly to his feet. "Driver!" he called out. "Come here."

"What's up, Charlie?" asked the Malay driver.

"I said, come here."

"Yeah. OK. I'm coming."

"'Yes, Corporal,' when you speak to me," snapped Charlie in a unfamiliarly stern voice.

"Yes, Corporal, when you speak to me," whispered the driver to LAC Roberts. "What's wrong with him? I don't like this, Reg."

"Nor me," said the puzzled signals operator.

"Come here, airman! At the double," shouted Corporal Charlie Brown.

"Yes, Corporal. I'm coming," said the bewildered Malay driver. Walking slowly across the clearing to where the dog-handler stood, he stopped in alarm when he drew near enough to see crazed eyes in a drawn face glaring angrily at him.

"You took your time coming," snapped the corporal. "Let's see if you can get a move on. Drive me and my dog into Singapore," he ordered.

On hearing the command, the driver's face showed amazement. "When, Corporal?" he asked nervously.

"Now, of course."

"But I can't, Corporal."

"Can't! Why not?"

"Are you crazy? You're on duty. And so am I."

"I said drive us into Singapore, Airman. You understand me, don't you?"

"But, Corporal!" and Hamid looked in bewilderment over to where the radio operator sat listening.

LAC Roberts butted into the conversation. "He can't do that, Charlie, and you know it."

"Rap up, you!"

"The orderly officer will be around soon, Charlie. You can't go off and leave your post, just like that," loudly protested the radio operator.

"I said, rap up. Shut your face or I'll shut it for you. I'm going to see the lights and so is my dog. Get over to your wagon and get the engine started," he ordered the driver.

"Christ, Charlie, you're crazy," shouted Roberts, the operator.

"Shut up! Get moving, driver."

"I can't leave here, except to take you to the guardroom or to the hospital," said the exasperated driver. "How about I take you tomorrow when we're both off duty?"

"No! You'll take me now."

"I can't."

"By hell! You will!"

"No, Corporal, I won't. Reg, ring up the guardroom. I think Corporal Brown is ill or something."

"Don't touch that phone, Roberts," the dog-handler ordered.

In dismay, both Roberts and the Malay driver watched as Corporal Charlie Brown's hand drop to his revolver holster, unbutton it and withdraw from it his heavy service revolver. The next moment the weapon was levelled at the now fearful driver.

"Don't be a fool. Put that away. Don't play games with that thing," shouted Roberts.

"I'm giving you to the count of five," Corporal Charlie Brown said to the horrified driver. "If your wagon is not ready by the time I reach five, you've had it."

"Put that damned thing away," screamed Roberts.

"One. Two."

"Don't, Charlie," pleaded the Malay driver.

"Three. Well, driver?"

"Let the three of us sit down and talk the matter over. But put the gun down first," said LAC Roberts, knowing that he must get to the phone, and fast.

"Four. One count left, driver."

"OK! OK! Anything you say."

"Five. Too late, driver. Sorry." And Corporal Brown squeezed the trigger. The quietness of the night was shattered, just for that one moment, and a bluish pall of smoke drifted away from the muzzle of the gun.

In horrified amazement the driver stood gaping at the dog-handler. He could not believe that he had been shot. He opened his mouth and gasped air into failing pumping lungs, like a fish out of water gasping air on a riverbank. His eyes were wide open, staring in shock and dismay at the corporal and at the gun he held in his hand. He had felt very little pain when the bullet hit him, just a thud in the stomach in the region of his solar plexus. Slowly his hand slid down to the spot, as if fearful of what it would find. He pressed the spot where he had felt the thud, then drew his hand away and held it up so that he could inspect the palm. It was dripping with his own warm blood. Already surprised and shocked by the events of the past few moments, the expression on his face did not change. Placing his hand to the spot again, he held it there, pressing, as if to keep the blood within his body. Staring at the dog-handler, he shook his head sadly from side to side. "No need for that, Charlie," he said, almost in a whisper. He then sank to his knees, and slowly rolling over fell on to his back, and became still.

"My God, you've killed him, you crazy fool," shouted the horrified Roberts. "You've killed him." It was then that he also saw those insane eyes. Right up until the corporal had fired, he had thought the corporal was playing some ghastly game. He had left it too late to intervene, even if he had been able. For moments he had become paralyzed with fright at the suddenness of the shooting, but now his senses were returning to him. He must quickly decide what to say, and what to do. "Put that gun down, Corporal Brown," he ordered. "I'm going to ring up for another driver." He thought it wise not to say he wanted to call the main guardroom, also the hospital to send an ambulance.

The corporal gave an insane laugh and pointed the revolver at Roberts. "Oh, no you're not. You're going to be next. Do you know why? Because you can't drive."

"No, Charlie! I'm not going to be next," said Roberts, almost casually. Then suddenly he shouted, "Look behind you."

Surprised, the corporal turned his head, lowering the revolver as he did so. It was the moment Roberts needed. With every ounce of energy in him, he sprang forward in a flying tackle, grabbed the corporal's arm and twisted it, hoping the gun would drop to the ground. But he immediately realized his attempt was futile. He was neither strong enough nor skilled enough to combat the highly trained police corporal. Charlie Brown shook him from his arm with ease, and at the same time swung the heavy revolver so that it crashed down upon LAC Roberts's head, smashing in his skull. As if lifeless, Roberts sank to the ground a few feet from where the Malay driver lay in the wetness of his own blood.

Corporal Charlie Brown looked down at each body in turn. "Too bad," he said, returning the revolver to the holster at his hip. "I only wanted to show Wicked Witch the lights of Singapore." Turning to his dog, he said to her, "Now, Witch, we shall have to walk, for we have no one to drive us to see the lights."

Amazingly, Wicked Witch, unsure of what was happening, and receiving no command from her master, had stood nervously at hand the whole time. She had not understood the action at all but her eyes betrayed her agitation and wonderment at what had taken place.

"Come, Wicked Witch. Heel!" commanded Charlie Brown, and away from the signals section strode the very tall Corporal, his faithful dog following a little behind and to the right of him. But they were not heading towards the road that led to the city. Instead, they were heading for the swamps lying between the camp boundary and Changi Gaol.

At three o'clock that morning the orderly officer, accompanied by the orderly sergeant, left the main guardroom to begin their tour of inspection of the fire pickets and the various guarded areas at Royal Air Force Changi. They were making their rounds in a Land Rover driven by LAC Joe Milden of the MT section.

The orderly officer decided that their first place of call would be the signals section hut, located at the far end of the airfield. On arriving there the three in the Land Rover were shocked to find the hut deserted, and the door, which should have been guarded, wide open. There was no one in sight.

A far greater shock awaited them. The orderly sergeant was the first to spot the two bodies lying motionless at the edge of the clearing. Clutching the orderly officer's arm, he cried out, "My God, sir! Look! It's the work of the devil, so it is."

"Good grief!" exclaimed the horrified orderly officer. "What in heavens name has happened here?"

"They're both dead, sir," said Cornishman Joe Milden matter-of-factly.

"How the hell do you know?" snapped the officer. "Sergeant, get on the phone. Ring through to the hospital and tell them to send an ambulance here immediately. And tell them to send medical officers and orderlies. Stress the urgency," he snapped.

The sergeant, springing to attention and saluting smartly, said, "Yes, sir," and then did a practiced precise about turn.

"For Christ's sake, Sergeant, stop the bullshit and get a move on. And call the guardroom while you're about it."

"Yes, sir," snapped the sergeant, already hurrying towards the phone in the hut.

Both the orderly officer and LAC Milden bent over the body of the Signals operator.

"This man's not dead, Milden. He's badly hurt, but look! See! He's breathing!"

"Just about a goner, though, I'd say, sir. Wish the blood wagon would hurry up. Look 'ere, sir," he said, pointing a finger at the fallen man's scalp. "It's blood."

The officer looked at the mess of matted hair and blood. "You're right. He's had a hell of a whack on the head by the look of it. Let's take a look at the other man."

Together, they crossed the few feet to where the motionless Malay driver lay on his back. Congealed blood had formed on the KD uniform covering the man's stomach. They both bent over the motionless airman.

"By the look of it, he's been knifed or shot in the stomach, sir," said Joe Milden.

"Yes, Milden. That's rather obvious."

"He looks dead, sir."

"Yes, I think he is dead."

The orderly officer lifted a limp wrist and felt for a pulse. "No, he's not dead!" he exclaimed. "He's got a pulse, very weak but still beating." Suddenly excited, the officer snapped, "Airman! Get to the phone quickly and ring up the hospital. Tell them to expect emergency operations. No, I'll ring up myself and I'll call the main guardroom."

"But the sergeant's calling them, sir."

"I know. But I want to make sure what's going on. You stay here. Don't touch anything. Just listen. There's a chance this man may say something that's vital to us."

"Yes, sir."

At that moment the sergeant returned. "Ambulances will be here any minute, sir," he said. "The hospital's ready to receive them. I've also notified the guardroom and spoken with the guard commander. He's on his way."

"Good show, Sergeant. What did the guard commander say?"

"He seemed more concerned about the dog-handler who's supposed to be on duty here, a Corporal Brown, sir. Said he'd like to talk to him but I told him there's no dog-handler here."

"Hmm," said the puzzled officer. "Yes, there should be a police guard here. I quite forgot."

"There's supposed be a dog-handler on duty here at all times, sir."

"If that's the case, then where is he? And where's his dog?"

The sergeant wanted to say, 'How the hell should I know?' Instead, he said, "I wish I knew." He rubbed a square chin with a heavy hand. "First time I've come up against anything like this. I don't know what to make of it. You know, sir, I wonder," he said thoughtfully.

"You wonder what, Sergeant?"

"I'm wondering if the corporal was here when whatever happened here happened. Could it be possible that he and his dog have given chase to the attackers?" he said, hopefully.

"He would have notified the guardroom first."

"Yes, sir. I suppose so."

"This certainly is a rum affair, though, Sergeant. It's a job for the SIB to sort out."

"Sir, look! This chap's eyes are open, and I think he's trying to tell us something," sang out the excited voice of LAC Milden. "Shh" and he held a finger to his lips seeking silence as all three men bent over the signals operator.

"Take it easy, son. You're going to be all right," the sergeant said in a gentle voice. "What happened?"

Bluish white lips trembled, and all three men bent closer.

"The corporal. The corporal," the signals operator whispered, wincing in pain.

"Yes. But what about the corporal?" eagerly asked the orderly officer.

"He did it."

The whispering ceased, the lips closed, the frightened eyes fluttered, and then they, too, closed.

"He's passed out again, sir. Did you hear what he said?"

"Yes, I heard him," said the bewildered officer. "The corporal did it."

"Yes. That's what I thought he said. It doesn't make sense, does it? If this man's words are correct, the corporal must have gone bonkers."

"I beg your pardon, Sergeant?"

"Nuts, sir! You know, crazy!"

"The corporal?"

"Yes, the corporal, sir. My Sherlock Holmes intuition tells me that he attempted to bump these two off, then footed it somewhere. See! He must have left on foot because their MT vehicle is still parked here. He did this then walked calmly away."

"Let's not jump to conclusions, Sergeant. Let's not say too much against the man, not yet anyway. We may be wrong."

"I hope we are."

"Corporal Charlie Brown should be on duty here tonight, sir," butted in LAC Milden. "He's a good chap. He's the last man who would do something like this. I know him well. Everybody likes Charlie Brown."

"Hmm." The orderly officer frowned, then sighed. "As soon as the Station Duty Officer arrives, we'll decide what action to take. Ah! Here's an ambulance now. And here come the police."

In a great cloud of dust, the blue-grey ambulance roared into the clearing and skidded to a standstill close to where the three men were standing over the two bodies lying motionless on the ground. Within seconds the two injured men were placed on stretchers and hoisted into the ambulances. Within minutes they would be arriving at the emergency section at RAF Changi Hospital.

It was now six o'clock in the morning, already daylight, with the sun rapidly rising up over the horizon.

The search for Corporal Charlie Brown was underway. The search party was made up of personnel from many sections: RAF police and fellow police dog-handlers accompanied by their vicious charges; civil police; medical orderlies; plus volunteer airmen from the fire section, catering section and motor transport pool. All were airmen who personally knew and liked Charlie.

Only the police carried revolvers, which they were compelled to carry as part of their uniform when on duty. However, on this morning no firearm would be used, not unless it was absolutely necessary. Corporal Charlie Brown was too well liked for any of his searchers to wish him harm. They wanted to safeguard him, to get him into the hospital for treatment. Actually, the majority of the searchers still could not believe that it was Charlie who had committed those brutal acts on two defenseless co-workers.

The massive search party formed a ring around the many acres of swampland and cautiously moved inward. There were five police dogs out there, too, tracking with their masters. The scents of Charlie and Wicked Witch were easy for the dogs to follow. Straining at their leashes, sniffing and snarling and eager and excited, but baffled occasionally when splashing through mud and water, they pursued their quarries through thorny bushes and tall coarse grasses. The place was alive with many species of snakes, mostly poisonous. Fortunately, most of these slipped discreetly away, to hide whilst the tide of men and dogs passed over.

Suddenly, someone shouted, "There he is. There's Charlie Brown. Over on that hillock."

All eyes turned to where a medical orderly was pointing. Sure enough Corporal Brown had risen from scrub bushes and stood his full height for all to see, watching his pursuers not fifty yards away encircling and closing in on him. He appeared to be quite calm and unconcerned, as did his dog, which stood patiently at her master's side. Slowly, Corporal Brown lifted his revolver and squeezed the trigger, aiming towards the circle of moving men but at no one in particular. The bullet, glancing off a rock, ricocheted, whining and flying wild. The searchers dropped as one into the mire and waited.

"Charlie! Put down your gun! We're your friends! We've come to take you back to the camp," shouted a fellow corporal police dog-handler. "We'll have breakfast together."

"Hey! Charlie! This is ol' fatty Ginger Brent. You gotta be hungry.

Let's go back to the kitchen. I'll fix you bacon and eggs and we'll have a mug of tea together," shouted the cook. Only an hour earlier LAC Brent had come off a ten-hour night shift in the airmens' mess kitchen. He'd had a busy night with three big transport planes arriving at Changi loaded with army chaps coming in from England en route to Korea. He'd helped cook and serve grilled spam, scrambled eggs, sautéed potatoes and toast for over two hundred men in transit, plus the normal late suppers and early breakfasts for night-duty personnel. He was tired and still in his cooks' whites, but on hearing the bad news about Charlie, had immediately volunteered to help in the search. He and Charlie were good friends.

Brent's words were greeted by another shot from Charlie's revolver, followed by a third, then a fourth, all seemingly fired aimlessly. Then, but for the yapping of the dogs, silence fell across the swamps.

"He hasn't reloaded. He can't have many more rounds left in that gun. I think it's empty, unless he reloaded it before we saw him," muttered Sergeant Chapman of the fire department. "Come on, Smithy," he said, addressing his corporal, "Let's move forward."

"OK, but take it easy."

Again the ring of men slowly closed in on Charlie Brown, but more cautiously than before, creeping through sharp-thorned willow-type bushes and crawling through stinking mud and over stones covered in slime. The two men of the fire section were now less than twenty yards from where Corporal Brown and his dog stood on the grass-covered hillock.

Sergeant Chapman raised himself from behind a bush and said in a fatherly and not too loud a voice, "OK, Charlie. Take it easy," and beckoning the dog-handler with a wave of his hand, he said, "Come on down here with us. We'll drive you back to camp."

Corporal Brown didn't acknowledge him, but instead stood staring out over the swamps as if seeing or hearing no one.

"OK! We're coming up, Charlie," shouted the sergeant. And he stood up, an easy target, but Corporal Brown ignored him.

"Charlie," the nasal voice of Corporal Smith rang out. "It's me, Smithy. Remember me? I'm your pal in the fire section. I'm coming up to you. I've no gun, so throw yours down. I'm coming up. Do you hear me?"

The provost police sergeant was now at Corporal Smith's side. "Steady," he said. "Don't do anything silly."

"Yeah. Don't panic him," someone else said.

"I'll go up and see if I can reason with him," said SIB Corporal Symes.

"I'll come with you," said dog-handler Corporal Ben Jones, Charlie's roommate. "I'll try to talk to Wicked Witch and keep her quiet. She could be a problem. She has only one master."

"I know," said Corporal Symes of the Service Investigation Branch. "OK. You come along, Ben. Maybe my judo will come in handy. I've always bettered Charlie at it. He may need pinning down."

"Maybe he'll come quietly," said Corporal Jones hopefully.

The two looked at one another. Both knew Charlie Brown well, or did they? If he could kill out of hand, just like that, he could kill again thought Corporal Symes, shrugging as they both edged forward.

As if in deep meditation, Corporal Charlie Brown was looking down at those around him, expressionlessly.

"Careful, you two," warned the fire section sergeant. "He's dangerous."

"I don't think he'd use his revolver on us, Sarge," said Corporal Ben Jones. "Anyway, I think it's empty. Unless he reloaded it after he left the signals section, he's fired the last round."

"Don't be too sure."

"I'll chance it. Wait! What's he doing now? Oh, my God!"

"Christ! He must have a round left!"

Corporal Brown was slowly lifting the revolver, higher and higher until the muzzle rested upon the bridge of his nose.

"Stop, Charlie! Don't do it!" screamed a horrified Corporal Ben Jones, and he began racing towards the hillock.

"Oh, fuck it!" shouted Symes, and following Jones, he too ran towards Charlie, bounding forward and ignoring the thorny bushes in his path. The two were on their way up the hillock and only a few feet from the corporal and his dog.

Both men saw Corporal Brown gazing for moments at them as if in puzzlement. He then lifted his revolver a fraction above and between his eyes, squeezed the trigger and dropped lifeless, his last round spent.

Too late, the men reached him, much too late.

Whimpering in grief, the faithful Wicked Witch positioned herself over the fallen body of her master and would not allow anyone to touch him. The commanding officer of the RAF military police shot her.

Peter Saunders was puzzled when the bus he was returning to camp on was stopped by RAF police at a barrier erected on the road near Changi Gaol. Being the only European on the bus, the police took one look at him, then waved the bus on. Peter didn't know that at that very moment his friend Charlie Brown was being tracked in the nearby swamps.

He arrived back at the camp much earlier than usual, having previously agreed with Sergeant Muldoon, who was taking the day off, that he would work both the early and late shift. Shortly after arriving at the sergeants' mess kitchen, he heard with dismay the news of what had happened that night at the signals section hut. Minutes later he was informed that Corporal Charlie Brown was dead.

At first Peter could not believe that Charlie, his friend who only yesterday had complained of a headache, and who was counting the days to going home, was dead. Stunned and depressed, he worked that day with a heavy heart, because Charlie Brown had been one of the best.

Several days later, Peter learned that after intensive care at Changi Hospital, both the Malay driver and the signal section operator survived their injuries, though the latter was medically discharged from the RAF due to brain damage.

19

Whistling happily to himself, LAC Peter Saunders reached the sergeants' mess kitchen at eleven o'clock in the morning on 1 April 1953 only to be confronted at the office doorway by a grim-faced Sergeant Muldoon.

"G'morning, Sarge. What's up?" Peter asked.

"Jeez, Pete, have I got bad news for you," the sergeant answered. "Bad news for me, too."

"Bad news! What do you mean?" asked Peter.

"Have you looked at the noticeboard lately, like in the last day or so?"

"No. Should I?"

"You haven't been keeping up with SROs? You haven't read them recently?"

"No, not for months. Not since I began working here. Why?"

"You best go and read them," said the sergeant, his face uncommonly solemn. "They've got you down for a posting to Negombo."

"What!" exclaimed Peter, aghast.

"I'm just as shocked as you, Pete. Thinking a mistake may have been made, I checked with Movements. They've got you down to be posted to Negombo next Thursday. That's the RAF station north of Colombo, the capital of Ceylon."

Completely taken aback and confused by this dreaded news, Peter could only mutter, "Yeah, I know where Negombo is. But I can't believe they'd do this to me."

"Well, check for yourself," said the sergeant. "Take a look at the lobby noticeboard."

"I will," said Peter dejectedly. Hurrying from the office, he passed through the kitchen without noticing the Chinese cooks and other kitchen staff preparing tiffin, and on through the dining room where white-coated Chinese waiters were laying the tables, until he reached the double-doored main entrance to the mess and lobby where the four-foot-square noticeboard was attached to the wall for all to see.

With pounding heart, his confused thoughts for the most part was on how to break the awful news to Rose. They just can't do this to me, he kept saying to himself. Why do they want to send me to Negombo when there's a shortage of cooks here at Changi? Quickly he scanned the many notices tacked to the board, seeing on it the usual roster of duty senior NCOs, guard and fire picket rosters, minutes of the last messing committee meeting, and a leaflet asking for volunteers to play RAF Seletar at cricket. Actually, the cricket match had already been played the previous Saturday, with Changi losing dismally, but the leaflet had not been removed from the board. The normal sheets of Standing Station Orders were also on the board, but Peter could find nothing relating to postings. Puzzled, he stood back and again studied every item on the board. No, there was definitely nothing on it that related to postings, for anyone to anywhere.

Totally perplexed, Peter returned to the kitchen office to find Sergeant Muldoon seated at the office desk awaiting him, a surprisingly different expression on his face from when Peter had seen him just moments ago. Then, he had seemed troubled by the news, but now his eyes were sparkling mischievously.

Puzzled by the change in the sergeant's expression, Peter said to him, "I couldn't find anything on the board to do with postings. What's going on, Sarge?"

"I didn't expect for one moment that you would," replied an amused

Sergeant Muldoon. "I thought I'd give you a bit of a scare."

"A bit of a scare?"

"Yeah, a scare," said the sergeant, chuckling. "Do you know what day it is today, Pete? It's April Fool's Day. April Fool, Pete. I really gotcha, didn't I?" whereupon the sergeant burst into a fit of laughter.

"Oh, for Christ's sake, Sarge, that was not bloody-well funny. Not funny at all."

"You should have seen your face," hooted the sergeant." I thought you were about to crap your pants."

Like a suddenly deflated balloon, Peter relaxed and breathed a heavy sigh of relief. "Well, it wasn't funny," he said, nettled at having had such an upsetting joke played on him.

The sergeant's laughter subsided as he soberly said, "Well, I won't be able to play that one on you this time next year, Pete. Neither of us will be here. God only knows where we'll be."

"You're right, Sarge," Peter agreed. "And there's one thing that's certain, I'm not looking forward to leaving here." Shaking his head sadly, he said, "I truly believe that I would've sat down and cried if I'd really been posted away from Singapore."

"It's surprising what a bit of skirt can do," said the sergeant, chuckling. "Anyway, changing the subject, I want you to check the rations and then write in the book the menus for the next three days. I've not had time. I've been down at the catering office most of the morning talking to the old man."

"About anything important?"

"Mainly about you. The catering officer said he's pleased with your progress here. He'd like you and a couple of the other LAC cooks to have a shot at getting your SAC. It would be a feather in his cap if at least a few of the cooks at Changi passed the SAC trade tests and got promoted."

"What about the ten-week catering course that's been talked about for so long, the one I'm supposed to go on?"

"For the time being it's been scrubbed. Instead, you'll be taking the practical test for your SAC over at the aircrew mess five weeks from now. There'll also be a written and oral test."

"Crikey! Do you think I'll pass? What sort of menu will I be required to cook?"

"It's here," said the sergeant, tapping on a sheet of paper lying on the desk. "The catering officer made it out, but I've altered it somewhat to include a couple of your favourite dishes, those you've prepared and cooked a few times since working here. Take a look," he said, handing Peter the sheet of paper on which the menu was written.

After studying the menu, Peter began reading it aloud and at the same time discussing the various dishes with the sergeant. "Consommé julienne. That's easy enough," he said.

"But everything's from scratch, remember, and must be as per the RAF manual of cookery, the AP87," said the sergeant. "Do you have an AP87?"

"I have one in the billet."

"Good. You're going to need it."

Peter shrugged and carried on reading the menu, "Fillet de sole au gratin."

"You can substitute any similar fish if you wish," said the sergeant. "Halibut, even cod if there's nothing else."

"OK. That sounds all right. I'm not so sure about the main dish though, chicken fricassée à la minute. I would have preferred a lamb dish, like à la Nivernaise."

"Well, there's still plenty of time to change the menu. You can manage the Vichy carrots and Duchess potatoes. Those are easy enough."

"Sure, there's no problem with those. And tarte aux apricots. I suppose that's just an apricot flan."

"Yep, that's right," said the sergeant. "There again you may substitute some other fruit, perhaps tinned peaches or pears if there's no apricots. The menu's simple enough, right?"

"Yes, Sarge, no problem."

"OK. However, you must remember to read up on your AP87. Really study it. Every question in the written exam will have its answer in that book, and there will be one hundred questions. Anyway, Pete, I've got to be going. I'll see you at noon tomorrow, and then you can take a couple of days off and work the weekend. Is that OK with you?"

"Yeah. Thanks, Sarge." Momentarily dwelling on how he would spend those two whole days and three whole nights with Rose, he suddenly remembered that in the walk-in refrigerator there was a plump hen sitting in a baking pan, ready for the oven.

"Hey! Sarge! There's a fresh chicken in the refrigerator," he shouted after the sergeant who was already on his bike and showing off the yellow and purple socks he was wearing as he pedalled out through the kitchen doorway. "It's just waiting for you to take home for Mrs Muldoon to cook for your dinner," shouted Peter.

"You can't catch me with that one, Pete," Sergeant Muldoon shouted over his shoulder. "One April Fool is enough for this morning." He was disappearing out of the courtyard as Peter shouted as loudly as he could, "Wait! I'm not kidding, Sarge."

The note of urgency in Peter's voice prompted the sergeant to stop, turn around, and return to the kitchen and watch as Peter opened the walk-in refrigerator, stepped inside and promptly emerged carrying a baking tray containing the fat hen ready for the oven. "This bird was running around the kitchen yesterday on the end of a piece of string," Peter said. "Charlie chopped its head off and Kah Seng plucked and cleaned it for you. That's how fresh it is."

The sergeant, dismounting from his bike, said, "Boy'o! It's been months since the wife and I had a fresh chicken." Taking the tray from Peter, he eyed the bird suspiciously. "Where'd you get it?" he asked.

Peter smiled but made no reply.

"Well?"

"Ask no questions and you'll be told no lies, Sarge. Just take it home and enjoy it."

Peter thought it best not to mention the deal he had made with the pig-swill man who owned a pig and chicken farm near Changi Gaol. Two ten-pound tins of dehydrated vegetables for one plump fresh hen seemed to him a reasonable trade, especially as there were at least another thirty tins of the stuff cluttering up the vegetable room. God knows how long they had been there. There were many more there now than when he began work at the sergeants' mess and weekly, when the ration truck arrived, one, two, and sometimes three or even more were added. With considerable imagination and ingenuity he had tried numerous recipes to make use of the dried confetti-like cabbage, the strips of carrot, the mixed vegetables, and potato strips and potato powder. He had make bubble and squeak with the cabbage and potato, potato pancakes, Duchess and creamed potatoes, and toppings for cottage and shepherd's pie. Delicious fish cakes had been made with tinned herrings and potato powder and a whole variety of soups and various other dishes created out of dried vegetables. But, regardless of whatever form of disguise the dehydrated vegetables were presented to the dining mess-members, they were neither well received nor enjoyed, the proof being that almost all that had been served ended up in the swill-bin for the Chinese farmer to cart away daily. So, had thought Peter, why bother wasting time and energy cooking the stuff. It was far easier and certainly more convenient for the swill-man to tote the stuff in its dry state to his farm via his three-wheeled bike than when it was cooked and swollen heavy with water. At the farm the owner himself could reconstitute and cook the quantity needed to feed his pigs and chickens without waste. The Chinese farmer, delighted with the idea, had kept his promise of delivering to Peter fresh eggs, live chicken and fresh portions of pork in exchange for the huge square tins of dried vegetables. Most of the fresh goodies found their way to Rose's home, where she promptly made them into delicious Chinese dinners for them both to enjoy.

Thus far, during the past six weeks, Peter had rid the vegetable room of almost two dozen tins of various dehydrated vegetables but the supply was constantly being replenished.

"That's a good looking bird," said Sergeant Muldoon approvingly.

"I'll wrap it up for you," said Peter.

"It's from the swill-man?" ventured the sergeant.

"He's happy to get the swill," said Peter nonchalantly.

"That's funny, he's never given me anything."

"Well, you don't speak to him in Chinese. I do."

Sergeant Muldoon laughed good-humouredly. "You're a bit of a devil, Pete. Nevertheless, this bird's going to look damned appetizing when it's a golden brown and sizzling sitting on our dining room table. You know, Pete, it really is a long time since I've eaten fresh chicken. Frozen stuff is never the same."

"I must agree with you there, Sarge."

Minutes later, whistling a merry tune, and with the hen wrapped in paper under his arm, Sergeant Muldoon again pedalled his squeaky bike out of the kitchen. "Thanks, Pete. See you tomorrow," he shouted as he disappeared, homeward bound.

Peter returned to the office thinking how he and Sergeant Muldoon were a good working team. Neither of them put up with RAF bullshit, and together they kept the kitchen running without undue problems. Of course, there was the occasional complaint from one or another fusspot member of the mess. Peter always allowed the sergeant to deal with these. But generally, all went smoothly. He sat down at the table and was about to open the menu book when the chief of the provost police, Flight Sergeant Cameron, strode into the office.

"Good morning, Cookie," he said, pleasantly enough.

"Oh! Good morning, Flight. How are you? Can I help you?"

"You can, by babysitting at my home this Thursday evening," replied the flight sergeant matter-of-factly.

"Oh, come off it, Flight. You know I don't babysit. I've told you enough times that if I did, I'd be the laughing stock of the catering section." Changing the subject, Peter said, "Would you like some bananas? A fresh supply came in yesterday." Peter was well aware that the flight sergeant was a living-out member of the mess and therefore not entitled to any foodstuffs from the mess, not even a few bananas. Regardless, Peter often supplied him with fresh fruit, especially when the flight sergeant was about to go on night duty, which was often. Also, because of the flight sergeant's ulcer, which at times played up, Peter cooked him soft boiled eggs and toast, which the flight sergeant ate in the office.

"Cookie, thanks, but no thanks. I don't want bananas today," he said, shaking his head and frowning. Always there had been a definite 'no' from Peter to his requests for him to babysit his two children. But Thursday night he and his wife were invited to a special event. He needed a babysitter he could trust and LAC Saunders was certainly that, and seemed to be the ideal person for the job. Smiling gravely to Peter, he said, "You're a hard nut to crack, Cookie."

"Well, I'm sorry, Flight, but I'm not cut out for babysitting. I'm not interested."

"Och, man! But you may become interested. I do have certain information which may change your mind."

"What do you mean, Flight?"

"Can't you guess?"

"No. You've lost me."

"Well, let's put our cards on the table. By visiting this girlfriend of yours, you must be aware that you are breaking at least one military regulation and quite a serious one at that."

Peter shrugged noncommittally. "Maybe," he said.

"There is no 'maybe' if the girl happens to live in an out-of-bounds area."

"Flight, you must catch a person in an out-of-bounds area before you can charge him or her with breaking that regulation."

"Perhaps, but don't be too sure. Your girlfriend lives in an out-of-bounds area close to Lavender Street, correct?"

"How do you know where she lives?" asked Peter, suddenly ill at ease at the flight sergeant's knowledge.

"It so happens that I am the head of the provost police on this island," answered the Flight Sergeant. "I know the Lavender Street area like the back of my hand. I know every brothel, almost every pimp and just about every woman who solicits in that area. I certainly ought to know your little girlfriend by now."

"You know her?"

"Och, man, of course I know her. As a matter of fact, I knew her long before you ever set eyes on her."

"You did," said Peter, amazed.

"We keep tabs on almost all the working girls, as well as where they hang out. Most of them are OK. Generally they are clean, almost always honest, and only a few use pimps."

"And my girlfriend, what do you know about her?"

From an inside pocket of his tunic, the Flight Sergeant calmly withdrew a yellow sheet of paper that had been torn from a legal pad. "Here, read this and correct me if I'm wrong," he said, handing the sheet of paper to Peter, a peculiar smile playing on his rugged face. "You'll read and find that all the facts are correct, Cookie, I assure you. I, myself, have checked every detail.

"You're a nosy bugger, aren't you, Flight?" said Peter. He carefully studied the contents of the double-spaced lines of typewritten words, his face not showing the surprise and indignation he felt as he finished reading. Then, slowly he reread the lines, his face expressionless. It was all there, everything about the girl he loved. Black typewritten words upon yellow paper. At the top of the page a heading seemed to scream out at him, followed by facts.

ROSE OF SINGAPORE

Name	Rose Chan Lai Ming
Age	28
Height	4 foot 10 inches
Hair	Black
Eyes	Brown
Race	Chinese (Indonesian)
Nationality	Singaporean

Address	Currently known
Marital status	Widowed
Children	1 son
Profession	<u>PROSTITUTE</u>

There followed a brief account of Lai Ming's activities: her main sources of contact were made at the Butterfly Club and the Raffles Hotel. It was all there in writing, even mentioning the date and facts concerning her last visit to the Social Welfare Department for a free-from-infection check-up. She had no known criminal record and had never been arrested. Below these remarks, written in ink were the words, "She's a good woman, Cookie. You're a very lucky man. But the fact still remains that her home is a brothel in an out-of-bounds area."

"Obviously it was you who wrote those last few words," said Peter.

"Och! Of course, mon. But do you find anything written there that's incorrect?" asked the seemingly jubilant chief of the provost police.

"Not quite," replied Peter acidly.

"No! Then what's incorrect?" demanded the flight sergeant.

"You've omitted the fact that she has a big brown birthmark on her backside," Peter said, his voice full of sarcasm.

"Och! Has she now? Well, you should know. I'll enter that wee bit of very important information into my records. Would you say that birthmarks come under 'other means of identification?'" the flight sergeant asked, a grin appearing on his face.

"Also for your records, Flight, and if you'd like to jot this down, she wears super-duper delux, sheer black silk knickers, lace-edged, zip-fastened, with 'all police are a shower of bastards' embroidered on them," said Peter, pouting.

"Cookie, there's no point in you getting up the pole with me," said the flight sergeant. "What I'm getting at is the fact that you visit her frequently. In fact, you more or less live with her. Unfortunately for you, her home happens to be in an out-of-bounds area. Do you catch my drift?"

"I do, Flight. But you must catch me before you can charge me or prove anything against me," Peter answered testily, his face tense and beginning to show anger towards the giant of a man confronting him.

The flight sergeant's rugged face barely concealed his amusement. Chuckling, he said, "It may interest you to know that a couple of my men tailed you to the home of the lady in question on or about your third visit to her. That was months ago. Since then the same two men could have nabbed you on several occasions but it was on my orders that they did not arrest you. On the night you had the attack of malaria they were sorely tempted to return you to Changi but at the time they were not sure whether you were sick or drunk. Regardless, so I was told, your little friend appeared to have the matter well in hand, so they simply waved her goodnight. You were much too sick to notice their jeep stopped behind your taxi when you stepped from it and staggered through the alleyway to the door of the lady's home."

"That's true," acknowledged Peter. "Rose did tell me some days later that RAF military police had seen me get out of the taxi. She wondered why I was not arrested."

"Oh, aye, it's true," smiled the flight sergeant. "Furthermore, Cookie, it may interest you to know that I, myself, accompanied by Corporal Symes of the SIB, trailed you one afternoon as you walked along Lavender Street towards the lady's home. It was a sort of relaxing fun game for us. But we could have nabbed you at any time."

"So! Why didn't you?"

"Och, man, I couldn't do that to our wee Cookie, now could I? Especially when he is so obliging to my needs. And can you imagine how The Muldoon would react if I put you away for a while? Live and let live, that's what I say, especially when dealing with the sergeants' mess cook.

"At least that's nice of you."

"Yes. We thought so, too. We considered the incident amusing. We both laughed about it and let you go unsuspectingly on your way, to enjoy, I presume, a delightful afternoon with your lovely lady."

Peter simply shrugged his shoulders, and apart from saying, "Thanks," he remained silent.

Flight Sergeant Cameron also paused from further speech. Instead, he stroked his chin and appeared as if deep in thought. Eventually, he said, "The two SPs who trailed you have since been posted to Kai Tak. And Corporal Symes has returned to the UK and is now demobbed, so you have nothing to worry about from those three."

"Therefore, I presume you're the only cop who knows."

"Yes." The flight sergeant coughed an artificial cough, as he was apt to do. "She's a lovely wee lass, Cookie, and I admire your taste. If I were single I'd envy your luck in having such a beautiful girlfriend. But I'm married and I also happen to be a cop so I should do my duty when need be. You are well aware that you're breaking SSOs, and if caught it means seven days over the wall for you. Twice caught and you'll get six months. You understand me, of course, don't you, Cookie."

"Yes, I'm reading you loud and clear, Flight. It's what's commonly known as blackmail."

"Oh, come now, Cookie, blackmail is such an ugly word. We mustn't use that word between us. We're friends."

"But that's what it boils down to. Either I babysit, or you eventually catch me out of bounds and turn me in."

"No, Cookie, I don't see it that way," said the flight sergeant, shaking his head, his granite-like face unusually solemn. "Let's talk man to man. You realize that I am in a position to get you into serious trouble and should that happen, it would considerably affect your whole way of life here."

"Yes, of course it would."

"Fortunately for you, however, I have no wish to cause you grief. I would never turn you in regardless of whether or not you babysit my two kids. You see, Cookie, I like you. You've always been more than helpful to me. I'm grateful to both you and The Muldoon for the many favours you've done me, especially before the arrival here of my wife and children."

LAC Saunders sighed wearily but he felt relieved and was no longer angry. "What day do you require my babysitting services, Flight?" he asked resignedly.

"This coming Thursday evening, if you can make it."

"I'll do it. But I still say it's blackmail."

"No, not at all. Let me explain further. I said I liked you, OK? Well, there are two other reasons why I prefer you to babysit my kids. It's because of your dependability and trustworthiness. Also, I'd like to show you my appreciation for all the little things you've done for me these past months."

"You've a funny way of showing your appreciation, Flight."

"No. I don't think so, Cookie. You've got me wrong. By babysitting for us, you'd not only be doing Floss and I a valuable service but you'd have a home away from camp life."

"But I already have a home away from camp, the home of my girlfriend, and that suits me fine. When off duty I can go to her home anytime I wish."

"Any time and on any day? Surely not."

"No. Not every day but on most days."

"In that case, on the days you remain on camp, you could enjoy the comforts of our home. The refrigerator is always well stocked and you could help yourself to beer. You'd be welcome at our home, not only to babysit, but anytime. Sometimes Floss gets very lonely so she'd welcome your company."

"Thank you, Flight," said Peter. "Yes, I can imagine how she must feel. It's a very different lifestyle here than in the UK."

The flight sergeant moved his huge frame from the doorway, and Peter followed him out through the kitchen door. "More rain this evening, I'm thinking," said the flight sergeant looking up at the sky.

"It looks that way," agreed Peter. "Cheers, Flight. Have a good night."

"Thanks. Don't poison anyone, Cookie. I'll probably call in tomorrow." With those words Flight Sergeant Cameron strode across the kitchen courtyard whistling the song "Rose, Rose, I Love You" as he headed for the main guardroom

On returning to the office, Peter Saunders sat at the desk, the open menu book in front of him. But he was not concentrating on it but just staring at the black ink written on white paper and thinking to himself, fancy Flight Sergeant Cameron knowing so much about Lai Ming and their affair.

Thus, deep in thought, Peter looked up quite startled when his friend Rick, dressed in a perspiration-soaked KD uniform and an RAF blue beret worn on his head at a jaunty angle, fairly crashed through the screen door of the kitchen and came rushing into the office, his face aglow.

"Peter, I've found myself a girlfriend," he excitedly exclaimed.

"You have? Where? Who?"

"A Portuguese woman."

"Really! Come on in for a cup of tea and tell me all about her. But Rick, have I got news for you! You won't believe this but Flight Sergeant Cameron knows all about Rose, knows that she lives in an out-of-bounds area, and he knows everything about our relationship."

"Christ, Pete, that is bad news."

Peter shrugged his shoulders. "Maybe, but maybe not. I don't think he'll let the cat out of the bag. Knowing that he's got me by the balls, I've agreed to babysit his two kids."

"Bloody hell! He's got a nerve."

"Maybe. But some good has come out of this. If I'm caught out of bounds by the RAF police, he's not going to let any charges go further than his own desk. The red caps and shore patrols are a different story. I'll have to watch out for them. Anyway, let's change the subject. Let's hear about your Portuguese girlfriend. What's she like? Do you think you're on to a permanent thing?"

"Yeah, I believe I am. She's a smashing-looking bird, Pete. You should see her."

"Where'd you meet her?"

"In the Blue Rajah Cafe. She's a waitress there. You know the joint, the Indian restaurant just off Dingham Road. Don't you remember the place? We went there once and had a curry dinner. That was before you met Rose."

Peter chuckled. "Yeah, I remember the place. We ate curried chicken, really hot stuff, the hottest curry I've ever eaten."

"So bloody hot we needed a gallon of cold beer apiece to wash it down, remember?" laughed Rick.

"Could I ever forget! The next morning that damn curry came out the other end so hot it burnt me a new arse."

Rick laughed. "But you've got to admit, Pete, they do make smashing curry. Anyway, about two weeks ago, my mate Corporal Jameson of my section and I, he thinks he's a connoisseur of good curry, went to the Blue Rajah for dinner. He ordered beef curry and I had the shrimp curry. Anyway, right from the beginning, what really fascinated me was our waitress. She smiled at us with big flashing brown eyes. She's a real corker, Pete, darkish skin, long and glossy black hair, and sex appeal splashed all over her. She took our order, served us, and as I ate my shrimp curry I watched her and made up my mind that I was going to get into her pants."

"And did you?" Peter asked with increasing interest.

"You bet I did. Last night, or should I say, in the wee hours of this morning, for the first time. I'll tell you what happened, and it's the truth, I swear it."

Kah Seng, bearing two cups of steaming hot tea, entered the office, his usual friendly grin creasing his aging, weather-beaten face. "Two teas, Chicko," he sang out as he placed the cups and saucers on the desk. "One you. One Mister Rick."

"Thank you, Kah Seng," Rick said.

Peter said, "*Do tze*, Kah Seng."

Kah Seng nodded his head, grinned and silently withdrew, returning to the kitchen to resume his task of dicing oranges for that day's fruit salad.

Rick, taking a sip of tea, stared at a blank page in the menu book as if in deep contemplation. Eventually, he said. "I've been going to that bloody restaurant for dinner every damned night, ever since I set eyes on that Portuguese woman."

"You mean you've eaten curry there every night?"

"Yeah, believe it or not, every night for two weeks. And I drank gallons of beer to wash the stuff down. Beef curry, chicken curry, shrimp curry, fish curry. My ass was on fire from eating so much damned curry."

"I bet it was. So, what happened?"

"She didn't take a blind bit of notice of me. Well, until a couple of nights ago. I went there the same time as usual, sat at the same table I've sat at for the past two weeks, she came to serve me but instead of ordering a curry, I ordered only coffee. She looked at me kind of funny-like, so I told her that I had been coming in every night, not to eat their blasted curry but only to look at her beautiful face."

"That must have really grabbed her. What did she say?"

"She gave me a big smile and as the place was not busy she sat down at my table, had a glass of coffee with me, and we talked for several minutes."

"And then?"

"Last night I went to see her, asked her for coffee, and as the place wasn't too busy, she sat down and we talked for quite a while, maybe an hour. I asked her where she lived. She replied, not far from Changi Gaol; so I asked if I could escort her home. She appeared to be a rather stuck-up type, so imagine my surprise when she said, 'I thought you'd never ask.'"

"Really?"

"I took her home in a taxi. Naturally I turned on the jolly old Gerald Rickie charm."

"Which didn't help one bit."

Rick ignored this remark. "She lives in a little wooden house behind the gaol," he said. "I told the taxi driver to wait for me as I fully expected to return to camp in it. Anyway, whilst wondering what might happen next, I walked her to the doorway, shook hands with her, told her I had had a lovely evening, and asked if I might kiss her goodnight. Instead, she invited me into her home. So I paid off the taxi and followed her in."

"So you made out with her there and then?"

"No. But this is all pucka gen, Pete. I'm not making anything up, not shooting a line at all. So listen."

"I'm all ears."

"OK. The house is very small. To be truthful, it's just a native hut with two rooms. In one room were two young kids and an old woman asleep on mats. It shook me for a moment. Marie, that's my girlfriend's name, whispered to me that the kids were hers and that the old woman looked after them whilst she was at work. She told me she's no longer married, Pete. Who knows? But that's what she told me.

"She said she didn't want to wake up the kids, and as it was such a lovely moonlit night, would I like to go for a walk with her as far as the nearby beach. Well, we walked past the main gates of Changi Gaol, and then she held my hand and led me through a Malay *kampung* built in a palm grove, and then along some wasteland until we reached a low cliff overlooking the sea. There was a nice sandy beach below the cliff."

"How romantic. But let's get to the gory details, the sex scene on the sandy beach."

"It didn't happen on the beach, Pete. On the edge of the cliff there's a concrete pillbox, a leftover from the war, built on a grassy bank. We both sat down on it."

"You sat on the pillbox?"

"No, idiot, we sat on the grassy bank."

"Oh! Of course."

"The setting was perfect. A full moon overhead, gentle waves lapping the shoreline, and the wind gently sighing through the nearby palm grove. It was gone midnight, the whole place quiet and deserted except for Marie and I."

"Well! What happened?"

Rick shook his head, "Patience is not one of your virtues, Pete."

"Oh, come on, Rick. Get on with it. Did she or didn't she?"

"Of course she did. You don't think for one moment that she took me to that secluded and romantic spot just to show me the scenery or to listen to the wind and the lapping of the waves, do you? She fell into my arms and looked into my eyes with those big beautiful eyes of hers, pleading like. But, believe it or not, I was still a bit doubtful as to what I should do. I've heard that if angered, Portuguese women have terrible tempers."

"But surely you could tell, Rick. She must have thought you awfully slow."

"A perfect English gentleman, that's what she thought. She told me so."

"Oh, bullshit! She can't be that daft."

"She wore a tiny gold crucifix hanging from a chain around her neck. She slipped the crucifix inside her dress and laughingly dared me to try taking it out. Of course, she was just asking for it. We playfully wrestled on the bank for a minute or two; then she gave in and lay quietly on her back with me sitting astride her. I opened her blouse, slipped off her skirt, and soon had her completely naked beneath me, the whole scene lit up as clear as daylight by the full moon. My God, Pete, you should have seen her. She's lovely! And what a body!"

"How did you get back to camp?" laughed Peter.

"I walked most of the way. Then some chap from the MT section came along in a lorry and picked me up. He dropped me off at the signals section block."

"You were lucky. How old is this girlfriend of yours?"

"About thirty. I'd say she's about the same age as Rose. Maybe a bit older."

"Are you seeing her again?"

"Tomorrow evening. She's got the evening off. She's going to meet me at the London Bar in Changi Village. Care to join us for a drink?"

"Thanks. I'd like to meet her, Rick, but I'll be at Rose's home. Perhaps we can make it a foursome some other time."

"Let's do that, Pete. Anyway, thanks for the tea. I've gotta get going. I'm supposed to be on duty."

As Rick rose from where he had been sitting on the edge of the table, the telephone rang at Peter's elbow. Picking it up, Peter answered it, saying, "Sergeants' mess kitchen. LAC Saunders, duty cook in charge speaking."

"Saunders, I'm glad I've caught you in. This is Warrant Officer Whitehead, Chairman of the Messing Committee. Do you have a minute?"

"Of course, sir."

"Good! Now listen! We're challenging the aircrew mess to a dart match this coming Saturday evening."

"Yes, sir."

"We're holding it in the sergeants' mess bar. I'm expecting over fifty senior NCOs to show up, and I'm wondering if it's possible for you to oblige us by putting on something to eat during the evening, say from eight to eleven. We're thinking of fish and chips, English style, wrapped in newspaper just like at home."

"Well, sir! Eh! We could do it at the mess but I can't use RAF rations."

"Hold it, Saunders. Let me finish. If you'll go along with this, what the mess members and I are proposing is for you to buy sufficient fish, potatoes, fat and whatever else you need to make fish and chips for at least fifty men, at the village grocery store with your own money. Probably there will also be WRAF NCOs present, as well as a few wives from the married quarters. You cook and serve the fish and chips whilst the darts match is in progress, and you can charge a fee per serving. Naturally, for all your extra work we expect you to come out of this arrangement with some sort of profit, and most certainly not a loss, so it would be up to you to charge what you think is reasonable. Of course, if you did make a loss the Messing Committee would reimburse you. If it's a success, then we expect to put on some sort of do every Saturday evening, such as a whist drive or a dance, with fish and chips laid on by you. It would be just like running your own fish and chip shop. How do you like the idea, Saunders? No, don't answer that right away. Think about it. At the moment I'm at SHQ, but I'm coming right over to discuss this matter more fully with you."

The phone went dead. Peter put down the receiver and turning to his friend who had been listening to the conversation, exclaimed, "God! What a morning, Rick! I've been posted to Ceylon, blackmailed into babysitting, forced to listen to your sex life, and now I'm expected to open up a fish and chip shop in my spare time here in the sergeants' mess kitchen. The president of the messing committee, old Warrant Officer Whitehead, is on his way here right now, I guess to give me the official go-ahead."

Rick, seeing dollar signs before his eyes, said, "You could make yourself a nice bit on the side, Pete, without even fiddling. Anyway, I'm out of here before that old geezer Whitehead shows up. I'll come around and sample your fish and chips on Saturday. Cheers. Good luck."

"Thanks. I'm going to need it."

Peter watched as Rick hurried from the kitchen. Alone now and seated at the office table, he was thinking of the sizeable quantity of fish, potatoes, cooking fat, flour, eggs and other commodities he would need to buy in order to feed fifty or more hungry people. In fact, he should be prepared to cater for at least a hundred. It just wouldn't do to run short. But what if much of what he bought remained unsold? What then? A brilliant idea suddenly came to his budding entrepreneurial mind. He could buy a small amount of the required foodstuffs at the village, and if need be he could use rations from the sergeants' mess. Better still, there were always sacks of seemingly surplus potatoes in the airmens' mess veg room, also there were boxes of frozen fillets of cod, halibut, turbot, hake and other fish stacked high in one of the three walk-in deep freezers. He could ask the ration truck driver SAC Jock Mackenzie if he would throw a couple of extra sacks of potatoes, a few boxes of frozen fish, a sack of flour, a twenty-eight pound tin of cooking fat, and a couple of dozen eggs onto his delivery lorry. All on the QT, of course. He was sure Jock would oblige him. They were good friends. When Peter was on duty, Jock often ate his lunch in the sergeants' mess kitchen office, at times washing his steak, lamb chops or whatever down with a cold Tiger beer from the bar. Yes, he was sure Jock would do it for him. However, and his mind was racing, he must be sure to create legitimacy by having bills of sale which, if necessary, he could present, meaning he must buy at least a small quantity of each commodity at the village grocery store. Ten pounds of potatoes and five pounds each of fish, flour and fat, a dozen eggs, some salt and a small bottle of vinegar should do the trick, he calculated.

Even the sergeants' mess Chinese staff could make a little extra money by working overtime at his fish and chip shop. Kah Seng or one of the other kitchen boys could peel and chip the potatoes, Charlie or one of the other cooks could slice the fish into reasonable portions and mix the batter, and one of them could stay late and cook the fish and chips. All he need do is serve the fish and chips and rake in the money. What a profit he could make! How much should he charge, he wondered. It must be a reasonable amount, say one dollar per serving. He would be selling his fish and chips cheaply, but as his financial outlay would be minimal, at a dollar a head he would be making a fantastic profit. And he'd have no overheads, such as rent, insurance or electricity bills, and he would use the sergeants' mess kitchen equipment.

He was thinking of the many extra dollars per week he could make when Warrant Officer Whitehead walked into the office saying, "Well, what do you think of the fish and chip shop idea, Saunders?"

"Since you rang, sir, I've been thinking about it and don't foresee any problems. Why don't you go ahead with your plans for the darts match on Saturday and leave the catering to me?"

"You're a good man, Saunders. Do you have any idea how much you'll charge?"

"A dollar per person, sir."

"That seems far too little. You'll never make a profit at that price."

"Just leave it to me, sir, and I assure you everyone will be satisfied."

"Good man, Saunders," said the aging warrant officer. "Well, as the sun's already over the yardarm, it's time for my midday gin and tonic. "Turning, he headed towards the sergeants' mess bar. "I'll let you know on Friday how many to expect," he shouted over his shoulder.

"The more the merrier, sir," Peter sang out. And raising his teacup, he whispered, "I'll drink to that!"

20

Like the wheel of life spinning out one's destiny, young British servicemen and women were being returned daily to the United Kingdom, their tour of overseas duty completed. They were 'tour ex', tour expired being the official words on British governmental documents.

The majority of departing Royal Air Force personnel had spent a full two and a half years at various RAF stations scattered throughout the Far Eastern Command. Others, the two-year National Servicemen and three-year enlisted men, spent considerably less time abroad before being returned home. However, regardless of the length of time personnel served with the Far Eastern Air Force, they were inevitably replaced by fresh personnel from home, lily-white and unacclimatized 'moon men' and 'women from mars', often straight out of RAF trade training camps in the UK.

As for Peter Saunders, his tour of overseas duty was gradually drawing to a close, the grains of time in his hour glass steadily but surely running out. It was now the middle of May, and he only had eight months remaining to serve before he too became tour ex.

Eager to return to the UK, the majority of service personnel stationed in the Far East were counting the days and scratching them off on calendars. Time passed too slowly for them, whereas for Peter Saunders, the days and the weeks passed far too quickly. He was not looking forward to that four-day flight home on a four-engine Hastings transport plane, and even less to the possibility of spending a twenty-six-day or more voyage back to Liverpool on one of those awful troopships such as the *Empire Pride*, the troopship he had sailed on from Liverpool to Hong Kong almost two years ago. He still had vivid memories of being repeatedly seasick, even within minutes of leaving every port. His major dread, however, was the unbearable thought of having to say goodbye, perhaps forever, to Rose.

He was now a senior aircraftman, having passed the written, oral and practical SAC catering examinations the previous week with the highest possible grades. The very informal and jolly catering officer, Flight Lieutenant Rogers, visually inspected all his prepared dishes in the kitchen of the aircrew mess, where the test took place, before adjourning to the dining room where Peter had carefully laid a table for six. Two bottles of wine, both gifts from the sergeants' mess bar, stood on a sideboard; one of the bottles, kept cool in a bucket of ice, was a white Chablis ready to be served with the fish dish. The other, a bottle of red Bordeaux, complimented the main course.

Two Chinese waiters who were employed at the aircrew mess seated the diners. The catering officer sat at the head of the table. On his right sat Flight Sergeant Jean Kelly, the gorgeous NCO in charge of the hospital kitchen. Flight Officer Kite, chairman of the aircrew messing committee, sat at the other end of the table. The three other places were taken by Warrant Officer Beaty, the senior NCO of the catering section, Flight Sergeant Bates, the gnome-like, bald-headed, and ready-for-retirement Cornishman who ran the aircrew mess kitchen, and a very young pilot officer who had just flown in from somewhere and needed a meal. The six sat down to judge and enjoy the superb luncheon created from scratch by LAC Peter Saunders who had worked diligently at the preparation and cooking of the meal since very early that morning.

The soup dish, consommé julienne with sorrel shredded into a fine chiffonnade floating on its surface, was judged superb. Likewise was the fish dish, fillet of sole au gratin, enhanced by the Chablis. The main course which Peter had eventually selected was a favourite of his, chicken Marengo, served with cauliflower à la Polonaise, vichy carrots and Duchess potatoes, accompanied by the very fine bottle of Bordeaux.

"By Jove! A gastronomic delight!" exclaimed the catering officer on tasting the chicken, a remark unanimously agreed upon by all the other five diners. Peter did not mention that he had obtained the two very plump fresh chickens the previous morning from the pig swill man, who had walked them alive and clucking into the sergeants' mess kitchen, where they were promptly dispatched and plucked and cleaned by Kah Seng for Peter's use. At the luncheon, both chickens and the rich sauce they were cooked in were soon heartily consumed so that on all six dinner plates only bones remained of his chicken Marengo.

A peach flan topped with chantilly cream followed the main course. And finally, coffee was served. Minutes later Peter was called into the dining room to be congratulated by the six diners on his presentation of a fine meal, and to be informed by the jovial and now well-fed catering officer that he had passed the practical test, using his words, 'with flying colours.'

On the written theory examination, Peter received a grade of one hundred percent, owing this unbeatable score to his having memorized the whole written works, even every recipe, of the AP87, the RAF manual of cookery. Ever since 1 April, the day Sergeant Muldoon had first mentioned the forthcoming SAC test to him, Peter had read over and over again his blue-covered RAF cookery book right up until the day of the test.

The oral catering examination was conducted at the catering office by Warrant Officer Beaty; Peter answered every question correctly.

Later that day, Peter was again called to the catering office, this time to be congratulated by Flight Lieutenant Rogers, Warrant Officer Beaty, Sergeant Muldoon, as well as several other members of the catering section on his success at passing the SAC catering test. And as the catering officer was saying, "By Jove, Saunders! You did an absolutely terrific job," glasses and a full bottle of Scotch appeared as if from nowhere, and a 'wee dram,' as Warrant Officer Beaty called it, was drunk in celebration by all present.

Two days later, Peter's new rank of Senior Aircraftman came through from FEAF, which meant that, instead of a red two-bladed propeller, SAC Peter Saunders now wore a red three-bladed propeller on the sleeves of his KD uniforms. Peter was proud of achieving his new rank, and chuffed with himself at having scored one hundred percent on the theory. His next step up the ladder would be corporal.

As can be imagined, the catering officer was extremely pleased with the results of his new SAC's catering exam, especially the one hundred percent theory paper, which he promptly and proudly sent to the Command Catering Officer. Not only was it a feather in his own hat but it also made the whole catering section at RAF Changi look good, especially as it was extremely rare for anyone to pass the AP87 written examination with an unbeatable score.

As for babysitting, on a number of occasions since the beginning of April, Peter had actually enjoyed visiting the Camerons' residence in the married quarters. He found the flight sergeant's wife to be a rather nervous but kindly person who welcomed him, and immediately put him completely at ease. He liked Mrs Cameron, and he also liked Derek and Megan, the two children. Megan insisted that he read books to her about bunny rabbits, and mice having tea parties, and other funny little stories whilst sitting on his lap. Derek wanted to show off his stamp collection and play with the impressive train set which took over the whole floor of one of the rooms. Peter, relaxing with a glass of beer in hand, would find himself fascinated by the whole layout and intricate workings of the model railway with its many engines, coaches, little railway stations and winding tracks running through countryside and villages. Never before had he seen, let alone played with, such an elaborate electric train set. At first he was concerned when Derek purposely crashed the trains but as no damage seemed to occur and it kept all three of them amused, he did not interfere. In fact, he crashed a few too.

Saturday evenings were now devoted to his fish and chips enterprise at the sergeants' mess. It had become a fantastic success, from bringing in sixty-three dollars at a dollar-a-head the first night, to now over two hundred dollars, catering to darts matches, whist drives, bingo and dances. Every Friday morning the ration truck driver would drop off at the sergeants' mess an ever increasing number of boxes of fish, sacks of potatoes, fourteen-pound cans of fat, cans of flour and an extra tray of eggs. And every Saturday morning the same standing order arrived from Jong Fatt's grocery store in Changi Village; five pounds of potatoes, fish, flour, and fat and half-a-dozen eggs, paid for in cash by Peter. He kept the receipts in case his financial doings were challenged by the powers that be.

Although his fish and chips enterprise was considered a great success by all his customers, it meant a considerable amount of extra work for Peter, who certainly earned the more than one-hundred-and-fifty Singapore dollars profit every Saturday evening, plus making between fifty and a hundred dollars in tips. The Chinese staff who helped Peter not only received overtime pay but also received an equal share of all tips. Thus, everyone was kept happy.

On one occasion, the chairman of the messing committee asked Peter, "How do you manage by charging such a trivial amount, Saunders? I've spoken to several of the mess members on this matter and they are all in agreement that one dollar doesn't seem enough for all the work that you put into it."

"Sir, if you are happy with our fish and chip arrangement, I'm happy. So don't worry about it."

"Very well, Saunders. But if you need to raise the price, do so."

Saturday evenings also kept Peter from dwelling on what Rose was doing, Saturday evenings being her busiest and most lucrative period of the week. She was glad that he had the babysitting and the fish and chip business, which now occupied his mind. Refusing all offers by him of financial assistance, she had instead suggested that he invest his money in the Post Office Saving Bank at Changi, which he did, and from that day on he became a POSB member. It was his first bank account.

Suddenly, from the bloody battlefields of Korea, and from numerous military hospitals in Japan, wounded British soldiers began arriving daily at Changi Airfield, flown in aboard RAF Hastings and York aircraft of Transport Command. At the terminal building, the wounded were met by medical personnel and driven in military ambulances the one mile to Changi Hospital where their wounds were tended and they were given a break, a period of recuperation before embarking on that final long journey home, back to the UK.

Now, with the hospital caring for far more than its normal number of patients, extra staff, including personnel from the catering section, were drafted in. Senior Aircraftman Peter Saunders was one of the first cooks detailed to work in the hospital's kitchen. There was now neither time for him to babysit nor to manage his fish and chips enterprise.

The wounded were arriving in constantly greater numbers. Ambulances and blue-grey coaches were pulling into the driveway and stopping in front of the emergency entrance. From a kitchen window, Peter would watch with great sadness the new arrivals being helped into the hospital. There were so many pitiful sights.

Every wounded man was first taken into the emergency room to be booked in, have his wounds checked and his bloodied bandages changed before being assigned and taken to one of the several airy, spacious wards. The medical officers, nurses and orderlies attending the wounded always seemed to have smiles and lots of cheerful chatter, but God only knows how they felt inwardly.

When working at the hospital and not busy in the kitchen, Peter would visit the wounded and, where needed, offer a helping hand. Again, what heart-rending sights he witnessed. Young men, really mere boys his own age, who just a short while ago had travelled out to Korea healthy and strong and completely innocent of warfare, were now in pathetic condition. Almost all had at least one limb missing, many had just stumps swathed in bandages. Some were on crutches, several on stretchers, and others pushed in wheelchairs. Heads were bandaged. Whole bodies were bandaged. There were those who were shell-shocked, those deafened, and those who had had their face partially blown away; they could not speak, and might never speak again.

At Changi Hospital the doctors, nursing orderlies, and nursing attendants of the RAF aero-medical service were doing a magnificent job of caring for the ever increasing number of incoming wounded, who were, because of their terrible injuries, in shock and more bewildered than down physically. The nurses were assisted by members of the WVS and by WRAF and RAF personnel. Everyone had a part to play. Eyes were needed to guide the blind, hands for those with none, help for those who could not walk, and many words of encouragement.

Senior Aircraftman Peter Saunders and several other members of the catering section, like so many other airmen and airwomen stationed at Changi, became volunteer helpers and hosts to the wounded. They assisted the medical orderlies in taking patients to the NAAFI, the camp cinema, the cricket and football field, and on short outings down to Changi Village, visiting the beach, and attending friendly gatherings at the Changi Yacht Club. But most of all they seemed to enjoy big beer-drinking parties at Changi's Malcolm Club, where jokes were cracked and there was much talk, laughter and song. It was difficult for Peter to understand how these wounded boys remained so cheerful, their misfortunes joked about, sometimes ruefully. They had survived Korea, not quite intact, but they had survived, and now it seemed as if all stress and tension was flowing from their patched-up bodies. They were alive, and they were returning home. Life ahead of them was tomorrow. Today they celebrated. Peter could only venture a guess as to their innermost feelings. Few spoke of Korea. That in itself was a tragedy left behind, and for them, best forgotten. They spoke of home, of mother, the old man, the missus, a girlfriend, and Blighty.

Now they were fighting a different battle, their own battle. Here, in transit at RAF Changi, they were being helped, but soon they must help themselves, both in mind and body, for the remainder of their lives. But for now, they were fighting, by singing and blotting out horrifying memories, trying to ignore pain and bouts of depression, at seeing a stump that had once been a healthy leg, or burn marks and shrapnel wounds that might never completely heal. Korea, for them, had to be forgotten. Ahead the future lay with wide open doors. It would be up to the wounded individual to make sure that those doors did not close. Peter wondered what his reaction would be if he were in the place of one of those boys. He could not answer such an awful question.

He was glad when the radiogram was turned on and the song "Moon Above Malaya", sung by a sweet-voiced, well-known and popular Chinese girl from Shanghai, floated soothingly through the beer fumes and cigarette smoke in that crowded great hall at the Malcolm Club. And when "Moon Above Malaya" faded away it was followed by, "Rose, Rose, I Love You", "Tell Me Why, Why I Love You Like This?", "Just One More Night, Alone With You I Must Create", "The Little White Cloud That Cried" and "Do Not Forsake Me, Oh My Darling".

These were the songs which headed the Hit Parade on Radio Malaya, songs that Peter Saunders enjoyed listening to. Those wounded British soldiers fresh from Korea will remember for the rest of their lives those few days spent in transit at RAF Changi, Singapore.

Day after day the wants of the procession of arriving wounded were tended to; evenings were reserved for entertainment. Meanwhile, as the days and weeks passed, the volume of wounded slackened until it became a trickle flowing through the camp; then that trickle thinned to a mere handful, the wounded having been rerouted home to the UK.

One of the last cases to depart from Changi, a frail, freckle-faced youngster who Peter escorted to the plane one scorching afternoon, said philosophically, "We can teach them a lot, and they can teach us a lot. If only we could get together peacefully with our enemies, it would be a happier world."

Peter agreed, and said, "Good luck, John."

Dwelling upon John's last words, Peter watched as the hospital plane took off for England, and he was still pondering them when it disappeared from view into a steamy haze hanging over the jungle of Johore.

And now, after weeks of caring for the wounded, it was time for him to return to work at the sergeants' mess, and to his profitable sergeants' mess fish and chips shop. Also, babysitting for the Camerons. But most enjoyably, to spending more time with his adorable Lai Ming.

21

On 2 June 1953, throughout the world, loyal subjects of the British Empire celebrated Coronation Day—the crowning in Westminster Abbey of their sovereign, their lovely young monarch, Her Majesty Queen Elizabeth II.

The citizens of the tiny British colonial island of Singapore celebrated this once-in-a-lifetime event in spectacular style. Boldly, and with great reverence to their new monarch, they transformed the already gay and colourful city into one bedecked with Union Jacks and buntings, red, white and blue streamers and banners, millions of glittering coloured lights and countless jewelled crowns all painted gold. Anticipating this memorable day, gardeners had worked diligently in every city park preparing the soil and planting millions of plants, which now bloomed red, white and blue in massive displays of colour. And in brightly illuminated shopfronts the message 'Long Live The Queen' was splashed across banners in red upon gold displaying the peoples' respect and goodwill towards their new ruler. On this day no talk was heard of independence.

In honour of the Coronation, Singapore's rich diversity of ethnic groups united as one to celebrate this day joyously and with devotion towards the island's new ruler. The British, Chinese, Indians and Malays were all her subjects, she their ruler. With warmth in their hearts towards their new monarch, the people of Singapore rejoiced.

The Chinese population accepted Queen Elizabeth II as their 'number one' even though she was a woman, and they showed their reverence and respect for her in their own special way. After dusk had fallen on Coronation Day, a two-hundred-foot dragon, belching great gusts of fire from huge nostrils to ward off evil spirits from the queen during her reign, weaved a crazy pattern through the waters of the outer harbour. Illuminated by a thousand coloured lights, the dragon was towed hither and thither by small boats without lights which, in the darkness of the vast harbour, could not be seen from the shore. Thus, the fiery dragon, an awesome sight, rode the swell in lone magnificent splendour.

Closer to shore, junks and *sampans*, coated in fresh, gay-coloured paint, lost their normal drab appearance, enhanced by new sails in red, purple and gold, and by great red banners splashed with gold Chinese character writings proclaiming 'God Save the Queen'. In a warm breeze, red and gold buntings fluttered gaily from mastheads, and fire-crackers hanging from yardarms loudly snapped and crackled as they leapt up the masts and spat sparks from off lowered booms.

Not to be outdone, the Indian population erected two man-made, illuminated, larger-than-life elephants on either side of one street, their trunks reaching inward towards the centre of the street. On their backs and heads the two elephants carried Royal Coats of Arms, and between the tips of their outstretched trunks they held a colossal replica of the crown which the queen would wear at her Coronation.

Mounted on the roof of the tallest building in Singapore, the newly opened Cathay Building, was a brightly-illuminated crown, where, immediately below the crown, a brightly-lit, intricately designed royal coach drawn by four horses moved clockwise electronically around the top of the building. And below, at the Cathay Theatre, the words 'A Queen Is Crowned' shone from thousands of clear, brilliant electric lights.

At the Capitol Theatre, where the picture 'The Miracle of Fatima' was being shown, the whole front of the building was adorned by Union Jacks and a colossal banner proclaiming 'Long Live the Queen'. An equally huge plaque of a Union Jack with a crown above it adorned the roof, reaching for the sky in majestic splendour.

The day was declared a national holiday. Many British colonial officials and military officers played cricket and drank gin and tonic, whereas British servicemen, other ranks of course, drank beer and played football, often against swift and agile Chinese players.

There were street parades, too, not only by the military but also by various ethnic groups, joyfully marching in colourful display, with bands blaring, flags flying and fire-crackers popping everywhere to ward off evil spirits.

All British military personnel, except for those detailed for parades or performing necessary duties, were given the day off. And all were issued a chit, which could be exchanged in the NAAFI for a free soft drink or a bottle of beer of their choice with which to 'splice the mainbrace' and to drink the Queen's health. Also, all military personnel were issued two hundred State Express cigarettes, twenty to a tin. These flat, gold-coloured tins, collectors items really, had the inscribed words 'State Express 555' displayed on their lids. Below these words was a picture of the Royal Coat of Arms and the words 'Coronation June 1953. HM Queen Elizabeth II.' At the bottom of the lid was the company's address, '210 Piccadilly, London' and finally, in small letters, the words, 'Made in England'.

Peter Saunders gave away eight of his ten tins of State Express cigarettes. Those he chose to receive a tin were Charlie, the number one cook, Yip, the number two cook, Kah Seng, the kitchen boy, Chuff Box, the junior kitchen boy, Wang, the head waiter, Yong, the barman, little old Sew Sew, the camp's seamstress, and Wan Ze, Lai Ming's *amah*. Lai Ming graciously accepted the ninth tin as a souvenir, and for the same reason Peter kept the tenth.

Now, hand in hand, Lai Ming walked with Peter Saunders along brightly lit Stamford Road, then along St Andrew's Road, passing a brightly illuminated St Andrew's Cathedral, and onward until they reached the waterfront where they could clearly see the fiery Chinese dragon.

"Queen Elijabef is my queen as well as yours, isn't she?" asked a serious Lai Ming looking up into Peter's face.

Peter chuckled. However much he corrected Lai Ming, there were letters in the alphabet, which she could never pronounce no matter how hard she tried. The letter Z became J and TH became F making the word Elizabeth particularly difficult for her to pronounce.

"Yes," Peter assured her. "Queen Elizabeth is our queen, yours and mine."

Lai Ming smiled knowingly, nodded her head in approval, and was satisfied.

Three months after the festivities surrounding the Coronation had died down, Peter, now back to his regular routine of afternoons at the beach, fish and chips evenings and the frequent nights with Rose, found himself sitting in the kitchen of the airmens' mess with his best friend Rick. Both now had girlfriends in Singapore and were enthusiastically comparing notes when the ringing of the phone at his elbow interrupted him. Lifting the receiver, he said, "Hello. SAC Saunders speaking. Duty cook, sergeants' mess."

"Oh! Hello SAC Saunders. So I've finally contacted you. This is SHQ Movements Section. SAC Williams here," came back the brisk reply.

Movements Section, those very words sent a sudden sickening shiver through Peter. "Oh, Christ. Now what?" he heard himself saying under his breath. A call from Movements could mean only one thing, a new posting. But it couldn't be back to Malaya with his malaria. Perhaps he was being posted back to Hong Kong. He didn't want to jump to conclusions but his mind raced. Could this call be merely a message advising him of impending new arrivals at the sergeants' mess? Normally such messages came through a different office at SHQ but perhaps procedures had changed and they were now coming through Movements. "Hello. Yes." Peter heard himself saying, his voice filled with uncertainty.

"Ah, yes, SAC Saunders. Could you report to Movements sometime today. You've been posted. I've a form here for you to fill in."

Posted. That one word hit Peter so hard he suddenly felt weak at the knees. "Posted!" he exclaimed in disbelief. "To where?"

"Oh, not too far away, and not for long. It's to a place called Fraser's Hill, up in the Highlands of Malaya."

"The Highlands of Malaya?"

"Yes. You're to spend a month up there on detachment from here. Changi will remain your parent unit."

"But why am I being sent to Fraser's Hill?" blurted out a dismayed Peter Saunders. "I'm not supposed to return to Malaya. I'm on medical repat' from KL. I've had malaria."

"I know. I have your file in front of me. However, there's nothing written on it about you working as a cook at Fraser's Hill. It seems they're sending you up with a bunch of other chaps who are marksmen with a rifle. You are a marksman, aren't you?"

"I haven't fired a rifle since I first joined the RAF nearly three years ago."

"Is that so? Well, I suppose the powers-that-be consider that once a marksman, always a marksman."

"But I'm a cook. I'm not in the bloody RAF regiment," said Peter, exasperated at the news.

"Look here, old chap, you sound pissed off over this posting but it's not my fault, this is Movements. We instruct you as to where you are going, by what means of transport, and when. Nothing more."

"I know. But where the hell is Fraser's Hill? And what am I supposed to be doing there with a rifle? And when am I supposed to be going?"

"Very soon is the answer to your last question. Can you come down to see me at SHQ this afternoon, say, before three?"

Dazed, Peter said, "Yes."

"Good. As for Fraser's Hill, there's a small RAF radar unit at the summit. The camp's main purpose these last few months, though, is a place for R and R, a health camp at a high altitude. It's about 5000 feet above sea level, so I've been told, where the climate is dry and cool."

"But where is it?"

"It's in the highlands in the southern part of Pahang, a little north of the Selangor border."

"God, I still can't believe it!"

"You can't believe what?"

"Oh, never mind. I never wanted to see that part of Malaya again."

"Well, unfortunately, you are going to see it."

"Fuck it!" exclaimed Peter, exasperated.

"I beg your pardon?"

"Oh, I'm just mad at being posted away from here."

"It'll only be for a month. Look, come over to SHQ and I'll give you all the gen. We'll get your clearance chit signed and you'll be able to collect your air passage form at the same time. You'll need to attend a casual pay parade tomorrow."

"Why the hurry?"

"Did you ever hear about Sir Henry Gurney?"

"I've heard his name mentioned. He was once the High Commissioner General of Malaya or something like that, wasn't he? Why?"

"Sir Henry was the High Commissioner of Malaya. He was also one of the first to be ambushed and murdered on the road to Fraser's Hill. Communist terrorists ordered him out of his car and then shot him dead at the side of the road. That was back in 1951, October the sixth to be precise."

"So? That's history. What's the connection? Why am I being posted to Fraser's Hill?"

"Unfortunately, ever since Sir Henry's death, there have been frequent acts of terrorism in that area. An army staff car was ambushed there only last week and three British soldiers and a high-ranking officer were killed. Now, marksmen are being used to help guard the twice-weekly convoy that makes the run. You're one of those lucky sods that's been chosen to help guard Thursday's convoy."

"Oh, for Christ's sake! This Thursday?"

"Yes. You'll be flying from Changi to Kuala Lumpur this coming Thursday morning, and from KL you'll travel by road to Fraser's Hill in the convoy. You're slated to arrive there Thursday evening."

"Thanks very much," said Peter dryly.

"I'll see you this afternoon, then?"

"Yeah. About three."

"OK. Cheers."

"Cheers," muttered Peter. Returning the receiver to its cradle, he said resignedly, "Well, Rick, that's that."

"Good Lord! What bloody bad luck," said Rick, who had overheard every word of the conversation and who was equally shocked at the news. Then, optimistically, he said, "You may enjoy the change. I've heard stories about Fraser's Hill. It's a rest camp where all you do is eat, sleep and relax. No shagging, of course, but you can still knock a few balls around. You can play golf. The Sultan of Pahang had a nine hole golf course carved out of the jungle there, so I've been told."

"I don't play golf! Can you picture me belting a stupid little ball around a golf course?"

"Well, not really. But I've heard there's also an English pub at the top of Fraser's Hill; darts and all that sort of twaddle, and real English beer. You'll probably have a damned good time up there."

"A good time, my ass, Rick. Hell, don't you realize that going there will mean a month away from Rose? Now, every day is precious to me and they want to take away a whole bloody month of my remaining time here." Angry now, Peter said, "A month, perhaps even longer. God knows how many men will sleep with Rose during that time."

"Well, while you're away you'll have to forget her."

"Don't be stupid, Rick. You know me better than that. How on earth do you expect me to forget her?"

"I don't know. But you'll have to forget her sooner or later, unless you marry her."

Marry her. The two words sank into Peter's numbed brain. On a number of occasions he had asked Rose to marry him, but always

291

she had refused his offer. Also, he knew only too well that if he put in an application to the commanding officer to get married to a Chinese woman, especially to a Chinese prostitute, he would be bundled aboard the next plane out of Changi. He'd probably never see her again; certainly not whilst still in the RAF. But, he thought, he would ask her again and, if she agreed, they could get married secretly. Why should he lose her forever? He could take care of her. He didn't convey his thoughts to Rick. The calendar lying on the desk caught his eye. Vaguely noticing a young and beautiful Chinese girl posing in a one-piece swimming costume on the cardboard cover, he picked it up, turned the pages to the month they were now in and began studying it, checking the dates.

"This leaves me only three days," and turning to his friend, Peter said, "I was hoping never to see KL again. I hated the place, not the town so much, but the camp and the jungle. I'm not looking forward to this trip, Rick, not one bit."

Rick shrugged, and wanting to get off the subject of the posting said, "Tell you what, Pete, after you've visited SHQ how about having a couple of beers together down in the village?"

"That's the best idea you've had all day, Rick," answered Peter. "I'll tell Rose the bad news tomorrow." And then a sudden thought occurred to him. Rick was also a marksman with a rifle. "Hey, Rick!" he began, and then he thought, 'no, I'll say nothing.' He'd check the list of names of those bound for Fraser's Hill later, when he visited SHQ. "Let's hear some more about your Portuguese bit of stuff," he said. "What happened last night? Where did you both go? I want to hear something that will cheer me up."

Rick laughed and said, "OK, I'll make it juicy. I'm really looking forward to having a couple of beers with you later. It will be just like old times."

Peter Saunders did not guess that Rick was thinking the same thoughts as himself, that he, too, was a marksman and was his name on that list of marksmen bound for Fraser's Hill.

22

L ai Ming studied the calendar hanging on the inside of her wardrobe door, and then looked at the clock on the bedside table. "Five o'clock," she murmured. It was the evening of 9 September 1953.

Walking to the window, she gazed down upon a moving mass of humanity in the street below, where a celebration of some sort was taking place. There seemed to be people everywhere, shouting, laughing and singing; whilst others were trying to get through the crowd, pushing, shoving and hurrying, always hurrying. The city was alive, as if it were a giant anthill, its population scurrying hither and thither, forever on the move. Beggars were crying out for alms whilst shuffling along the street. Trishaw *wallahs* weaved their machines slowly in and out of the crowd. There were many shouting hawkers touting their wares, which lay displayed on sheets of newspaper and in boxes on the pavement, taking up much space on the five-foot way that lay directly beneath Lai Ming's window.

Sighing, Lai Ming looked towards the sky to where the sun was already slipping down over the western horizon, its final rays of that day casting red and silver dancing shadows wherever they touched. The sky had lost its blueness. Now, high in the sky, there was a greyness, though there were no clouds. But towards where the sun was sinking, the greyness gradually melted away to become not one but a diversity of colours: turquoise and silver streaked with orange and reds, and smudged with a bluish haze rising over the distant skyline.

The sounds from the street below grew fainter as her thoughts again turned to Peter. Her mind dwelt heavily upon him and upon last night when he had again asked her to marry him. Indeed, he had begged her to marry him, and at this very window where she now stood. However, as with his previous proposals of marriage, she had refused him. She loved Peter, of that she was sure, and except for her son, he meant more to her than anyone else in the world. But as for marrying Peter, it would not be fair to either of them. She, Chinese and almost ten years older than him, a widow, and a mother with a child sick with polio. A marriage between them could never be.

The National Health Service in England would provide excellent care for her son, Peter had repeatedly assured her. But she had no wish to leave Singapore, especially now that her son was beginning to show signs of recovery. Anyway, she told herself, she could not start life afresh in a cold and foreign land among strangers who could well be hostile towards her and her son. Everything in England would be so vastly different from Singapore: the culture, the food, the climate. Marrying Peter and travelling to England was too great a risk, especially now, after she had worked so hard, had repeatedly degraded herself but had watched with cold satisfaction the balance in her bank book growing with every passing month. Soon after being paid her first fee working as a prostitute she had decided upon her plan, and she must stick rigidly to that plan. Within a matter of months she hoped to have enough money to buy her first bungalow in one of the new suburbs springing up on the island. This she would rent to the British Government who would pay without question the amount she asked, and always on time. The British were always in need of good rentals for their civil servants and military personnel, and the house would be safe in their hands. She was determined to eventually buy three, four, or even more homes before retiring, and then live off her rentals. Marrying Peter and going with him to England was completely out of the question, yet, when the time came for his leaving her and returning to his homeland, she knew she would be heartbroken. She loved him far too much for him to simply say goodbye to her forever. She smiled to herself and thought, I love him, yet he is still a little boy full of childlike curiosity. He knows so little of life, yet he knew far less when we first met a whole year ago.

However, in ten years from now, especially if they were married, would he still want her, and would he still love her, she wondered. Or would he despise her and think what a fool he had been to marry a Chinese prostitute almost ten years his senior? What then? Would he shun her, cast her from his home and find himself a white girl his own age? And what would become of her son?

Even now, she knew Peter was far from being content. Indeed, at times he was miserable, lying silently at her side brooding, depressed and tormented, ashamed at how little he could do for her. Yet, without her ever asking for one dollar from him, he was spending most of his fortnightly pay on her in one way or another. She was so moved by his unselfishness in giving all his hard-earned savings from his fish and chip enterprise to the hospital to help pay for her son's medical expenses. His thoughtfulness caused her to cry, but not in his presence.

In many respects both were guilty of interrupting each other's path through life, she thought. She had, in her mind, abducted Peter, had seduced him and had led him from his proper path. But was it entirely her fault, she wondered. She loved him and took care of almost his every need. She had at all times been kind and loving towards him, and he needed her as much as she needed him, for companionship and a loving partner.

Now, she wondered, how would her relationship with Peter end? Before knowing him, her road had been much easier to follow and her goal definite. Now, she must still aim for that goal, but to navigate the road ahead had been made far more difficult. Soon, though, in about four months, Peter would have completed his overseas tour and would be returning to his home in England, then her road should be easier to follow again. She knew that when eventually he bade her that final farewell, she must put him from her mind, as all that would remain of him would be memories, nothing more. But she would always remember him, and treasure those memories.

Sighing, with Peter still in her thoughts, she moved from the window and, so as not to awaken the baby she held, she carefully sat down upon the edge of her bed. She did not expect Peter to leave Singapore on his exact tour expiration date, but that his departure from the island would be reprieved by a few weeks. The signing of the truce agreement just six weeks ago on 27 July, hopefully ending the Korean war, could be thanked for that, because for several months to come the troopships and military transport aircraft would be full to capacity with servicemen who had fought in Korea. Ex-prisoners of war and the wounded had first priority, followed by the tens of thousands of British army boys, the lucky ones who had come away from the battlefields unscathed. Already troopships were passing through Singapore full to capacity. The servicemen and women stationed in Singapore could wait. But most of these did not mind the wait. For the majority, Singapore was paradise.

Nevertheless, regardless of those few reprieved weeks, she knew that. Peter's time in Singapore with her was fast running out. Soon he would be at home with his mother and brothers. Would he forget her, she wondered. She wished so badly that he could stay with her. In just another year, perhaps two, she could retire comfortably from this dirty business, buy her dream home, and live with nice ordinary people outside the city. She would visit the theatres, the amusement worlds, the racetrack, parks and beaches, and no one then could smirk and whisper for all to hear, "She's a prostitute!"

Her thoughts again turned to Peter. Tomorrow he was going away for a whole month, perhaps longer, and worse, back into the jungle. She had prayed that he would not leave her during his last few months in Singapore, and she dreaded the thought of him returning to the jungle. Concerned for his safety, she knew he would be sick with malaria again. Also, she had heard that there were terrible dangers lurking in the jungle. But what was the use of worrying, she told herself. Other servicemen went into the jungles of Malaya and came out unharmed, so why shouldn't Peter? And why shouldn't his good friend Rick, who was going with him, come back unscathed, too? That Rick's name was on the same Movements order of those airmen detailed to go to Fraser's Hill was to her the only piece of good news Peter had brought her regarding his impending journey. She knew he had a good friend and companion in Rick, for although she had never met him, Peter often talked to her about Rick. She wondered how Rick's girlfriend was taking the news, and if she had the same dread she herself now felt.

"He must come back. He must ..." she heard herself saying, when suddenly she heard his special knock on the door below. Excited more than normal by his arrival, she listened, hearing the old *amah*'s gritty voice asking, "It is you, Chicko?" And she heard Peter's voice answer, "Momma. *Hoi mun ah. Fai di ah.*" 'Open the door quickly' he had asked her, for it was evening, and already the provost police would be patrolling the streets. Lai Ming heard the rasping voice of the *amah* who was swearing loudly as she unlocked the door. The *amah* often swore at Peter, but always in jest and in a friendly manner. She had a fondness for Peter, and would allow no other man entry into the house when he was expected or whilst he was present, especially on this day, which she knew was a sad day for her mistress.

Lai Ming smiled as she heard Peter say in English to the *amah*, "Here, Momma. Take these brown eggs. My chickens laid them this morning especially for you. And here's some sardines and a tin of cigarettes." She heard the *amah*'s delighted squeals of thanks, and then she heard Peter's hasty footsteps on the narrow stairway leading up to her apartment.

Later that night, Peter and Lai Ming lay in bed together, talking, touching, loving each other, their final hours together slipping quickly away. Eleven o'clock came, time for him to dress and depart if he was to catch the last bus back to Changi. Reluctantly, he got up off the bed and began to dress.

"No, Peter, you no go bus tonight, you take taxi," Lai Ming said, also rising from the bed. "But first I wash you. You must be nice clean boy, not dirty boy go back camp. Come, Peter," she was saying as she entered the bathroom.

Peter followed her in and allowed her to perform the ritual of washing his private parts whilst they both squat over the white enamel bowl three-quarters filled with warm water laced with Dettol disinfectant. He liked the feel of her touch. It tickled and felt good after sex. Normally she giggled as he played with her nipples while she performed the ablutions, but on this occasion he felt in no mood to play, or she to giggle. Both were too sad. After Lai Ming had completed the ablution and Peter had begun to dress, Peter finished a second bottle of Carlsberg beer. The time was approaching half past eleven but he was in no hurry now that he was to take a taxi back to Changi.

Outside, the night had grown quiet. The hawkers and beggars had retired for the night and very few citizens now roamed the street. Those who did were mostly prostitutes standing alone or in pairs in doorways, waiting to be approached by men looking for a short time or an all-night session. There was very little vehicular traffic passing below the window now, and those few were mostly whining jeeps, which regularly passed to and fro, the military police in them vigilantly seeking straying British servicemen. Also, there were numerous taxis, which passed slowly beneath the window whilst cruising the area, their alert drivers waiting for bargains to be settled between prostitutes and their potential customers before making their approach. Trishaw *wallahs* also waited for bargains to be settled. Their conveyances for hire were usually cheaper than the taxis but rarely used by British servicemen in the red-light district, because to do so would be folly and just asking to be picked up by the military police.

Dressed now and ready to depart, Peter held a *sarong*-clad Lai Ming in his arms. "A last kiss, Rose," he said, and their lips met. They broke away, seeing each other in the glow of the bedside table lamp.

"Don't take anyone tonight, Rose. Please, I ask you not to. Let my thoughts be at rest tonight," Peter pleaded.

"Shh. No talk about dirty business. I no want break spell of evening's happiness."

"You're my lovely little lady, Rose. I love you so very much."

"And I love you, Peter, much more than you think. I won't ever love anyone else. I know I won't, ever. You will come back to me the day you return to Singapore?"

"You know I will."

Opening the drawer to her bedside table, Lai Ming took from it a pen and an unused white envelope with a ten cent red Malayan stamp already stuck to its top right hand corner. Her name and address was written in Chinese on the left-hand side of the envelope. "Peter, this my name and address," she said. "Now you write my name and address in your writing."

Questioningly, he took the envelope from her.

"When you get to where you go, you put inside picture postcard of place and post to me, OK. Then, I know you OK."

"All right. That's a good idea," said Peter, and placing the envelope on the dressing table, he carefully wrote in English Lai Ming's name and address on the right-hand side of the envelope. "How's that?" he said.

"It is good," Lai Ming answered.

"I will post it as soon as I'm able. I may be able to send you a picture postcard of Fraser's Hill. It will be a memory."

"Yes, a memory," she said, holding back tears she knew must flow. A thought suddenly occurred to her. Supposing there were no postcards where he was going. "Peter," she said. "If there are no postcards, send only the envelope. I shall understand, and I shall know you arrived safely. But you no forget send envelope."

Folding the envelope, Peter slipped it into his pants back pocket. "I won't forget," he said. "I shall post it as soon as I arrive at Fraser's Hill." He looked into her sad, bewildered eyes. Or were they frightened eyes? He believed he understood her feelings. She wanted to hold on to him, and not let him go. Again he took her into his arms, feeling her warmth pressing against him and soft tresses of her hair sliding between his combing fingers. He did not want to leave her. Her soft cheeks were against his lips as he sincerely said, "You know, Rose, I shall always love you."

Hugging Peter to her, Lai Ming lifted her face for a final farewell kiss. "We belong to each other, though it's a love that can never be," she whispered. "A little Chinese woman and an English boy." And she tearfully said, "Take care of yourself, Peter. Remember your mother's words. Yourself first, second and third. Always think of yourself, your own safety. And Peter, come back to me as soon as you can. I shall be waiting for you."

"You're a darling. We should get married. Let's discuss it again when I return."

"No, silly boy, remember, I am a mother and I'm too old for you. Let's not talk of marriage, but always you can be my lover."

"OK. Have it your own way."

She gave him a peck on the cheek. "The *amah* will get you a taxi as soon as she hears your footsteps on the stairs."

"Thanks."

"And don't forget to post the envelope as soon as you arrive at the camp. If no picture, OK. I want envelope. It says you OK."

"I'll remember to post it."

"Goodbye, Peter. Be careful. Look after yourself."

He saw tears running freely from Lai Ming's eyes and rolling down wet cheeks, and he realized that he, too, was not taking the parting easily. He felt heavy at heart at leaving her, as well as a strange uneasiness. Damn the RAF for posting him back to Malaya, especially during his last few remaining months with her, he thought.

With a lump in his throat, he said, "Bye-bye, Rose. I'll be back as soon as I can."

Standing in her apartment doorway, Lai Ming tried to smile. "Goodbye, Peter," she said, and now she was sobbing even more.

Peter turned from her. He did not like to see her cry. Feeling much sadness in his heart at parting from her, he slipped quietly down the stairway. And now, the other feeling that he had felt much of the day returned to him, a foreboding feeling of the forthcoming trip, a feeling of impending disaster. It lay hard upon his spirits as he let himself out of the house and walked the alleyway towards the road where a taxi had stopped, flagged down by the *amah*.

"Thank you, Momma," he said, as he passed the old *amah* in the alleyway.

"Good travels, Chicko," she replied in Chinese.

He climbed into the taxi. This night he would lie in his own bed, but tomorrow? He could not answer that question. Anything could happen.

PART FOUR

23

Unperturbed by all that was happening around him, young Pilot Officer Anthony Graham carefully surveyed his immediate surroundings. Satisfying himself that he had found a suitable spot, he pulled out a putter from his golf bag that lay amid his other luggage— two new suitcases and an ancient-looking violin case containing an equally ancient violin which his grandfather had left him in his will. Taking a golf ball from his trouser pocket, he ambled over to a patch of scrubby grass growing alongside where the perforated steel plate runway ended and the concrete apron of the dispersal area began. There, using the heel of his shoe, he stamped an indentation into the soft wet soil, walked back four paces, dropped the ball to the ground, and putted it towards the hole he had made. The ball stopped within an inch of the hole. Tapping the ball into the hole, he casually retrieved it, and then practiced the shot a second time, this time scoring a hole in one. Smiling with satisfaction, he again retrieved the ball and retreated six paces. A Vampire fighter took off, its jet engine screaming as it flew low over his head, but Pilot Officer Graham did not look up; he was far too engrossed in putting the golf ball into that little hole he had created.

Between the budding golfer and the recently landed twin-engine Valletta, on the hot tarmac of RAF Kuala Lumpur in Malaya, waited Peter, Rick and the remaining arrivals from RAF Changi in Singapore. Some stood in small groups chatting and smoking cigarettes, whilst others sat on suitcases and kitbags, watching the young officer showing off his putting skill, and all appearing unconcerned about the journey ahead.

Suddenly, a three-tonne Bedford lorry appeared heading in their direction. Careering off the camp's main road, it bounced its way towards them in a cloud of dust along a dirt track, slowing only on reaching the tarmacked dispersal area, and finally stopping close to the groups of airmen waiting with their luggage alongside the stationary Valletta.

The cab's door flew open and out sprang the lorry driver, a senior aircraftman, about thirty years of age, freckled and with a mop of unruly red hair. The airman's blue beret was stuffed under an epaulette, the normally shiny brass RAF badge pinned to it blackened so that it would not glint in sunlight. Pulling a Sten gun from behind the seat of his cab, he casually clipped a full magazine into it and returned the weapon to behind his seat. He then turned to face the crowd of gathering airmen.

"OK chaps, all those for Fraser's Hill, chuck your gear aboard and jump on the lorry. Our first stop is the airmens' mess," he shouted. Spotting Pilot Officer Graham swinging his golf club and about to putt another ball, he shouted, "And that means you, too, sir."

At that moment, KL's grey-haired Movements NCO, Flight Sergeant Philpotts, arrived on the scene in a jeep driven by a military police corporal. Seeing the young officer wielding his golf club, Flight Sergeant Philpotts, who had flown as a rear-gunner aboard Sunderlands and bombers during World War II, was thinking, 'What's this bloody RAF coming to?' Aloud, he said, "No time for golf now, sir."

The young officer, twirling his golf putter as if he were a cheerleader twirling his baton, strutted towards the Movements flight sergeant, an ingratiating smile on his face.

"Good morning, Flight Sergeant. A lovely day, what!" he said, turning on the charm.

"Good morning, sir. Yes, it is a lovely day. But we've got to get moving."

"Oh! Of course, Flight Sergeant," the young officer beamed. "Just practicing a little, you know." On seeing that his was the only luggage remaining on the tarmac, he said, "I say, Flight Sergeant, can someone help me with my luggage?"

"Your luggage, sir?"

"Yes. My luggage."

"Well, it's not like Changi here, sir. There's no bearers at KL."

"No bearers! I say, Flight Sergeant! That's frightfully inexcusable. What am I to do?" Looking across the airstrip the young officer espied two suntanned airmen clad only in khaki shorts busily working on the engine of a Beaufighter. Two other airmen, similarly clad, were standing on metal mesh beneath the wing, handing up tools when needed to the two aircraft mechanics. Confidently, he turned to the flight sergeant. "Those airmen over there, Flight, the two fiddling around underneath the wing. Could you detail one to help with my luggage?"

The flight sergeant looked over to where the young officer pointed, and on recognizing the two airmen working under the wing, said, "Them, sir! Them's mechanics. They can't go shiftin' peoples' gear around. They've got their own work cut out."

"My luggage is awfully heavy, Flight Sergeant. That's mine over there. No one's bothered to put it on the lorry."

The Movements flight sergeant, looking at the pile of luggage, couldn't help smiling to himself. "Sir, do you think it's wise to take golf clubs and a violin to Fraser's Hill?" he asked.

"And what's wrong with bringing my golf clubs and violin along, Flight Sergeant?"

"Well, sir, you are going up into the jungle. It's not exactly a pleasure trip."

"I don't expect the actual trip to be too pleasant, Flight Sergeant, what with this damned heat and humidity. But the climate at the summit of Fraser's Hill should be delightful. It's quite cool and bracing there, so I've heard. More importantly, are you aware that Fraser's Hill boasts a spectacular golf course, built out of the jungle by the Sultan of Pahang?

It's highly regarded in the golfing world and is definitely the largest and best golf course in Malaya. And since I'm to be the officer in charge of the radar unit at Fraser's Hill for the next six months or so, both my violin and my golf clubs will come in jolly handy."

"Sir! I'm well aware of the golf course at Fraser's Hill, but do you know that much of the surrounding area is infested by Communist terrorists?"

"Oh, phooey to a few terrorists."

"Well, sir, good luck to you. I hope you do manage to get in a few rounds of golf. But don't underestimate the terrorists. I'll get a couple of the lads leaving with you to put your gear aboard."

"Good show! Thank you, Flight Sergeant. By the way, where's my transportation?"

"You'll be travelling to Fraser's Hill in this lorry, sir," said the Flight Sergeant.

A sudden look of indignation appeared on the young pilot officer's face. "That lorry is to take me to Fraser's Hill?" he exclaimed.

"Yes, sir."

"I thought there'd be at least a coach laid on for such a long journey."

"No, sir. That's it," the flight sergeant said, pointing a finger towards the Bedford lorry.

"Oh well!"

"As I've already said, sir, I hope you'll have a good trip. But don't keep the boys awake at Fraser's Hill with that violin of yours. And mind you don't lose your balls."

"I beg your pardon, Flight Sergeant?"

"Your golf balls, sir. Mind you don't lose them in the *ulu*."

"The *ulu*?"

"The jungle."

"Ah! Yes! The neutral jungle."

Muttering to himself, "Some mothers do 'ave 'em," the flight sergeant strode over to where a couple of hefty-looking airmen were smoking, sitting on the tarmac near the officer's luggage. "You! Airmen! Get rid of those fags and stow those four pieces of gear up on the wagon," he ordered.

The officer's luggage, including the beat-up violin case and the bag of golf clubs were tossed unceremoniously aboard the lorry by the two hefty airmen, where they fell on top of all the other pieces of luggage stacked behind the cab of the three-tonner.

"OK lads, all those going to Fraser's Hill get aboard," shouted the flight sergeant.

A rush followed, the airmen clambering up over the sides and rear of the lorry, a few swearing on knocking themselves against metal parts, others swearing because of the heat and the humidity, and some because of not knowing where they were going or what to expect. Several had suddenly become apprehensive on seeing the driver with a Sten gun, and more so at having seen him nonchalantly load the weapon. Keyed up, they were letting off steam.

The young pilot officer, aloof and alone, approached the lorry driver. But before he could utter a word, the driver said to him, "If you take a seat up in the cab, sir, I'll first take you to the officers' mess."

"Oh, thank you, airman. Is it far?"

"The officers' mess? No, sir. It's just up the hill past them rubber trees," he said, jerking a thumb towards a distant rise. Turning his attention again to the airmen seated in the back of the lorry, he shouted, "OK chaps, after I drop off the officer, our first stop will be the airmens' mess. It's not the best of grub up there. It was until the cooks fucked it up. Now listen carefully. As soon as you've finished your meal, you're to collect arms from the armoury. That's over there," he said, jerking the same thumb towards some single storey buildings, which appeared to be at the entrance to the airfield. "I'll be picking you up there in exactly one hour from now, so eat fast. There ain't no latrines along the route, so take a shit if you need to before we head out. Some miles outside KL we'll be joining a convoy. That convoy can not be delayed by us or by anyone else. So remember, no one must be late getting to the armoury.

Is that clear?"

Much muttering followed among the airmen seated on two rows of slotted wooden benches facing outward and running down the length of each side of the open lorry. A few questions were shot at the driver, who shot back only the one answer, "You'll find out soon enough." Returning to his cab, he sat down next to the young pilot officer, and with everyone seated, restored the engine to life. The Bedford three-tonner moved away from the parked Valletta and headed towards the exit of the airfield, and to the officers' mess and the airmens' mess, both being situated upon the hillside half a mile or so away.

Memories flooded Peter Saunders as he sat next to Gerald Rickie on a bench at the rear of the lorry, where both gazed out over the closed tailboard.

Peter knew that a modern RAF camp was in the process of being built at KL but he was not too interested in seeing it, just curious. And as the lorry drove away from the airstrip, he could see numerous remains of the old camp but as yet nothing of the new. Very little seemed to have changed since that day, just over a year ago, when he had departed from RAF Kuala Lumpur. Now, the weather was just as hot and humid as it had been then, and he travelled the same narrow, dusty road lined on his left by tall, rank grasses, and on his right the abandoned rubber plantation; land which was already being reclaimed by fast-growing jungle. There must be some life left in those gnarled, shapeless old rubber trees, though, he thought, because he had spotted an aged Tamil Indian woman among the greenery carving a downward curve in the lower part of a tree trunk and setting a crescent-shaped cup beneath the fresh wound. By morning that old lady rubber tapper could be rewarded by perhaps half a cup of pure latex for her efforts from that one tree and, most probably, she would have tapped many of the trees during the course of the day.

Peter noticed that there were still some remains of the old camp. Among undergrowth to his right he could see two of the old bashas as the chaps called them, dirt-floored huts made out of rough-cut, bug-infested palm planking. The rotting doors were made of the same material and hanging on rusted hinges. There were no glass windows, just square openings in the sides of the huts, with heavy wooden shutters, which were supposed to keep out the torrential afternoon rains. However, these shutters, equally bug-ridden and hanging on rusted hinges, were rarely closed. The shutters were literally alive, the myriad holes and crevices in the woodwork swarming with inch-long black ants, maggots galore, and huge hairy spiders with bodies the size of a man's thumb nail. The many lizards that scuttled hungrily through the palm-thatched roof and among the woodwork were man's best friends at the old camp at KL, Peter recalled, and were often kept as pets in mens' jacket pockets, and in their lockers, too.

Originally, the bashas had been built to house native rubber tappers. Much later, during the brutal Japanese occupation of Malaya, the huts had housed British and Australian prisoners of war, many of whom died there from brutality, starvation and neglect. And after the war ended the same run-down huts were used to house RAF other ranks stationed at Kuala Lumpur. Now, though, the few huts that Peter saw appeared to be uninhabited. He would have burnt the lot to the ground, bugs and all, if he'd had his way. The hut on the hillside that he had lived in was obscured from his view by jungle that had taken over the old rubber plantation. But he could see the beginning of the rutted, muddy path that led to it, winding its way along the mosquito-infested hillside.

The lorry passed close to a derelict shack considerably larger than the other shacks, its palm-frond roof caved in. This bigger shack had once been the SHQ, the nerve centre of the old camp. Its innards had been partitioned off to form hot and smelly offices with very little ventilation. A beehive that had outlived its usefulness, it had become quite inadequate for the many and varied tasks the clerks had had to cope with to meet the demands placed upon them by the Communist uprising.

Peter well remembered how he had felt that last day when he walked down this same dusty road to the airstrip with his suitcase and kitbag, to board the aircraft which took him to RAF Changi and to a completely new life in Singapore.

At the time of his leaving, the camp at KL had begun to be revolutionized. Architects had already designed a new, modern camp, and builders were busily beginning its construction.

Now, as the lorry left the remnants of the old camp behind, Peter caught his first glimpse of the new RAF Kuala Lumpur. Through the sweat and toil of Chinese coolies, much had already been completed within that one year; a modern military base had risen out of cleared swampland, jungle and a part of the abandoned rubber plantation. RAF Kuala Lumpur could finally feel proud of itself, thought Peter. The majority of those journeying with him would see only the new camp. They would not know of the old SHQ, the health-breaking kitchen and dining room, the filthy old bashas, all of which were now covered by living growth but which soon would be demolished, the land and everything on it cleared to make way for progress.

The lorry stopped outside a modern, white, two-storey brick building in front of which proudly fluttered the blue RAF flag from the yardarm of a tall flagpole. The driver got out and, pushing his way through a mosquito-proof screen door, entered Kuala Lumpur's new Station Headquarters. Through screen-protected open windows Peter could see clerks busy at their desks, and he could hear telephones ringing, and the fast clickety-clack of typewriters. There was an imposing air of efficiency about the whole place.

Within minutes, the driver returned, climbed back into his cab and the lorry resumed its short journey. It stopped next at the officers' mess, where Pilot Officer Graham alighted, before proceeding to the airmens' mess, passing new, white, brick bungalows that Peter guessed had to be the airmens' billets.

Even though Peter could not see inside these bungalows, he had learned from a cook recently posted from KL to Changi that each spacious room had sleeping accommodation for four airmen. Every modern comfort had been installed in them such as bedside reading lamps, electric fans, wardrobes, bookshelves, shoe cupboards, easy chairs and a writing table in every room. There were even bedside mats, ashtrays and coat-hangers provided. What a vast difference to those bad old days that he had experienced, he thought. And as for the toilets, he had heard that they were as good as at any first class hotel. Hot and cold water, tiled floors, towel racks, soap trays, mirrors above washbasins. Take your pick as far as baths were concerned. He had heard that there was a foot bath per bungalow to soak one's weary feet, a shower bath for those who felt hot and sticky with sweat, and a deep, full-length bath in which one could wallow in soapsuds. One could even use the lavatory without a mosquito biting one's ass or seeing a snake slithering across one's feet. The RAF chaps had never had it so good as now at KL, thought Peter.

Even with all its modern buildings, the camp was not yet fully complete. A sports centre and a NAAFI was halfway constructed, and a library and a swimming pool was in the planning stage. RAF Kuala Lumpur was becoming quite a holiday camp.

The lorry drew up at a pathway leading into the airmens' mess dining room. The driver, as he had done on both previous occasions, jumped down from his cab, backwards.

"OK men, this is the airmens' mess," he shouted. "Remember what I told you. Meet me in an hour at the armoury. And don't be late."

The men jumped down from the lorry onto the hot tarmacked road. On entering the mess they lined up at the servery, taking from their small packs RAF issued brown enamel mugs, and their eating irons comprising knives, forks and spoons. Peter noted how sullen the two cooks appeared to be who were standing behind the gleaming, stainless steel servery waiting to serve the incoming men in transit. Perhaps, thought Peter, these in-coming men needing early lunches were delaying the cooks from getting on with the preparation and cooking of the main lunch. Perhaps there was still a shortage of cooks at KL. Without a hint of a smile between them the two cooks sloshed food onto outstretched plates. Soon, all those bound for Fraser's Hill were served and seated.

Rick gulped a dollop of powdered potato down his throat and

swallowed hard. He prodded the leathery roast beef with his knife, and then attempted to cut it but could not. "God, either my knife is blunt or this beef is damned tough," he complained. Pushing sickly-looking dehydrated cabbage to one side of his plate, he then tried the dehydrated turnip. That too he found unappetizing. In disgust he pushed the plate aside. Peter did likewise. In silence, both then ate their serving of a few cold prunes and stodgy rice pudding.

When both had finished eating, Rick grumbled, "If that's a sample of lunch at KL, roll on teatime at Fraser's Hill."

"I agree," said Peter. "I wouldn't give that stuff to my pig-swill man."

They both cleaned their knife, fork and spoon by wiping them off on pieces of bread before returning them to their small packs.

"Fucking ironic, isn't it, Pete?"

"What is?"

"Here they have a brand new, all-electric kitchen, and the cooks have the audacity to lash up worse muck than you and the other cooks ever did up at that pigsty on the hill. Come on. Let's go."

Together they rose from the table and made for the exit.

"Just like home cooking," Rick remarked to a sour-faced corporal cook standing in the exit doorway. For a moment a smile flickered on the corporal's face as the remark sank in. "Yeah, my mother can't cook either," continued Rick, and he was out of that dining hall, and gone, fast, with Peter Saunders hot on his heels.

24

The party of twenty-two airmen, that was about to depart from Kuala Lumpur on the dangerous journey to the summit of Fraser's Hill, comprised Pilot Officer Graham, Warrant Officer Jack Perkins, Corporal Hicks and seventeen airmen, plus two motor-transport drivers, both senior aircraftmen. One lorry was insufficient to carry the men, their luggage, necessary stores, plus equipment requested by the outgoing officer in charge of the radar unit at Fraser's Hill, so an additional Bedford three-tonne open lorry had been laid on. Both were now pulled up on the dusty road outside the armoury.

There were a number of reasons why the two lorries and twenty-two RAF personnel were making the sixty-three mile journey from Kuala Lumpur to the isolated RAF camp at Fraser's Hill. Relieving the officer in charge at Fraser's Hill, who was tour expired, was one. Airmen due leave and who were being replaced was another. Also, foodstuffs, stores and equipment had to be delivered there.

Transporting airmen who had spent at least a year down in the hot and humid lowlands, up into the renowned, temperate and healthy climate constant on Fraser's Hill, where the air is free from humidity and always bracingly cool was another reason. Hence, for some considerable time now, the lonely radar station also served as a health spa and recuperation centre for RAF personnel of all ranks. For the duration of one month, it was a place where one was supposed to relax, where one's vigour was expected to be restored, and one's blood thickened back to normal after being thinned during a prolonged stay in the heat of the East. The airmen who were sent to Fraser's Hill were considered 'lucky bastards' by those sweating their guts out down in the tropical lowlands of Malaya. These few were getting a break in their two-and-a-half year overseas tour, a break from work, from the incessant heat, even from culture shock and the excitement of the mind brought on by the mystic environment of the East, which is so vastly different from that of their homeland.

There was a grimmer reason, too, why seven of these airmen, all marksmen with a rifle, were making the journey. During the past months, Communist terrorists had, with increasing frequency, ambushed not only military vehicles but also private cars making the journey up jungle-clad Fraser's Hill. Seldom showing mercy, the terrorists robbed and murdered those they ambushed, especially British men, both civilian and service personnel, regardless of their rank or status. This period of terrorism began in the late 1940s, and from then on had gradually escalated. One of the most vicious acts took place on 6 October 1951, when Sir Henry Gurney, the High Commissioner of Malaya, was forced out of his chauffeur-driven car at gunpoint, and there, at the side of the road, halfway up Fraser's Hill, he was shot dead. His wife and chauffeur were ordered to remain in the car, and after Sir Henry was murdered they were allowed to proceed unharmed.

In order to counteract the intensifying violence of the terrorists, armed convoys were being formed before making journeys through known Communist terrorist danger zones in Malaya. For their protection, private vehicles mingled with military vehicles in the convoys, the latter carrying armed guards. Now, all military personnel making the trip to Fraser's Hill carried weapons, but in this convoy the seven airmen who were marksmen were considered more able to spot and pick off any aggressor.

Also, it was rumoured that the powers that be were considering using these seven RAF marksmen, plus scores of British army marksmen, in a massive seek-and-destroy manhunt for those responsible for the recent murder of a high-ranking British officer and three British soldiers.

SAC Peter Saunders and LAC Gerald Rickie arrived at the armoury just as both Pilot Officer Graham and Warrant Officer Perkins were each being issued a service revolver and a carton of ammunition. Corporal Hicks signed out a Sten gun and a dozen magazines, and every airman was being issued a .303 Enfield rifle and a belt of ammunition. Immediately on issue, both SAC Saunders and LAC Rickie thoroughly checked their rifles, especially the bolt action and the forward sight. Satisfied, each made sure that the safety catch was on and clipped a ten-round magazine into place. Just like old times, thought Peter Saunders grimly.

While the airmen had been at breakfast, a Bren gun had been mounted and secured to the cab roof of each Bedford lorry. Now, manned by a corporal of the tough RAF Regiment, each gun, loaded with twenty-eight rounds of .303 ammunition was ready to spit death at any foe.

The military transport drivers, with loaded Sten guns at their side, were seated in their cabs, impatiently waiting to get started; they preferred to be moving. Only too well did they know that if the convoy should be ambushed, they would almost certainly be the first to die. The drivers were almost always the first to be shot at. These two drivers, though, showed no apprehension towards the hazardous journey ahead. To them it was just one more trip, one more duty to perform. Both had driven this same route without incident many times before. Actually, they gave their safety little thought, both preferring to think of the pints of draught beer served at the Rose and Crown, a little English pub that had suddenly materialized near the golf course at the summit of Fraser's Hill.

Clutching their weapons, the airmen again clambered up into the back of the first lorry. Some were apprehensive, others wondered what was going on, and a few thought it a big joke; but all were interested, even excited, just at the thought of the nearly seventy-mile journey that lay ahead. A few knew what to expect geographically—native villages and farmlands, rubber plantations and vast acres of jungle in the lowlands, followed by a winding road up green, jungle-clad Fraser's Hill. Only a few of the airmen had visited the mainland of Malaya before this day. Several wondered what lay ahead, but all were perspiring freely and wanting to be moving. The jungle was completely foreign to the majority of them, its beauty, the strange and exotic noises exuding from it, the contrasting colours. Likewise, only a few of the RAF personnel journeying to Fraser's Hill that day knew of the jungle's treacherousness, where one seldom sees the enemy, and the hunter often becomes the hunted. But not one of these airmen was afraid, although some were troubled at seeing such a great amount of arms and ammunition issued. The lorry they were in fairly bristled with weapons, not only from both sides of it but also from its front and rear, like quills on a porcupine, only infinitely more deadly.

Peter Saunders sat at the rear of the lorry, at the side of his friend Rick. Both of them, as well as the few other veterans of the jungle, had very mixed emotions. They had experienced the cruel, neutral jungle, and were not ignorant of the potentialities that lay concealed amidst its tranquillity. During this period of time, danger always seemed to lurk there. As for Peter Saunders, the sense of foreboding he had felt when with Rose yesterday evening remained. But, except for this nagging feeling and the thoughts of being away from Rose, on looking at Rick, he felt both happy and thankful at having him at his side. Not only would it be a pleasant trip together, he told himself, but also they would enjoy a happy-go-lucky month at Fraser's Hill. He had heard that at the camp there was an archery range and a small sports section where one could borrow a bow and a quiver of arrows. He smiled to himself as he thought of Rick and himself playing at being Robin Hood and Friar Tuck, although it was no Sherwood Forest surrounding the small village and RAF camp at the summit of Fraser's Hill, but instead the almost impenetrable jungle.

Guarding the rear, both Peter and Rick rested their weapons on a pile of new mattresses bound for the camp at Fraser's Hill. Again Peter checked the safety catch on his rifle to make sure it was on. A flick of the finger, rapid bolt action and a squeeze on the trigger was all it needed for instant action. He was about to speak to Gerald Rickie, who was squinting towards the guardroom and camp exit, when, in a cloud of dust, a jeep drew up at the armoury and out climbed a tough-looking flying officer of the RAF Regiment. A heavy service revolver hung in its holster from the officer's hip, and an impressive bushy black moustache hid neither the scowl nor the deep scar on the man's weather-beaten face. Drawing on a black cheroot, he strode between the two lorries in which the men waited, puffed out a cloud of smoke and stood there, almost menacingly, his long arms hanging down his sides like those of an ape.

Looking up at the many inquiring faces peering down at him, he greeted them with, "Good morning one and all," in a loud, regimental tone of voice.

"Good morning, sir," came mumbled replies from both lorries.

"I'm your officer in charge of this party. My name's Morgan. Flying Officer Henry Morgan. No relation to Henry Morgan the pirate but just as much a bastard to anyone who don't follow my orders. Is that understood?"

Murmuring followed among the men in the back of the lorries, and a few said, "Yes, sir."

Again they became silent as the flying officer exhaled more smoke and gave a dry sort of cough, as if clearing his throat, before continuing in a loud voice, "OK, chaps, just a little pep talk before we move off. As your officer in charge, I expect each and everyone of you to obey any and all commands I give without question, and at the double. This must be understood by all, right from the beginning. You must pay attention to everything I'm about to say. If you don't, lives may be at risk, perhaps your own. Is that understood?"

"Yes, sir," answered many voices in unison.

"Good. As you probably know, we are bound for Fraser's Hill. The route can become quite sticky at times, and when I say sticky, I mean downright dangerous. We shall be travelling through areas occupied by terrorists whose sole aim is to kill you. Therefore, I expect every one of you to keep your eyes open. And when I say open, I mean for you to be fully alert from the moment we leave here until we arrive at our destination. Once we are on the road, you will look outward the whole time. You will note everyone and everything, and you will consider everyone and everything a potential life-threatening danger. So remember, you must remain alert."

"He's no joker," whispered Peter Saunders to Rick.

"Silence," roared the flying officer. "Once we're moving, there'll be no smoking, as little yapping as possible and keep your hands on your weapons. But no rounds in the breech, not yet. Those with rounds already in the breech, unload them. Now!"

Peter and Rick looked at each other and shrugged. An airman sitting next to Peter withdrew a round from the breech of his rifle. Other airmen were doing the same.

"OK. Next!" Swivelling around, Flying Officer Morgan indicated with a wave of his cheroot the stoic corporal of the RAF Regiment standing behind each of the two Bren guns. "Both you Bren gunners are old hands at this job," he continued, "but you must not be complacent. I need not remind you that you must remain behind your weapons at all times. Remember, peoples' lives depend upon you." He turned to young Pilot Officer Graham who was standing at the cab door of the first lorry, a bored and indifferent look on his face. "You, sir, will be the driver's mate in the first vehicle. Forget your revolver. You'll keep the Sten gun in your hands ready at all times for instant action. Is that clear, sir?"

"Oh, yes," said Pilot Officer Graham. "But I don't know how to use a, what did you call it?"

"A Sten gun," barked Flying Officer Morgan. "Don't worry, you'll learn how to use it when and if the time comes. Just point the weapon at the enemy and squeeze the trigger."

"Oh!" exclaimed the young officer. Forcing a smile, he said, "I hope there'll be no reason for me to use it. Shall I climb aboard now?"

"Yes, by all means, but please stay alert." Then, turning his attention to the riflemen who lined the sides and rear of both lorries, he said," I want your rifles at the ready as soon as we're the other side of KL. Each lorry must have a complete circle of armament protection, also a complete circle of visual protection, so stay alert. There will be no sleeping. Anyone I catch sleeping I'll deal with immediately on reaching our destination. Is that fully understood?"

Answers of, "Yes, sir," came from the ranks.

Nodding his approval and with his bushy moustache twitching, Flying Officer Morgan pushed forward a square, stone-like chin as he surveyed the two lorry loads of men he was about to conduct up Fraser's Hill. All were greenhorns as far as he was concerned; just little boys recently weaned from their mothers' titties. They were not like him, and never would be. Life in the Regiment had certainly given him the sort of life he loved during the five years he had served in the toughest section of the Royal Air Force. Previously, in World War II, he had worn a red beret, had parachuted into Arnhem, and there, single-handed, had destroyed three German Tiger tanks and killed twenty or more German soldiers before being captured and imprisoned. Then came the end of the war, his release from a POW camp, and his return to England as a civilian, only to find his wife of four years seeking a divorce from him and living in luxury with a top politician. Disgusted with his homecoming and with the feeling that never again could he settle down to England's boring lifestyle, he had, within weeks of his demob from the parachute regiment, enlisted in the RAF Regiment. He had no regrets. The Regiment gave him the chance to make use of his power of command, and his shrewdness and coolness when in action and facing danger. Long ago he had realized that there was something about him that all those under his command admired, respected and trusted, even though he did appear to some of his men as a five-foot-six, broad shouldered, arrogant little ape in an RAF uniform. His ex-wife had called him a bald-headed, bombastic little bastard. But, nevertheless, he was a genuine leader of men, so much so that all those in the two lorries that morning immediately felt safer by having him in command. Their eyes were riveted on him, his weather-beaten face, and the heavy service revolver hanging loosely in its holster almost to the man's knee. For the most part he wore an RAF uniform, meaning khaki drill long pants and jacket. But instead of an RAF blue beret adorned with a shiny brass badge, he wore his old red beret with his paratrooper badge still pinned to it, plus a black metal RAF badge that would not glint in the sunlight.

"By Jove, he's another little Napoleon," someone quipped.

There were titters of laughter, followed by another roar of, "Silence," from Flying Officer Morgan, which brought immediate results.

"OK, men, you've had your little joke, now pay attention." Flying Officer Morgan then continued by saying, "We shall be travelling north from here, just our two trucks, to an army unit at a place called Kuala Kubu Baru. There, we shall join a convoy of both military and civilian vehicles, and from thereon we shall be ascending Fraser's Hill where the likelihood of meeting trouble will be at its highest. Regardless, immediately after passing the guardroom of this camp, I want you to be on your toes. Then, once we've passed through KL, you must remember that every tree, every shrub or bush, every patch of tall grass, every hillock, slope or even a ditch by the roadside, all are potential ambush positions. When we pass through rubber plantations or areas of jungle you must be even more vigilant. Remember, in any of these places may lurk the man who is about to kill you or the man sitting next to you. It is up to every individual here to study all he sees, quickly, taking in every detail, every movement. Where there is jungle, your eyes must attempt to penetrate it, to seek a hidden enemy. Any questions so far?"

There was a silence among the men at first, then a rather timid voice asked, "Sir, if we see something suspicious, a movement for example that we believe is or could be the enemy, what should we do? Do we report to you, or do we fire at it?"

"Good question! If you believe it's a man attempting to conceal himself, or if you should see someone in the jungle, immediately open fire on him. He should not be there. And shoot to kill. OK! Are there any more questions?"

There was some muttering among the men but no further questions.

"No? Well, in that case, I'll now explain the route we're about to take. First we'll be passing through the town of Kuala Lumpur. Then, with KL behind us, we'll be heading along a road that will take us past the Batu Caves. Be especially on your guard when passing through this whole area. The RAF has bombed the shit out of the place but the remnant of a murderous gang of Communist bandits still lurks there. So watch out! After Batu Caves, we shall pass a tall peak known as Tiger Tooth Rock. That whole area has been heavily bombed too, both night and day, so I don't expect trouble there. Regardless, keep your eyes open. After Tiger Tooth Rock we'll pass through farmland, mainly paddy fields and flat, low-lying land, until we arrive at Kuala Kubu Baru. There we'll join an armed convoy and proceed along a road winding upward through thick jungle. From there onward we'll be climbing continuously until we reach the RAF station at the summit of Fraser's Hill."

With cold steely eyes, Flying Officer Morgan gazed around him at the many young faces listening intently to his every word. "The Gap!" he suddenly shouted. "The Gap is a death trap. It has one hell of a reputation for ambush attacks, and if today we are to encounter the enemy, the Gap is where we are most likely to meet him. So listen carefully to what I say. The Gap is roughly halfway between Kuala Kubu Baru and the summit of Fraser's Hill. It's a narrow passage we must take along a road overlooked by hills coated in thick jungle. On the left-hand side of the road there is a drop-off of thousands of feet covered in vegetation. In places the drop-off is sloping, but mostly it's sheer; straight down. On the right hand side of the road there's steep hillsides of jungle, which seem to almost hang over you. Later, when we are about to approach the Gap, I shall remind you that this place is a death trap. You must be on your guard the whole time. Don't relax your vigil for one moment or it may well be your last. Any questions?" Again curt words were being uttered from an impassive face studying those on the two lorries.

This time there was no murmuring, no questions; instead, there was an uneasy silence except for a rifle butt scraping on a lorry's wooden floor.

"Good! Now everyone pay attention. Should we get ambushed, and by that I mean fired upon, this is what I expect every one of you to do. First, you will return the fire regardless as to whether or not you can see the enemy. You will fire at the point of the gunfire flashes which you may see coming from the jungle or from behind trees or bushes. If you see no flashes, fire into the vicinity of where you believe the firing is coming from. If you just don't know where the firing is coming from, keep on firing anywhere into the jungle. You may not hit an enemy, but you may check his rate of fire, or even cause him to retreat. He won't show himself, I assure you. Our lorries will keep moving, and you will not cease firing until I give the order."

Looking to where the drivers sat in their cabs, he again gave a short cough, as if again clearing his throat, and then continued. "If we, or the whole convoy, should get stopped, halted shall I say, by a driver getting shot and we are still in the ambush area, everyone of you will get clear of the wagon you're in as fast as you can; every man-jack of you. And when you jump, you will go over the side facing downhill, even though it may be quite a drop. You must go over the side and downward. Don't worry whether you roll, slide, fall, or do a couple of somersaults; panic if you will the first few yards down into the undergrowth, but get concealed quickly. And don't forget your rifle or whatever weapon you're supposed to be carrying. Your gun is your best friend. I say go downhill because the enemy is almost certain to set their ambush facing downhill. Don't try going uphill towards him. He will pick you off before you can say 'fuck it'. And don't think you're safe by crawling underneath a vehicle. Ricocheting bullets will soon finish you off. Remember, go downhill, and fast. Once you are under the cover of the jungle, remain quiet and motionless for a while. Get your breath back. Get your bearings. Then try to form up into parties of threes and fours, and, if possible, proceed to stalk the enemy and to retaliate. Once again, though, if we're ambushed and your vehicle is stopped, go downhill. Let the enemy lose you. Then, you find the enemy."

He gazed upward at the many faces peering down at him from the backs of the two lorries. He moved his eyes slowly from face to face.

"Are there any questions?" he asked. But none came. "No?" He shrugged his broad, ape-like shoulders. "Remember, no nodding off." Then, "All right, men, that's all."

"That's enough," said Rick, under his breath.

"Yes. 'Twas quite a mouthful," acknowledged Peter.

Turning to Warrant Officer Jack Perkins who still stood by his side, Flying Officer Morgan said to him, "Warrant Officer Perkins, you'll sit up front with the other driver."

"Very good, sir."

Climbing aboard the lorry Peter and Rick were in, Flying Officer Morgan positioned himself at the side of the RAF Regiment Bren gunner. "OK drivers. When you're ready," he shouted.

Engines moaned as bottom gears were engaged. Then, slowly, the two Bedfords headed towards the camp exit. There, the camp barrier pole was raised by an SP who saluted them as they passed him at the guardroom. Proceeding along a narrow, winding road, with RAF Kuala Lumpur behind them and the town of Kuala Lumpur two miles ahead, the two lorries gathered speed amid great clouds of dust. It hadn't rained yet that day at Kuala Lumpur. But it would.

25

In great heat and swirling dust, and exactly on schedule, the two Bedford lorries left RAF Kuala Lumpur for Fraser's Hill. The wooden seat on which Peter sat was uncomfortable but so far only the juddering and jolting of the Bedford lorry as it struck potholes in the road caused him any discomfort. The high-pitched whine of the Bedford's engine dropped in tone as the driver changed to a lower gear and swung the wheel sharply to the left; the truck veered off the narrow road from the airstrip and onto the main Malacca-Kuala Lumpur highway.

Suddenly a near-deafening roar drowned out all other sound as three RAF bombers streaked low overhead, their wing-racks loaded with rockets and bombs as they headed towards yet another strike at known Communist terrorists' hideouts.

Minutes later, the two lorries reached the outskirts of Kuala Lumpur where, on each side of the road, there were dirty, old wooden shacks crammed with Chinese families. Peter glanced at the deep monsoon drains running parallel with the road, noting that they were still cluttered with garbage and swarming with flies.

Among the shacks grew clumps of banana trees that had wide, tapering leaves shading doorways and open windows. Peter noticed that not one of those plants bore fruit, perhaps because they were too young. But they were not too young to shade the many thin and wiry men, clad only in cotton shorts, bronzed and aged by the sun, squatting in the dust on bony haunches, playing mahjong. These men were much too absorbed in their game to look up as the two lorries passed them by. Only when they needed to spit, to swear, or when the wooden tiles were shuffled did they look up from the game. Children were everywhere, playing, laughing, shrieking and screaming. Many of the children appeared to be undernourished, almost all of them bore sores, scabs and scars on neglected bodies, and all had shaven heads. Chinese mothers looked on, appearing neat and clean amid the filth of the place. Almost all these women wore dark blue or black cotton suits or *samfoo*, the wide trousers known as 'foo' needing no belt to hold them up, just a twist and a tuck in at the waist. The jacket or 'sam' was buttoned up to the neck, generally with a high collar, and done up by tiny cotton buttons slipped into little loops of cotton thread. The whole two-piece garment hung loosely about the wearer, a cool shading dress sensible in a climate such as that of Malaya.

Tethered to a pole by a long rope, a water buffalo, dangling a bell from its stumpy neck, grazed on scorched, yellowish grass. Most probably, thought Peter, its owner now drank tea in the nearby coffeeshop, which did business next to a Chinese temple. Glistening with sweat, two near-naked coolies jogged along a dusty trail, both burdened down by a huge bale of thatching reeds slung at each end of a bamboo pole lying diagonally across pitifully bony shoulders. Vendors of peanuts and sweetmeats squatted beside their wares, but there appeared to be few customers. Minutes later the village was passed through, and forgotten.

On entering the city, they passed Kuala Lumpur's railway station, designed in the British 'Raj' style, the imposing General Post Office building and several more government buildings and hotels until they arrived at the clock tower across from which lay a broad expanse of green, the Padang, where men of many nationalities, all dressed in white, played a very British game of cricket. At the far side of the field, shaded by trees, was the Mock Tudor-style Selangor Club where many a gin and tonic was downed.

The lorries then passed close by a grove of coconut palms, which almost hid from view a mosque built upon a promontory between two rivers, both sluggish and muddy-brown. These dirty-looking rivers gave the city its name, '*kuala*' meaning 'river confluence' and '*lumpur*' meaning 'muddy'.

The lorries sped onward along a congested Batu Road, the bazaar and shopping centre of KL, where Indian merchants and shopkeepers all but forced those customers who were passing their doorways to enter their gaudy markets; naturally, in a most polite manner and with beaming smiles. "Just look, Johnny! Just look. Come inside," they would urge. Often, the passer-by, generally a British serviceman, would simply smile and ignore the invitation. But not to be outdone, the wily shopkeeper would then say, "Come in and have a cold beer, Johnny. No need to buy. Just look." Many potential customers would readily accept the offer of a cold beer, and some time later would emerge from the shop burdened down by purchases they had never intended to buy.

Soon into the countryside again, the two lorries sped past an old Chinese man dressed in the traditional black cotton suit, trudging along the side of the road, burdened down by strings of freshly gathered vegetables hanging from a bamboo pole bouncing upon his narrow shoulders. A few yards behind him, garbed in a black smock, her head completely shaven, trotted a small girl of about ten years of age carrying tools of farming. They look like father and daughter, thought Peter.

Rick interrupted his thoughts by saying, "Look over there! Those must be the Batu Caves," he said, pointing at a distant mountainous area. "And that must be the Tiger Tooth Rock."

"So it is!" exclaimed Peter. "Quite a sight, isn't it. No wonder it's called Tiger Tooth Rock. It really does look like a gigantic tooth."

Indeed, Tiger Tooth Rock did appear somewhat like a gigantic tooth, covered in vegetation and standing tall, its base hidden in the depth of the jungle. The Communist terrorists had long used Batu Caves as their hiding places until blasted out by continuous night and day bombing by planes of the RAF. The caves had almost been demolished, or so it was thought, although it was strongly suspected that terrorists still hid and plotted within the sanctuary of those caves, the entrances camouflaged by rubble from the heavy bombing, and now overgrown by the jungle.

Onward the two lorries sped, rattling and bouncing when their wheels struck potholes. But the road was mostly level and wide, with few bends, and running parallel with the railway line for mile after mile. These first thirty miles were a driver's dream.

On their arrival at a deep gorge between jungle-clad hills known as the Kanching Pass, the road became narrow, twisting like a giant snake beneath cliffs overgrown by sweating green foliage and sweet-smelling flowers growing in a blaze of colour. Also, there were banks of tangled vines, tall grasses and green shrubbery, and everywhere was serene and would have been quiet but for the singing of many birds. It was all so beautiful, yet so very treacherous, with potential ambush positions within every square foot of those hills. There was, though, no movement to be seen; nothing, not even a breeze stirred the undergrowth.

Perhaps it was too quiet for Flying Officer Morgan's liking. "OK men, shove a round up the spout," he suddenly shouted. "There could be trouble waiting for us in this area."

Rifle bolts were immediately pulled back and rounds of ammunition pushed into breeches. Men tensed, their anxious eyes seeking hidden enemies. Several slipped the safety catches off their weapons and kept their finger on the trigger. They sweated freely, the seats of their KD pants sticking to the wooden forms on which they sat. Carefully scrutinizing the jungle around them, many of the men expected to hear shots fired at them but Kanching Pass, with all its hidden enemies, was soon left behind, and the two lorries roared out onto an open plain where there were more rice fields.

The lorries passed through the village of Serendah before it too was left behind, and they were on the open road again. Here, rice fields were dotted by islands of banana trees, heavy with hands of green bananas.

As the lorries sped onward, and as the paddy fields were gradually left behind, the awful smell of sun-ripened excrement diminished until eventually the air became breathable again. Now they had arrived among rubber plantations; mile after mile of avenues of trees, each tree bearing a latex cup attached beneath a long, sweeping, freshly made cut on its scarred trunk. Every day those trees had to be tapped, their barks scarred afresh in order to produce the milky sap that would eventually become rubber. Barebacked native tappers moved quietly among the trees, some collecting the cups of latex and transferring it into larger containers, whilst other workers followed, tapping afresh the trees with sharp machetes. The tappers did not look up to wave, smile or shout greetings to the servicemen in the two lorries. Even if they had wished to, they dared not. These rubber tappers, mostly Tamils, were constantly intimidated and often murdered by the terrorists, more especially if they showed any sign of friendship towards the British.

Onward rode the men, in choking dust and scorching heat, with dirt and sweat combining and sticking to their hot, sweating bodies. What had started off as starched and neatly pressed KD uniforms had now become crumpled and saturated by perspiration. Talking ceased except for the occasional whisper, or at times a grunt or a curse as buttocks changed position on a hard, uncomfortable seat. By now, almost midday, it was far too hot to waste energy on idle talk. Some sipped on water, others iced tea, from hip flasks filled at KL.

More rice fields and more stench. Then the lorries roared through a palm grove and a Malay *kampung* of *atap* huts where papaya trees, heavy with fruit, were growing. Copra had been spread out on mats to dry in the sun. Chickens scratched for their lunch and, on a grassy plot, several white goats grazed. A wizened old Chinese woman, bent almost double beneath a great bundle of hay, slowly jogged on bare feet along the edge of the road, the long bamboo pole slung across her bony, narrow shoulders bouncing up and down in rhythm to her jiggling trot. A mongrel dog sniffed at her ankle. Cursing it loudly for all to hear, she spat upon the dog and kicked at it angrily. Peter observed much as the lorry sped onward along that dusty highway.

Within another few hundred yards, they came to open shopfronts and thatch-roofed dwellings on both sides of a dusty, potholed street;

more smells, many dogs barking, children screeching, street traders hawking their wares. They arrived at a barbed-wire fence and an open gateway where, to one side of the gateway, a British soldier with a rifle and fixed bayonet stood guard. Inside the gateway, painted in big black letters on a square, red-painted wooden board was the name of the British army camp the lorries were about to enter. Peter Saunders read out the name aloud. 'KUALA KUBU BARU.' He then read, "'ONE STEP FROM HELL'. How charming!" he said to Rick.

"It looks like one fucked-up place to me," was Rick's only comment.

The army camp at Kuala Kubu Baru was the rendezvous for all transport about to ascend Fraser's Hill, a transit camp where armed convoys were formed.

An army military policeman lifted a pole at the gateway and beckoned the leading driver to proceed into the camp. Once inside, a British soldier took over, directing both lorry drivers to stop at an empty, dusty, sun-scorched parking area. They were the first to arrive.

Looking about him, Peter Saunders turned to Rick. "Bloody hell! I'd hate to be stationed at this God-forsaken place," he said.

"Me, too," Rick replied. "It really is a hell-hole."

The camp was built upon a cleared and now barren hillside overlooking jungle. The army billets were constructed of rough unpainted planking and corrugated sheeting. Everything looked very old and dilapidated, and was probably used during and even before the Japanese occupation. The camp roads were nothing more than dirt tracks of fine dust and loose stone. Peter shuddered as he thought of how it must be when the rains came.

Hovels, mostly whorehouses and bars to supply the needs of soldiers, lined the dusty, stony street across the road from the entrance side of the British army camp at Kuala Kubu Baru. To the rear the scene was completely different. There, the camp, built on a man-made hillside plateau, overlooked a wide, steamy valley. Gazing through tangled barbed-wire fencing, Peter Saunders could see tall coarse grasses, burnt yellow by the sun, striving to exist on the high, dried-up mountainside. Lower down, the slopes of the hillside were green and well watered, and from them a continuous bellowing of bullfrogs could be heard, a cacophony dominating all other noises. Thick jungle covered the lower areas of the valley except where a brown, sluggish river meandered through steamy marshland. Peter shuddered as he thought of the milliards of mosquitoes, which must infest those lowlands.

With no sign of any other military vehicles to make up a convoy, the airmen in the two RAF lorries grew increasingly hot and restless. Yet, in fact, only ten minutes elapsed before the first vehicle, a light tank, made an appearance. Rumbling and clanking into the compound, it eventually swivelled around on heavy tracks and, facing the gateway it had entered, came to a standstill, its turret gun slowly revolving until the barrel pointed towards the far hills on the other side of the valley. The turret hatch opened and from it climbed a young British army officer who jumped from the tracks of the tank to the dusty ground. A lance corporal followed. Wearing jungle-green uniforms and black berets, both were perspiring profusely as they drank the contents from a shared canteen; and then both lit up a Players cigarette.

An armoured car followed the tank into the camp. It too carried a heavy turret gun, also machine guns that peeped out through slits in its armour. On coming to a standstill, its turret hatch was immediately flung open, and from it emerged a pair of young British soldiers, a corporal and a 'squaddy', also wearing jungle-green uniforms and black berets. Sweating, they sat on their hot war machine and they, too, lit up Players cigarettes.

Three bullet-proof lorries filled with heavily-armed British soldiers were next to enter the camp, followed by several Land Rovers and Jeeps, each with a mounted Bren gun manned by the driver's mate. After these, an assortment of other military vehicles, including two British army dispatch riders, straggled into the camp.

Arriving in a jeep, a fiery, ruddy-faced, British army captain took charge of forming the convoy. Appearing as if angry with everyone in that dusty compound, with much waving of his arms, in an Irish brogue he shouted orders mixed with profanities at the drivers of the many vehicles about to be formed into a convoy.

After a brief spell of sitting on the turret of their armoured car smoking, the crew were ordered by the army captain to return to their hellishly hot cramped confines, and to immediately position themselves as leader of the convoy. With its engine whining and aerial swaying the armoured car exited the camp and, cruising along the dusty street for a hundred yards or more, came to a halt upon reaching a predetermined marker.

The driver of an armoured army lorry was ordered into second place. Next, the drivers of the two RAF lorries were ordered to take up their positions behind the armoured army lorry, making them third and fourth in line. Behind these the convoy was made up in the following order: an empty, open army lorry, an armoured lorry, a Land Rover, an army staff car, another armoured army lorry, another Land Rover, and two army servicemen-filled lorries, their open backs protected from thrown grenades by a wire mesh canopy. Following one another the vehicles took up their allotted positions until finally the convoy was formed. The two dispatch riders, eager to start the journey, sat astride their motorcycles ready to kick them into life. They could ride where they wished within the convoy. Both inside and outside the camp there was much noise and movement.

The light tank, however, remained at a standstill, its engine switched off. But now that all the other vehicles had moved out of the camp and into their designated places, the tank's crew, sweltering within the hot confines of the tank, awaited orders to take up the rearguard position. Within the small circular opening of the gun turret, a young army officer could be seen as he acknowledged the army captain's order to move. At the same time he talked into a walky-talky to the corporal in charge of the armoured car which headed the convoy.

Peter Saunders surveyed the line-up of vehicles with considerable interest, noting that with the armoured car in the lead, followed by the armoured lorry and the luggage-laden RAF lorry, the lorry he was in was fourth in line. An empty open army lorry followed, which gave protection to neither the vehicle ahead nor the one following. Peter felt some apprehension at being fourth in line. He would have preferred to be somewhere in the middle of the convoy.

The British soldier on sentry duty at the gate leaned on his rifle, a bored expression on his deeply suntanned face. Looking at his watch, he then looked towards the guardroom. His relief was due, and he was fed up with standing in the heat of day doing guard duty. Once the convoy departed, the camp would be dead, but he was glad of that, thinking of the time he could spend drinking and screwing at Molly Wong's little whorehouse just across the road. The minute hand on his watch seemed to move forever slower. He shifted his weight from one foot to another, spotted a black, hard-backed beetle, and crushed it with his rifle butt. That made him feel better. Then he saw his relief coming out of the guardroom smartly marching towards him.

Now, the sun was even fiercer, its rays dancing upon the glinting metal of many weapons. A shimmering haze of heat rose above the dusty road adjacent to the camp compound. Everyone in the convoy sweated, and all wanted to be moving.

'One step from hell.' Rather an appropriate description thought Peter Saunders, seeking whatever scant shade there was in front of the tailboard of the lorry. He could see the slopes of Fraser's Hill far in the distance, rising majestically out of the steaming jungle. Mist clung tenaciously to the lower slopes. Higher, the air appeared to be clear, and he could see in places what he believed to be the road meandering upward. Wisps of cloud embraced the summit. He glanced at Rick who was seated at his side, and their eyes met. They had spoken little since taking their place in the convoy, both feeling too hot and sweaty to make conversation.

"Christ, it's bloody hot," said Rick, wiping sweat from his brow with the sleeve of his jacket.

His remark brought those men sitting nearest him suddenly to life.

"It may get hotter," whined a Brummie. "We ain't goin' on no picnic."

"Och, away wi' ya, mon," butted in Jock Campbell. "Ya bin gettin' your knickers in a twist."

"Ah, so he is, Jock," chirped Paddy Jones from where he sat close to the Bren. "He's a big lassie, so he is. A proper dogsbody."

"Just wait an see. We all may be proper lassies and shitting in our pants before the day is out," whined the Brummie.

"Och, mon, ya worry a right lot about nothing," said the Scotsman.

"Less talking," barked Flying Officer Morgan.

"Captain Henry Morgan has commanded," whispered Peter to Rick. "If we don't behave ourselves, he'll have us all walking the plank."

Rick laughed. "He seems quite a character," he said.

"He's the rit mon for this wee jobby," said the Scotsman.

"You're right there, Jock," said Peter Saunders; and he meant it.

"We're in a bad position here, Pete, aren't we!" whispered Rick.

"Yes, we are," admitted Peter. "I realized that as soon as we had taken up our position."

"If we should get ambushed, the bandits will allow the armoured car to pass around a bend and then open fire on the rest of us. That's how I see it." said Rick.

"Yeah, you're right. The road is sure to be narrow, so if they manage to stop one lorry, they'll stop the whole convoy."

"And riddle these open lorries with bullets."

"Then make good their escape before the armoured stuff has a chance to come on the scene. That's what I'm thinking. I think we should hand in our resignations right now, Rick."

The corporal, overhearing the conversation, said, "You're both getting the wind up over nothing. The convoy's been making this run for months without incident."

A piercing whistle was suddenly heard, blown by the army captain who stood surveying the scene from the side of the road. The whistle was his signal for the convoy to move out. The armoured car, pulling away from all the other vehicles, slowly made its way along the narrow road skirting the camp, and then gathered speed on reaching the junction, which brought it onto the main highway. At set distances it was followed by the armoured army lorry, the two RAF Bedfords, and by all the other vehicles which seemed to be playing a game of Follow The Leader away from Kuala Kubu Baru's camp exit. It was here, at the junction, that at least twenty private cars carrying civilian passengers of many races awaited the convoy. Seeking protection during the potentially hazardous journey, one by one they found a place for themselves among the many passing military vehicles.

In an otherwise clear blue sky, a few wisps of cloud now floated lazily overhead. Soon, in the lowlands, it would be raining again. But here, where the land was caked and dry, clouds of brown dust billowed up around the wheels of the many vehicles as the convoy gathered speed and streamed out of Kuala Kubu Baru. The village was soon behind them, its smells, its noises, the dusty camp, everything. Here there were no rice fields or rubber plantations, instead only jungle with a thin ribbon that was the road twisting like a never-ending snake beneath overhanging growths of greenness. Now, the sun was often lost from sight, only to reappear where there was no mantle of jungle covering the road.

On a rare, very long sweeping clear curve in the road, Peter Saunders attempted to count the number of vehicles strung out one behind the other. On arriving at twenty-one, he lost count; the convoy was much too long. Actually, the convoy consisted of forty-seven vehicles.

"Thirty-one. Z.V. Fifty-two," Peter suddenly said.

"What's that?" asked Rick.

"Oh, I was just reading the registration number on the armoured car. Quite a sizeable gun they've got on it, eh, Rick? What size do you reckon it is?"

"I dunno. I've no idea," answered Rick. "But big enough to knock the bloody head off a frigging bandit."

Peter Saunders chuckled at his friend's remark. "You can say that again," he said.

After another mile of jungle they were out in bright sunlight again. Here the convoy began to climb the hill, slowly, for the narrow road literally clung to, and had been carved out of, the stony hillside. To the left of the road was a steep drop-off into jungle; and to the right loomed an almost perpendicular wall of dense foliage—a matting of greens, yellows, browns and golds glistening and sweating in the sunlight. Orchids grew wild in great profusion on the hillside as did many other flowers, species unknown to Peter Saunders. Twining vines interwoven with shrubs and wild sickly-looking banana clumps all jockeyed for position in order to survive in that beautiful yet treacherous jungle.

Among the airmen in that fourth vehicle there was scant conversation. Only eyes, and fingers on triggers, betrayed some nervousness. Glinting muzzles were aimed to where eyes could not penetrate.

All vehicles had now engaged lower gears, the faster hanging back for the slower in order for positions to be maintained. Slowly, the convoy wound its way upward, around hairpin bend after hairpin bend. Those in the vehicles ahead could frequently look down a hillside of jungle and see six or seven vehicles on the winding, narrow road below. Far down the mountainside the road could be seen again, with vehicles travelling upon it that were perhaps twentieth or more in place, all winding their way up the face of that hill, skirting ravines, edging between great gaps, clinging upon that hillside road hundreds of feet above the lowlands. Far below, how green and fertile the valleys appeared to be from the mountainside. Up here, there was not a house to be seen, nor sound or movement of man or animal. An occasional bird winged its way overhead, singing a greeting, it seemed, to those travelling the road below. But those birds were the only show of life. Except for them life in that green hell remained silent. Even snakes and rodents remained hidden whilst the noises from many engines passed them by.

Two miles from the Gap the convoy drew to a halt at a police outpost, where, nearby, a huge palm-thatched shack advertised coffee and orange drinks for sale. Here the sweating men were allowed to leave their vehicles to stretch and relax awhile. Many trooped into the shack and soon a queue formed. Peter and Rick were two of the first to enter the shack, to be served by an aged Chinese woman help by a girl who appeared to be her daughter. They both ordered a Green Spot orange drink, and stroked a big ginger tomcat that sat aloof upon a stool. No one thought of moving the cat, and it purred contentedly when allowed to lap lukewarm coffee from someone's mug. Much fuss was made of that ginger tomcat.

Far above the outpost loomed Fraser's Hill; the road could be seen only until it disappeared into the jungle less than a hundred yards further on. A silence hung over the hill. It's too quiet, Peter Saunders thought. There was no chatter of monkeys to be heard, neither squeaks nor squeals from other smaller animals, no buzzing noises from grasshoppers, and not even the honking of bullfrogs in the nearby grasses. Even the birds were without song. The quietness was suspiciously ominous to country boy Peter Saunders. Here, the grown-over hillside should be full of animal and insect noise. Glancing apprehensively at Flying Officer Morgan, he noticed a definite state of nervousness written on the man's rugged face as the officer's eyes searched through binoculars the side of the hill for movement. Turning suddenly, the officer espied the young airman watching him.

"What the hell are you staring at?" he snapped.

"Sorry, sir," said Peter Saunders, not knowing what else to say.

"Get back up on the wagon."

"Yes, sir."

Noticing the experienced way the young airman carried his rifle, Flying Officer Morgan asked, "Airman, are you one of the marksmen?"

"Yes, sir."

"Good. I thought you were. Now remember, from now on make sure you've a round in the breech. And once we're moving, keep a finger on the trigger and your eyes alert for the slightest sign of movement."

"Yes, sir."

"OK! Good man! Now get back up into the wagon," Flying Officer

Morgan ordered. He then shouted, "All right men, all aboard. And remember, keep a damned good look-out from now on until we reach the summit."

Following Rick up into the back of the lorry, Peter sat down beside him and checked his rifle, making sure the safety catch was off. Intuition, a sixth sense; casting his eyes upon those green slopes once again, he shuddered, suddenly fearful of the journey that lay ahead.

26

A stirring in the undergrowth was all that betrayed his presence; a few leaves rustled, and beneath his feet dead twigs crackled as Fong Fook, hiding behind a low bush, stealthily changed his uncomfortable squatting position. Whispering curses, there were more agitated movements as he massaged a cramped foot, and then, after awhile, quietness returned, so that the jungle-clad hillside appeared devoid of human life.

With nothing but the faintest of breezes stirring the hillside, several minutes passed before movement again disturbed concealing leaves and thin branches as a wizened human face, barely visible, cautiously rose from among the tangled mass of greenery growing entwined and around the low bush. Peering between its twigs, furtive eyes scanned the winding narrow road that lay a hundred feet or so below. As regular as clockwork, the convoy would be on time today; three-thirty, zero hour. The ambush was set, there would be no slip-up; no mercy given and none expected, neither by himself nor by any of his thirty-five men hiding in the undergrowth fifty to a hundred feet apart upon the hillside overlooking the road.

Fong Fook, the senior area committee member of the Malayan Communist Party for the State of Pahang, gripped his rifle in readiness, a grim, vengeful look on his face as he waited to kill and destroy more of those who had brought his downfall, and who now ruled Malaya. Not one iota of love or goodwill towards mankind showed in those peering eyes; instead there was hate and a burning desire to kill. Killing had long become Fong Fook's single pleasure. Indeed, killing had become an obsession as well as his profession. No longer did he find passion in loving a woman, not since the last woman he had loved, more than two years ago, had given him the gift of syphilis. And now, through living in the jungle, a wanted man with such a high price on his head that he dared not visit civilization, the disease, remaining untreated, was assisting in killing him. The yearning he once had for women had long turned to bitterness, and any feelings of sexual want brought only pain. Now, deeply implanted into his crazed mind was the need to kill. He lived only to kill.

Though not quite twenty-seven years of age, already Fong Fook was an aged-looking, sick and dying man. Living, hunting and being hunted in the jungle these past twelve years had completely ruined him, mind, body and soul. Often he suffered from deep, black depressions to the point of his being on the brink of insanity. His body, emaciated through years of neglect and undernourishment, was covered with festering sores on parchment-like skin. His hollow cheeks and sunken dark eyes revealed the other deadly disease he suffered from that was already advanced and obviously killing him, tuberculosis. A filthy army beret, taken from a British soldier he had killed, did not conceal his tangled mass of unwashed black hair. Protecting his feet were worn-out sandals held on by dried *lalang* grass, and covering his body he wore a pair of sun-bleached, ripped and filthy blue trousers and a matching sleeveless jacket. Back at his base camp there were several pairs of boots and many items of clothing taken from the dead—mostly British military personnel they had killed. But neither he nor any of his fellow guerillas would wear military clothing on this day and risk mistaking each other for the enemy.

Thus, Fong Fook, the notorious Communist Party leader and head of a gang of terrorists and murderers, had become the grand possessor of the clothes he stood up in and those stolen from the dead. Gripped

341

in bony hands he held a .303 Enfield rifle, and strapped to his waist he carried an old Malay *kris*, a short, wavy-bladed dagger, its bone handle chipped and seemingly ready to part company from the pitted and badly rusted blade. At his feet lay a pile of hand grenades and a box of .303 ammunition. Only the government's price on Fong Fook's head gave him worth, whether brought in alive or dead.

This was the great Fong Fook, the ruthless bandit who, at the height of his fame controlled over two hundred men, all Communist Party members. Now he was leader of the remnants of his brigade, all the others having been wiped out by the relentless bombing by the RAF, the bullets from the guns of British servicemen, and the knives of Dyak headhunters and the fearless Gurkhas. Many more had been hanged in the gaols at Penang, Kuala Lumpur and Changi in Singapore. Also, there were those who had died from untreated wounds and diseases. Each and every one of Fong Fook's remaining men was wanted for murder and numerous other offences by the ruling British authorities, and all had prices on their heads. Here, under wretched conditions, as outcasts, they lived in makeshift camps hidden in the pitiless jungle; just one step away from a fate, which they all knew would eventually catch up with them, as it had their brethren. Fong Fook did not fear a violent and quick death. He was more afraid of dying from malaria, which often wracked his body, from malnutrition or from starving to death, or from that constant dull ache in his chest which at times burst into great pain as if within him a fire had been kindled. He knew the lower portion of his body was being eaten away by the syphilis he had contracted, but he had no penicillin with which to check the devastation going on in his body; he also knew that it was unthinkable for him to visit a clinic for treatment. Being far too notorious to show his face in a public place, someone would surely recognize him, inform the authorities and collect the very high reward for his capture. He could only wait for death in the jungle, as could his fellow terrorists, tuberculosis and venereal diseases being rife among them and as frequent a killer as the security forces themselves.

One might ask, why would Fong Fook wish to kill? Fong Fook himself believed he had every good reason for his actions. Certainly he was no coward, nor did he consider himself braver than any other member of his remaining miserable body of men. Receiving his orders from a higher-ranking party official, he carried them out as efficiently as he knew how. He was a mere pawn to this killing art, but there was much more to it than that. He had been no murderer, no thief, no arsonist, not until the Japanese invasion of his homeland in that disastrous year of 1941, when so many fled before the advancing hordes of yellow men from the islands away to the east. Those who did not flee from these ruthless men were killed by bullets or by the sword and the less fortunate were tortured and butchered.

At the beginning of that tragic period Fong Fook was a mere sixteen years old, a farmer's son who diligently tended the family's two water buffalo, fed the pigs and chickens, planted rice, and caught fish from both the sea and from the clear, sparkling river that flowed passed his family's home, on its way to the sea. He had been a handsome youth, with big brown intelligent eyes, and a square face, proud and honest. His parents had two other sons very much like him in appearance but older and of heavier build; and they had a daughter who was named Lily, because her skin was white and unblemished like the flowers growing in great profusion on the village pond. His father, old Tak Wah, and his father's wife, Mei Ling, were in their teens when they had journeyed together from Shantung in China to settle in Malaya. Quite rightly, they became proud of their four children and the home and farm they had created out of the swamps bordering the river which flows past Lumut, a little town nestling on the west coast of Malaya. Around their farm a village of Chinese houses had gradually formed, and with it a market place and a temple. And nearby, was a great square of green, close to the beach, where the children played and upon which a school was built.

Then came the Japanese armies, invaders who were not interested in hospitality, but instead dealt out brutality and death, and lay total destruction in their wake. Fong Fook's memory served him well. Fong

Man, his eldest brother, had killed a Malayan traitor who had caused the death of several of the Chinese men in the village. The Japanese dug out his brother's eyes and slashed off his ears with their bayonets in front of the villagers, then, still not satisfied, and with the tide being low, they lashed him to the base of the village wire and bamboo fish trap. How they laughed at his tormented cries. But they did not bother to watch as the tide rose slowly about and above his head, to finally cover and drown his screams; the Japanese soldiers were much too interested in other bestial acts they could and did commit.

Fong Fook had gone fishing that day the Japanese army arrived. He lay hidden in tall grass by the side of the river and had watched horrified as the males of the village were rounded up and tied to palm trees. Helplessly he witnessed mothers and daughters being raped by that horde of evil men time and time again on the village green in front of their menfolk. And when the females were half-dead and useless to the Japanese soldiers, they were slashed to death, writhing and screaming, by ceremonial swords and bayonets streaming with blood. Then the boys of the village were stripped naked and used as women before being bayoneted or beheaded. Babies were fixed upon bayonets and whirled out to sea, the soldiers laughing fiendishly and shouting to one another, wagering bets of money on who could toss the dead and dying babies the furthest. Then, every man in the village was put to death by various barbaric means. Some were buried alive in the sand until only their heads were showing. The incoming tide soon stifled their cries. Some had their innards ripped from them, screaming in agony and terror while still lashed to the palm trees. The invaders used others in gruesome games of tug of war, the victim's hands being secured by ropes attached to two tanks, which were then driven slowly, in opposite directions, tearing the wretched person's body apart. Finally, after cutting the bonds of those remaining alive, they then ran them down with their tanks. They murdered everyone in that village, and then they burnt every building to the ground. Everyone in the village was dead, everyone, that is, except for Fong Fook who, after the Japanese had departed, wandered away, completely insane by all that he had witnessed.

Three days later he returned to the village, and to his burned-out home. The carnage was incredible. He found the body of his brother, Fong Man, black and swollen, half-eaten by crabs and other sea life, still lashed to the fish trap. He found what had been his mother, naked and split almost in two. He failed to recognize any other member of his family among the torn and dismembered bodies that lay grotesquely everywhere; on the beach, the green where he had so recently played, and within and without the burned shells that had once been homes. Many had also died within the destroyed temple. The smell from the dead was awful, but Fong Fook knew the smell would soon be gone and the air as he had known it would be clear and sweet again. Birds of prey, carrion-eating birds, dogs and even pigs that had escaped slaughter were busily feeding on the already putrid flesh of the villagers. Soon, there would be only bones remaining of those he had known and loved.

In just a matter of a few hours the village had been wiped from the face of the earth, and all its inhabitants slaughtered; all but that one boy, Fong Fook.

Alone, with no food, no shelter, and no one to comfort him in his sorrow, in anger and madness he wandered into the jungle. Knowing that he alone had been spared, he realized that it was now up to him, his duty to his deceased family and to all the dead villagers, to revenge them by killing as many as he could of the barbaric foe. Within the week he met others in the jungle—men, women and children from other villages who, like him, had escaped the oppressors. They talked and consoled one another, and a guerilla force was formed among them to fight the evil tyrants; the revengeful fight against the Japanese had begun.

Because of his coolness and bravery in action, Fong Fook rose quickly to become the leader of more than a score of men, women and children whose sole aim in life was to obstruct and kill the hated invader. They blocked roads, blew up bridges, railway lines and electrical installations. Informers and traitors were put to death slowly in brutal manner. But the guerillas' main goal was to kill Japanese officers and soldiers. The majority of Japanese, those on sentry duty and the like, were quietly and speedily garroted, their bodies hidden in the undergrowth where they became food for wild animals. Seldom were the dead found by the Japanese.

Fong Fook's foremost thoughts, however, were not to speedily kill the enemy, but to capture the enemy alive, and if it were an officer, so much the better. First he would gouge out the man's eyes with his *kris*, then slowly cut off the ears and force the wretch to eat them. He showed no mercy to any Japanese, but treated them as they had treated his elder brother. Most received the same fate, lashed to a fish trap somewhere along the coastline, where he would watch them scream and die as the tide came in and covered them. Every Japanese soldier's fate was sealed the moment he was captured by Fong Fook or any of his followers. When raiding inland, where there were no fish traps, Fong Fook led his captives to a swamp he knew. Once there, he tied them to water-level objects in the swamps, then cut off their genitals, which he tossed as bait to the many hungry crocodile inhabitants. How he laughed at the screams of his victims as the crocodiles glided near to take that first bite.

Many of the women in Malaya were forced to become comfort girls for the pleasures of the Japanese oppressors, and there were a few who willingly became mistresses to the Japanese. The latter, when caught by the guerillas, were seduced by anyone in the gang who wished to make use of them. And when no longer of use these women were taken to the edge of town, tied to palm trees, gagged to muffle their screams, and there disemboweled alive, their bodies slashed open from the vagina upward so that their entrails fell from them. There they remained as a warning to others willing to be mistresses of the Japanese, for them to see and to heed. Cooperating with the enemy meant certain death.

The war ended as suddenly as it had begun, with the Japanese offering their ceremonial swords in surrender to the British down in Singapore. But for Fong Fook the war in the jungle against the hated murderers of his family was not over. He killed many more Japanese officers and men before the last one was finally withdrawn from Malaya. It was not until then that he left the jungle's sheltering cover to start a new life, but as what? How to kill was all he knew.

For a few months he tried his hand at various jobs, mainly as a labourer working long, back breaking hours. He detested this means of livelihood, so that when the Communist Party sought him out and found him doing manual labour, they offered him a paid position of rank within their party. Eagerly he accepted the offer, only to discover that he had signed his name to a group who had recently murdered an English rubber estate owner down in Johore. Also, an uprising against the British had begun and atrocities were being committed against them almost daily. The British quickly reacted. They discovered that Fong Fook was a member of the illegal Communist Party, and its members guilty of murder. Thus, promptly, Fong Fook found out that he was wanted dead or alive by the British authorities, also by the Malayan police, and that there was now a high price on his head.

Hence his return to the sanctuary of the jungle, to be joined by others, many of whom had fought with him against the Japanese and who had become disenchanted by the false promises of their new rulers, the British. Every one of his men became a member of the Communist Party, though none knew exactly why, or what they were fighting for. They were told, 'it's freedom from the British yoke, and towards our independence.' They received their orders from officials living quietly and unobtrusively in the villages and towns of Malaya, and on the island of Singapore. To disobey the orders of those Communist officials meant death at the hands of his fellow man.

Now, several years had passed since Fong Fook's return to the jungle. His health had deteriorated badly during that period, both in mind and body. Death, one way or another, had already claimed most of his old comrades, but new recruits had steadily joined the gang, though by no means replacing in number those that had departed. Members of the Communist Party had murdered innocent families, slashed hundreds of acres of rubber-bearing trees, destroyed newly planted trees, intimidated the tin-mine workers, butchering one or more occasionally to frighten the others. They had ambushed trains, buses, and even motor convoys, always with order to destroy and kill, which they always did. To kill was their way of life.

Neither did Fong Fook heed the 'Talking Bird', which flew over him almost daily, nor the millions of leaflets dropped from the plane offering full amnesty. He did not trust the British. He trusted only the Communist Party whom he believed would eventually bring justice to the land of his family.

Now, he and the remaining survivors of his group, about thirty-five of them, lay hidden, spaced out at intervals among the greenery overlooking and bordering the slopes of the Gap. Every man was armed, mostly with weapons taken from those they had killed during earlier ambushes. Most possessed .303 Enfield rifles, some shotguns, and all possessed hand grenades, which lay within their reach. At the last bend in the road, at the far end of the Gap, concealed gunners manned two Bren guns that had recently been obtained from an ambushed British army lorry. Positioned strategically at the turn into the bend was another Bren gun. These guns would create an awesome crossfire, most certainly enough to stop the leading vehicles on the narrow, single lane road, which in turn would bring the whole convoy to a halt. Once that happened, every man in the group would immediately open fire with his small arms, then rain hand grenades down onto the stopped vehicles. As many vehicles as possible would be destroyed, and as many people as possible killed during that initial attack. In the expected ensuing panic, previously chosen guerillas would leave their hiding places and storm the convoy, firing their weapons and hurling the remaining grenades into the vehicles. Once free of their grenades, they would take the arms and ammunition from the dead and the dying. They would then stealthily retreat, to return to their camp in the safety of the jungle, their mission accomplished.

Now, impatiently they waited. It was still too early, but only by a few minutes. It was almost three-thirty.

Visible below, amid jungle, was the entrance to the Gap and portions of the road meandering its way upward to where it would pass directly beneath the ambushers' positions.

Suddenly, at the entrance to the Gap, a billowing cloud of brown dust rose above the greenness; and now could be heard the steady throb of many engines; a droning noise growing louder as the convoy neared.

Waiting men tensed. No longer calling to one another, every man became still and silent. Gripping their weapons, they lay concealed behind shrouds of foliage. Safety catches were released as straining eyes caught movement below. Some loosened the fasteners on grenades. A few more minutes and the convoy would be directly below them, travelling on a narrow road clinging to the edge of a jungle-clad ravine, where, in places, on the left hand side, was a sheer drop of hundreds of feet. For miles on the right-hand side of the road, the hillside had been cleared of vegetation from the road upward to about one hundred feet, so that it was now barren and incapable of hiding attackers. But upward, beyond that one hundred feet, the jungle remained as it had always been, where, at this moment, the ambushers hid and silently waited.

Mosquitoes had once been a major problem to the terrorists, but now they were accustomed to having their unprotected skin bitten; they were far more concerned with snakes biting them than mosquitoes. Now, there was not even a whisper among them, and every man tried his best not to make movement, even when forced to change position because of cramped muscles. The armoured car leading the convoy was now only two bends away in the road below and unprotected men could be clearly seen in the lorries following it.

Fong Fook knew this day would bring a massacre upon the oppressors. He badly needed arms and ammunition from the convoy. Perhaps his men might also obtain food or even medications. Mainly, however, he wanted to kill, yet he found no remorse, no glory, no feeling at all towards the deed he was about to commit. He would kill many people this day, both military and civilians, but he had killed far too often for such trivial thoughts to enter his sick mind. At any moment now he would fire a single shot from his rifle, the prearranged signal for the Bren guns to commence firing.

27

Thus, after a brief rest period, the convoy again took to the road, in great glare, heat and dust. The police outpost was soon left behind, and an isolated village of a dozen or so *atap* huts perched on the hillside was quickly sped through. The Gap and the narrow road meandering up the mountainside to the summit of Fraser's Hill lay invitingly open to the long string of forty-seven vehicles.

Carefully making its way around the hairpin bends, and holding well its position in the convoy, a Silver Wraith Rolls Royce purred its way upward, ascending the hill smoothly with hardly a whisper audible from its well-nursed engine. A satisfied smile creased the handsome face of Lim Seng Yew, the middle-aged Chinese chauffeur and valet to billionaire industrialist Ng Kwok Wing. Seng Yew loved driving the new Rolls Royce, more so than any of the other luxury cars in the personal fleet of his employer.

Seng Yew loved his job and was proud to be the servant of such a good master as Mr Ng; just as proud as his father had been when personal servant to his master's father. During the Japanese occupation, both fathers had suddenly departed from this world. They were executed in front of their families by the swords of the invaders; each leaving behind a son, one now the wealthy employer, the other a faithful and trusted household servant.

Looking into the rear-view mirror, Seng Yew said to the diminutive, aged Chinese woman sitting behind him, "See how well my beloved holds the road, and how well she climbs the mountain. Do you not feel the power surging through her magnificent engine as she waits like a tiger ready to leap forward? My beloved does not like to follow others but prefers to lead."

"Yes, she leads on an open road, but here I prefer others to lead. How many more miles must we cover before we reach the safety of the hilltop? My heart misses a beat whenever I see the swaying of a blade of grass or the movement of a twig."

"Have no fear little grey-haired one. Soon you will relax at the master's mountain home. You will become invigorated by the mountain air, as will the worthy daughter of our master."

"The climate here has not suited her. She was as fresh as a young flower when she arrived from Nanking. Perhaps she should have remained there with other relatives of the family."

"No, little woman, I cannot agree with you. Her departed parents would have preferred her to live with us. Our master was their closest relative, and he loves the girl as he would his own. She will surely enjoy a much better life with him than if she had remained in China."

"My negative thoughts are only on the climate in Kuala Lumpur as compared with that of Nanking. I hope her health improves when she lives in the big house in Singapore. Yes, it is true our master loves Ah Ho, and he dotes lavishly upon her. In my thoughts Ah Ho means more to him than all his empire. It is good that he has adopted her as his own daughter. I, too, love her as if she were my own child."

Silence fell between the two as the chauffeur eased the Rolls Royce around yet another hairpin bend, causing Ping Jie, the trusted and faithful *amah*, to nervously grind her teeth and fearfully turn her head away from the sheer drop to her left. Instead, she gazed down upon Ho Li Li, the adopted and only child of Ng Kwok Wing, who lay asleep stretched out on the back seat of the car, her head contentedly resting in the old *amah*'s lap.

Eventually Ping Jie asked, "Lim, do you feel nervous driving upon this hillside?"

"No! Should I be nervous?"

"I feel frightened. My eyes attempt to pierce the matting of green and brown, yet they see nothing."

"We are safe here in the middle of the convoy."

"I feel no safety," the old *amah* said.

The chauffeur turned his head towards her, a reassuring smile upon his face. "You must not fear," he said. "The military might in this convoy is far too great to stir the men of the jungle into action against us. Relax as does your mistress, and think of only what lies ahead, of where the air is cool and sweet, and of where we shall drink cooling iced tea upon our arrival."

The chauffeur's voice was calm and reassuring, but he too felt a nagging uneasiness, even though this was his third journey to the house at Fraser's Hill within the last two years. On those previous occasions he had felt no nervousness. Often, though, he had wished that his employer would sell the house built on the hill's summit. Once again Lim Seng Yew cast his eyes above the line of cleared vegetation and into the gloom of matted jungle which, being so still and quiet, was pregnant with menace. The convoy was now in its final approach to the Gap. His thoughts flashed to the late High Commissioner of Malaya, Sir Henry Gurney, who had been murdered on this road, and in this very vicinity. He had known Sir Henry well. He also knew that during the past few years the Gap had seen the loss of many lives at the hands of the Communist terrorists. This particular stretch of road was lined with potential ambush positions too numerous to count, even though the vegetation had been cleared from the hillside for many yards upward from the road. However, as all those who travelled the road knew well, it was impossible to clear the whole mountainside overlooking the road of potential ambush positions.

Seng Yew's thoughts suddenly turned from all the madness that was taking place around him to his own peaceful, beautiful little home in Johore Bahru. Sighing wistfully, he thought of his adoring wife, and of the three perfect children she had borne him. Sighing again, he wished he were with his family now instead of being here driving through the centre of Malaya. As chauffeur to his master, he was often away from home for several days at a time but a whole month would be the longest period ever for him to be away from his wife and family. He was, however, content with his lot. He owned a villa near the water's edge in a lovely area not far from the Sultan of Johore's palace. His two elder children, both boys, attended school and were learning fast. And his salary was certainly enough to clothe, feed and entertain his family well.

Smiling to himself, he thought of how, out of all her eagerness and passion, and from such a little body, she bore for him twins, two sons; and two years later, a daughter that was the image of her mother. He wondered whether the child she now carried within her belly would be another daughter. He sighed wistfully, wishing he were home instead of driving up this dangerous mountain road.

Suddenly, a single rifle shot brought him out of his reverie. Shocked, he saw a uniformed figure tumble from an open army lorry two vehicles ahead. Almost immediately all hell broke loose as simultaneously three Bren guns opened up firing long bursts. There was rapid fire from almost thirty rifles, blasts from shotguns, plus loud, sharp explosions from tossed hand grenades.

Traumatized by what he was seeing and hearing, Seng Yew's eyes opened wide in amazement and his mind became numb. Closing his eyes and shaking his head, he brought himself back to reality, to distinctly hear the exploding grenades, which on detonation momentarily drowned out the noise from the guns firing all around him. When there were no exploding grenades, he could hear the loud, long bursts of fire from the Bren guns above the rapid fire from the rifles. He winced when sharp fragments of glass tore into his face and hands as the car's windshield shattered. Above the din, many screams rent the air. Appalled, he saw a blonde-haired lady, the driver of the open-topped little blue sports car ahead of him, suddenly slump over her steering wheel. Horrified, he watched as the car, now out of control, veered across the road, paused as if undecided at the edge of the cliff, then slowly toppled over. Moments later, caught in the embrace of jungle below, the car exploded into a giant ball of fire.

"Ambush!" gasped Seng Yew. "What shall I do?" He reached for the pistol, which he always kept in a pocket of the driver's door but he felt no safety as he held the inadequate weapon tightly in his hand.

The terrorists had allowed the leading vehicle in the convoy, the armoured car, to pass the ambush position unscathed, and it had already turned the next bend in the road before the guns opened up their terrific barrage of fire. The driver of the second in line, the armoured army lorry, most probably never heard the long burst of fire from a Bren gun that shattered the so-called bulletproof windshield, killing him instantly. The vehicle, with no one steering it and still travelling at twenty-five miles an hour, struck rocks at the edge of the hillside, careered from off these, struck the hillside again, to finally stop, broadside across the road, its front wheels wedged between rocks. Immediately, the whole convoy was forced to slow down and then come to a standstill.

Both Warrant Officer Perkins and the driver seated at his side in the leading open-backed RAF Bedford lorry were killed instantly by the first hail of bullets. The lorry they were in, on striking the armed army vehicle ahead, glanced off it and toppled over the cliff's edge. Slithering at first, it then bounced and rolled over and over, to somersault down the steep, jungle-clad slope, with supplies and equipment, and the three airmen who had been seated in it, hurtling in all directions from the open back. A couple of hundred feet down the mountainside the lorry hit rocks and disintegrated. The second RAF Bedford also struck the army lorry and became wedged, its driver sitting at the steering wheel, dead.

The horrified driver of the oncoming empty army lorry swerved and braked to avoid colliding with the two stalled, wedged-together lorries the same moment as a hail of bullets smashed into his cab killing him instantly. With a dead driver in the cab, the army lorry hurtled off the road, plunged into the abyss, and followed the path the Bedford had taken, until it, too, was swallowed up by the tangled mass of greenery far below.

The din was awesome. People were jumping and throwing themselves clear of their vehicles, slithering over the edge of the road and down into the cover of the jungle. Several jumped from their vehicles where there was no slope but just a sheer drop-off of hundreds of feet. They disappeared to their death over the edge of the cliff. And all the while the murderous bruuuttttttttt, bruuutttttttt, bruuuutttttt came from the three Bren guns, the rapid fire from the many rifles, the distinctly different blasting noise from shotguns, mingled with the heavier crash of exploding grenades.

A dispatch rider, his service revolver in hand, was bravely firing back from behind the cover of his motorcycle. A grenade hit him in the chest and exploded, causing the petrol tank of his motorcycle to explode in a great flash of flame, leaving no signs of the dispatch rider—his shattered body had been blown over the cliff.

Above the road the ambushing Bren gunners gloated over the sight of so many reeling bodies. Here, no skilled aim was needed. They could not miss. They had only to keep their fingers on the triggers and swing their guns from side to side. When the guns ceased firing because their ammunition was spent, other terrorists were on hand to immediately unload the empty magazines and promptly replace them with full ones of twenty-eight rounds apiece. Then the Bren guns began firing again.

The Silver Wraith's Chinese chauffeur wiped blood from his eyes and face with the sleeve of his jacket. He, like all the other drivers in the convoy, had been forced to come to a standstill. Now, instead of surprise and shock showing upon his face there was fear, not so much for himself but for his two passengers. He was responsible for their safety and wellbeing whilst they were passengers in the car he drove, and he alone would be held accountable should any misfortune befall either. Thrusting the pistol into a trouser pocket, he threw open the door of the car and sprang out onto the road. Wrenching open a rear door, he saw that the *amah*, petrified with fear, had sunk deeply into the far corner of the seat, the child, now sobbing with fright, clasped tightly to her bosom.

"Come, woman!" he yelled at her. "Get out! Get out! And bring the master's child with you. We must go down the hillside to safety."

The *amah*, as if hypnotized by the terrifying noises all around her, did not move. It was all too much for her. She lay back in the seat as if dead; only the slight quivering of her thin lips betrayed life from death.

Again the chauffeur shouted at her. "For the master's sake, come, give me the girl!"

The *amah* did not move but instead stared up at him, a terrified look on her face. Her mouth dropped open as if she wanted to speak but no sound came.

Hurling himself upon her, Seng Yew wrenched the crying child from the *amah*'s arms. The child began to scream but he heeded her not. Dragging the little girl from the car, he picked her up in his arms, hurried to the roadside, and there carefully studied the vertical drop-off, which was at least thirty feet. Below this he could see thick jungle that sloped gradually downward away from the edge of the road. There was no deep drop-off here of hundreds of feet such as he could see further along the road, or which he had seen in many places along the route. Looking down upon the tangled mass of greens and browns, he noticed that directly below him a broad-leafed bushy tree stood higher than all other vegetation, and that clinging to the tree were many webs of tangled vines. The topmost leaves of the tree, though several feet away, grew almost parallel to the road. That tree, he knew, could well be the child's only chance of survival.

"Ah Ho, go to safety. May the master forgive me if I do wrong." Uttering these words, Seng Yew carefully gauged the distance between himself and the topmost leaves of that tree, and then tossed the screaming child from him. He agonized as he saw her terrified face and her little arms and legs kicking and clawing at nothing as she passed over the chasm and fell among the topmost leaves of the tree. He watched her, for what would be the last time that he would see her, sinking from sight within the sanctuary of the jungle covering. In his mind he measured the distance that she would fall within the shelter of that tree. At the most thirty feet, he thought. But, he told himself, she had to take her chances. She was much safer down in the jungle than up here on the road. Ricocheting bullets and shrapnel from exploding grenades whined noisily near him. Ragged holes suddenly appeared in his beautiful car's bonnet. Loudly he cursed the gunner and dived back inside the car, intending to pull the *amah* from it and throw her, too, into the comparative safety of the tree and the jungle-clad slope below the road. The *amah* had not moved but instead sat as if in a trance.

"Wake up, foolish woman. Let not noise dull thy senses," he screamed at her.

Stooping over her, in great desperation he grabbed her by the arms and began pulling her towards the open door of the car, when, suddenly, a chill ran in cold shivers throughout his body as he sensed that he was being watched. He now had a feeling that death was close upon him. Lifting his eyes, he looked out of the window and up the roadside embankment but saw nothing there to cause him alarm. He was puzzled but relieved.

"Do not leave me here to die," he heard the plaintive voice of the *amah* beseeching him. "I am coming with you."

"Good! Come quickly!"

Whilst pulling her through the doorway, he looked behind him and up the hillside to reassure himself that they were safe, and was startled to see a movement high up among the bushes. He watched as the branches of a low bush parted. Just the wind, he thought. But, no, there was no wind; not even enough to stir a leaf. Troubled, he stared intently at where he had seen the movement then he stiffened and, in great fear, held his breath.

"My God! Be this not my day!" he gasped.

He watched as the skinny figure of a man staring at him out of hollow eyes rose slowly from behind the bush, with arms extended towards him, the hands holding a rifle pointed at him.

Sickened with fright, just for a moment he wondered if it was too late to dodge and to cheat death. With his eyes held firmly upon that lone figure, Seng Yew sank slowly to the floor of the car, his hand feeling for the pistol, hoping, praying, but he was too slow and too late. He heard the loud report of the rifle the same moment as he saw a side window fly into a million fragments and felt a stinging blow strike his chest. Reeling backwards, he clutched at the spot. The bullet had ploughed through his clothing, his flesh, smashed a rib, grazed his heart, and had embedded itself in a lung.

Shaking his head to free himself of the mist that was engulfing him, he told himself, I must not pass out. He tried to get up from the floor of the car but his knees sagged from under him. He was swaying but he did not want to drop. And he could not clear away the mist that was all around him, a bluish, orange and greyish mist. He tried to blow it away, but could not. It encircled his eyes and numbed his brain. He felt himself as if on a cloud, drifting into eternity. His blood, deep red and streaked by white foam crept from the corners of his mouth, to drip upon the plush carpet of his new Rolls Royce; and now blood began to spurt from his nose. He was fast losing consciousness. He felt neither pain nor fear, the cloak of death having cast itself over him and was already bearing him upwards, upwards. A second shot rang out from the rifle. But the chauffeur neither heard the shot nor felt the bullet. His body jerked just once before toppling over and falling across the passed-out *amah*. Seng Yew was dead, the back of his head blown off.

Fong Fook smiled to himself, gave a grunt of satisfaction, patted the rifle fondly, and then again levelled it at the car. He had seen the woman. She might as well join the other in death. He put an eye to the sights, squeezed the trigger and watched as the little woman twitched in her death throes before she, too, became still.

Ping Jie, the faithful, reliable *amah* and nurse to Ho Li Li, a good mother, a grandmother, and a person who in life had caused grief or hurt to no one, was dead. And through a ragged hole torn through her neck her life-blood oozed, where it mixed with that of Seng Yew, the chauffeur, in an ever-enlarging puddle on the white lambs-wool carpeted floor of the new Rolls Royce.

28

When the single rifle shot rang out, followed immediately by the horrendous barrage of terrifying gunfire and exploding grenades, most of those travelling in the convoy, civilian and military personnel alike, froze in shock, and for precious moments did nothing. Many died during those crucial first seconds.

The two airmen, SAC Peter Saunders and LAC Gerald Rickie, were two who sat thus, unable to do anything but stare in horrified disbelief, hearing the agonizing screams of their comrades as bullets thudded into them, and watching as they twitched and died. Precious seconds had already ticked by since the leading RAF Bedford plunged into the abyss to the left of the ill-fated convoy. Both airmen, though, in total shock, sat as if paralyzed and could not even remember being told that if ambushed they must immediately get clear of the lorry and down into the jungle.

Then, amid the chaos around them, and even above the terrifying din, the thunderous voice of Flying Officer Morgan could be heard shouting orders at his men.

"Get out! What the fuck are you doing sitting on your asses? Get out and get down into cover! Come on! You! You! And you! Move, man, move! Move your fucking selves."

His bellowing commands brought many of the airmen from their stupor. Grimly hanging on to their rifles, they began dropping over the sides and tailboard of the lorry, some to leap and some to fall into cover. The RAF Regiment corporal Bren-gunner was now returning fire in long bursts.

"Quick, man! Quick!" Flying Officer Morgan shouted as he heaved a terrified youth over the side. The youth was Tulip whose left hand had been hit by a bullet, and he had sat there staring in horrified amazement at the mangled bloody stubs where his fingers had been shot away leaving only a blood-splattered thumb. In shock, and hurt by the fall from the lorry, he was sobbing and crawling along the edge of the road when a hand shot out from the roadside undergrowth, grabbed him by the ass of his pants and pulled him down into cover. At that same moment a hail of bullets riddled the road where he had been.

Peter Saunders, thinking clearly now, was about to jump from the lorry but found that his foot had become wedged in the damaged and twisted metal seat on which he had been sitting.

"I can't move my foot, Rick," he gasped in dismay.

"You've got to, Pete," agonized his friend.

"Christ, Rick! It won't come out."

"Shuddup and heave. Come on! Heave!"

"It's out, Rick! It's out!" Peter screamed.

"Come on, then. Let's go."

Both airmen were about to jump off the back of the lorry when Peter turned and saw Flying Officer Morgan manning the Bren, sending short bursts of fire up into the jungle overlooking them; the corporal RAF Regiment Bren-gunner lay dead at the officer's feet. In between short bursts, Peter actually heard Morgan give a grunt of satisfaction, and he watched as a man's body pitched from behind a bush high up on the hillside to crash head first down onto the road. "One," Peter clearly heard the officer say. A moment later, he heard, "Two," and Peter saw another man rise from behind cover. This one rolled down the slope accompanied by his rifle, which he held onto until he hit the road.

Rick screamed, "For fuck sake, Pete, let's go!"

"OK. I'm coming," Peter answered, and he was about to leave the lorry when a grenade exploded within the lorry's cab, the blast from it shattering the rear window and sending Flying Officer Morgan staggering backwards. Peter heard him grunt, and watched dismayed as the officer sank slowly down onto the floorboards of the lorry, a jagged piece of glass and chunks of shrapnel from the grenade embedded into his chest. Flying Officer Morgan feebly but tenaciously sought to regain his feet, and almost managed to do so, by picking up a rifle from the floorboard of the lorry and attempting to use it as a crutch. Weakly, and as if mechanically, he managed to draw the bolt of the rifle back and slide a round into the breech. But the rifle dropped from his hands with a clatter, and Flying Officer Morgan sank down across the body of the Bren-gunner, and died.

"You bastards," shouted Peter, now almost in tears of anger and frustration. "I'm not going now, Rick."

"You're what?"

"I want to get one of them bastards."

"Don't be a bloody fool."

"You go."

"I'm going."

Scrambling across the dead and wounded, Rick stooped down at the side of the dead officer and withdrew the heavy revolver from its holster. "I'll take this," he said. "It may come in handy. Come on, Pete!" With those words Rick sprang over the side, his rifle in one hand, the revolver in the other.

Half-crazed with anger, Peter Saunders looked around him and noticed the violin and bag of golf clubs stacked neatly in a front corner of the lorry. Young Pilot Officer Graham, thinking they would be safer travelling in the same lorry as himself, had transferred them from the other Bedford during the rest period at the police post. The young pilot officer, himself one of the first to die, had fallen dead from the cab and now lay on the road in a pool of blood. Peter gaped at the dead man, his anger intensifying and all fear momentarily forgotten. Noticing the sun glinting on metal in the undergrowth above him, Peter suspected that a terrorist lay in hiding there behind his weapon. "I'll get you, you bastard," he muttered. Lusting to kill, he wrenched a blood-splattered Sten gun from the hands of badly wounded Corporal Hicks, aimed the quick-firing automatic weapon from his hip and squeezed the trigger. The gun vibrated violently in his hands but he held on, the muzzle aimed at that glinting spot. Suddenly, as if in surrender, a man rose from his hiding place amid the greenery, his hands held high above his head—his surrender to death. And as he stood there dying with still more bullets thudding into him, Peter Saunders snarled, "Die, you bastard, die," and he managed a grim smile of satisfaction as he watched clothing and flesh being ripped in shreds from the man's body. Raising the muzzle of the Sten gun ever so slightly, Peter watched as the man's face splattered and the head disintegrated. The body, finally keeling over, tumbled from among low bushes and slithered down the cleared embankment to land in a messy heap at the side of the road below. Seeing more movement in bushes above and farther back the road, Peter fired at the spot until there was silence from the Sten gun, its last round spent. Peter tossed the weapon aside. For the first time in his life he had killed a man.

Grabbing his rifle, he winced as a bullet thudded with a heavy thump into the Irishman, Paddy Jones. But Paddy Jones did not feel a thing. He was already dead, killed in the first bursts of gunfire.

Corporal Hicks, moaning horribly, lay stretched across a seat, with blood pumping from his stomach and forming a widening pool on the floor of the lorry. A determined gleam shone in the eyes of Peter Saunders as he hissed, "You're one poor bastard that's not going to die, not in this lorry."

Attempting to drag the corporal by the arms, Peter gasped, for the man was so big and heavy and he felt so weak and inadequate for the job. He somehow managed to haul the corporal as far as the tailboard; but the man was not helping himself any, just groaning and feebly waving his arms in the air. There was only one way of getting the corporal off the lorry. Placing a foot against the man's behind, determinedly Peter Saunders shoved with all his strength, so that the heavy body slowly slid over the tailboard and dropped to the ground like a sack of potatoes.

Peter watched as the corporal, rolling over once, fell off the edge of the road and disappeared into the sanctuary of the jungle.

Now, it seemed to Peter that every gun on the hillside was aimed directly at him with bullets coming from all directions, splattering woodwork, thudding into bodies, and ricocheting off steel. So far, he had remained unscathed. Groaning loudly, he gritted his teeth and stood undecided, not knowing what to do. Several badly wounded RAF personnel still remained in the back of the lorry and he didn't want to leave them to their fate. But now his anger left him and was replaced by fear, he felt terrifyingly alone. Feeling as if he must at any moment empty his bowels into his pants, he was stopped from doing so by a sudden searing red-hot pain as a bullet ripped through his scalp and slid across his skull. Wincing, he cried out, "Christ, I'm hit." He had to get off the lorry and down into the relative safety of the jungle. It was now or never. Carrying his rifle, he jumped in one mighty leap from the tailboard, not even touching the road but seemingly to fly over it, to drop over the edge and to land on his feet with a jarring thud among low bushes growing upon a soft, wet, moss-covered slope.

As he was regaining his balance an explosion behind him rent the air, followed immediately by a loud 'whoooshhhh', and then another explosion. Fearfully he looked towards the road and gasped in horror at the spectacle he witnessed. The RAF lorry's petrol tank had exploded engulfing the vehicle in a great ball of fire, the screams coming from within the flames were terrible.

"Poor bastards." Peter said, talking to himself.

Fearful and sickened by all he had seen, he plunged downward, panicking in his headlong flight through the undergrowth. He fell, dropping into a mass of creepers and nettles. Freeing himself, he tried to calm down, telling himself that he must not panic. But it was no use. Unable to control himself, he again crashed his way downward, fighting against all that tried to trip him, tear at him and hold him back. Nauseated and sweating with fear, he slashed a path with his rifle, not caring about the cuts and bruises received in his headlong flight, or about the noise he created, and expecting at any moment to feel bullets ripping into his body. On colliding with the trunk of a spindly tree, he grabbed a hold on it for support, feeling as if he was about to faint. Dropping his rifle, he leaned heavily against the slender trunk, holding onto it whilst trying to pull himself together.

On the lower side of the road the scattered security forces were regrouping, taking up positions and returning a massive barrage of gunfire against the terrorists hidden in the jungle-clad hillside a hundred feet or more above them. And now the armoured car, the leader of the convoy, having reversed back around the bend in the road, began firing back at the enemy, its heavy turret gun thumping and its twin machine guns chattering.

Replaying the awful events in his mind, Peter wasn't sure whether he was about to shit his pants, vomit or both. He vomited, spewing the contents of his stomach down over the tree and onto the jungle floor. Now he felt better and in more control of himself. Wiping his wet face with the sleeve of his jacket, he was surprised to see the sleeve covered in blood. Previously, the only pain he had felt was the moment the bullet ripped through his scalp and he had forgotten the wound. Now, though, knowing that it bled, it hurt. Removing his beret, he examined it and stared in disbelief at the two bullet holes in the blue cloth, one in the front, the other in the rear.

"You bastards. I'll get more of you before this day is over," he shouted. He felt his mouth dry and twitching and his whole body shaking in both fear and anger. Leaving the sanctuary of the tree, he took up his rifle and cradled it almost lovingly in his arms. "You're going to do your stuff today," he was saying, wiping muck from it with the cuff of his jacket. He decided to work his way upward, back to the edge of the road and once there take up a firing position.

The constant din of firing guns was now even more intense, most probably caused by the convoy's armament answering back, Peter thought. Yet, as there was such a continuous din of gunfire coming from the direction of the road, it seemed to him that the terrorists were still shooting up the stalled vehicles. Perhaps he could pick off a terrorist or two with his rifle, he thought. Through wet jungle, he began to make his way slowly upward towards the edge of the road.

Ammunition in a burning army lorry exploded near him, the blast knocking him to his knees. Dazed and unable to regain his feet, he began to crawl upward. He came upon several dead bodies, military personnel and civilians, some almost hidden in the thick undergrowth, others, with body parts missing, hanging in the bushes. Close to a burned out and still smoking car, two bodies lay, charred almost beyond recognition as once being human. At least two of the recognizable dead wore RAF uniforms. He came upon a turned-over jeep, its dead driver, a British soldier, crushed beneath it.

That's strange, Peter thought. Here there are only dead but a number of the airmen travelling with him had managed to get clear of the lorry and down into the jungle unscathed. But he was alone, and he wondered why. Some living members of his squadron must be nearby. He thought of Rick. He had seen him jump from the lorry. He must be close by. I must find him, he told himself. Regaining his feet but stumbling now, and finding no one alive at the edge of the road immediately in front of him, he turned to the right towards where the convoy was stalled, and from where there was still the noise of exploding grenades. Cautiously pushing dense foliage aside, he eased himself between creepers as thick as his arm. Thus, he worked his way slowly through the undergrowth, trying his best to keep parallel with the road. Suddenly he tripped and stumbled over a British soldier lying still and obviously dead. Regaining his feet, Peter kept going.

He found Jock Campbell, that sure-of-himself, dependable Scotsman, lying on his back with his eyes closed as if in slumber, and half hidden by the broad leaves of wild bananas. A grim, frozen smile played upon the face, yet the spirit had gone from the body. To Peter, it looked as if a hand grenade had exploded against the man's chest, killing him instantly. Much of the interior of the body lay exposed in one bloody mess of busted rib bones, heart and lungs. The stomach had been torn apart causing the entrails to fall from it in a nightmarish mess near the body, everything interwoven by ragged pieces of the man's KD uniform.

Sickened and dismayed, Peter stared incredulously at the mess at his feet. Shutting his eyes he turned away from the awful spectacle. When he looked again he gasped in amazement. An army of half-inch long brown and white ants had already found the body and were swarming over it in their thousands, eating their way into warm intestines and clotting blood, and already carrying away minute pieces of the body to their nest.

"My God!" Peter whispered. "My God!" With his booted foot he scuffed at fallen leaves covering the soil, and finding the soil soft and pliable he dropped to his knees, and using his hands and the rifle butt he began burying the body. "You poor devil," he was saying, sobbing in anger and despair. "You poor devil." Now, working in a state of frenzy, sweating profusely he scraped and tore at the loose soil, throwing it over the bloody remains of the body, to slowly cover it, inch by inch.

"No ants are going to get you, Jock. Not whilst I'm here. I'll get the bastards."

Slowly but thoroughly he covered the entrails lying on the ground, and then the bloody mass protruding from the man's gaping chest wound. He then began covering the remainder of the body with whatever came to hand—soil, stones, twigs full of leaves, grass which he tore up by its roots, leaves snapped off the banana clump and then more soil. Finally, on completing the job, he stood and surveyed the heap at his feet, and with bowed head sadly said, "So, Jock, I did my best. Now go with God. Rest in peace."

And as Peter stood there with bowed head, he realized that his vision was blurred. Taking off his glasses, he examined them and saw that the lenses were not only smeared with dirt and blood, but one was also cracked. He took a clean white handkerchief from his pants pocket, the only thing on him that was not filthy dirty, and spitting on the lenses, he very carefully cleaned them with the handkerchief. Though a simple task, it helped steady his nerves.

Their cleaning complete, he put his glasses back on and returned the handkerchief to his pocket. Then, with rifle in hand, he carefully made his way back towards the edge of the road, passing a dead British soldier and two RAF chaps, neither of which, to his relief, was Rick. Nearer the road, shaded by low bushes, he came across the corporal whom he had shoved off the lorry. He was dead. Tulip was close by, crying and holding up his mangled hand still dripping blood. An uninjured RAF senior aircraftman who Peter did not know was trying to comfort him. Seeing the uncovered bloody mess that had been a hand, Peter pulled the white handkerchief from his pocket. "Let me put this on your hand, Tulip," he said.

In shock, and quivering with fear and pain, without saying a word Tulip held out his mangled hand. Carefully, and as best he could, Peter wrapped the bloody mess in his handkerchief. "Just hold the handkerchief on there, Tulip," he said. "Help will soon be on the way." He turned to the other airman. "Have you seen Rick?" he asked.

"Who's Rick?" asked the airman.

"The fellow who was sitting with me at the tailboard."

"No, I haven't seen him," was the reply.

"Stay with Tulip," Peter said. "I'm going back to the road."

Just feet from the road he came across two more airmen, alive, uninjured but obviously very frightened, whispering to one another. He asked them the same question. "Have either of you seen the fellow who was sitting with me at the tailboard?"

One of them, an LAC, said, "He got clear. I saw him going that way," and he pointed towards where the centre of the convoy should be. "He wasn't going downhill. Looked like he was keeping parallel with the road."

"Thanks," said Peter.

"What a fuck-up," said the LAC

"Yeah, it is," agreed Peter. Turning his back on them, he headed in the direction the airman had pointed, coming across more bodies as well as several wounded; some were civilians, some military, but there were no RAF personnel among them. Peter hurried onward, through more tangled undergrowth until he came to an opening where he could look up and see a burning jeep on the road above. Unsure as to where he was along the length of the convoy, he cautiously approached the road's edge and peered over.

An awesome sight met his eyes. Crashed and burning vehicles, both military and civilian, littered the road. Many were jammed together. Dead bodies lay strewn about upon that whole stretch of road, while others hung like limp rag dolls from bullet-riddled and wrecked vehicles. There was no sign of any living person.

Suddenly, to his amazement, Peter saw a near-naked Chinese youth, a machete in hand, run down the steep bank and leap onto the road almost opposite to where he crouched behind the road's edge. On impact with the road the youth staggered, regained his balance, then ran fleet of foot to where a man and a woman's body lay on the road close to an expensive looking white car with a flag, a British Union Jack, fluttering from its bonnet. The couple was middle-aged, obviously of European descent and well dressed in light-coloured clothing. First, the youth ran to the side of the woman and without hesitation and with one whack from his machete, he slashed off all her fingers from a hand. Stooping, he picked up rings and those fingers still adorned with rings and slipped these into a pocket of his sole garment, a pair of dirty khaki shorts. So quick and so audacious was he, Peter was astounded, and for moments watched in horrified amazement.

The young Chinese terrorist, who could not have been older than Peter, cast furtive eyes about him and must have thought there was no one near him except the dead because, almost casually, he bent over the body of the man and removed a watch from the limp, dead wrist. The watch followed the rings into his pant's pocket. A Sten gun lay at the side of the dead man. The Chinese youth bent forward to pick up the gun. In another moment the rapid-firing Sten gun would be in his hands.

"No, you can't have that gun," Peter yelled, standing up in full view and firing his rifle from the hip. The youth, knocked backward by the impact of the bullet, screamed in sudden terror and pain. The second bullet caught him between the eyes and immediately silenced him. His dead body fell across that of the dead woman. "That'll teach you, you bastard," Peter said. "That'll teach you," he repeated.

Peter was sorely tempted to retrieve the Sten gun, and was about to do so when a bullet smacked into the road inches from where he stood. Pretending he was hit, he dropped back over the edge of the road and froze, and remained thus for more than a minute. Then, cautiously, he peered through long grasses, his eyes methodically sweeping the hillside overlooking that stretch of the road. He was now the hunter. "Ah! That's where you are," he said softly on locating his prey. He had seen a slight movement behind a low shrub high up the hillside, almost to the next ridge. Then he spotted a face peering between branches of the low shrub. "You're as good as dead," he whispered, sighting his rifle so that the bullet would strike the centre of that face. "Here's one on your nose," he said, squeezing the trigger. His eyes, not leaving that spot high on the hillside, watched as a man with his head blown away fell out of the shrubbery and rolled then bounced down the steep embankment. "Sorry about that, old chap," Peter said. He then slid deeper into the undergrowth.

Keeping parallel with the road, he resumed his search for Rick, and had not gone far when he suddenly tensed. "That's odd," he said to himself. "I could have sworn I heard a baby crying. I must be going bonkers." Holding his breath, he listened, but at first could hear only the noise of gunfire. Seconds passed, and then there was more crying, coming from quite near to where he crouched. "Yes, there it is again," he said quietly to himself.

Pushing the undergrowth aside with his rifle, he stealthily made his way towards the plaintive cries. Soon, he could distinctly hear words spoken by the child, that sounded like Chinese but in a dialect he could not understand.

More Chinese words flowed from the child, and then Peter realized that the child was now speaking in Malay. He had learned several words of Malay when stationed at KL, also from Rose. "*amah*! *amah dimana*? *Mari sini*," the child was calling out. Her words were followed by a burst of sobbing.

"*amah*! Where are you, *amah*? Come here." Peter whispered to himself, translating the Malay into English.

"*amah*!" wailed the child.

"There it is again. I must be going around the twist," Peter muttered. "But that's definitely the voice of a child. I swear it is."

There were more plaintive cries in Chinese followed by words in Malay. "*Cepat mari amah. Tolong saya.*"

"Come quickly, *amah*. Help me," Peter translated. Creeping forward he carefully pushed aside tall grasses that had impeded his progress. Now, the whimpering of the child came from directly ahead, and very near him. Parting more tall grasses ahead of him, he whispered as loudly as he dared, "*Kamu dimana?*" (Where are you?)

There was no answer, just the noise of gunfire coming from the vicinity of the road. Had he imagined that he had heard the cries of a child, he wondered. Was his mind playing tricks on him after all he had seen and been through this last hour.

As loudly as he dared, he repeated, "*Kamu dimana?*"

"*Sini atas,*" came back the reply.

Peter froze as he translated the two Malay words. "Up here!" he exclaimed in puzzled surprise. Parting a mass of undergrowth growing in profusion above his head, he stared upward, his eyes barely penetrating the thick greenery. Then, astonished by the sight which met his eyes, he exclaimed, "What the hell are you doing up there?"

High in the bushes, as if caught in a giant spider's web, hung a little girl clad in a white dress, her arms and legs outstretched, her feet ensnared in a mass of tangled vines clinging to a bush-like tree, which appeared to be taller than all other nearby vegetation. Peter could not see the face of the child, just black hair which was the back of her head, and little bare feet and legs, and tiny hands which clung tenaciously to supporting branches of the main bush. There was no answer from the girl, but she did turn a frightened face towards him.

"Well I'll be damned! A baby Chinese girl! How did you get up there?" Peter asked. It seemed all too silly. He was staring up at her, and she looking down at him with fear in her eyes, watching his every movement.

Peter Saunders looked down at his filthy uniform, knowing that his hair and face was matted in blood and dirt. "Christ, no wonder you're scared of me shitted up like I am. We'll I'll be damned, I still can't figure out how you got up there."

The girl whimpered, her tiny hands clutching at higher creepers as if she was trying to escape from him.

Peter gazed up at her. "You're sure in a rotten predicament. Of all the daft things possible, this must be just about the screwiest. Fancy me finding a little Chinese girl caught up in the middle of a tree in the heart of the Malayan jungle." Tension flowed fast from him. He wanted to talk. He wanted to free his mind from all he had seen and heard that day.

"Well, girlie, there's one thing for sure, somehow or other you'll have to come down from up there. You can't go hanging around in the treetops all day, can you? It beats me, though, how the hell you got up there in the first place."

Then, suddenly, understanding came to him as he noticed a gap in the dark mass of greenery immediately above the girl, a gap through which he could just make out the drop-off from the road above.

"So you came down from the road, eh, sweetie pie? You jumped down, I suppose. That's some jump for a little girl your size."

The girl began to whimper again.

"Do you speak English?" There was no response from the girl. Next, Peter spoke to her in Cantonese, which she did not seem to understand either. Finally, he spoke to her in broken Malay. "*Tunggu. Saya tolong kamu.*" (Wait a minute. I'll help you.)

The whimpering ceased. And now the gunfire had suddenly lessened. Peter wondered if any terrorists remained on the hillside. Surely, he thought, with their mission accomplished and with the element of surprise gone, they would be hurrying away from the massacre. Had they already departed from their ambush positions and at this very moment were hurrying quietly and unseen through a maze of jungle paths they alone knew, to their jungle encampment? Perhaps the security forces were now firing at no one.

Except for the occasional shot ringing out, and the shouts of men in the distance up on the road, the jungle was strangely quiet. The birds, bullfrogs, praying mantis, and all other creatures of the jungle hid and uttered not a cry, their quietness their sanctuary. Those creatures would bide their time before making sound again.

Peter leaned his rifle against the moss and creeper-covered trunk of a rotted fallen tree. It should be safe now to allow his rifle out of his hands, he thought. Thrusting his hands and arms up amid tangled wet creepers, he caught hold of a thick vine and, hand over hand, pulled his body upward. He cursed the thick web of plant life that seemed to grasp and hold onto him, yet at the same time, as he made his way higher, he used them as if they were rungs of a ladder. He was now no more than a few feet below the girl, looking up at her with a stupid sort of grin on his face. She was staring down at him, frightened and wanting to keep her distance.

"Don't be scared. I won't hurt you," he tried to reassure her. She didn't understand his words, but now she seemed a little less frightened of him. "Just a baby, a little Chinese girl. Well! This really is some kettle of fish. Hold on, ducky! Your Uncle Peter is coming."

She lay among the branches quiet and still, watching with those big brown eyes his every move. Now he was close enough to reach out and touch her. She did not shrink from his touch but just stared at him. Now, she was almost in his arms. Her ankles, both badly scratched and bruised, were jammed between a criss-cross of creepers, which had kept her from falling. Now, because of her struggle to free herself, her position was precarious. One wrong move and she would topple over and hang upside down.

Reaching for the creepers that trapped her feet, Peter tugged at them, all the while prepared to catch the child should she fall. He stopped for a moment to reassuringly stroke a tiny hand and to look as friendly as he knew how into her frightened little face. "I'm not going to hurt you, little girl. I'm going to help you down from this big old tree," he said in Malay.

A first smile suddenly appeared on the little girl's face. "*Terima kasih, tuan,*" she said in a whisper. (Thank you, sir.) And then again, "*Terima kasih.*"

"That's all right, ducks. Anything for a little lady." And Peter was surprised to see that she had suddenly begun to giggle, as if she thought him funny. "Some bloody sense of humour you've got!" he said, holding on to keep himself from falling. "Anyway, girlie, your Uncle Peter will soon have you down from here."

29

A gloating Fong Fook had watched as the little blue sports car careered off the road and plunged down the jungle-clad hillside. He fired next at the male driver of the vehicle that had been ahead of the sports car, but missed. Cursing, he fired again, this time hitting the driver in the shoulder. Scrambling from the car and throwing up his hands as if in protest, the man screamed obscenities as he fell off the edge of the road and disappeared from Fong Fook's sight.

Cursing again, Fong Fook switched his attention to the occupants of the Rolls Royce the same moment that Ho Li Li hit the top of the trees and sank from sight within its greenery. All Fong Fook saw of her was a disappearing flurry of whiteness. Shooting the chauffeur twice, he then shot the old lady who lay petrified on the rear seat of the car, and on seeing a military police jeep draw alongside the Rolls, he tossed a grenade so that it hit the road and rolled between the two vehicles. The ensuing explosion ruptured and ignited the jeep's fuel tank, which went up in a flaming 'whooosh'. Almost immediately the Rolls Royce did likewise, the two vehicles becoming one flaming inferno.

Concealed in his ambush position, Fong Fook watched with grim amusement as a military police corporal, his whole body ablaze, crawled from the burning jeep and staggered a few feet before collapsing in a flaming, twitching heap. Fong Fook then continued to toss grenades at stalled vehicles and to fire round after round from his rifle at the panic-stricken unfortunates desperately seeking safety beyond the roadside drop-off. Fong Fook seldom missed his target. Below him the dead and the dying lay strewn the whole length of the road. Fong Fook was enjoying this massacre no more or no less than during the many other killings in which he had participated. On this occasion, however, his curiosity was aroused by the flurry of whiteness that he had glimpsed disappearing amid the topmost leaves of the jungle opposite. Why was the object so important that the driver, at the risk of his own life, should attempt its safeguarding? These questions nagged him even as he continued shooting at those unfortunates fleeing and seeking cover.

Suddenly, during a momentary lull in the gunfire, he heard the faint cries of what sounded like a young child in distress. Listening intently, he heard more cries, which seemed to come from the treetops directly across the road from him. My curiosity is answered, he told himself. A child had been a passenger in the shiny new car, and now she is alone and hidden somewhere among those trees beyond the road.

Although within the last ten minutes the destruction of vehicles and loss of life on the road below had been great, Fong Fook's enemies were now not only taking up defensive positions just beyond the road's edge but also were returning the fire in rapidly increasing intensity. Fong Fook knew only too well the security forces superior armaments, also their accuracy at finding their targets was not to be underestimated. Already, on either side of him, he had seen several of his men topple down the steep embankment after being hit by enemy gunfire. If his comrades were not dead on hitting the road, they were dispatched quickly by the avenging security forces. He could not afford to lose a single man much less several men; the time had come for him and his men to retreat to their jungle encampment, content in their knowledge that their mission had been accomplished. He had plundered no arms, ammunition, nor even medicines from the enemy. He had, though, accounted for at least a score of lives—not mercenary killings of military men, but by murder, half his victims being civilians, both men and women, as well as a Chinese couple with three young children who, one after another, he had picked off with his rifle. He was satisfied.

Three miles east of where the road began its winding climb up Fraser's Hill, six Daimler armoured cars bounced and rattled their way along a neglected dirt road meandering its way through swampland and patches of jungle. This same road, which was really no more than a muddy, potholed path had once been a main commercial highway for the local rubber and tin industry. But that was many years ago, even before the Japanese invasion of Malaya.

Within the cramped confines of these stifling hot armoured vehicles sweated a commando-trained British Army patrol of the little known Special Forces Seek and Destroy unit or SAD.

On that hot and humid afternoon, the patrol, accompanied by an Iban tracker from Borneo, had already covered twenty miles on the dirt road, passing through a government-controlled native village en route. Except for a few inhabitants peacefully going about their business in the village and a number of civil police guarding the place, there had been no other sign of human life for the last twenty miles. The whole area, though, was still considered to be a 'black area'— infested and controlled by Communist terrorists.

Corporal Bill 'Killer' Burns, on lookout from the leading armoured vehicle's specially designed gun turret, suddenly spotted a wisp of smoke curling upward from a patch of thick jungle less than half a mile away. Like an oasis in a desert, the small patch of jungle was surrounded, not by sand, but by a wide area of waist-high *lalang*-covered swampland.

"Hey! That's smoke!" exclaimed Corporal Burns. "Take a look over there, sir, to our right."

He was speaking to Lieutenant Gates, commander of the patrol, who was riding in the same vehicle.

Lieutenant Gates stuck his head out of the gun turret, took one look at the wisp of smoke, and then raised an arm signalling the vehicles following to stop and for all engines to be silenced.

"What do you make of it, Killer?" the officer asked the young man at his side.

Southampton-born Corporal Bill Burns, a five-year man who was already a two-year veteran of the Malayan conflict, answered dryly, "Well, sir, where there's smoke there's got to be fire. And from my experience, where there's fire in the jungle, there's got to be people. I bet there's a hideout right smack in the middle of that patch of *ulu*."

"You're probably right," replied Lieutenant Gates, a forty-two-year-old officer who had seen warfare in many parts of the world, mainly with the Eighth Army in North Africa, Italy and Germany, then a brief spell in Korea, and now in Malaya. "Let's investigate it." It had been such a boring day for him, he was impatient to see something exciting happen. He was thinking, I'd like to take a patrol on foot through the grass and see what's over there. However, he was well aware that under very few circumstances should he or his men leave the armoured cars to go chasing on foot after Communist terrorists.

Reading his thoughts, Corporal Bill Burns said cautiously, "Sir, if there are people over there, then they'll have look-outs. In that case, they've already seen us."

"I know, Killer. You're right. The moment they see us moving in, they'll be gone. Our best plan is to send Selso over to that patch of *ulu*. Let him see what's over there."

"You're right, sir."

"Well you tell him. He understands you."

Corporal Bill Burns smiled to himself at that last remark by his officer in charge. Yes, Selso, the Iban tracker, did indeed understand him, as much as any Iban tracker would understand a corporal in the British Army. Having shared each other's company in Malaya these past two years, fighting alongside each other and often living together in primitive jungle encampments, they understood each other well.

Disappearing into the bowels of the armoured car, Corporal Bill Burns got on the radio to the Daimler armoured car stopped next in line behind his vehicle and in moments he was speaking in Malay to Selso.

Now Selso, like all other Iban trackers used in the Malay uprising, was from Borneo. The Sarawak Rangers is the official name for their small regiment. They are not only brave and dependable warriors but are also keenly observant and able to tell just by looking at grass or at surrounding jungle whether or not man or animal has passed that way, how many and how recently. Often used by British units, especially infantry units unfamiliar with jungle warfare, the Iban tracker almost always went ahead of British foot patrols.

On his return to the turret, Corporal Burns reported to Lieutenant Gates, "He'd already seen the smoke, sir. There he goes now."

The two men in the turret watched as the Iban tracker sprang from the armoured car to the ground. Clad in jungle-green trousers tucked into soft running shoes, Selso, whose only weapon was a razor-sharp machete, was indeed a fearsome-looking warrior. His ears were pierced and stretched into long loops almost to his shoulders, his whole body, that which could be seen, was almost completely tattooed in colourful leaves and flowers, and his black, shaggy hair hung in ragged strands from beneath a jungle-green army hat. Just the sight of this man was enough to put the fear of death into any enemy.

Crouching down as he entered the *lalang*, Selso quickly slid from sight among the tall grass. To those watching from the patrol vehicles, it was as if the *lalang* had swallowed him up and was now devoid of human life. Across the swampland, as far as the eye could see, not a blade of grass moved.

Lieutenant Gates and his men patiently waited.

Inside the stationary armoured cars the heat soon became stifling. The minutes ticked slowly by until almost an hour had passed. The lieutenant, Corporal Burns and Sergeant 'Basher' Rusk, the commander of the second armoured car had by now got out of their vehicles and were standing talking together at the head of the column.

"Well, where the fuck is he?" asked the sergeant.

"He ain't gone for no haircut," replied the corporal. "He can take care of himself."

"Yes, just relax," said the lieutenant. "We'll see him when he's good and ready to be seen."

Suddenly, out of the waist-high *lalang* grass emerged a grinning Selso accompanied by a Dyak head-hunter who, through broken black teeth, was also grinning and proudly wearing a recently gained trophy, a severed woman's head hanging by its hair from a belt of dried grass worn around the man's waist.

"Damn it! The Dyak's broken government regulations," snorted the lieutenant. "Recent orders are that bodies are to be left whole and taken back to camp for identification purposes without bits and pieces being chopped off them."

"Well, I suppose we can't blame them if they don't follow all our orders. Anyway, the Dyaks have beaten us to it," said Cpl, Burns ruefully.

"Yeah. We'll find no living enemy over there now, that's for sure," said the sergeant.

Selso and the triumphant Dyak warrior approached them at a jogging pace, the woman's head bouncing up and down grotesquely.

"We're too late," Selso said to Corporal Burns in Malay. And, nodding to the Dyak, he continued, "He and his friends found the camp first. Nobody was there apart from one old woman and two old men. They're dead now."

"What did he say?" asked the sergeant.

"I think he said they're all dead, didn't he, Killer?"

"You're right, sir," and with those words Corporal Burns translated into English what the tracker had said.

Selso then continued, "There's much to eat at the camp. Cooked pig, cats, monkeys, yams, a big pot of rice. Enough to feed an army."

Corporal Burns translated what the tracker had said.

"Really!" exclaimed the lieutenant, with growing interest.

"I think plenty of men went hunting. Return soon very hungry," said Selso.

Again Corporal Burn's translated every word to both the officer and sergeant in charge.

"All right. Let's go in and have a look around," said Lieutenant Gates. "Sergeant, this might be an ambush meant for us. Also the approach may be mined. Therefore, I'm going to do the unusual. First I'm going to send in a foot patrol, led by you, Killer."

"Right, sir," said Corporal Burns.

"Selso and his blood-thirsty cohort can lead the way. They'll know if there's any danger to our men," said the lieutenant. "We'll use a couple of mine detectors on that higher ground over there. If it's clear of mines, we'll follow the patrol in. Corporal Burns!"

"Yes, sir."

"Go over and inspect the place. Something fishy is happening, and I don't like it. Take as many men as you need."

"Yes, sir," acknowledged Corporal Burns. "I'll ask for volunteers."

Every one of the men immediately volunteered. Anything to get out of those stifling hot vehicles. Corporal Burns chose eight.

"All right men, let's go," Corporal Burns said quietly. "I'll be behind Selso and his pal. Thompson, you and the others follow at ten paces apart. You, Apa Kayu, you take up the rear."

Apa Kayu's real name was Watwood, but as the word 'what' in Malay is 'apa', and 'wood' is 'kayu', Lance Corporal Watwood became fondly known as Apa Kayu by everyone, including his commanding officer.

"I always guard your bloody arses," Apa Kayu jested. "I never get a chance to shoot anybody."

"You've shot your share," said Corporal Burns. "Right then, fellows, now remember, as little noise as possible, and once we're out in the grass, no talking. Let's go."

A black cloud of mosquitoes rose from the ankle-deep watery swamps as the patrol from the SAD unit entered the waist-high *lalang* grass, each man following the other at about ten paces apart, their Sten guns held in sweaty hands, their fingers babying hot triggers ready to kill. But no opposition was met except for the myriad of whining mosquitoes, gooey water and mud sucking at their boots, and the long, sharp *lalang* grass that seemed intent on ripping their camouflaged jungle uniforms from their bodies.

A huge python measuring at least twenty feet in length, slid silently through the grass across Lance-Corporal Thompson's path.

"Fuck you," Corporal Burns heard Thompson fearfully mutter. Turning, he was quick enough to see Thompson levelling his Sten at the snake.

"No!" Corporal Burns hissed. "Stay quiet."

Unharmed and unharming, the snake slithered its huge body through the long grass within spitting range of Thompson.

Apart from the loud grunting of a startled wild pig running away from them, the patrol arrived at the outskirts of the patch of jungle without further incident. Now, at least, the ground underfoot was reasonably dry. Selso and his Dyak companion were met by another fierce-looking Dyak who grinned at the soldiers and held up for all to see a grisly, blood-dripping, man's head. The Dyaks then led the soldiers almost a quarter of a mile into the interior, to where rude huts, or bashas, made from dry *lalang*, palm fronds and branches of trees had been built, the living quarters, it seemed, for a sizeable regiment. Also, latrines had been dug. Shielded by cut brush, a fire of about eight feet in diameter smouldered, with very little flame or smoke to it; just that tell-tale wisp. On the fire, in its glowing embers, sizzled and baked at least fifty yams. A wild boar on a spit cooked over the fire, also what appeared to be two big wild cats and several monkeys, all skinned and hanging from tripods over the fire and already baked a deliciously golden brown. The aroma from the cooked meat was mouthwatering. Keeping hot at the edge of the fire stood a huge iron cauldron brimming with cooked rice, and nearby was stacks of about fifty empty rice bowls and a paraphernalia of eating and cooking utensils.

A headless old woman dressed in a ragged, bloodied *samfoo* lay near the fire; the body of the camp cook, it seemed. A scrawny old man, also dead and headless, lay a few yards away.

About six more Dyaks who had been searching the camp appeared the same moment as the six armoured cars entered the encampment and stopped some yards from the fire. The lieutenant, on getting down from the leading vehicle, disdainfully prodded the body of the old man with the toe of his polished shoe. "They shouldn't have severed their heads," he said, shaking his head in disgust. "However, it's not our fault." Turning to Corporal Burns, he asked, "What do you make of it, Killer?"

"Well, sir, there's enough food here to feed an army," replied Corporal Burns solemnly. "It seems as if our luck's in. During their absence, we've stumbled into the Commies' lair."

"I'm sure you're right. Maybe as many as fifty of them," said the lieutenant.

"It could be that we've run smack into their district headquarters," ventured the corporal.

"I think you're right, Killer. But where are the bastards? Their lunch looks just about ready," said the lieutenant.

"Yes, that's what's bothering me." pondered the corporal.

"They can't be too far away," said the sergeant.

"That's true," said Corporal Burns. "And there must be a hell-of-a lot of them or there wouldn't be this much food being prepared. Where the hell are they, I wonder?"

Suddenly, what sounded like the sharp crack and rumble of thunder in the distance made him say, "Christ! That's gunfire and exploding grenades."

"Yeah, you're right. And I bet I know from where," shouted Corporal Burns.

"From Fraser's Hill, that's where it's from, God damn it! I don't believe it! They're hitting the convoy!" the sergeant exclaimed angrily.

"I bet it's happening at the Gap," said Corporal Burns.

"It's too late now to race over there and help," said the exasperated lieutenant as the noise in the distance intensified.

"The Gap's about three miles from here," anguished Corporal Burns.

"We'd never make it in time, not on a dirt road. They'll be retreating back into the jungle by the time we get anywhere near them."

"That right, they will be retreating, and they'll be returning here," said Lieutenant Gates. "By God, we can't help the poor sods at the Gap, but we sure as hell can stop those Commie bastards from ever eating this meal."

"You're right, sir," said the sergeant. "They'll all come back here, and they'll be returning in dribs and drabs; ones, twos and threes, hungry, tired, and off their guard. That's when we'll ambush them, a few at a time."

"Yes, that's what I'm thinking, Sergeant," agreed the lieutenant. "That's what we'll do. We'll catch every one of them as they return. This is indeed where the hunter becomes the hunted. Detail the men as you see fit, Sergeant."

"Right, sir! I suggest that we form into groups and surround the whole encampment," said the sergeant.

"There are three paths leading into the camp," said the Iban tracker to Corporal Burns.

Corporal Burns translated the tracker's words to both Lieutenant Gates and Sergeant Rusk.

"Good. That makes our job much simpler. I'm sure these Dyaks will be only too happy to assist us. We'll line the paths with hiding men and wait there for the bastards to return. And as they straggle back to camp, we'll kill them as quietly as possible. Now remember, I want silent killing, no screams and no gunfire. We'll use just our knives and machetes."

"Good thinking, Sergeant," replied the lieutenant.

"Yeah, you're right. We could get the whole fucking lot of 'em," said Corporal Burns.

"Rock on, Killer! But first, Sergeant, let's get our vehicles under cover," said Lieutenant Gates.

"Yes, sir!"

"And keep the bloody smoke rising from that fire so that they'll see it. The smell of cooked pig and monkeys will tempt them in fast enough.

The gunfire and sharp crack of exploding grenades had intensified, and for almost twenty minutes there was a continuous din coming from the direction of the Gap. Eventually, however, the noise gradually subsided, and it was not too long before the hiding, waiting, commando-trained men of the SAD unit heard the approach of the first returning Communist terrorists.

Tired and hungry, unsuspecting and carrying their rifles unconcernedly at their side, three terrorists walked single file along a path and into the trap.

During a lull in the gunfire, Fong Fook eased himself stealthily upward, on his back, through tall grass and low shrubs, like a snake slithering silently away from danger. Once again he heard the faint cries of a child in distress. Pausing and sinking his skinny body flat to the ground, he listened. There followed more heavy gunfire, then another lull during which time he distinctly heard the plaintive cries of a child, a baby girl calling out in Chinese, but in a dialect which he could not understand except for one word, "*amah*!" Was the old woman he had killed the child's *amah*, he wondered.

Fong Fook resumed his snake-like glide through the concealing undergrowth, slithering on his stomach now whilst dragging his rifle at his side. Full well he knew that beyond the road below him, searching the hillside with alert eyes, were many angry men, with nervous trigger fingers ready to fire at anything that dared move on the facing hillside. Sliding among more tall grasses, he eventually came upon a narrow, rarely used path, so overgrown that it had become tunnel-shaped by masses of foliage. Fong Fook knew all the paths in this part of the country. Tired and hungry, his body wracked with pain from his diseases, he gave a long sigh of relief, and stood up, knowing that now he was well concealed from the eyes of those below. From here on he had only to follow the correct zigzagging path through the maze of paths in the surrounding jungle to be far enough away to escape entrapment by the security forces. He knew only too well that soon they would throw a cordon of their men, the head-hunting Dyaks and the blood-thirsty, fearless Gurkhas included, around the whole area, with orders to search and destroy.

Yet, he was curious as to whose child now cried for her *amah* from the jungle. Had she travelled in the shiny, expensive-looking car? Dare he attempt to find her? He cursed himself for being such a fool, realizing that it would be as good as suicide to attempt such a crazy venture. To risk crossing the road safely would be madness. And should he manage to cross the road unseen, it would necessitate him moving among the enemy. The risk was too great. He hurried onward, his rifle in hand, along the narrow, overgrown path, in the direction of the setting sun slipping from sight behind far hills.

Thus Fong Fook made his retreat, crouching to avoid thorny overhanging branches whilst jogging at a half run along the narrow path.

After covering a hundred yards or so, he suddenly stopped and listened as more heavy gunfire broke out behind him. It would be gunfire from the security forces now. His men would have already left the ambush area and would be making their way in ones and twos back to camp. Seating himself upon the trunk of a fallen tree, he relaxed and gloated over this day's work. The ambush had succeeded better than even he had anticipated; his ego was enormous. Fools! Fools! How could such greenhorns to the jungle hope to win over him and his men who were such veterans of this form of warfare? Were not the majority of the oppressors mere boys who had never been tried in battle; who had never before faced death? Contemptuous of his enemies, he spat on the ground, a supercilious smirk appearing on his gaunt face. Yes, he would go among the enemy, and he would seek and find the child. He would gain nothing from the foolhardy venture, he knew, but this would be his supreme test. Very soon he would learn whether or not he had lost his former hunting skills acquired when tracking-down and killing jungle-trained Japanese soldiers.

Refilling the magazine of his rifle with ten rounds of .303 ammunition, he clipped it back into its place. Satisfied, he got up from the fallen tree trunk and jogged onward. Now he must take a different path, but like all others in the area, it was a path he knew. On reaching the junction of that path, he looked both to the left and to the right but saw no one. So far, so good, he thought. The path, tunnel-shaped, was lined by tall creepers which had woven themselves together overhead so thick the matting of foliage blocked out even the sunlight. Carpeted by spongy moss and dead leaves, it ran for a hundred yards or more parallel with the road.

Bent almost double, Fong Fook ran along this path which would take him past the rear of the convoy. He knew that he must cross the road somewhere behind the last vehicle in the convoy, then stealthily double back to where he had heard the crying child.

On and on he ran, pausing occasionally to listen and then cautiously peer between creepers to see if the road was clear. Finally, parting creepers and tall grasses overlooking the road, he saw that he had reached the rear of the convoy. To his right the stopped convoy trailed its way up the hill. He could see men manning gun positions; but here their guns were silent. Immediately below him was the light tank, its turret gun pointed straight at him, its gunners staring through narrow slits seeking the invisible foe. A hatch in the light tank opened and a head emerged, followed by broad shoulders with 'pips' on each epaulette. The head wore earphones and was speaking into a walky-talky, loud and very clear. Fong Fook heard every word, but not knowing English, understood nothing. This was his chance of a lifetime, he thought, drawing back the bolt of his rifle and pushing a round into the breech. Just the click of the bolt action was audible; nothing more. Grinning evilly, he levelled the rifle and squinted down the sights until he had them aimed between the man's eyes. This was just too easy, he told himself. This officer was about to earn himself a medal, posthumously.

Fong Fook's finger slid to the trigger the very same moment that the head and shoulders withdrew back into the turret, and the hatch clanged shut.

Cursing to himself, Fong Fook relaxed his grip on the rifle. The hatch remained closed. He cursed again at having missed the chance to avenge fallen comrades killed by the murderous tank crews who had blasted jungle hide-outs into heaps of rubble with their terrible cannon fire, and who had swept whole areas clear of human life by their deadly machine guns.

Shaking his head in annoyance, he flipped on the rifle's safety catch and then crept back to the tunnel-like path. Cautiously looking in both directions, with no one in sight, he resumed a crouching, jogging run, and covered another hundred feet or more when he arrived at another bend in the path. Here he halted, and for several seconds listened intently. Hearing nothing, he carefully parted bushes and tall grass so that again he could look down and see the road.

To his left the road was empty, and to his right the road was equally deserted all the way to the distant bend; a high bank, stony and cleared of vegetation at the bend shielded the tank from his view, as it also shielded him from the whole convoy.

There was still the occasional sharp crack of rifle fire, also spasmodic short bursts from Bren guns to be heard coming from beyond the bend in the road. His nerves being on edge, Fong Fook suddenly jumped in alarm as a bullfrog honked within inches of his face, the loud rasping noise momentarily startling him. Yet, except for the myriad of mosquitoes whining all around him, all else where he hid remained silent. Even the many colourful birds held their songs in check, or had long sped from the shattered silence of their sanctuary. Nothing but mosquitoes stirred near him, and no human voice broke the silence where he now hid. He surveyed the greenness of the jungle on the other side of the road. There, not even a leaf seemed to stir. Now was his opportunity to cross the road.

Pushing concealing undergrowth aside, he emerged cautiously

into sunlight to find himself at the topmost edge of a cleared, stony embankment, which slanted downward until it reached the mountain's narrow road. Completely exposed now, Fong Fook had to act swiftly. First he ran, and then he slid as if skiing down a snow-covered slope, sliding on dry dirt, shale and stones down the steep embankment until, tripping up at the bottom, he fell, sprawled out upon the road. Regaining his feet, and without looking to his left or right, he quickly ran across the road and noiselessly entered the jungle's green covering. Once there, pressing himself against the trunk of a tree, he panted heavily, his bony chest heaving in and out from all the exertion, his eyes nervously darting in all directions; yet he saw nothing to cause him alarm. He gave a smile of satisfaction. He had safely crossed the road.

Carefully and quietly parting sticky wet creepers, he slipped among them and began edging his way back towards the stalled convoy and to enemy occupied terrain. Now, with no path for him to scurry along nor tunnel of foliage to conceal his movements, the going would be much more difficult than before. With every yard covered his heart seemed to miss a beat as dead twigs crackled beneath his feet, and leaves and creepers rustled in protest at being parted and pushed aside. Suddenly, he stopped, startled at hearing the loud and clear voice of the tank commander again, speaking into his walky-talky from his stationary tank positioned on the road above. Silently Fong Fook cursed the man. The fool was simply asking to be eliminated. But he dared not take a shot at him from the lower side of the road.

Sinking deeper into cover, Fong Fook inched his way stealthily forward, hardly daring to breath, his eyes darting in all directions. Hearing voices approaching, he sank out of sight amid creepers and watched as armed men in military uniform slashed their way through the jungle, so close to him he could have hit one by a throw of his *kris* if the jungle had not been so dense. Other armed, uniformed men followed, passing within feet of where he was hiding, and he could hear voices coming from the edge of the road. He cursed himself for his rash action. Crossing the road had been a foolish move. By now he could have been almost back at the camp where he knew hot food awaited him. A wild suckling pig, two wild cats and several monkeys on spits would be roasting over an open fire, and freshly dug yams would be baking in the fire. Also, there would be a giant pot of white rice, all prepared and cooked by a faithful old woman camp guard, to feed the returning famished men. Next to monkey, wild cat was his favourite dish. Now, though, he was not hungry but angry with himself. To allow himself to be just a few feet away from so many of the hated enemy had been foolhardy. He waited until a second lot of men had distanced themselves from him before wiping a grimy hand across a sweating brow and thinking, 'Dare I go onward, or should I quietly retreat?' Brushing a big black spider from his leg, he rubbed a growing spot of redness where the spider had bitten him.

Onward he would go, he decided. Perhaps a fool, but he was no coward, and he was too near his goal to turn and run. He would reach his objective. He would seek and find that child now crying for help in the jungle.

30

A frightened girl dressed in a torn and bloodied white silk dress stood looking up at him out of big brown unblinking eyes, wide with both fear and wonderment. Filled with mingled awe and helplessness, she was uncertain; the unfamiliar man towering over her had rescued her from the treetops, and he was not angry with her or using loud words of reprimand.

Puzzled and shaking his head in disbelief, Peter Saunders stared down at the little girl. He tried to smile, wanting to reassure her and gain her confidence. Then, because the top of her head reached only to just above his knees, he squatted down in front of her so that their faces were level.

The little girl's face was coated in dirt, bloodied where scratched and swollen from weeping, yet by her delicate features and ivory-white skin, she could very well be the daughter of a Chinese aristocrat, thought Peter. Also, although now dirty and dishevelled, her hair obviously had been groomed by caring hands. It was as black as ebony and flowed in soft and shiny waves around delicate shoulders. She had cute little dimples and a tiny heart-shaped mouth, but it was her eyes, which impressed Peter the most. Almond shaped, they were brown and beautiful, and they reminded him of how his Chinese girlfriend Rose looked when perplexed or appealing to him when wanting her own way.

"Hello, little girl," Peter said to her, in English.

The little girl, not understanding and looking obviously puzzled, simply stared back at him and said nothing.

"So you don't speak English, eh? In that case let's try Cantonese. *Ne hou ma, siu mui mui*?" (How are you, little girl?)

Unblinking and watching his every move, the little girl, still not seeming to understand him, remained silent.

"So, you don't speak Cantonese either. That's damned odd. I suppose you speak Mandarin," said Peter Saunders. "Well, I don't, so we'll have to stick to Malay."

She looked at him questioningly.

"*Boleh cakap Melayu*?" (Do you speak Malay?) he asked.

Instantly, the little girl's face brightened. "*Boleh*," she answered.

Wanting to reassure her that he was a friend and not going to harm her, Peter said, "*Saya kawan. Orang Ingerris.*" He smiled to himself. He did not know too many words in Malay, but speaking to this little girl, his vocabulary seemed adequate. He told her that he was a friend and an Englishman.

The girl nodded her head in understanding. "*Saya Cina*," she whispered shyly.

"*Bagus*. That's good. Now we're getting somewhere. I can see that you're a little Chinese girl, but I find it strange that you speak Malay and not Cantonese."

Having understood not a word of the last long sentence, the little girl gave him a coy look and shrugged her shoulders. Peter then asked her name, saying, "*Nama siapa*?"

This drew an immediate response. In the same shy whisper, the little girl replied, "Ho Li Li."

"Ho Li Li, eh!" said Peter. "Well, that is a lovely name. Ho Li Li," he repeated.

The girl nodded her head.

"Well, Miss Ho, I shall call you Li Li. How's that?"

She was smiling at him now, almost to the point of giggling "I suppose I do look a funny sight," Peter said, forgetting for the moment his throbbing head-wound, the chaos all around him and the horrifying sights he had just witnessed. But now, at long last, the din was subsiding. Ammunition exploded in a burning vehicle at the rear of the convoy, and orders in English were being shouted from another direction. But except for the occasional rifle shot and some short bursts from a Bren gun coming from somewhere in the distance, the gunfire had ceased. Now, the stillness of the air was broken only by a whispering breeze that rustled the topmost leaves of the trees surrounding the odd couple facing each other among the greenery.

"I must see if we can get back onto the road. If we can, then I'll try to find out who you belong to."

Rising to his feet, and whilst stooping to pick up the child, he was startled by the sound of snapping dry twigs behind him, as if from under someone's feet. Turning, he gasped in dismay. His hands dropped from the girl. Already it was too late to take defensive action, much too late. He had committed the cardinal sin of allowing his rifle out of his hands. It stood where he had propped it, against the skinny trunk of that rotting tree six feet away; it may well have been six miles for all its usefulness to him now.

Fong Fook had reached his objective. Not only had he found the crying child but also a defenceless military enemy. Stepping out from behind a covering of jungle vegetation, he smirked and, forgetting the child for the moment levelled his rifle at this easy kill.

Realizing the hopelessness of his predicament, Peter Saunders did not move a muscle but instead stared stonily back into a villainous face full of hate. He saw the skinny man's cobra-like eyes dart to where his own rifle stood propped against the tree. He saw the man's lips part and heard a low snarl coming from the mouth of a sallow, shrunken face leering evilly at his helplessness. Peter Saunders stood as if stone. There seemed nothing he could do except await certain death.

It was Li Li who gave him his chance. Both he and Fong Fook had momentarily forgotten her presence. Sensing and fearing great animosity between the two men facing each other, she gave a loud fearful cry and ran whimpering to hide behind a mass of tangled creepers.

Fong Fook's eyes followed Li Li's passage for just those few fleeting moments but not so those of Peter Saunders. He dived forward, straight at the man, at the gaping muzzle of the rifle, with his hands outstretched ready to grasp and slew the weapon to one side. But he was not fast enough. Too late, he saw the finger squeezing the trigger. Then he saw the finger fumbling with the trigger. He could not understand why there was no exploding report, no pain. His mind would not allow him to believe it as he reached his adversary, was upon him, grappling with him and throwing him to the ground. There, the two combatants writhed and rolled, wrestling and clawing at each other, each seeking the other's throat for a strangle hold. And except for Li Li's loud sobbing, the jungle surrounding the two men locked in mortal combat became strangely quiet.

Fong Fook, his rifle lying on the ground where it had fallen, now attempted to reach his *kris*; so did Peter Saunders. Suddenly seeing his chance, Fong Fook kneed Peter in the groin and sprang to his feet. Lashing out a foot, he kicked him in his solar plexus, knocking the wind out of him. Gasping for breath, Peter rolled over, hauled himself to his knees and desperately crawled towards his own rifle.

By now Fong Fook had not only regained his rifle but also knew the reason why it had previously failed him. He had clipped on the safety catch after the tank commander's head had disappeared down into the turret and had forgotten to release it. Snapping the catch forward, he fired at Peter and then drew back the bolt, freeing the spent cartridge. Violently he slammed the bolt forward again, so violently a round jammed across the open breech.

Peter Saunders felt a searing pain in his thigh as the bullet tore into flesh and bone, the impact jarring him, spinning him around and knocking him on his back. Clutching at the wound, he gasped in agony and for moments could do nothing to help himself. Horrified, he watched as the veteran Chinese terrorist fumbled with his rifle. He heard the man cursing in Cantonese, saw his own blood soaking through the hem of his

KD jacket, and all the while seeing his rifle so near, almost within reach. Desperately he flung himself upon it. It was in his hands, but too late. Fong Fook had already managed to clear the breech, had slipped another round into it and fired at point-blank range, the bullet tearing into and embedding itself in Peter's chest. Peter collapsed, writhed in agony for some moments, then lay still, almost unconscious and as if dead.

On regaining his mental faculties but still dazed and in great pain, he heard screams. His mind cleared, and on looking towards where the screams were coming from, to his horror he saw the terrorist holding the baby girl by the hair with one hand, and in his other hand the *kris* with which he was about to cut the child's throat. Then, surprisingly, he dropped the child who fell sprawling upon the ground, and returned the knife to its sheath. Blood began to trickle from Peter's mouth but he gave it no heed as he anxiously watched the little girl who lay sobbing bitterly at the feet of the terrorist. He was going to spare her life Peter was thinking. But, no, that was not the terrorist's intention. Suddenly, to Peter's dismay, the man stooped and with both hands caught the now screaming child by the throat and lifted her off the ground, where she dangled, kicking and squirming in a pitiful manner. Her screams ceased. The man was strangling her, wringing the very life out of her young and innocent body, and all the while he was grinning fiendishly as the little girl's movements became more feeble.

"You bastard!" Peter shrieked at him, and in savage fury, he forgot pain, forgot everything except that which he must do. "No!" he screamed as he hurtled himself upon his rifle and pulled the butt savagely towards him. But the child was shielding the man, and Peter's hands were shaking far too badly for him to take any proper aim. He saw an opening and fired but the bullet only grazed the man's face. His strength ebbing fast, Peter feebly drew back the bolt and slid it forward again, but too late.

Flinging aside Li Li, Fong Fook drew his *kris* and sprang at Peter who, seeing the enemy upon him, swung up the muzzle of the rifle to meet him. He squeezed the trigger the very moment the terrorist loomed over him, the recoil tearing the weapon out of his weakening hands. He groaned aloud. He had shot the man in the stomach, but not a shot that would cause instant death. The terrorist, with blood pumping from his wound, fell astride him. Lying helplessly on his back, Peter saw a skinny arm rise, *kris* in hand, poised now and about to strike. Feebly he raised an arm in a futile attempt to ward off the inevitable death blow.

Suddenly, two shots rang out in quick succession. Peter heard the terrorist scream and felt him slumping heavily down over him, the *kris* falling to the ground within Peter's reach. Dazed, he freed himself and rolled away from the body, hearing as he did so a familiar voice saying, "I said this gun might come in handy, Pete!"

Peter looked up from where he lay on his back. He turned his face and vomited blood. "Rick!" he gasped. "Rick, is that really you?"

"I thought I'd lost you back there, Pete." Gerald Rickie staggered out from where he had been concealed in the undergrowth. "I've been following him, but I lost him for awhile. Someone was following me, Pete. He got me first, before I shot him."

"What do you mean, he got you?"

"Pete, I'm hurt. I'm hurt bad." Rick's voice was gradually fading away.

"Where are you hurt? What's the matter with you, Rick?"

"He got me, Pete. I'm finished."

"What do you mean, you're finished?"

"I've had ..." Without completing what he was about to say, Rick's voice became a wheezing, gasping cough. The heavy revolver slipped from his fingers and dropped with a dull thud to the ground.

"Rick! Rick!" groaned Peter as more blood ran from the corners of his mouth.

But LAC Gerald Rickie did not answer him. Instead, his knees buckled under him and he sank to a kneeling position as if in prayer. He gave a long drawn-out sigh and then pitched forward face downward and became still, the hilt of a knife protruding from the centre of his back.

Peter's mouth hung open in amazement and despair. He couldn't believe what he was seeing. He must not believe what he was seeing. Yet Rick was there, in front of him, lying on the ground, not moving, the back of his KD jacket soaked in blood.

"Rick! Rick! Oh, my God! What have they done to you?" His words were hardly audible, and he began to sob. Next, he was on his hands and knees scrambling forward in a terrible frenzy of wretchedness, to fall weeping upon the dead body of his best friend. Peter felt no pain now; grief had overcome all feeling. He didn't feel the wound in his scalp, the bullet lodged in his thigh, nor the bullet in his chest. He took no notice of the blood welling out of his own wounds. He did not realize that he, too, was dying.

"Oh, Rick, you can't be dead. You must not be dead," he implored. "You just can't be," and he sobbed bitterly. "Why did we have to come to this bastard of a country? Why did you have to die?"

Hearing movement nearby, he turned his head and saw the badly injured terrorist slowly slithering a hand along the ground towards the revolver.

A grim smile came to Peter's face. "So you are not dead yet, you bastard, and your hand still seeks to hold a gun." He looked down at what had been his best friend and a murderous need for revenge filled him. He crawled towards the revolver, grasped it and withdrew it from the other's reach.

Fong Fook lay on his back watching him through half-open eyes, a pool of blood forming on his stomach and running in rivulets down over his near-naked body. Peter studied the wound and watched as a miniature fountain of blood pumped out of it. Then he watched as the man struggled to a sitting position, his back against a tree. The man could not live much longer, thought Peter, but he wanted the satisfaction of killing him himself. He could hardly lift the heavy revolver but managed to do so and to point it at the man's head. "Die, you bastard, die," he was saying and was about to squeeze the trigger when, in his half-crazed mind he was again shooting pheasants in the woods on Lord Mildmay's estate near Yealmpton. Distinctly he could hear Stan

Medcock, his gentlemanly workmate and poaching friend, shouting to him, "Not on the ground, Pete! Give 'im a sporting chance! Shoot 'im on the rise!"

Peter slid the revolver towards the fallen terrorist, exclaiming as he did so, "So you've a bullet in your guts and God knows where Rick shot you. Well, I'm about to blow your fucking head off, but I'm giving you a sporting chance. We'll see which one of us is the marksman." Groaning with pain, he managed to haul himself to a sitting position facing Fong Fook. Slowly, he reached for his fallen rifle, laboriously lifted it and aimed it at the Fong Fook's nose. "Come on, bastard, pick up that gun," he heard himself screaming.

Fong Fook did not reach for the revolver. Instead, he suddenly lashed out with his feet, sending a shower of dirt into Peter's face. He then grabbed the revolver. Blinded for the moment, Peter fired, then wiped his eyes enough to see that the man's face had disintegrated. "That one's for Rick, you bastard," he cried out. He did not wait for the body to slump to the ground but instead continued a rapid fire at the same spot until the magazine was empty and there was only a click of the trigger. Fong Fook's headless body lay twitching convulsively where it had fallen, and all that remained of what had been his head were fragments of skin, pulpy bone, splattered brains and some bloodied hair spread over the soft mossy soil. The body finally became still. The rifle slipped from Peter's hands.

Li Li began to scream. With much effort and feeling great pain, Peter slowly got to his feet and began to stagger around, not knowing where he was going, losing blood all the while, and feeling as if a red-hot iron was being thrust into his thigh. He looked to where the body of his friend lay and tears came to his eyes. He turned away and looked to where the girl was standing among tall, broad-leaf creepers, watching him wide eyed and screaming all the while.

"That's right, girl, scream your bloody head off. Someone's bound to hear you," he said.

He touched his shattered thigh and groaned with pain. The bullet in his chest did not hurt. That whole area had become numb. His whole body was covered in muck and blood.

His stomach retched again but he could not throw up, only spit blood. Blackness engulfed him. For moments he stood swaying slowly to and fro over the headless corpse, his strength ebbing fast. Swaying forward one more time, he crashed to the ground to sink into peaceful unconsciousness over the body of the dead terrorist. Now, he could not even hear the terrified screams coming from Ho Li Li, the little Chinese girl.

31

A platoon of the 11th Hussars was the first to reach the devastated convoy. The platoon, comprising twenty-six men in two six-wheel-drive, Alvis engine-powered Saracen 604 armoured personnel vehicles and five Daimler armoured cars, had that day already accomplished without incident their two missions. Their first was to escort a food convoy from Kuala Kubu Baru to an army outpost fifty miles to the north. This was called a food run. Their second, their prime duty, was to safely escort a number of VIPs, including the High Commissioner, through a thirty-mile 'black area.' Their two missions accomplished, they were heading back to camp when, over their radio, they received news of the ambush at Fraser's Hill. The seven vehicles carrying the platoon of the 11th Hussars immediately raced to the scene.

They arrived at the rear of the convoy just as a burning army lorry loaded with boxes of small arms ammunition began to explode, sounding like a million fire crackers going off during Chinese New Year.

Among burning and abandoned vehicles the dead, the dying and the wounded lay scattered all over the road as far as the eye could see. The Saracens and armoured cars immediately began to rake the scrub-covered upper hillsides with their machine guns. However, after several minutes of 'bank firing', as it was called, and receiving no return fire, the officer in charge gave orders to cease firing. The officer then ordered a number of his men to assist the wounded where possible and to place them in the shade of the hillside. The dead they placed at the drop-off side of the road.

Once the centre of the road was cleared of bodies, the leading Saracen moved forward and pushed the stalled, disabled and burning vehicles to one side to make way for the many ambulances and other emergency vehicles, which were already arriving.

The famed Royal West Kent Regiment was next on the scene. Within minutes of the signal coming through confirming the ambush at the Gap, Sergeant Jack Westcott, Lance-corporal Williams and Privates Bob Miles, Jim Alinton and Roy Mervin, plus thirty-five other soldiers of the Royal West Kent Regiment had set out from a British Army camp near Kuala Kubu Baru. They were accompanied by a platoon of veteran jungle-fighting Gurkhas and a dozen Dyaks, and all travelled in tanks and armoured cars to the Gap.

Their orders were to seal off the area surrounding the Gap, to assist in bringing in the wounded and dead, to get the convoy moving again, and to track, capture and bring to justice the ambushers. Those were their written orders, but most everyone knew that the Dyaks or the Gurkhas seldom brought in prisoners. A Dyak might very well bring in the heads and hands of those he had killed, to prove his kill and for identification purposes, but there would be very few, if any, prisoners taken.

The shooting was over when they arrived at the Gap. The terrorists who had survived the ambush had already fled. Charred and burned-out vehicles were still on fire or smouldering at the edge of the road, and an army lorry filled with detonating ammunition was well alight and burning a great black hole in the jungle many feet down the hillside. British army servicemen were positioned along the whole length of the convoy, guarding piles of ownerless firearms, equipment and luggage. The many dead that lay on the road were covered by sheets, blankets and articles of clothing. Medical officers and orderlies flown in by numerous helicopters began arriving and attending the wounded as best they could. However, there were not nearly enough medics to care for the scores of wounded. Blood flowed like red wine from a thousand ruptured barrels on the road to Fraser's Hill that day.

The whole length of the convoy was strangely quiet when Sergeant Westcott and his men arrived on the scene. Noting that the 11th Hussars had already taken charge of the dead and the caring for the wounded on the road, and assuming that there were still many more unaccounted for in the jungle, Sergeant Westcott detailed the majority of his men into small groups, their sole task to search the jungle and to bring the dead and wounded they found up to the road.

Lance Corporal Williams was ordered to form one such group. He chose Privates Bob Miles and Jim Alinton, plus two Gurkhas whom he had been on patrol with on previous occasions and a fierce-looking Dyak tracker. Once formed, the group immediately left the road and entered the jungle, the Royal West Kent soldiers armed with Sten guns, the two Gurkhas their knives, and the Dyak a machete. One of the Gurkhas also carried a fold-up stretcher.

First, the observant Dyak leading the way found the partially covered body of Airman Jock Campbell, who was immediately carried to the road. On returning to the jungle they found several dead soldiers, three airmen and several civilians, but no wounded. One at a time the bodies were placed upon the stretcher and carried up to the road, where the most badly mutilated and burned were covered by whatever could be found such as jackets, dresses, blankets and sheets. After each trip to the road the rescue party immediately returned to the jungle to their grisly task of searching for the wounded or more corpses secreted within the camouflaging undergrowth. So far, though, they still had found no wounded; only the dead.

An almost inaudible moan first drew the Dyak's attention to Ho Li Li. He stopped, listened for moments, and then cautiously approached the area where the sound was coming from. He found Li Li, exhausted and asleep in a patch of wet knee-high grass. Silently he beckoned the others.

Moaning in her sleep when they found her, she awoke screaming and trembling with fear at the sight of the new dangers that surrounded her; the machete-wielding, near-naked, fearsome-looking Dyak, the two sinister-looking Gurkhas, and the three Sten gun-carrying British soldiers. All were peering down at her—a little girl wrapped up in white silk covered with blood and dirt. A few feet from her lay the body of LAC Gerald Rickie, and close by, one on top of the other to form a grotesque cross, lay SAC Peter Saunders and the headless corpse of Fong Fook, the Communist terrorist leader.

"Blimey!" a wide-eyed Bob Miles gasped. "It's a little girl!" Then, looking at the bodies, he exclaimed, "Bloody 'ell! What the fuck 'appened 'ere?"

Li Li, sobbing bitterly now, was momentarily forgotten as the mens' attention was riveted on the three bodies.

"Holy Moses!" gasped the lance corporal. "What a horrible sight."

"'E ain't got no 'ead," said Private Bob Miles. "Got it blown right orf."

"Do ya think I'm bloody well blind?" snapped the lance corporal.

Private Bob Miles didn't answer. Instead, he said, "'e's one of them, ain't 'e?"

"He looks like one. Them's two RAF bods," said Private Jim Aliston. "Looks like the Chinaman and this one's bin fightin' a bloody duel."

"It looks that way," agreed the lance corporal. "Funny! The only one left alive here is the kid. You better see to her, Bob."

"OK. I'd rather look after 'er than look at that bloody mess."

The lance corporal nodded. "Jim, let's take the two RAF blokes up to the road. We can collect this other character later."

"Look! The Dyak's cuttin off 'is bleedin 'ands already. It makes you sick ta watch, don' it?" said Private Bob Miles.

"Well, don't watch, Bob. They need the hands for fingerprints. Anyway, you're supposed to be looking after the kid. How is she?"

"Scared shitless."

"S'pect she is. Wonder how she got here," said Private Jim Alinton.

"Your guess is as good as mine. What is it, Haka?" the corporal suddenly asked one of the short but burly Gurkhas.

The Gurkha named Haka turned to him and pointed a finger at the backward-flying red eagle sewn on the shoulder of the KD tunic worn by the airman lying across the body of the dead Chinese terrorist. "RAF" he grunted.

"Yes, Haka, I know he's RAF."

Haka's broad nose twitched as he bent over and gently lifted and cradled the body of the blood-soaked airman in his arms. "Bad business," he said, his voice surprisingly full of compassion.

"It is, Haka," agreed the lance corporal. "Very bad business."

The brave Gurkha did not conceal the pity he felt for the young man he held so gently in his arms when suddenly he stiffened and stared intently at the young face. Had he seen an eyelid flicker? Had he imagined it, he wondered. Puzzled, he did not take his eyes from the pallid face. No, no life there, he told himself. It must have been his imagination. Sadly, he looked down over the blood-soaked khaki uniform, and was about to place the body on the stretcher when he saw a slight movement in the young airman's little finger.

"Corporal! Look! He moves!" cried out an astonished Haka. "Look, Corporal! Look! He moved!"

"You saw him move?" said the corporal questioningly. "That's just nerves. He's dead."

"My old man had a pig once, and its nerves were still twitching hours after my old man killed it and split it in two," volunteered Private Jim Alinton.

"Thank you for that marvelous bit of information," said the corporal sarcastically. "Haka, put that fellow on the stretcher and let's take him up."

"See!" Haka shouted again. "He moves!"

"Look! His finger is moving," gasped Private Miles. "'e's still got a chance."

"Hamen! Get the stretcher under him," snapped the lance corporal. "Let's get him up onto the road, and fast! Haka, and you Hamen, can you manage him between you? We must get him to the road as quickly

405

as possible. He'll have to be taken to Fraser's Hill. This is an airlift job."

"OK, Corp, but what about her?" said Bob jerking a thumb towards the little girl who, still very frightened, but now not crying, was sitting on the damp ground watching wide-eyed their every move.

"Hell! I'd forgotten her."

"We'll 'ave to take 'er along," said Private Miles.

"Course we will," said the lance corporal. "Look here, Jim, she'll have to be up front with us. You can look after her."

"Huh! Trust Jimmy to be the bloody babysitter," said Private Alinton.

"You'll have to carry her. If she gets too heavy, I'll take her."

"Well, ain't that just too considerate of you, Corp." Private Jim Alinton bent his huge body over the little girl. "Now take it easy, ducks. I ain't gonna hurt you." He scooped her up into his arms. "That's a good little lass," he was saying to her.

Scarred and full of holes, and with many vehicles missing from those that had set out earlier that day from Kuala Kubu Baru, the remainder of the convoy had by now arrived at the summit of Fraser's Hill. Numerically, though, the number had been made up again by the addition of military ambulances, patrol wagons, tanks and armoured cars that had rushed to the grim scene from various army outposts. Most of the vehicles were now parked upon a football field which also served as a cricket pitch, next to a nine-hole golf course, all of which had been carved out of the jungle, it was said, by the Sultan of Pahang. Adjoining the golf course and football field was the RAF camp consisting of a few wooden huts, radar equipment, and a small garden where those stationed at the camp could potter and attempt to grow flowers and vegetables if they so wished.

The football field and a part of the golf course were alive with movement. On stretchers, in two long rows, the many wounded, both military and civilian, lay awaiting their turn to be taken by helicopter to British Military Hospital Kinrara, located on the outskirts of Kuala Lumpur.

Medical officers and orderlies of the three services, the Royal Navy, Army and the Royal Air Force, were tending the wounded. Every so often there would be a shake of the head, and yet another dead would join the forty or more covered by sheets in a tree-shaded far corner. More dead and wounded were being brought up from the jungle every few minutes.

Many of the more seriously wounded had already been flown to Kinrara; others, the less injured, had to wait their turn; the majority of the helicopters could airlift only two wounded at a time.

Two helicopters had just lifted into the sky, and another was waiting its turn to become airborne yet again, to make its third flight to Kinrara. The rotor blades of Her Majesty's Royal Naval helicopter SN 186 revolved slowly, fanning the short grass and a cluster of assisting naval medics, the flying-machine itself standing as if an oversized beetle at bay, glinting silvery blue in the fading final light of day enhanced by moonlight. A full moon had already risen over a faraway hill and was sweeping the dark greenery of the surrounding jungle with its pale, watery light.

On his arrival at the golf course, SAC Peter Saunders was promptly examined by a medical officer who, confirming that he was still alive, though barely, gave him priority and immediately ordered his stretcher to be placed in a sling and hoisted to the doorway and slid into the waiting helicopter SN 186. The stretcher was placed alongside another occupied by an unconscious soldier, and then the two stretchers were secured to the aircraft by leather safety straps.

An RAF medical officer carrying a peacefully sleeping Li Li in his arms climbed aboard the helicopter. He sat down near the two stretchers in the wide body of the craft.

"All right, Captain, they're secure," the medical officer shouted above the din of the engine to the pilot sitting up in the cockpit. Nodding towards the airman, he said, "I don't think this one will make it."

The pilot, looking back over his shoulder, shouted, "Sir, we'll get him to Kinrara as fast as we can." He then said, "What a bloody awful mess here today." He sighed and shaking his head, said, "I've never seen anything quite like it. I'm used to hoisting guys out of the water from downed aircraft. Never anything like this."

Revved up, the motors roared even louder, and the whole craft vibrated and became enveloped in a great cloud of dust that billowed up from the dry grassy sward beneath where SN 186 stood. Finally, as the rotating blades became rings of flashing silver, intensified by the flood lamps lighting that one small area, the helicopter's four wheels lifted off the ground. Quickly rising to one hundred feet, the helicopter swerved and banked like a great bird changing course in flight, to immediately swoop downward low over the mountainside and the moonlit jungle-clad slopes of Fraser's Hill. In a matter of minutes the helicopter would be landing at the British Military Hospital at Kinrara.

32

In the quietness of that upper room, an American merchant seaman, a young man in his late twenties, lay naked on Lai Ming's bed brooding and staring vacantly at the ceiling. His baleful eyes were weak and watery, and on his face there was an expression of quiet but seething rage, as if he had been cheated out of something he had paid for. It was not forthcoming, and now he was sulking and clearly showing feelings of venom boiling within his intoxicated mind. Within easy reach, on the bedside table, stood a half bottle of whiskey and an empty glass.

Sitting on the far side of the bed, with her back to the wall and a *sarong* wound around her body, kept in place by a corner tucked within the cleavage of her breasts, Lai Ming eyed with disgust and contempt the naked man lying in front of her. She loathed the very nearness of his presence.

He had been an easy pick-up, this American sailor. The moment he had approached where she sat at a table in the Lucky World Amusement Park, it was obvious to her that he was looking for, and needing, a woman. A friendly smile, coy flutters of her eyelids, a cheeky nod of her head beckoning him to sit down at her table, that was all it took to attract this client.

Before meeting him, she had already unsuccessfully solicited for almost two hours whilst keeping company with Mary Lau, a prostitute and long-time friend of hers, at Mary's pitch at a coffee stall at New

World. Sipping until she finally finished her second glass of coffee, she began to get downhearted at not being approached by any potential customers. Mary accosted a young, handsome British soldier and had the good fortune of taking him to her home for an all-night session. And she, Rose of Singapore, alone now and eager to earn money, became restless. Contemplating taking a taxi to the Raffles Hotel to sip on a green Creme De Menthe at the hotel's Long Bar, she had already paid for the coffee, gathered up her handbag from the table, risen from her seat, and was about to leave when she suddenly spotted him.

Of course he was an American, even a fool could see that. He was a big man, tall, heavy-set, his hair cut short to the crewcut style of the day, and he was chewing on an expensive-looking cigar. Wearing a gaudy Hawaiian shirt half buttoned and hanging loose outside faded jeans made him stand out among the milling crowd, mainly Chinese, as he walked towards her with an exaggerated roll which seaman are apt to do. She had smiled to herself, thinking of Maxwell Clinton, her American sailor friend, the radio operator from the Southern Star, and wishing that it were him who was approaching. Comparable to, or even better than almost all other Americans she had taken to her house, 'Maxel' was a kindly man, gentle and very generous. Here, definitely, was a Maxwell-type customer, an American with plenty of money to spend. Returning her handbag to the table, she had sat down again, smiled up at him, and he had smiled back and said, "Hi, babe," in return to her nodded invitation for him to join her. Sitting down opposite her, he ordered a fifty-cent glass of coffee for her and a beer for himself. They had then talked and bargained until a price was agreed upon, had taken the short taxi ride home, and immediately got down to business.

He hadn't argued her price and had paid her in American dollars. She had been pleased that he had not argued or given her a hard time as did some of her customers. There followed the usual procedure on her bed, the labour of a loveless union between a man and woman. For him, a sex-starved sailor, it was lust, a few minutes of blissful ecstasy, then satisfaction. For her, it was the weight of his sweaty body flattening her

410

to the bed, fat clammy arms embracing her, hands mauling her, kisses that reeked of his obnoxious cigar, and meaningless words uttered lasciviously from garrulous lips. Satisfied for the moment, his limp, heavy body had rolled from her, and he had then wanted to talk, which was all right by her.

After the man left later that night, Lai Ming returned to her bed and lay down. Outside, light rain had begun to fall, and menacing black clouds rode the night sky. Faraway lightning flickered and there began a grumbling of distant thunder. Suddenly, a terrific flash of brilliant white light illuminated the whole room so that all within it became clear, with no shadows. Startled, Lai Ming looked towards the window, and wide-eyed saw what appeared to be a white flare hovering high in the sky. Now, frightened, she could not take her eyes from that bright light. Then the flare seemed to rent the sky apart in one great terrifying flash of lightning and deafening peel of thunder. Her room shook. Clamping her hands over her ears, Lai Ming slid into the sanctuary between the bed sheets. There followed more brilliant flashes of lightning, illuminating the room and causing weird dancing shadows, followed by one, two, three, four more deafening claps of thunder, a cannonade rending apart the stillness and quietness of the night, shaking the house with its fury and rattling everything within it. Then, suddenly, there was darkness again, and the sky became silent.

Lai Ming sighed, her thoughts again turning to Peter, and on what, during these past weeks, she had contemplated doing. Now, there would be no further contemplation. Her mind was made up. The American sailor had made it up for her. That sailor would be the last man to pay for the use of her body. There would be no more short times or all-night sessions. From now on there would be no man in her life except Peter, at least not until he had said his final goodbye and had departed from her. As soon as he returned from Malaya, she would tell him she had given up prostitution. She smiled to herself, knowing how happy he would be, and seeing his face light up as she explained her intentions to him. That was what he had wanted all along, and that is how it would be during the remainder of the all-too-little time they had left together before his departure to England. No other man but Peter would have sex with her during that short period. Again she told herself, he would be so very happy.

She was still smiling as she fell into a sound non-dreaming sleep.

Some four or five hours later she was awakened by a military police patrol car stopping beneath her window. She knew it had to be a military vehicle simply by listening to the note of its engine. The engine, suddenly switched off, became silent. Puzzled, Lai Ming stirred, sat up, yawned and listened.

Getting up from the bed, she went to the window and was surprised to see at this hour of morning an RAF police patrol car parked beneath her window. The roof of the car hid from view the driver and any other occupant it may contain. For a brief moment she wondered if the military police were waiting for Peter to step from the alley, so that they could arrest him for being out of bounds. No, that was not possible, she told herself. The driver was probably simply killing time and had stopped for a cigarette.

With an uneasy feeling she turned from the window, adjusted her *sarong*, sat down at the make-up table and looked into the mirror. Picking up a comb, she ran it through her hair, and was about to do so again when she was surprised to hear a loud knocking on the front door. All those who knew her used the alley door. Putting down the comb and turning and looking at the alarm clock standing on the bedside table, she wondered who it could be at this early hour. It was not yet seven o'clock. Surely it was not the military police raiding her home. Most of the police knew her, several had been her customers, at cut-price rate, of course, and all liked her. Never once had the military police bothered her. Puzzled, she heard the door's heavy iron bolt being drawn back by the *amah*, and the door creaking as it opened. Next, she heard the *amah*'s nasal voice demanding of someone the meaning for disturbing the house at such an early hour. Lai Ming was surprised to hear a girl's voice answer, first in perfect English and then in Malay.

Quickly going to the head of the stairs from where she could view the front door, Lai Ming became even more surprised to see a young and beautiful Indian woman standing in the doorway. The woman was of about twenty years of age, had very dark skin, and glossy jet black hair that flowed down her back in one great wave to her slim waist.

From the top of the stairs, with a quizzical smile playing on her face, Lai Ming greeted the young lady, "Good morning. Can I help you?" And as the eyes of the young lady rose to meet hers, she saw black glittering pools of beauty in a warm, serene and friendly face.

"Oh! Good morning! Are you Chan Lai Ming?" asked the young lady.

"Yes. I am," replied Lai Ming, puzzled. "Why do you ask?"

"Please, I wish to speak to you."

A moment of silence followed as Lai Ming studied the upturned face. What was she doing here? More and more puzzled, with a wave of her hand Lai Ming beckoned the young lady to enter the house. "Please, come up to my room," she invited.

"Thank you," and the young lady, a flurry of darkness clad in a colourful cotton frock, carefully ascended the narrow stairway.

When both were in the room, the two women studied one another. Looking into each other's eyes, Lai Ming saw mingled awe and pity. The young Indian lady saw only curiosity.

"Now, who are you, and why do you wish to see me?" asked Lai Ming. She could see that this young lady calling on her was no prostitute as were the majority of her female visitors.

"My name is Irene, Miss Irene Bothany. I am here on behalf of the Social Welfare Department in Havelock Road," she began. And on seeing that Lai Ming was about to interrupt her, she held out a delicate hand for silence. "Please, one moment," she said graciously, and she gave a hint of a smile, showing off pure white teeth in a perfect mouth. "I know your medical card is stamped up to date and that you have had your monthly check-up, but it's not your welfare that we're concerned with at the moment."

"Are you acquainted with a British Royal Air Force serviceman named Saunders, a Senior Aircraftman Peter Saunders?" she asked.

Lai Ming's heart sank at the very mention of his name. "Yes," she quietly answered. "I know him. Why?"

"I have news of him. Please, you will need to compose yourself because I bring you bad news."

"Bad news! What bad news?" snapped Lai Ming. "Is Peter sick?"

The young Indian lady reached into her handbag and took from it a torn, soiled and bloodstained envelope which she handed to Lai Ming. "As you can see, your name and address is written on this envelope in both Chinese and English. It was delivered to the authorities at RAF Changi late last night by a dispatch rider that had ridden all the way from a hospital near Kuala Lumpur. A military police officer stationed at Changi brought this envelope to the social welfare department. He has requested our help.

Numbed, Lai Ming stared wide-eyed at the bloodstained envelope she held in her hand. Her head was swimming. She felt dizzy and about to faint.

"He is dead," she said, finality in her voice. "My Peter is dead. That is the bad news you bring me."

"No. Peter Saunders is not dead," Irene Bethony answered in a gentle voice, putting an arm around Lai Ming and steadying her, because she, too, thought the little Chinese lady was about to faint. "No. Peter is not dead," she repeated.

"No?"

Perceiving the wretchedness of the woman at her side, the young Indian lady said compassionately, "No, he is not dead, but he is hurt. He is very badly hurt." She allowed Lai Ming, sobbing her relief, to fall across the bed.

"He is not dead. He is not dead." Lai Ming gasped between sobs.

"No, I promise you he is not dead." Irene Bethony did not dare say that she was not sure whether Peter Saunders had died or not since the envelope had come into her hands only an hour ago. The welfare department had called Kinrara Hospital immediately, only to be informed by the hospital staff that SAC Saunders lay in a deep coma.

"Then, if he is hurt, I must go to him," said a wild-eyed Lai Ming. "Where is he? What can I do?"

"That is the very purpose of my visit here this morning. I have come here to ask you to go to him. He is in a coma. His doctor thinks that your presence might possibly give him a chance of survival."

Burying her head in her hands, Lai Ming moaned. "Yes, I'll go."

"Madam Chan, please dress. You have a long journey ahead of you. A military car is waiting outside your door. The RAF will take you to him."

In the driver's seat of the military police patrol car, big, tough, square-jawed Flight Sergeant Cameron, head of the Singapore Provost Police, chewed the end of an unlit cigarette. He wondered how Lai Ming, Rose of Singapore, was taking the news. He wondered if she was already preparing herself for the long, two-hundred-mile journey ahead. He knew that she would go, and that she would travel with him. He had never spoken to her before but had seen her often enough. She was quite a girl for young Peter Saunders to handle, he thought. He smiled grimly to himself. I'm really taking a prostitute for a ride this time, he was thinking. Normally, it was his duty to separate the airman from prostitutes. This was the first occasion that gave him cause to bring the two together. He prayed that it would be worth the long drive up through Malaya to Kuala Lumpur escorted by the regular nine o'clock military convoy, which left from the Johore side of the causeway. Damn the Communist terrorists for pock marking the airstrip at KL two nights ago. To his knowledge it was the first time mortars had been used by them. If it wasn't for the terrorists the airstrip would be in use and Lai Ming could have flown up to Kuala Lumpur on a DC3. It would be at least a couple more days before the airstrip would be in service again, or so he had been informed.

Of course, all of Changi, in fact all Singapore had heard of the massacre at Fraser's Hill. Later, Flight Sergeant Cameron had been handed the bloody envelope and had seen the name of the airman on the report sheet the dispatch rider had brought around to the main provost office. It was he who had contacted the Social Welfare Department to ask their help, and it was he who had volunteered to make the drive to Kinrara.

The powers that be in the Royal Air Force had not exactly sanctioned this Chinese woman accompanying him on the long journey to Kinrara Hospital. No woman was mentioned when an officer at SHQ Changi handed him sealed documents supposedly required immediately at Kinrara Military Prison situated close to the hospital. On this occasion the RAF would look the other way and not see the pretty Chinese lady seated at his side in the patrol car.

He was curious to speak to the woman that Cookie had so often spoken of and bragged about. He wondered if she was as nice as Cookie had made her out to be. It should be quite an interesting journey. It was strange, though, he thought, that his ulcer was not playing up. His thoughts went to Cookie feeding him softly boiled eggs in the sergeants' mess kitchen office, and supplying him with fresh fruit. He and his wife thought the world of Cookie, and their kids loved him, too. He had turned out to be a wonderful babysitter even though he emptied the refrigerator of beer during his each and every visit. He now hoped and prayed that Cookie would survive and that it would be worth the effort put into it by all those involved.

The door was creaking open again. They were coming. Tossing the unlit cigarette onto a pile of roadside rubbish, Flight Sergeant Cameron restarted the engine.

33

"Nurse Mason!"

"Yes, Doctor?"

"What's the time by your watch, please? Mine seems to have gone haywire again. The wretched thing still shows eight o'clock."

Chuckling, Nurse Mason looked at her watch. "It's precisely twelve noon, Doctor, time for my lunch. I'm starving."

"Thank you, Nurse Mason. I must get rid of this damned thing, it's never kept good time. I'm hungry, too. Oh, by the way Nurse, as I've yet to complete my rounds of the wards, how's that boyfriend of yours progressing?" The good doctor had a sly grin on his face as he asked the question. "Wendle, Rendles, or some such name. I never can remember it. Come to think of it, Nurse, I haven't heard you mention his name once today. Is there a problem between the two of you?" and his face beamed with delight at his teasing.

"You mean Captain Vernel, Doctor," the nurse corrected him, blushing. "He's improving, but his temperature is still a wee bit high."

"Ah! Only when you're near him, I'll be bound," laughed the doctor. "Mark my word, he'll be as fit as a fiddle before this week is out. Then, Nurse Mason, watch your step. It's just a touch of malaria, that's all he has." Then he asked, "How serious is it, Nurse?"

"The malaria, Doctor?"

"No, my dear girl. The romance blossoming between you and the captain."

"Oh!" Startled by his blunt question the nurse hesitated before saying, "I really don't know, Doctor. I like him a lot, but at times I wonder if I'm his 'Miss Right.' He speaks so often of other women, those whom he knew in the past, so much so that I wonder at times whether his thoughts dwell more on them than on me."

"Oh dear, that doesn't sound good. However, I'm sure that by feminine wiles you can rectify the situation."

Fortyish, fat and jolly, Doctor Henshaw, an army medical officer at British Military Hospital Kinrara was a doctor not only respected by everyone at Kinrara but also liked by all the hospital staff, and patients, too. He was one of those rare officers with whom other rank service personnel could talk frankly man to man; a person who would listen to their problems, he being a doctor and not a military type man.

Standing on the wood-planked steps leading up to his personal quarters, a pile of papers stuffed untidily under an arm, and wearing no hat which showed off his bald suntanned head, Dr Henshaw reminded Nurse Mason of someone she had once seen in a film, but she couldn't remember which film. To her, he looked somewhat like a cheeky gnome, or was it Happy, the dwarf in Snow White and the Seven Dwarfs, minus his pixie hat?

Nurse Mason, the baby of the nursing staff at Kinrara Hospital, was petite, had a curvaceous figure, flashing, laughing brown eyes, chestnut-brown hair, and lips meant for kissing. As well as being the youngest staff nurse she was decidedly the favourite. In the wards, the bed-ridden young servicemen loved to see her flit from patient to patient, their needs happily attended to by her. She was never grumpy. And now there were rumours of her big romance with young Captain Vernel, a patient at the hospital, another malarial victim. Recently, it had been learned that the two had known each other for years, and were born and raised in the same farming village that was within walking distance of Bugle, a small town in the county of Cornwall. In fact, both had gone to the same hilltop village school at Treverbyn, which overlooks a valley of hedged fields, open moors, and many clay mines from where white china clay or kaolin is still being extracted, much of which is made into the finest bone china in the world.

Now, a trifle nervous, Nurse Mason stood on the steps at the medical officer's side. "Yes, Doctor, I shall have to do something about it," she said thoughtfully. "Unfortunately, I really don't know if I mean anything to him. He doesn't seem to encourage me."

"He doesn't? He must be a bit of a twit." Doctor Henshaw cleared his throat with a short cough. "I wish I were his age again. I would compete with him," he said.

"Would you, Doctor?" Nurse Mason blushed as she heard herself saying, "Knowing you as I do, Doctor, you'd stand a good chance of winning."

Laughing, the doctor did not carry the conversation further but instead nodded his head towards a rosy-cheeked woman of generous proportions, dressed in a white nursing uniform, who puffed and panted as she hurriedly approached the pair. "Ah! Here comes my dear friend Matron Finch, and hurrying, too. And by the look on her face, she brings happy tidings." He waited until the matron reached the foot of the steps before singing out, "Good morning, Matron. You're looking positively radiant this morning. Has the major been telling you yet another of his rather risqué jokes? If so, let's hear it. We all need a good laugh."

Her arms swinging, her cheeks aglow, and with everything bounceable bouncing, the good matron happily ascended the stairs, and on reaching the top she stopped and confronted the pair. "Good morning, Doctor Henshaw. Good morning, Nurse Mason," she said, a gleeful expression on her face. "No, the major has not been telling me jokes, risqué or otherwise."

"No? Then you must have something devilish up your sleeve, I'll be bound," said Doctor Henshaw, a note of curiosity creeping into his voice.

Beaming with merriment, the matron said, "It's the patient in the post-surgery room of ward five, the young airman, Saunders. I'm happy to say that about an hour ago he came out of his coma and is now fully conscious."

"Is he, by Jove! Well, that is excellent news!" exclaimed the obviously delighted Doctor Henshaw.

"Yes, it is good news. Doctor Hogan's with him now."

"What excellent news, Matron," the doctor repeated. That young fellow has had me worried. We've had to pour gallons of blood into him, or so it seemed. How long ago, did you say, Matron?"

"About an hour, Doctor. Doctor Hogan says he believes Saunders will survive, that's if there are no complications. It's a miracle he's alive. I suppose it's God's will."

"I believe his lady friend has played a major part in his survival, and she could play an equally big part in his full recovery," expressed Nurse Mason.

"I think you're right," agreed Doctor Henshaw. "I believe that our first ever volunteer supernumerary nurse is a great asset to the young lad's recovery. I'm so glad we managed to have her brought here. I was afraid that military red tape would interfere. By the way, Matron, how is she taking it?"

"The poor mite is shedding tears of relief."

"Is that so? Is she still with him?"

"She hasn't left his bedside since she first set foot in the ward.

"When Saunders was delirious he kept repeating the name, Rose." said Dr Henshaw. I presume he was referring to the same Rose who is now seated at his bedside."

"That's correct, Doctor." replied the matron. "Rose of Singapore, that's whose company we have the pleasure of here at Kinrara."

"Rose of Singapore?" repeated the puzzled medical officer. "Is she a film star? Of course she's definitely of the Chinese upper class. She's most refined. Where does she live in Singapore?"

"Just off Lavender Street, Doctor. She lives in what one might call a brothel," replied the matron matter-of-factly.

"I beg your pardon, Matron," gulped the surprised medical officer.

"She lives in a brothel, Doctor," the matron repeated. "She's a prostitute. Quite a noted prostitute, too, so I've been told. Noted enough to earn her the title, Rose of Singapore."

"A prostitute! Really! I find that hard to believe. Why don't the three of us pay a visit to ward five? Lunch can wait."

Doctor Henshaw led the way along a narrow concrete pathway bordered by flowering hibiscus and well-tended green lawns until, eventually, they arrived at a flight of planked wooden steps leading up to a wide verandah encircling ward five, one of several white painted, one-storey wooden huts built in rows.

Mounting the wooden steps, the doctor pulled open a screen door and held it for the two ladies to enter. He then followed them down between a double row of beds all occupied by military personnel, many of whom were those wounded at the Gap. Giving the patients words of encouragement as they passed through the ward, the three came to a door at the far end. Pushing open this door, they entered into a room specially equipped to treat patients needing intensive care. Senior Aircraftman Peter Saunders occupied the only bed. Lai Ming sat on a chair at his bedside holding one of his hands whilst gazing into the ashen face peering upward from a snow-white pillow.

On hearing the door open and seeing the approach of the three, Lai Ming turned her head, smiled timidly, and then rose slowly to her feet, a tired, appealing look on her face, her cheeks swollen and wet from weeping.

"Good morning," Doctor Henshaw greeted her in a kindly manner, a reassuring smile upon his gnome-like face.

Respectfully, Lai Ming bowed her head. "Good morning, sir," she replied softly.

Matron Finch also said, "Good morning," and Nurse Mason said, "Hello."

"Please, sit down and relax, my dear," said the medical officer.

"Thank you, sir." Lai Ming sank wearily back into the chair. "I am in your way, yes?" she asked.

"In our way? Oh, no, not at all! On the contrary, we're glad you're here."

"I am happy. I am honoured to be here," and Lai Ming turned and smiled down upon the wan face peering up from the pillow. "Peter will be all right? He is going to be all right, isn't he?"

"Oh, good gracious me, yes. Before you can say 'Jack Robinson,' he'll be on his feet and as fit as a fiddle again."

A ghost of a smile appeared on the patient's white face; the first smile.

"You see! He's smiling already. It appears that you have performed a miracle. Therefore, young lady, I thank you. We all thank you."

"Peter is my boyfriend. I love him very much," Lai Ming softly said, dabbing tears from her eyes with a tiny colourful handkerchief.

"Hmm! Yes." Doctor Henshaw coughed a dry cough. "Hmm, yes," he repeated, coughing again and not knowing what else to say. "I suppose you must," he finally said.

A weak voice from the patient suddenly surprised all present by asking, "Did they bring in the other airman, sir? His name was Rickie. Gerald Rickie."

Puzzled, the doctor thought for moments before replying. "I cannot recall seeing a Rickie on any medical report of mine, but he may be in another ward under the care of a different doctor. I'll see if I can locate him."

"He's dead, sir. He was a friend of mine." The voice faltered and tears came to his eyes. "I just wanted to know if his body had been recovered."

"Oh!" Lost for words, the doctor eventually said, "I will make enquiries." And seeing the horrified expression that appeared on Lai Ming's face, he asked. "Did your lady friend know him?"

"She knew of him."

"I'm sorry, for both of you."

"Thank you, sir."

"I will make enquiries. Now, no more talk. You must rest."

"I must ask about someone else, sir."

"You're going to rest, my boy," said Matron Finch adamantly. "That's the doctor's orders."

"Just the one question. I found a little girl up there. I'm wondering if she's all right?"

"The Chinese girl? Oh, yes! That girl who was brought in with you," said the doctor. "We treated her for shock and minor injuries. She told a remarkable story. Yes, we looked after that little girl until her father sent for her. She's safe and well, back in her home in Singapore."

"I'm glad. Am I in Kinrara hospital?"

"That's right. You're in good hands. And now it's time for you to sleep." The doctor turned to Nurse Mason. "A mild sedative," he said quietly to her.

"Yes, Doctor."

Stooping over Peter, Lai Ming kissed the lips of the white face. "Sleep good sleep, Peter. I come back soon," and she lifted a dainty hand and brushed it lightly over his cheek, whilst trying to smile and not to cry. Then, bowing to the three gathered around the bed, she said to them, "I am now so happy, I don't know what to say. But I do know that I have much gratitude to everybody here."

"We are grateful to you, young lady," said doctor Henshaw. Then, turning to Nurse Mason, he said, "Don't take Rose through the ward. I don't want the boys to see her right now. Take her out the back way."

"And take good care of her, Nurse," whispered the matron. "Take her to my bedroom. She can sleep there."

"Your bedroom, Matron?"

"Yes. She'll be more comfortable there, and it's a quiet room."

"Certainly, Matron. Thank you." Nurse Mason put an arm around Lai Ming, "Come, love, I'm going to look after you." Exiting the room, the two were followed by the eyes in the deathly white face.

"You're going to be all right, son," said the medical officer gently, "Both of you. If you need anything, ask a nurse or the matron here. But remember, whilst you are here, Matron Finch is your boss. You'll have to await your discharge before your lady friend takes over again," he said, smiling. "I'll come to see you this evening," and he waved a long finger at the patient. "Rest and sleep is what you need. The more rest and sleep you get, the sooner you'll be leaving Kinrara to return to Singapore."

34

Ah, my memory serves me well, thought Tan Kah Hin, the chauffeur, smiling to himself as he scanned the red and white road sign a hundred yards from the hospital's main entrance.

He had passed this way before, but that was well over ten years ago; even before the Japanese invaders set foot on Malayan soil. He still had recollections of the area, however, even though many reminders had long disappeared, obliterated, he presumed, by the Japanese. The Malay *atap* village was no longer there, nor were the coconut palms that had shaded the village; also gone were the many acres of rubber plantations which had dominated the area. Now, rolling manicured lawns, shade trees, flowering shrubs and masses of colourful flowers graced much of the land on both sides of the twisting road. He remembered the road solely by its many twists and turns, but now it was much wider. And where there had been barking dogs and Malay children playing in the dirt outside thatch-roofed huts, there were many new buildings; villas mainly, which surrounded the grey, foreboding military prison and the military hospital complex.

Breathing in the sweetly perfumed air of his surroundings, Kah Hin approached a black and white sign, which stated 'Security Guardroom'. Below these two words a long red arrow pointed towards a turning in the road. Kah Hin swung the new, black, R-type Bentley Continental into the turning. Approximately a hundred yards further ahead he could see a small brick building in front of which was a green painted sentry-box and a lowered black and white pole that stretched the full width of the road.

Coming to a stop in front of the sentry-box, Kah Hin's eyes dwelled for moments upon the glinting, highly polished black bonnet in front of his windshield. Proudly and with great satisfaction he knew that the whole exterior of the car would have the same highly polished appearance; his reward for two hours of labour carefully spent, although it had meant rising from his bed that much earlier than usual.

From the sentry-box a uniformed Malay guard emerged and greeted Kah Hin, "*Tabik*."

"*Tabik*," Tan Kah Hin replied.

"What is your business at Kinrara, please?" asked the sentry in English.

From the driver's seat, Kah Hin looked without expression up into the face of the obviously curious Malay sentry.

"I bring my master, the venerable Ng Kwok Wing, who has reserved audience with a patient at this hospital," said Kah Hin.

Now the sentry had heard stories of Ng Kwok Wing, of his great wealth and power in Malaya, and of his many philanthropic deeds, so he said in a surprised voice, "The Ng Kwok Wing?"

"The Ng Kwok Wing," replied the chauffeur, his face remaining, as always when with his master, inscrutable.

"Ng Kwok Wing," repeated the sentry in awe. It was his duty, however, to check all occupants of incoming vehicles before he could give information or lift the barrier. He took a step forward and peered into a rear side window. A black lace curtain obscured his view, but he could make out the dark figure of a man sitting in the back seat, not looking at him but seemingly towards the hospital at the end of the road. "Ah! Please excuse me, sir," he said in a respectful voice. Bowing his head, he stepped back a pace. He had done his duty. Addressing the chauffeur, he said, "Please, move forward to the security guardroom ahead. There you will need to see the officer in charge who will take particulars and direct you." The guard then saluted the chauffeur and raised the barrier.

"*Terima kasih, tuan*," replied Kah Hin, thanking the guard in Malay. Engaging a low gear, Kah Hin drove the car slowly the short distance to the front of the security guardroom. Here, he stepped out of the car, immediately to be confronted by a white man in a British army uniform who had stepped out of the guardroom. "Are you a visitor?" the man asked.

"Yes."

"OK. See that white hut at the corner of the road. Please report to the officer in charge there."

"Thank you," said Kah Hin. The uniformed figure was already disappearing back into the guardroom.

Tan Kah Hin returned to his driving seat, restarted the engine, and again proceeded slowly towards the hospital. Driving on a freshly tarmacked, straight but narrow road carved between more manicured lawns and flowerbeds, he approached the hut. At one-hundred-foot intervals gravel paths led from the road towards white painted wooden bungalows surrounded by wide wood-decked verandahs. These were but a few of the many wards of the hospital. Further along Kah Hin could see more buildings, but made of stone, with wide concrete corridors between them, and no verandahs.

Comfortably seated in the back seat of the Bentley, preoccupied with his own thoughts, Kwok Wing had neither seen the Malay guard's face at the window nor the soldier at the guardroom. He still grieved the loss of Lim Seng Yew, his number one chauffeur, manservant and lifelong friend; also old Ping Jie, the much loved, respected and trusted *amah*. His thoughts, though, dwelt this moment on the young British airman who had saved the life of his daughter Li Li, and on the young man's Chinese lady friend whom he hoped soon to meet. He certainly knew of both their pasts; not so much about the airman's, but much about the young lady's.

It had been a wise move, he thought, having the investigative branch of his personnel office conduct a discreet investigation of the young airman, the sole purpose being for him to evaluate how best he could reward the young man. His investigative branch had been very thorough, not only learning details such as the airman's name, age, rank and trade in the RAF, but also, surprisingly, that he spoke some Cantonese, and that his constant companion was a Chinese woman, a noted prostitute almost ten years his senior. Astonished at first, then curious, Kwok Wing then had the investigative branch delve into the woman's past. Thanks to records, the Social Welfare Department and other agencies in Singapore, and also officials in Sumatra, his agents had collected an ever-thickening, incredibly interesting dossier on the woman named Chan Lai Ming. Finding and checking details of her years spent in Singapore had been relatively easy compared with the difficulties encountered tracing her life back through the years to when she was born in Palembang, Sumatra, to very respected parents bred from families of honourable ancestry. Though he must never mention his investigations, Kwok Wing was pleased that they had been conducted so thoroughly.

Already he felt as if he knew the two and was impatient to finally meet them. He had hoped that they would be informed of his intended visit but the medical authorities decided such notification would be unwise, that it might cause unnecessary emotional stress to the recovering patient, who had already spent three weeks in the hospital. He had been advised, however, that a Doctor Henshaw would greet and escort him to where he would finally meet the man who had saved his daughter from certain death. Deep in thought and staring with unseeing eyes at the world without, Kwok Wing sighed and sank back into soft, velvet cushions.

A gentle breeze was blowing that afternoon, taking away much of the humidity in the air and seemingly lowering the almost ninety-degree temperature by several degrees. For Malaya, it truly was a balmy day, with as yet not a cloud in the sky, a rare occurrence at two o'clock. The thunderstorms and rains to follow would surely come before the afternoon was out.

In a wheelchair, rolled out onto the wide wooden verandah of Ward Five, SAC Peter Saunders, clad in military pajamas and a towelling robe, watched with keen interest the approach of the two men who were walking together towards the wooden steps leading up to the verandah of ward five. One he recognized as short, pixie-like Dr Henshaw, who was actually clad in a natty, lightweight grey suit, and even more unbelievably, he was wearing a conservative silk tie. Rarely did Dr Henshaw wear a suit and tie at Kinrara. When not in medical uniform, he preferred to wear white shorts, a white sleeveless shirt and a pair of rather worn white plimsoles. His companion was a tallish Chinese gentleman dressed in an expensive-looking, tailor-made, dark blue suit and a tie of similar colour. The two were an odd-looking couple, thought Peter Saunders. Nudging Lai Ming, who was seated in a wicker chair at his side, he looked at her questioningly and whispered, "I wonder who the Chinese gent is. I've never seen him before."

Lai Ming, dressed in a light blue *cheongsam*, and looking relaxed and happy, shrugged her shoulders and shook her head, replying, "No, he must be a visitor. He looks very distinguished."

"Yes, he does," Peter replied.

Indeed, the Chinese gentleman, Ng Kwok Wing, was not only of considerable means and importance but also was liked and loved by many, and most certainly well respected. He owned several of the largest and most modern oil tankers in the world, was a building contractor of roads, bridges, office buildings and hotels throughout Malaya and Singapore, and now, in Singapore, he was the builder of whole suburbs of reasonably priced homes for an exploding population. Also, he owned considerable amounts of shares in several thriving businesses throughout Malaya and Singapore. Undoubtably, Ng Kwok Wing was one of the wealthiest and most powerful men in the Far East who, not content with his great wealth, constantly sought ways to increase his millions by making use of his extraordinary business sense and power.

However, regardless of his ruthlessness in business, Kwok Wing was a good man, kind and charitable, a benefactor to cancer research, the TB clinics, to hospitals and schools, and to the leper colony situated on a small island off Singapore. Unknown to them, many hundreds of poor and destitute people in Singapore were fed, and the sick treated, all through the aid of this man's generosity. Rightly so, Kwok Wing was proud of his many achievements in the interest of public welfare. Seeing and understanding the immediate needs of Singapore and Malaya, not only was he philanthropic towards them but also he was a visionary predicting the needs of the future. On paper and in his head he had many ambitious plans. Ng Kwok Wing was justly proud and a true gentleman of the Far East.

At that moment the swing-door behind Peter Saunders and Lai Ming swung open and a male nursing orderly came through the doorway carrying a round wicker table.

"May I help you?" asked Lai Ming, getting to her feet.

"No, but thanks all the same. You've volunteered enough these past three weeks," laughed the orderly, placing the table in front of them. Another orderly and Nurse Mason brought two wicker chairs. These they put down facing the table. The two orderlies smiled at the pair as they made their exit. Nurse Mason remained.

"Nurse, are we having company?" Peter enquired.

"Yes," replied a smiling Nurse Mason. "You have a visitor."

"Really!"

"Yes. And believe it or not, I've volunteered to play waitress for the afternoon, just for you and your guests." She laughed saying, "But I won't be serving ice-cold beer or Singapore gin slings, not this afternoon. I shall be serving lemonade only."

Puzzled, Peter asked, "But why? And who's the Chinese gent?"

"Ah! You'll find out soon enough," sang out Nurse Mason, as she too departed through the swing door.

Dr Henshaw was the first to speak as the two men reached that part of the verandah where Peter Saunders and Lai Ming waited. Waving a hand indicating Lai Ming should remain seated, for she had begun to rise, he smiled impishly at the pair.

"Good afternoon, Miss. Good afternoon, Saunders," he cordially greeted them.

Peter Saunders replied, "Good afternoon, sir."

Lai Ming smiled and said, "Hello, doctor."

"How are you feeling, Saunders?"

"Much better, sir, thank you."

"That's what I like to hear. Guess what! I've brought you a visitor!"

Peter stared at the two men with growing curiosity, but was lost for words.

"Please, allow me to introduce you to Mr Ng Kwok Wing," began Doctor Henshaw. "He has come all the way from Singapore to visit you." Turning to the Chinese gentleman, he said. "Sir, this is the young man whom you wish to meet. This is Senior Aircraftman Peter Saunders. And this young lady is his friend, Miss Lai Ming."

Kwok Wing smiled benevolently. "I am deeply honoured to have the pleasure of finally meeting you both," he said, bowing a greeting to Lai Ming and then extending a well-manicured hand to Peter. "I am most honoured," he repeated.

Attempting to rise from the wheel chair, but ushered back by a vigorous shake of the head from Doctor Henshaw, Peter cordially shook the extended hand. "The pleasure is mine, sir. Won't you both please sit down," he said, gesturing towards the recently brought chairs.

"I would very much like to join you, but you must please excuse me," said Dr Henshaw. "I have a patient to see in ward six. Nurse Mason will take care of your needs." Turning to Mr Ng, he said, "I shall return in one hour, sir, when your visit is concluded." With those words, he departed through the swing doors.

Kwok Wing sat himself down in one of the wicker chairs and faced the pair, silently studying both for several moments before saying to Peter Saunders, "I expect you are wondering who I am and why I am here!"

"Yes, sir." Peter answered.

Kwok Wing clasped his hands together and rested them upon the tabletop, displaying on long fingers several gold rings encrusted with jewels, and on his wrist he wore a gold, diamond-studded Rolex watch. The man's cufflinks, too, were of gold, a large diamond embedded and twinkling on each.

"I had hoped to visit you sooner," he began. "But the hospital authorities would not permit it. Until yesterday I was continuously informed that you were too ill to receive visitors." With compassion in his eyes, Kwok Wing studied the young man seated in the wheelchair. "I am saddened that you had such a terrible encounter at Fraser's Hill," he said, sincerely. "However, I was thankful to hear from Doctor Henshaw that you are making such excellent progress towards a full recovery."

"Thank you. Were you at Fraser's Hill on that day?" asked Peter.

"No. I was in Singapore. But do you remember a little Chinese girl you chanced to meet in the jungle during that terrible day?"

"Yes, of course I remember her."

"And do you remember her name? Do you recall the name Ho Li Li?"

"I do remember her telling me her name. It was just before ... He stopped in mid-sentence. "If it wasn't for Rick," and he stopped again, his eyes brimming with tears. "I lost a good friend up there, my best friend." Wiping his eyes on the cuff of his pajama sleeve, he said, "Please excuse me. I'm still very upset over his death."

"Yes, I can well understand," said Kwok Wing, who would like to have said, 'I, too, lost two good friends on Fraser's Hill that day. I am also sad.' Instead, he said, "I am very sorry. I have heard that you suffer from a bereavement."

Peter sighed deeply. "Yes. I'm very sad about losing Rick," he said. "He saved my life, and for that matter, he saved the little girl's life, too."

"My young friend, you have my deepest sympathy. You see, I have heard from a witness the tragic story of what happened to you on Fraser's Hill that day; a story told to me by my young but very bright and observant daughter."

"Your daughter!"

"Yes. Li Li is my daughter."

"Well, fancy that," said an astonished Peter, staring at the man seated opposite him. "Is she OK?" he asked.

"Thankfully, yes. Thanks to you and to that other brave young man my daughter is in good health except for tormented memories. I know she has such memories because she awakens at night screaming, and I must go and comfort her."

"She will eventually forget bad memories," said Peter. "We must all try to forget bad memories and remember only those that are good."

"You speak wise words, those of a true man, a man who was brave enough to save my daughter from certain death."

"Well, honestly, I didn't do such a lot for her," Peter answered modestly. "I helped her down from a tree. I bandaged her leg. Then that bastard ... excuse me," he muttered apologetically. "Then that fellow came along, appearing from nowhere."

At that moment Nurse Mason pushed her way through the screen door, balancing on the palm of one hand a round tray with a jug of lemonade and three glasses on it. "Lemonade anyone?" she called out, her face all smiles.

The three at the table smiled back, nodded a reply, and in turn said, "Thank you," as she poured a glass for each. Nudging Peter, she whispered jokingly, "Where's my tip?" as she made her exit.

Kwok Wing sipped awhile on his lemonade before continuing. "Though very young and truly not much more than a baby, my daughter has been able to tell me the full story, not once but a number of times. It is always the same story, of you climbing the tree and helping her down, of a terrible man hurting her, strangling her, almost killing her. And of you getting angry with that awful man, so much so that you attacked him, causing him to throw my daughter from him. And then he had a big fight with you. As I previously stated, she has tormented memories, but they will eventually pass. Thankfully, she is alive and in excellent health."

"Thank God for that," said Peter. "I have wondered at times whether or not she remembered that day. I was told that she had been flown home to Singapore. Perhaps I shall meet her again some day."

"You shall indeed," said Kwok Wing. Turning now to Lai Ming, he spoke to her in Cantonese, who answered him in the same Chinese dialect.

When about to speak to Lai Ming again, Peter interrupted him, saying, "Excuse me, sir, but I'm puzzled. I'm wondering why it is that you speak Cantonese, yet your daughter does not. She spoke to me in Malay, and also in a Chinese dialect that I could not understand. It certainly wasn't Cantonese."

"Yes, the difference in our language has puzzled many people during the six-month period Li Li has lived with me. You see, the child is my adopted daughter. Her departed father was my first cousin. She was born in China, near Nanking, a city in the northeastern part of that great country. As she grew from babyhood to being a young child she learned to speak a little of what is considered the real Chinese language. She has yet to learn how to speak Cantonese."

"She speaks no Cantonese, yet she speaks Malay! I find that puzzling, too."

Ng Kwok Wing chuckled, saying, "Yes, I admit it is most unusual, but really, there is a simple explanation. My daughter plays often with Malay children who are our neighbours, and as the Malay language is not as complicated as Chinese, she has quickly learned many Malay words. And that's why she speaks very little Cantonese. Now, with your consent, let us return to the purpose of my visit."

Peter glanced at Lai Ming. Their eyes met but they said not a word.

"My visit here is to thank and reward you for saving my daughter's life," they heard Mr Ng saying. "As I have already stated, I know the full story. Therefore, what can I do? I can thank you, yet I cannot thank you enough with mere words. I can clasp your hand in gratitude. I can weep my happiness upon your shoulder, but neither would satisfy me. Should I seek to bestow money upon you, would you be offended? Or if I offer you a gift as a token of my thanks, would it be sufficient? I know not."

Peter held up a hand. "Sir, have you travelled this far simply to thank me for helping your daughter when she needed help?" he asked. "I would have done the same for anyone in such a predicament as she that day. You have come to thank me, sir? Very well, your words of thanks are sufficient. I'm glad to meet you, and I'm happy to know that Li Li is well." Peter paused for a moment, conscious of being stared at and studied by Kwok Wing's steely grey eyes. Peter sipped on his lemonade before saying in a lowered voice, "As I have said, sir, I would, though, love to see your daughter again some day."

"Oh, you shall! You shall indeed!" exclaimed Kwok Wing, adamantly. "However, I do wish to show you my gratitude. I am a wealthy man, one of the wealthiest in this part of the world. There is much on this earth that is obtainable to me, yet out of your reach. I ask you to think, Peter, and I hope you will allow me to call you Peter. Please think of something that money can buy, and if it be in my power, it shall be yours."

"Wow! Just like in a fairy tale," laughed Peter. "Are you serious?"

"I have never been more serious."

Suddenly confused, Peter passed a hand across his damp brow. He closed his eyes. Was he dreaming? Was this Chinese gentleman an illusion, a mirage? He opened his eyes. The man was definitely there, sitting opposite him at the table sipping lemonade, watching him and awaiting his answer. He thought of Rose, and in a flash he knew what he wanted.

"Anything?" His voice was tense from withholding the excitement he felt welling up within him. "Anything?" he asked again.

"Anything that is within my power."

Peter sat back in the wheelchair. "Please, give me a few moments to think this over," he said.

"Of course. Take your time. If you'll allow me, I should very much like to speak with your lady friend."

"Please do," said Peter, lapsing into thought and not listening to the pair who were now conversing in Cantonese. Not until several minutes had passed did Peter open his eyes and study the two Chinese people seated at the same table; he so prosperous and she so poor.

"Sir," he began, "In just a few months from now I shall be returning to England. I truly require nothing for myself. However, if you wish to help me in any way, then I ask you to help the lady seated at your side. She needs help, not I."

A whimsical smile appeared on Mr Ng's face. "And how, pray, may I help this lady?" he asked.

"Sir, I dread to think of the years ahead for her," said Peter quietly. "You have said that I may ask of you anything in your power. Therefore, I ask you this, and should you grant what I ask, it would be the reward of which I would be truly grateful, for then, when I am ordered to leave Singapore to return to my homeland, my heart and my mind would be at rest."

"Speak of what you desire," commanded Kwok Wing.

"Well, sir, I hardly know what to ask, but I do know that I would like to see this lady financially independent with a home of her own. Perhaps, in your organization, you could find her suitable employment. Truly, she has many needs. I have none."

"My honourable friend, I believe I already know the lady's needs. The honourable doctor who introduced us believes that your survival is largely due to this lady being brought here from Singapore. You had much need of her, and still have need of her."

Peter nodded his head. "Yes, you are right. I'm glad she is with me. I always want her to be with me, but that remains difficult. I am out of the woods, but as for my girlfriend, there are many brambles in her path and the way is dark."

"Fortunately, I am able to clear her path free of brambles as well as light her path. Tell me, do you speak some Chinese, Peter?" He asked the question in Cantonese, knowing already the answer.

"Yes, I speak some Chinese, thanks mainly to Rose here," Peter answered in Cantonese.

On hearing this acknowledgment, Ng Kwok Wing resumed the conversation in Cantonese, speaking the language slowly and correctly, and not using words difficult to pronounce or seldom used.

The two conversed thus for several minutes, until the Chinese gentleman, beaming his pleasure, clasped his hands together and exclaimed in English, "I am truly amazed at your knowledge of Cantonese. You speak the language almost as if you were a native."

Peter laughed. "As I said earlier, I have a good teacher," he said, nodding towards Lai Ming.

"Yes, the lady has taught you well," said Kwok Wing, a thoughtful expression suddenly appearing on his face. Moments later, in a surprisingly elated voice, he said, "I believe I have a solution to many problems." Turning and gazing intently at Lai Ming, he said to her, "You speak English quite well. You speak Cantonese very well. My daughter does not speak Cantonese. My daughter is in need of a teacher. Would you, Lai Ming, take on the challenge of teaching my daughter Cantonese?"

"Oh, I couldn't," said a surprised and flustered Lai Ming. "I'm not a teacher, I'm a … I have no qualifications," she said adamantly, thinking, 'he would never allow me to be in his daughter's company if he knew the truth about me.'

Reading her thoughts, Kwok Wing said in a sincere and gentle voice. "Ah Ming, the past is behind you. I think only of your future."

"You know?" Lai Ming asked weakly.

Kwok Wing had not intended to admit that he knew of the woman's past lifestyle. He had journeyed to Kinrara for one reason only, to thank and reward the young Englishman. Now, he realized that he had to reassure her, that her way of life would not be mentioned ever again. "An acquaintance of mine, an English gentleman employed by the Social Welfare Department in Havelock Road, has assured me that you are very much a genteel lady. Your past is behind you. We shall never discuss that part of your life again. It is time for change. A time to begin anew. Are you in agreement?"

"Yes," whispered Lai Ming in a faraway voice.

"Excellent. Then that's settled. This is the present situation. My wife, whom I brought from Shanghai, speaks very little Cantonese; and I, unfortunately, cannot devote as much time as I would wish with my daughter. My sudden idea, therefore, is that my daughter has need of a Cantonese tutor, and I believe that you, Lai Ming, have the desired qualities and qualifications to fill such a position. The position is open for your consideration. Of course, to take on such a responsibility, the remuneration will be fitting, of that you can be assured."

Both Peter and Lai Ming looked at each other in wonderment, but said nothing. They did not wish to interrupt and break the spell of this moment. Peter sank his head back into the pillow and closed his eyes, thinking, 'Perhaps I am dreaming.'

"You will need a suitable home, a place where you may quietly and safely tutor my daughter," Kwok Wing was saying. "Finding the road journey tiring, I shall return to Singapore by plane. However, I shall leave my business card with you. If you decide to accept the position, call my office and I shall have you flown down in a company aircraft, in fact both of you, if that is at all possible. On your return to Singapore we shall tour my new estates in the Upper Serangoon Road area. All my new homes are one-storey villas. You, Lai Ming, may choose a villa from any one of my estates, and I shall immediately transfer the deed of the house into your name."

"Sir, are you serious?" Peter asked incredulously.

Lai Ming, lost for words, simply stared at Mr Ng in disbelief.

"I have never been more serious in my life," said Kwok Wing. "Anyway, I ask you please to consider my offer."

Almost inaudibly, Lai Ming said to Peter, "I go, yes?"

"Yes, you must."

"Good!" exclaimed Kwok Wing. "Now, Peter, to discuss your future. You have considerable time still to serve in the RAF, I believe."

"Yes, I'll be demobbed in January '56," Peter replied, wondering what was coming next.

"Do you enjoy living in Singapore?"

"Oh, yes, I love Singapore. It's the most wonderful place in the world."

"And you have much affection for this lady."

"Yes, very much."

"In that case, on completion of your military service career, you will wish to return to Singapore."

"If possible, yes, of course."

"Do you know what the word Singapore means?"

"I have heard it mentioned, but I'm not sure."

"Actually they are two Sanskrit words, *singa* and *pura*, together meaning Lion City."

"That's interesting. And I do know that Singapore is known as the Lion City," said Peter.

A faraway look came into the steely grey eyes of Kwok Wing as he was saying, "During these years since the departure of the Japanese, Singapore slumbers like a sleeping lion. But that sleep has become restless. Soon, only a matter of a few years from now, Singapore will gain her independence. And then, my young friend, we shall see the awakening of the lion, the awakening of Singapore the Lion City. And when the lion awakens Singapore will prosper as never before. Singapore will increasingly need young people of your calibre. I want you to work with me, to assist me in making my dreams come true."

"But how can I assist?" asked Peter.

"You are of material that builds, not destroys. Together, we can help make Singapore the finest city in the world, a city and an island of which we shall be proud, a clean city where crime will not be tolerated. I would like you to be already settled in Singapore on our Independence Day. I want you to see the awakening of the lion. Think about that which I have said, and when you are discharged from this hospital and return to Singapore, please honour me by a visit. We have much to discuss, and I am sure that Li Li will be truly delighted to see you again."

Seeing Dr Henshaw approaching, Ng Kwok Wing rose from the table and extended a hand to Peter. "It has been a rewarding meeting for the three of us," he said. "And for me it has been delightful. But I see my time is up. The honourable doctor does not allow me to bother you further. Here is my business card. In the very near future we shall meet again."

Turning to Lai Ming with a smile, he shook her hand, saying. "Regarding your son. Please, have no worries concerning future hospital bills. There will be none. I have donated a sizeable grant to the hospital in which your son now receives treatment. My donation is sufficient to build a new wing as well as to take care of all your son's medical expenses."

With those words, Kwok Wing smiled and bowed to the pair, then turned and walked slowly towards Doctor Henshaw who was already climbing the steps.

35

The words of the song, "Just One More Night" flowed softly, sweetly, but with a melancholy air from a radio in a neighbour's villa at the junction of the road leading to Lai Ming's home.

With a heavy heart, Peter Saunders stopped walking and listened to the words of the song. "Just one more night," he whispered sadly, "alone with you," and standing on the curb of the sidewalk, he sighed deeply as he drank in the singer's voice, that of a young Chinese woman who often sang on Radio Malaya. She sang so beautifully, he thought. Waiting until the song had ended and the voice of the male radio disc jockey announced the name of the next number, Peter resumed his walk slowly towards the red-roofed villa standing in shaded greenery halfway along Meadowlark Road which junctions on to Dickens Avenue. Mr Ng Kwok Wing had named all the roads in this new suburb after birds; and having been an avid reader of classic works by British authors in his youth, he had named the crossing avenues alphabetically after famous British authors and poets. Abbott, Byron and Carlyle were the first three avenues in the huge development. Dickens was the fourth.

"The three o'clock Hit Parade," Peter murmured to himself, pausing again to listen as that sweet melody 'Moon Above Malaya' filtered through thick banana clumps lining the road. Again he sighed; this night would be the last time for at least two years that he would see that lovely yellow moon flooding Singapore with its light. And he told himself that he would think on the lyric 'Moon Above Malaya' whenever the moon shone its ray upon him, no matter where.

He was out of the city and far away from its many noises and smells, its rush and tear, its bright lights and gaudiness. Here in the outer suburbs of Singapore tranquillity reigned, the peaceful silence of the afternoon broken only by the occasional honking of bullfrogs hidden in nearby grass, the sleepy murmuring of birds in the tree tops, and the soothing voice of the male singer on that unseen radio.

Overhead, the sun rode high in a cloudless sky, flooding the young palm groves and banana clumps in their warmth of yet another tropical afternoon. Except for himself the road was deserted of people, and there was not even a stray dog or cat to be seen. At this moment Singapore seemed incredibly empty to Peter Saunders.

Treading on springy short grass growing in a long narrow strip parallel to the gravel sidewalk, he slowly made his way, limping noticeably and walking with the aid of a cane. He knew that it would have been quicker and less tiring to make the whole journey by taxi, but this being his last visit he wanted to walk the last half-mile. A taxi journey would have been too fast; he would have missed some small detail in this peaceful, lovely area that he now knew so well. He wanted to remember this, his last day in Singapore. And especially he wanted to remember this suburb that he had visited so many times during these past ten weeks; the neighbouring houses and gardens, and, of course, the beautiful new villa here in Upper Serangoon Road so kindly deeded to Lai Ming by Mr Ng Kwok Wing. He wanted to see and to remember everything, for fond and loving memories.

He arrived at a silver-painted wrought-iron gate, which he opened, passed through and closed behind him with a click of the latch. Sadly, he gazed upon the carefully tended colourful display of orchids growing in hanging baskets of charcoal, sand and moss. He looked at the ruby red bougainvillea reaching upward from beneath a loquat tree, and at the young papayas which Lai Ming had grown from seed and had planted out just a few weeks ago. He sighed and walked towards the front door.

The villa was a low-built bungalow nestling between two tall coconut palms which, bending towards the house, hung as if sentinels over the sloping, red-tiled roof. At the front of the house, even the doorway was partially screened from view by a cluster of tall zinnias of mixed colour, sunflowers and marigolds surrounded by a recently mown green carpet of grass. This was Lai Ming's home, almost a replica of the house she had dreamed of and had described to him during their first day together when they had met on Changi Beach. Here, she lived her life as a lady, secure from want, and enjoying tutoring little Li Li, who was brought to the house in a chauffeur-driven Rolls Royce or the new Bentley. Occasionally, especially when the weather was bad, Lai Ming was driven the short distance to her young student's home, a mansion built in a park-like setting.

Peter tried the handle on the front door. As he expected, it was locked. Lai Ming would be asleep, this being her siesta hour during the days when she was not teaching. He had no wish to wake her. He walked around the outside of the house until he was at the rear of the garden where there were more carefully tended lawns, three young coconut palms which took up much space, and a rockery encircled by a walkway of stone. Pale blue forget-me-nots dominated the rockery, although here and there natural bouquets of tiny white flowers broke through the blueness. At the bottom of the garden, beneath the tallest of the three palm trees, a heart-shaped lily pond, with tall, thick bamboo growing in its centre, glittered where falling water from a fountain fell. Lily pads covered much of the pond, hiding from view the numerous bullfrogs, which seemed to croak unceasingly. In the few open spaces goldfish lay still in the water or glided silently to and fro. When they rose to the surface, their scales of silver and gold glittered like jewels in the sunlight. The bungalow itself was entirely secluded from other properties by carefully landscaped ornamental trees and flowering bushes, mostly hibiscus of numerous varieties and colours. The house and gardens were Lai Ming's home, her pride and joy.

Peter let himself into the house by the rear door, and into the kitchen of a modern, all electric house. Just a flick of a switch for almost everything: oven, grill, water heater, washing machine, a sizeable refrigerator, and an electric kettle; and Lai Ming now owned a radiogram from which she derived much pleasure.

The house was comprised of three attractively decorated bedrooms, all in sunny positions, and each in a different colour. The master bedroom had its own spacious bathroom, and another bathroom was located off a short hallway which led into every room: a lounge, dining room, and a library in which Li Li not only took lessons in Cantonese from Lai Ming, but also English lessons from Peter. She was learning fast. At times Peter had wondered if she would be the only Chinese girl who would speak English with a strong Devonshire dialect. He had become very fond of the little girl. Yesterday he had given her a final hug, and in return had received a tearful goodbye kiss. He would miss Li Li.

Tip-toeing quietly into the main bedroom, Peter found Rose as he had expected to find her, lying nude, curled up on the bed, very small and lovely, a sleeping Chinese doll. A *sarong*, which she must have cast off in sleep, lay near her. Sadly, he gazed slowly down upon all four-foot-ten inches of her beautiful body, which was so full of love and laughter, and upon a face that rarely lost its exquisite smile. Today, though, there was a total difference. There was no smile on that little face, but instead a look of sadness, her cheeks stained by dried tears. She had, this day, cried herself to sleep. He would not disturb her. Instead, he would make himself a cup of tea and wait for her to awaken.

Returning to the kitchen, he plugged in the kettle, waited for it to boil, then switched off the current and reached for the hand-painted periwinkle-decorated china teapot from the house-warming tea set he had bought Rose. Rose would like a cup of tea; she always liked tea on awakening.

Minutes later, carrying two cups of tea and a plate of biscuits on a tray, he went to the bedroom and placed the tray on the bedside table. Stirring at his entry, Lai Ming's eyes flickered open, and seeing him standing at the side of the bed, she said in a dreamy voice, "Hello, Peter," and like an awakening cat she yawned and stretched out her arms and legs to their full length.

Peter knew full well her needs when she stretched herself in such a manner. "Did you sleep well?" he asked, sitting down beside her and caressing a naked thigh. "I'll pour you some tea," he said, already knowing the one word that would be her answer.

"After," she said.

"After what?" he asked, grinning boyishly at her naked body.

"You know what after." She gave him a mischievous smile and encircled his waist with an arm. "Undress and come on top of me," she said, almost in a whisper.

"No tea? Are you sure you want no tea?" Peter teased.

Laughing, Lai Ming shook her head. "No tea."

"How about a biscuit?"

"No, no biscuits. We take tea and biscuits, after."

Peter felt the arm pulling him towards her. Naked and with the sun streaming in upon her through the open window, her creamy-coloured body lay invitingly beneath his gaze. Always enraptured by her beauty, he sank his lips to her breasts, kissed them in turn, kissed her navel, then kissed her all the way down her smooth belly until he finally playfully plonked a kiss amid her thick bush of black pubic hair.

Grasping the hair on his head, she pulled him away from kissing her further. "Come, silly boy. Undress!" he could hear her saying.

Crawling up over her, he gazed down into her face. The softness of her bosom lay beneath his chest, and dark eyelashes swept his cheeks as she nestled with eyes closed within his embrace. This was how he loved to hold her, to know and to feel her giving herself to him so completely.

"Rose," he whispered.

"Yes, Peter."

"I shall ask you this question for the last time before I leave for England. Will you marry me?"

Lai Ming's eyes opened. "I have been thinking much on that question, Peter," she replied. "This is my answer. You have two more years in the RAF. During that time you will be able to think clearly what is best for your future. Mr Ng has offered you a good position within his empire, and I believe that you will return to Singapore and accept that position. As for me, Peter, if after those two years you want me as your wife, return to me, see if I have changed, see if you still love me and want me as your wife. If you then ask, 'will you marry me?' I shall reply, 'Yes.'"

"That is a promise?"

"That is a promise. I also promise you that I shall take no other man during your absence. I shall await your return. I do not want or need another man in my life."

Peter kissed her lightly on the forehead. "Rose, you're my little darling. I love you so very much," he said, cuddling her to him. "I shall return, and I'll always want you as my wife. I shall love you until the day I die."

"And I, you, Peter."

She lay watching him as he undressed and untidily dropped his clothes on the floor, just as he had done that very first day they had met. She smiled up at him as he climbed on top of her. And as he mounted her and she felt the weight of his body bearing down upon her, she opened her legs wide. Now they were kissing and embracing one another, he tenderly caressing her, she exploring him, slipping a tiny hand so lightly over his body it tickled, to eventually feel and hold that which must soon dominate her.

Soon it was time for him to leave the house. Lai Ming telephoned for a taxi. Peter would take it only as far as the Capitol Theatre he wanted to travel the fourteen-mile remainder of the journey back to Changi by bus, just for memories. Lai Ming suddenly decided she wanted to go with him, as far as the bus terminus at the Capitol. Together they would wait for the cab at the front gate.

As they walked along the gravel path, Peter looked sadly back at the house. He wondered when next he would see it. The taxi's headlights fell on them as it rounded the corner and drew up alongside them.

Peter opened the rear door, and when both had got in and were seated, Lai Ming said to the driver, "Capitol Theatre." The driver grunted an acknowledgement, the taxi sped on its way, and all too soon drew up at the Changi Bus Terminus situated between the Union Jack Club and the Capitol Theatre on the corner. Peter paid the driver two dollars. Both he and Lai Ming got out. Peter looked at his watch. Three minutes to twelve. Three minutes to when the last bus back to camp would leave the terminus.

Taking Lai Ming in his arms, Peter pressed her warm and cuddly body to him, crying, "Oh, Rose, I don't want to go. I don't want to leave you."

"You must," she whispered, sobbing against his chest.

Holding her tightly to him, his lips met hers for a long last kiss; then Lai Ming drew herself gently away from him.

"You must go, Peter," she said in a husky voice, "Before I break down on you."

He again took her in his arms and embraced her. Passers-by stopped and stared, but neither Peter nor Lai Ming cared; they did not see the many smirking faces.

"I don't know how to say goodbye, Rose. I just cannot say goodbye. You are with me now, but in moments you'll be gone; and tomorrow we shall be hundreds of miles apart." Choking back tears, he gave her a wry smile. "Be a good little girl, won't you," he said.

"I will," she promised. "Look after yourself, Peter, and always do what you think is right. Goodbye, Peter."

"Goodbye, Rose." He bent over her weeping face and kissed her lightly on the cheek. "Goodbye," he repeated, and was gone from her, walking with the noticeable limp to the waiting bus, his heart breaking.

"Goodbye, Peter," she whispered after him. But he did not hear her or turn around. She lingered on the sidewalk waiting for the bus to depart, seeing him seat himself in the rear seat. She could see only the back of his head. Why would he not turn around and wave a final goodbye? She wanted to board the bus herself, to be with him, but she checked herself; to do so could only worsen these unhappy moments.

The driver climbed into the cab and started the engine. The conductor pressed the button, which rang the bell. Then, on an impulse, Peter stood up, faltered for a moment, then making up his mind, stepped off the bus. He watched as the last bus back to Changi that night moved away from him.

"I couldn't do it, Rose," he said in a hoarse whisper. "I just cannot leave you."

"But you must, Peter. You must go, or you will get into big trouble."

"We'll go by taxi. We can catch the bus up and I can catch it when it stops at Geylang. There I'll leave you."

She was smiling up at him with tears streaming from her eyes as she said, "You fool, Peter. You darling fool."

A taxi cruised by. "Johnny!" Peter shouted. He turned to Rose and said, "This will be our last journey together for a long time."

"Perhaps forever."

"No, don't say that. It'll be January 1956, and then we'll be together again, forever."

He opened the door of the cab for her, and she got in. He sat down beside her and said, "Geylang," to the driver, and sat back in the seat, brooding, feeling the warmth of Lai Ming's body pressing against his, and not knowing what to say. He inhaled the sweet fragrance of her; it all saddened him. He watched in silence as she dabbed her eyes with a tiny purple handkerchief. Eyeing the handkerchief, he said, "Rose, let me have that for a little souvenir," and he reached out a hand. "Please," he implored.

She understood. Opening fully the tiny handkerchief, she pressed the centre of it to her lips, so that when she drew it from her, her lip marks were clearly imprinted on the cloth.

"A little memory," she said, smiling through tears. "I have another handkerchief in my handbag."

"Thanks."

"And Peter! I must give you something else! Something you may return to me when you return to Singapore."

Holding up a tiny hand, she took from a finger a gold ring with a dullish green stone embedded in it.

"Only now I think about this ring, Peter. It is Chinese gold. The stone is jade. Hold out your hand."

Peter did as bid.

"See! It fits your little finger. It is for you, not given, but loaned. You understand?"

"Thank you, Rose. Yes, I understand." And as he kissed her he noticed the eyes of the driver watching them through the rear-view mirror fixed to the windshield. Peter didn't care. Nothing mattered now; time was too precious and too quickly running out on them to care. He had existed on its terms; now it was coming to an end. It was all he could do to stop tears forming in his eyes. They had shared a short spell of time of each other's very existence in harmony of temperament in love and sex and companionship. They had been happy and had become completely content in their loving partnership. Two whole years away from her! It seemed an eternity. He knew that during those two years he would look back and think to himself, 'I really lived when with Rose. And I shall begin to live again when I return to her.' Life was going to be empty without her. But, fortunately, it would not be goodbye forever. He would return to Singapore immediately on completion of his RAF commitment and work with Ng Kwok Wing in his thriving business organization.

"Rose, I shall write to you as soon as I get home," he said in a hoarse whisper.

"Impatiently I shall await your letter," Lai Ming replied. "And I shall reply immediately. We must write often to each other."

"Yes, we must."

"I am happy that our correspondence is in the hands of Mr Ng's secretary. She translates well. Mr Ng is so thoughtful to suggest her as our go-between," said Lai Ming.

"Yes, we both owe Mr Ng such a lot. If it were not for him the burden of leaving you would be far greater. It would be devastating."

"Yes. For me, too," and Lai Ming squeezed Peter's hand and leaned over and kissed him on the cheek. The taxi driver glanced at the pair in his mirror, then again turned his attention to driving his cab, for although midnight had passed, milling crowds of people swarmed over the sidewalks, spilling out over the road in thousands, especially at road junctions.

The taxi passed banks where armed, bearded Sikhs stood guard at the entrances. There were shops still open, owned mostly by Indian merchants. Huge neon advertising signs in glitzy Chinese character writings lit up the night. On the arcade pillars more Chinese characters were splashed in crimson and gold. The taxi stopped for a traffic light. A group of Chinese men squatting in a doorway rattled and banged mahjong pieces. The Lion City, even though past midnight, was full of noise, colour and excitement, a city very much alive. Peter realized he was going to miss all this, the familiar sights, noises and smells. Taxi drivers cruised hooting after fares. Mingling trishaw *wallahs* peddled their three-wheeled conveyances in and out among the dense traffic. Friendly crowds of Indians, Malays, a few Europeans, and hordes of Chinese swarmed and jostled in all directions, dallying at food and drink stalls after coming out of picture houses or an evening's entertainment at one of the amusement worlds. It was late but hawkers still tended their stalls of sweetmeats, fruits, and curios, and were doing a brisk trade. Coolies, their bodies brown and glistening with sweat, jogged among the masses beneath great loads slung across their shoulders on long bamboo poles. There was the constant clickety-clack of a million wooden clogs upon the sidewalks.

The light turned green. The taxi was moving again, passing through a junction which led into Lavender Street. Lai Ming glanced down the familiar street. Turning, she gave Peter a wry smile. They were now on Geylang Road, passing the entrance to the Happy World Amusement Park, one of the three world parks where cosmopolitan Singapore has its fun. Tailor shops, photo studios, bazaars, barbers shops, eating houses and other such establishments lined the opposite side of the road. From the majority of side streets bamboo poles draped with laundry protruded from window ledges, to stretch almost across the full width of the street. There were the smells of dried fish and curry and joss sticks; smells, noises and colours. How Peter loved Singapore. To him there was no city its equal. Here he felt completely at home.

The taxi turned to the left, passing Kallang airport on its right, then down a dual carriageway, and within minutes arrived at the bus shelter at Geylang.

"Well, here we are at Geylang," Peter remarked almost casually. "And there's my bus waiting."

"Yes, I see it. Please go, Peter," Lai Ming begged. "Go quickly."

With a hand on the door handle, and with an aching heart, Peter bent over and kissed Lai Ming lightly on her lips, looked sadly into her eyes, then hardly able to force the words out of himself, whispered, "I love you, Rose."

"I love you, Peter."

Their eyes met and held for only seconds. Then Peter pushed the door open and got out, feeling sick and unsteady on his feet. He stepped across a water-filled monsoon drain and onto the sidewalk. He did not want to look back. Stiffly, he climbed aboard the bus, the conductor looking surprised at seeing him again. He sat down in the same rear seat as before. The bus moved off. He turned his head. The cab had swung around and was facing the opposite direction. They were moving away from each other, and the gap was widening. He caught a glimpse of her shiny black hair, and her face peering through the rear window, a tiny hand waving to him. He lifted his hand and waved back. Then she was gone, the taxi disappearing amid the mêlée of pedestrians and dense traffic; and he found himself alone, returning to RAF Changi for the last time.

Two stops before reaching the terminus at Changi Village, Peter dejectedly got off the bus and took a seldom used, short cut along a narrow,
grass-lined path. He passed the rifle range to his right and, further on,
passed close to the rear of the sergeants' mess and kitchen, all in darkness. Such a short time ago, just a matter of twelve hours or so, he had
said goodbye to Sergeant Muldoon and to the Chinese staff who were
on duty at that time. "I'll see you again, Charlie," he had said to Dai
Yat, the number one Chinese cook. "I'll drop in to see you all again one
day."

He walked the road which led to number 128, the block which
housed personnel of the catering section, and which had been his RAF
home ever since his arrival at Changi. This night, though, he would not
be sleeping in the catering block. Already he had shifted his kitbag and
suitcase out of block 128 and around the corner to the transit block
where he would sleep for a few hours before getting an early morning
call. Before entering the transit block he decided to first call in at the
kitchen for a mug of tea and to say goodbye to friendly Corporal 'Jock'
McKnight and the two LAC cooks working the night shift.

No sooner had he stepped behind the long servery, he heard the voice
of Corporal McKnight shouting from within the kitchen, "Pete, where
the hell have you been? Have you heard the news?"

Peter found the corporal preparing meals for a plane load of airmen
in transit, fresh out of the U.K. and bound for RAF Kai Tak, Hong
Kong. "What news, Jock?" he asked.

Corporal McKnight shoved a tray of bacon into a very hot oven and
closed the door. Looking up, he exclaimed, "Hey! Pete! The corporal
in charge of the transit block has been looking all over for you. He's
waiting for you at the transit block."

"Why?"

"You're flying home on tomorrow's Comet."

"What! Are you kidding?"

"No. I'm not kidding, mon. You're going to fly home in style."

Astonished but not too elated by the news, Peter asked, "Is there any tea on the stove? I could use a cup."

"Tea! Away wi' ya, mon, ta see the laddie in charge of the transit block, before he gives the wee ticket to some other laddie."

Calmly, Peter Saunders said, "Thanks, Jock. Keep the tea hot. I'll be right back."

On walking around to the transit block office, he met there the corporal in charge, seated at a table, poring over a stack of papers.

"G'evening Corp'," Peter said.

"Hi!" responded the corporal, looking up from the stack of papers.

"I'm SAC Saunders. Corporal McKnight in the airmens' mess said something about me flying home on tomorrow's Comet," said Peter.

"Oh! So you're SAC Saunders," said the corporal in a relieved tone of voice. "I've been wondering when you'd show up. Yeah, there are four vacant seats on the Comet," he said, reaching across the table for a lone pink travelling form and handing it to Peter Saunders. "You're one of the four lucky stiffs chosen to fill those seats," he said. "Does that make you happy?"

Peter shrugged his shoulders. "I suppose it should, Corp," he said. "I haven't had much time to think about it."

"OK. You'll be getting an early morning call at four-thirty, so you'd better get some kip."

"Yeah, I'll do that," replied Peter, shoving the pink slip into his pants pocket. "Goodnight, Corp," he said.

"Goodnight and good luck," replied the corporal, already settling back to again study and work on the piles of forms in front of him.

So Corporal McKnight was right, thought Peter. His news had been confirmed, numbing just a little more his tired and depressed mind. He really should get some sleep, he told himself, because within only four hours from now he would be getting an early morning call.

Within six hours, SAC Peter Saunders and three other airmen were due to fly out of Changi, Singapore aboard the first commercial jet aircraft ever, British Overseas Air Corporation's sleek, fast and beautiful Comet 1 G-ALYP, manufactured proudly by the de Havilland Aircraft Company.

36

It was dawn on the tenth day of January 1954. Torrential rain had fallen during the night but it had abruptly ceased an hour ago leaving the tarmacked apron of the dispersal unit glistening in the early morning light.

From the isolated, white stucco, one-room building which served as customs and immigration as well as an arrival and departure lounge, the passengers walked in a ragged file, in ones, twos and threes, to where the silvery-looking Comet 1 G-ALYP, the pride of British Overseas Airways Corporation, awaited them.

With mixed emotions, SAC Peter Saunders watched as a trim, neatly dressed, young and efficient-looking BOAC stewardess shepherded her flock across the fifty yards or so of rain-wet tarmac to where a flight of metal steps on wheels led up to the entrance of the plane. A BOAC air steward greeted the passengers at the doorway of the plane. Peter wondered just how many of those passengers, like himself, were sad to be leaving Singapore.

"Too bad we couldn't be among them," said a freckle-faced leading aircraftman to Peter, who was standing next to him amid a group of between twenty and thirty other airmen watching as the passengers boarded the Comet. "We'd be arriving in England within hours from now, instead of days."

"I suppose we would," said Peter, indifferently.

"Wow! Listen to this!" exclaimed the LAC "After leaving here, the Comet is going to touch down at Bangkok, Rangoon, Calcutta, Karachi, Bahrain and Rome, and will be landing at Heathrow in a matter of hours; not days, like our old Hastings. We won't get to England for at least three days, maybe four. God! I'm so disappointed at being bumped from the Comet. Aren't you?"

"It doesn't really matter," said Peter, sighing and hoping there would be something wrong with the Hastings so that his flight would be delayed a day, perhaps two.

In fact, Peter really didn't care how long it took the Comet to fly to England. Neither did he care nor was he disappointed that four paying passengers had purchased tickets during the night to make a full complement aboard the Comet. This meant that he and the other three airmen who, only late the previous evening, were told that they were the lucky ones chosen to fly home on the sleek jet aircraft, were bumped from its passenger list. Instead, the four airmen would be flying home on an RAF prop-driven, four-engine Handley Page Hastings aircraft of Transport Command, which was due to take off shortly after the Comet's departure.

Feeling depressed and sad about leaving Lai Ming and Singapore, Peter watched with little interest as the remaining passengers and a couple of the crew climbed the metal steps and boarded the Comet. He watched as the stewardess waved to a BOAC official standing on the tarmac, and saw the doors of the Comet being closed and the steps being pulled away. Within moments an increasingly loud whine of jet engines broke the quietness of the early morning, and the first commercial passenger jet aircraft ever moved gracefully forward across the tarmac, to begin, what could be, yet another world record speed-breaking flight. He watched as the plane headed towards and then onto the perimeter strip. He followed her with his eyes as she taxied towards the Changi Gaol end of the main runway until she eventually disappeared from his view. Minutes later, he heard the whine of her jets reaching a crescendo, and seconds later saw her reappear, just for moments, streaking down the runway, until she became lost from his view behind hangars and palm trees as she headed out over Changi Beach and the Johore Strait.

Then it was their turn.

Orders were given by the NCO in charge, and SAC Peter Saunders walked with other airmen across the tarmac to where the Hastings aircraft awaited them, its huge silvery body glinting in that day's first rays of sunlight. He presented his pink travelling form to the Movements Officer standing at the bottom of the flight of metal steps. Ascending the steps, he entered the plane and walked down an aisle between tall, leather-bound seats. He sat down near a thick glass porthole looking out over wing flaps, and strapped himself in by the safety belt.

Minutes later the double doors were slammed shut and secured. A red light came on in the cabin. The plane shuddered as an engine started. A pall of black smoke and red flames belched from the exhaust. Then, one after another, the three other engines spluttered and came to life, and the plane trembled as the engines ticked over. Minutes passed. To Peter Saunders those minutes seemed an eternity. Eventually, the heavy wooden chocks were wrenched from beneath the wheels, and the aircraft trundled forward from the dispersal unit towards the number one runway, the main runway that stretched the whole length from Changi Gaol to Changi Beach overlooking the Johore Strait. The Hastings swung to starboard before cruising at a fair speed down the long perimeter track until she reached the far end. There she swung around to port and taxied to the beginning of the runway. Behind her stood a grove of palm trees and behind these the notorious Changi Gaol. On the perimeter track, less than a hundred yards away, an ambulance and a fire tender stood by ready and waiting in case of an emergency.

All four engines were revved up, in turn and then in concert. Now, no black smoke came from the exhausts, but instead, a haze of greyish-white fumes and a lot of sparks. The engines roared at full throttle, brakes came off, and the aircraft lurched forward, steadied herself, then gained speed rapidly as she raced faster and faster down that very long runway. The dashed white line appeared to speed beneath the aircraft's broad belly. Flickering lamps of the flare path still spluttered, though it was already daylight. At an ever-increasing speed the plane reached where the runways crossed. The white control tower on the hill to the left seemed to flash by as she sped down the runway parallel with the green embankment carrying the two-lane road that ends at Changi Village. Peter watched as they flashed past the tiny post office, and next, the billets of the RAF Regiment Malay Squadron to his left. Halfway down the runway the tail wheel lifted. The plane no longer bumped on the tarmac but gracefully skimmed the flat, even surface until, pushed forward by her four powerful engines, she lifted and gradually ascended into an azure sky. The runway at RAF Changi quickly slipped away below. Just for moments, as the plane flashed over them, Peter Saunders stared sadly down at Pop's coffee-shack, the fish trap and upon a deserted Changi Beach. It was far too early for sun worshippers to grace its sands warming in that day's first sunlight.

Wisps of cotton-wool-like cloud flashed past the ports as the plane headed out over the Johore Strait, the water below twinkling and looking cool and calm, with fishing *sampans* dotting its surface and a Chinese junk chugging its way towards the mainland. The aircraft altered course and approached the city's boundary. Quite clearly Peter could see the detached mole, Clifford Pier and Telok Ayer Basin in the Inner Roads. He spotted the Raffles Hotel and the Union Jack Club, and of course, but further away, he could see the tallest building in Singapore, the Cathay Building, towering above the city. Fort Canning in the King George the Fifth Park seemed to glide silently by below; and to the north, he could make out Institution Hill. He continued to look down, sadly wondering where Lai Ming might be.

Lai Ming entered the wide, silver gates. Slowly, taking her time, she crossed the concrete forecourt then stopped for a few moments at the doorway of the main entrance to the Taoist temple. Looking about her, she involuntarily shuddered as she gazed upon the two ferocious-looking stone tigers, which stood one on either side of the doorway, guarding the entrance. She did not stand and stare as would a tourist but instead turned quickly away and entered the building.

Lai Ming wore her pajama-like, black two-piece cotton *samfoo*, the jacket buttoned up to the neck, and the trousers wide and flapping. On her feet she wore red wooden clogs. In one hand she carried a bone fan, and in the other a large wicker basket.

Fantastic carvings greeted her, and elaborate colourful glass ornaments glinted wherever she turned her eyes. She saw what must be the caretaker–priest in silent meditation at the entrance to the subterranean room beneath the seat where an effigy of Kwan Yin stood.

Placing the wicker basket down upon the stone floor of the temple, she clasped her hands together and held them towards the statue. Her lips moved slowly but no sound came as, with head tilted upward, she looked long and sadly into the Goddess of Mercy's eyes.

As she looked up into the face of her deity, her lips trembled. She hoped Kwan Yin would forgive her and answer her prayers favourably. For a fleeting moment a hint of a smile appeared on her face, accompanied by a bow of her head. She then bent down and drew from the wicker basket joss sticks in a ceramic vase. These she placed upon the altar. She lit the joss sticks then bowed three times in worship. Next, she took a bowl of cooked rice and one of sweetmeats and placed these also upon the altar, and bowed again. She then took from the basket a bowl of white loquat blossoms with yellow hearts, deep red in their centres—sweet-smelling flowers picked by her from her own garden very early that morning. These, she scattered upon the altar immediately in front of the Goddess.

Lai Ming picked up the two fist-sized wooden objects shaped like small elongated bowls, known as *yao bei*, and threw them onto the temple floor. She closed her eyes tightly and held her breath as they rolled across the ground before coming to a rest. She opened her eyes, hardly daring to see the result. One faced up and one faced down. "*Seng bui!*" whispered Lai Ming in her native Cantonese dialect, "how fortunate, the gods are looking down on me today." The *yao bei* were showing different sides, which meant Lai Ming could proceed to the next stage of the divination reading. She reached for the worn bamboo canister, which contained a sheaf of numbered sticks. On bended knee she held the small canister in both hands and shook it gently forwards and backwards. After only a few seconds one of the numbered sticks fell out of the canister and landed on the floor in front of her knees.

She would now have to throw the two wooden *yao bei* again to confirm she had the right stick. She stood up and fetched the same pair of *yao bei* before tossing them once again into the air. Should they land the same way up, she would know her numbered stick was not the correct one and she would have to begin the whole process again. "*Seng bui!*" she exclaimed, relieved to see yet again that the two *yao bei* were showing different sides. But one *sheng bei* was not enough; Lai Ming would have to get three consecutive *sheng bei* in order to be totally satisfied that her numbered stick contained the answer to the question she had posed to Kwan Yin, the Goddess of Mercy.

Again she performed the *qiu qian*, and again she was lucky, the two halves showed different sides. Gathering up the wooden *yao bei* for the final time, she rubbed them gently to her bosom. She did not speak, but silently prayed. Three times, and this was the third, the last. "They must! They must," she whispered to herself. She kissed and whispered to each block, her eyes wide and pleading. Casting both halves from her, they fell with a loud clatter on the stonework at the base of the altar. And when she looked down to where the two halves had fallen, she sighed a heavy sigh of relief. *Sheng bei* again. Lai Ming now knew the numbered stick that had shaken itself free from the canister contained the answer she so desperately needed to know.

She picked up the stick and memorized the number. Eighty-eight! With such a lucky number she felt confident of a favourable reply. She made her way to the back of the temple where she found the temple custodian, and she told him her number. The priest tore a strip of paper from a worn divination book that correlated to Lai Ming's number then studied it closely. Lai Ming held her breath as the old priest stared at the paper intently, his face completely devoid of expression. "The answer is yes," was all the priest said before handing the strip of paper to Lai Ming, turning and shuffling away. Had she heard correctly? Yes, he had said. Breathing freely now, all tension flooding from her weary, heartbroken self, Lai Ming was suddenly elated. "He will return! He will return!" she whispered passionately, the words rolling over and over in her mind. He would not forget her. He would return.

Gaining altitude all the while, the aircraft circled the city once, as if deliberately giving the passengers a final look at Singapore. Then, with her course set west northwest, she left the island behind. Johore, the most southerly state of Malaya, now lay below, steaming jungle bordered by a brown muddy coastline.

"This is Flying Officer Carpenter, your captain on this flight," began an up-beat voice on an intercom. "Welcome aboard. I'd like to gen you up on what's ahead. We are now flying at approximately four thousand feet. In a few minutes we'll be banking sharply to port, heading for the western tip of Singapore. From there we'll be climbing to ten thousand feet and a northwesterly course will be set, which should take us over northern Sumatra and across the Indian Ocean to the island of Ceylon. There, in approximately ten hours from now, we'll put down to refuel at RAF Negombo Airstrip. The weather ahead looks good but don't unfasten your safety belts until the red light goes off. Your quartermaster, Sergeant Price, will attend to your needs. Enjoy the flight."

Whilst walking down the narrow aisle of the plane, the quartermaster, an oldish, heavy-set, beery-faced sergeant, noticed SAC Peter Saunders peering anxiously out of the porthole.

"Are you feeling all right, son?" asked the sergeant.

"Yes, thanks, Sarge. I'm all right."

"You don't look all right to me. Are you on medical repat'?"

"I am all right, Sarge. And I'm not on medical repat'. I'm tour ex."

"Oh! My mistake! You just don't look well."

"I suppose it's because I'm sad at leaving Singapore."

"You've left someone behind?"

"Yes, Sarge, I have."

"A Chinese girl?"

"Yes."

"They're always Chinese."

"Mine's a very nice girl."

"A prostitute?"

"No! She's a real lady!"

"I've a Chinese girlfriend in Hong Kong. She's from Shanghai. She escaped the Communist takeover a couple of years ago, couldn't get a job in Hong Kong, had no money, so she became a prostitute."

"Just like the thousands of other Chinese girls who've flooded into Hong Kong," said Peter.

"Yes. My girlfriend's a prostitute, but she's also a lady," said the sergeant. In a friendly gesture he placed a hand upon Peter's shoulder. "Well, lad, I guess you'll just have to keep the memory of her."

"Yes, the memory. But I'll return to her as soon as I'm out of this mob," said Peter.

"They all say that. You'll soon forget her," said the sergeant. "During your leave at home you'll find yourself another girlfriend. You'll forget the past."

Peter forced a laugh. "Wise words, Sergeant," he said, looking up into the kindly face of the aging quartermaster. "But I'll not forget my girlfriend, not ever. Two years from now, when I'm demobbed, I'm returning to her."

"I hope you do. I'll get you a lemonade. Perhaps it'll make you feel better."

"Thanks, Sarge."

The other airmen seated inside the long passenger cabin sat in silence, each dwelling on his own thoughts, many staring out the portholes at fast receding Singapore. Soon, its long beaches and strips of mangrove fell astern, to be quickly lost in a misty embrace, leaving only memories for those returning home in that plane.

Now, below, on a broad expanse of twinkling blue water, the shadow of the lone aircraft flashed across a surface of rippling, tiny waves. Twenty minutes later the green and brown hills of Sumatra came into sight, and farther ahead, more water, and a greyish shadowy heat mist blurring the horizon.

The four piston engines droned in concert as the Hastings aircraft headed towards RAF Negombo, Ceylon. There it would be refueled, and refueled again at Karachi, Pakistan, then at an RAF base near Baghdad, Iraq, and finally at an airstrip in Libya, North Africa. Eventually, after four days, or almost fifty hours of actual flying time the plane would arrive at RAF Lyneham, England, and home.

EPILOGUE

The Rose of Singapore was first written in 1955, while I was based at RAF Fassberg in Germany. Although the story is a fictionalised account of my life in the RAF in Singapore and Malaya, it is based on true experiences.

Readers may be interested to know that the fruit seller who peddled her wares around RAF Changi, and who appears on page 97 of this book, was later awarded an OBE (Order of the British Empire). Having lost her husband to the Japanese during World War Two, the real Mary Tan smuggled food, drink and cigarettes to the desperate prisoners of war in Changi prison and other POW camps, defying death by the Japanese guards daily. She was an Angel of Mercy to the prisoners, many of them starving and owing their lives to her great courage.

Also, of great significance to the ending of this story, the BOAC Comet 1 G-ALYP, the jet aircraft which Peter was supposed to leave Changi on, exploded in midair ten miles south of Elba after departing Rome. There were no survivors.

ACKNOWLEDGEMENTS

I owe thanks to the staff of the British War Museum, for their assistance during my research of this book. Also to Grace Forbess whose great encouragement, also proof-reading of my work, helped me immensely with the writing of this, my first novel. Thanks are due also to Becky Ning Wang, for sharing with me her knowledge of Chinese customs.

Finally, I wish to thank my British Army and Royal Air Force friends who served in Malaya and Singapore during the early 1950s, for the many interesting stories they shared with me, some of which I have included in this book.